I0582191

TOUCH DOWN

TOUCHDOWN

Sonia Birdy

WARM PUBLISHING

WARM PUBLISHING
El Paso, Texas
www.warmpublishing.com

Original title: *Touchdown: Campus star*
published by Edisource
Paris, France

Copyright © 2020 Edisource
Copyright © 2025 Warm Publishing

Interior design by Warm Publishing
Cover design by Scarlet Lovell
Art by Scarlett Lovell
Translated from French by Iris Clark

ISBN: 978-1-958447-02-4

All rights reserved. In accordance with the U.S. Copyright Act of 1976, the scanning, uploading and/or electronic sharing of any part of this book without the permission of the publisher constitute unlawful piracy and theft of the author's intellectual property. If you would like to use material from the book (other than for review purposes), prior written permission must be obtained by contacting the publisher at warmpublishing@gmail.com.

Thank you for buying an authorized edition of this book and for complying with copyright laws by not reproducing, scanning, or distributing any part of it in any form without permission. By doing so you are supporting our French authors and allowing Warm Publishing to continue publishing them.

This novel is a work fiction. Names and characters, places and incidents are either a product of the author's imagination or are used fictitiously. Any resemblance to actual persons, living or dead, business establishments, events, or locales is entirely coincidental.

Publisher Notes

For the purpose of the story's scenario the author changed some aspects of the football world in the United States, this novel is fiction, and was created without wanting to offend the football fan public.

PROLOGUE

Rocky, 13-years-old

"You'll see, Rocky, we'll be happy here in Providence. Sam is a bank teller. He has a nice house where he lives alone," my mother says, a cigarette in her mouth, at the wheel of her Volvo 240; an old car that is not even sold anywhere anymore because it's so unreliable and has broken down hundreds of times, causing a lot of problems and humiliation.

"So, say something! Aren't you happy your mom has finally found love?"

I roll my eyes and just stare out the window.

How many times have I heard this speech? How many times have I seen that hopeful look on her face? I often wonder why my mother continues to believe it. After all these disappointments, you have to be fool not to give up on love. I make a solemn promise to myself that I will never be that stupid.

For my part, I am the most cynical teenager on earth. It's been a long time since I believed all that bullshit or her poor attempts to embellish reality by pretending that our messy life on the road, going from state to state, from guy to guy, is a wonderful adventure! A road trip! A movie like *Thelma & Louise*.

As a child, I obviously fell for it. I thought my mother was a heroine of modern times, a free woman, an emancipated woman. I felt like I was lucky. I saw beautiful landscapes, while other children of my age were bored at school.

But little by little, through fatigue and trouble, my innocence evaporated. I discovered the other side of the story. The slums where we landed, the nights spent in our car. Bars where mom tried to find a new lover, while I played with coasters, hunger tugging at my stomach.

From all our misadventures, I have concluded three fundamental things: life is a succession of problems to be solved, men are assholes to be avoided, and promises are only binding on fools who want to believe in them.

"You'll even have your own room!" she continues without worrying about my silence.

"Nice," I say ironically.

As if I was a spoiled brat and my main concern was not sharing my room. If she only knew! In my head, the waltz of questions has already started. Will my new stepdad leer at me or try to corner me as soon as Mom's back is turned, like jerk number four? Will he make it clear that I'm not really welcome in his house, watching my every move and rationing my food, like ex-jerk number three? Will the new place I'm going to go to be as horrible as the previous ones?

Until then, my schooling had been a succession of difficulties of understanding and problems of integration. *You have to try to fit in, Rocky*. Easier said than done!

To be accepted in a school during the year requires a lot of energy. And I have neither the motivation to make an effort or the patience to give the right people a helping hand. So, I prefer to be alone.

Being alone saves you a lot of disappointment. And that is rule number four.

Rocky

Today

My phone vibrates in my pocket, and I get a few sideway glances. Breaking the silence of the library is sacrilege. Especially at Brown, the prestigious university in which I have the chance to study. I give an apologetic smile, grab my contemporary architecture book, and bolt out of the room.

"Rocky, are you still coming with us tonight?" asks Allison.

"Yes of course! But I have to pick up Maxwell from school. Just enough time to make him dinner and take him to his babysitter, and I'll meet you at the dorm."

"Is your mom still not back from her business trip?"

"No."

I don't go into any more detail. Lying to my friends, I hate it, especially since Isabella and Alyson are the only two girlfriends I've ever had, and they don't deserve my fibs.

"Okay, that's cool. That way, we can get ready together. Grab your sexiest outfit, we're going to the Kappa Omega party."

"Another frat party? Why don't we go to Shamrock? It's been a while since we've been there."

Shamrock is an Irish pub just off campus. There are both students and locals hanging out there. The atmosphere is relaxed, you can drink beers, play pool, darts. There is even a small dance floor and a jukebox for those who wish to let off steam.

And God knows I need to let off steam!

And I can't even rely on sex for that anymore. Being a student and taking care of my 6-year-old brother also means that there aren't enough hours in the day to do everything I need to do. So, since this summer, I have given up any social life. The only pleasure I allow myself is one night a month with my girlfriends, so I don't completely forget that I'm only 19.

"We can't miss the Kappa Omega party tonight, it's 'Athletes night!' All the hottest guys on campus will be there. And you know Isabella wants to see Alec."

"You know how this is going to end, Alyson! Drunk and crying."

"I know, but what do you want? She's crazy about this guy! Dissuading her from going there is impossible. So, as we're her good girlfriends, we go there to prevent her from throwing herself on him and embarrassing herself."

A glance at my watch tells me it's three forty-five! I need to go.

"Well, okay, we'll talk about it tonight. See you!"

Without further ado, I hang up and rush to my car parked in front of the library. It looks bad next to the other vehicles. Most of Brown's students are well-off. That's why I had no problem finding a job in the cafeteria. When I saw the hourly rate, I was speechless. How could such a well-paid job stay open?

The truth is that students want to avoid the shame of wearing a hairnet in public. I admit that, glamorously, there is better, but the university pays twice as much as the minimum hourly rate. The location allows me not to miss too many classes, so too bad for my brand image.

I start my car, praying that it complies. Last time, I had to call a tow truck, and it cost me an arm and a leg. I know I need a new car, but I also know I can't afford it, so praying to God it won't let me down is all I have left. I close my eyes, turn the key with a sharp movement. The car groans to a start.

Thank, God!

A few minutes later, I am standing in front of my little brother's elementary school with other moms. The school bell rings. A crowd of children rushes through the door, shouting and cheering. My heart warms when I see Maxwell's little blond head, his *Ninja*

Turtle school bag, and his toothless smile.

When he was born over six years ago, a few months after our arrival in Providence, he changed my life. I loved him right away and immediately started taking care of him. We had this little magical, invisible bond that only siblings have. I, who used to be alone, I discovered the unconditional love of this little angel. After years of loneliness and the feeling that I didn't matter, it was a lifesaver.

It was the happiest and most stable time of my life. Sam and mom were also filled with happiness. The jerk number five that I feared so much turned out to be a good man. An perpetual bachelor, as the neighborhood liked to call him, but a bachelor with plenty of love to give. For once, my mother was right.

He took care of us like no one before, and Mom calmed down, forgetting her penchant for drinking to better equip herself to make this new family work. She still had occasional crises, but Sam had the ability to calm her down. It was thanks to this stability and the very good high school I went to that my grades soared and allowed me to get into Brown. I was no longer an outcast but a girl like the others, with a room of her own and a good dinner every night. Turns out that was all I needed to succeed. The universe was giving me a break, I was finally touching happiness with my fingertips. I believed it, I really believed it. Unfortunately, things took a tragic turn.

An unknown number, a shocked silence, then my mother's wolf-like screams, dropping her cell phone and collapsing on the kitchen floor. That's how I got the news: Sam had died of a sudden heart attack. At age 57, at his desk. That very morning, he was making plans for our Christmas vacation.

In an instant, our existence turned into a nightmare again. The hardest part was explaining to my little brother that he would no longer see his father. Death is an absurd concept for a child.

As for mom, her fall was slow and painful. At first, she faced up to the situation with an unfailing smile. She took care of the funeral, thanked the neighbors who came for the ceremony. Sam had no family to rely on. For months, she held on, and I never saw it coming. I was finishing my senior year in high school, starting college, and she was still going strong.

I moved to the dorm, came home once a week. She didn't talk much, but the cupboards were full, dinner was on the table, and Max smelled like soap. Then in April, something changed. I recognized the signals, little by little, pernicious. It started with bottles stashed in the garage and shaking hands, breath that smelled a little too often of whiskey. Mom had fallen back into her habits, that was for sure. But she continued to wake up in the morning and go to work. I still wanted to believe that all hope was not lost, that I would be able to continue my carefree life as a student. It was completely selfish of me to be blind, but I couldn't bring myself to face it. In May, I was forced to see the extent of the damage. The house was upside down, the fridge empty. Alcohol, antidepressants, and opiates had overcome my mother's last attempts to keep up appearances.

June, I was coming home for the summer and took over everything. Mom was just a shadow of herself. She was going into psychotic delirium. We fought, I slapped her, she scratched me in rage when I emptied all her bottles and made her painkillers disappear. I begged her to go to rehab, but she wouldn't listen. She would disappear for days, weeks, come back thinner and even more confused. The descent into hell never ended and, in the middle, there was Max. I tried to preserve him as much as possible, but he saw and heard things that a little boy of his age should not see or hear.

Then one day she left and never came back. I should have reported her missing. Instead, I ignored the problem, cursing her irresponsibility and selfishness. I was angry, I was so mad at her. I replayed in my head the different scenarios of her return. I wouldn't let her get away with it this time. She was going to pay! She was going to have to go to rehab! A week, two weeks, three weeks later, she still wasn't back. Going to the cops was tempting, but I didn't want to attract the attention of social services. I was a student, without a job, in charge of a 6-year-old child.

I was too afraid that he would be taken away from me and placed in foster care. So, I gave up trying to find her and dealt with the situation. At first, I thought I had to find a full-time job and quit school, but it was our neighbor, sweet Mrs. Johnson, who convinced me otherwise.

She told me it would be a mistake to quit college, given the great opportunities that Brown would give my resume, and the great life I could give my little brother if I went all the way through architecture school.

I thought about it a lot, weighed the pros and cons, and finally agreed with her. Since then, she has become Max's official babysitter on the rare evenings when I take some time for myself. I trust her blindly, and Max loves going to her house. It must be said that she spoils him a little too much.

"How was school, my little man?" I ask Max, who has managed to join me by making his way through the children in a hurry to get home.

I place a long kiss on his cheek. He strongly protests, because he hates that I treat him like a baby in front of his friends. Max is a year younger than the others, but he already knew how to read in kindergarten, so we skipped a grade to keep him from getting bored. Since then, he does everything to look bigger.

"Great! We had nuggets at lunch."

His answer makes me smile. My little brother's school stories always revolve around the same topics: food and recess. I'm glad that his innocence hasn't yet been damaged by the tragic circumstances of his young life.

"Great. Do you have homework?"

"A little."

"Okay. Let's go home, you'll have a snack, you'll do your homework, and then you can watch a movie at Mrs. Johnson's."

"Yes, so cool! Can I watch Jurassic Park?"

Max has an obsession with dinosaurs.

"No, you know how I feel about that."

"Please! I'm not a baby. It's not even scary."

"How do you know?"

His little guilty face tells me he's seen it somewhere before.

"I may have read a magazine in the school library that talked about it."

I ruffle his hair. My little brother is a genius and a little opportunist sometimes.

"Can I sleep over? Please, Rocky! She always makes homemade pancakes in the morning."

"I can make you homemade pancakes too."

"Yes, but she adds strawberries and blueberries."

His comment makes my heart ache a little. I would love to treat him with fresh fruit, but my budget is tight. My paycheck as a kitchen clerk at university doesn't allow me to cover everything, bills, cafeteria, clothes. He is growing up so fast. Often, I have to choose between a new pair of shoes for Max or a full shopping cart. I push these foggy thoughts out of my head to better focus on the task at hand: buckling my little man into his car seat.

When I got home, there was no time to procrastinate. Daily tasks take over and anesthetize my brain. Max eats his snack while I check his homework. Our ritual runs smoothly now. He has a few words to write and some reading to do. It should go quickly. Next is bath time, in which he likes to linger to play with his dinosaurs. I hear him growling and making little voices every time I walk down the hall. That makes me smile. I love him so much, my little man.

I get his things and put them in the laundry room for a quick wash. I then prepare his dinner. There's not much left in the fridge except onions, eggs, and spinach. I start making an omelet. I'm not a great cook, but I manage, mainly because of the internet.

I'm often tempted to buy ready-made meals at the supermarket. It would save me time and sometimes even money, but Max is growing, I have to feed him properly. I wouldn't want him to suffer from the same deficiencies I did at his age.

Max devours his eggs like a little glutton.

"Is it good?"

"Yes, very."

"You don't eat it?"

"No! I'll eat later."

I'm lying. I won't eat, except for a cereal bar or two that I have in my bag, but I'm used to skipping meals. Especially at the end of the month.

"Do you want your dessert?"

"Yes! Yes! Yes!"

"Okay! Don't get excited, it's just a yogurt."

He devours it as quickly as the rest, then it's time to drop him off at Mrs. Johnson's."

She opens the door with a big smile.

"Hello, Rocky! Hello, big boy! So, ready for a night out at your favorite neighbor's house?" asks Mrs. Johnson.

"Yes!" answers my little man.

Max quickly rushes inside, happy to find his dinosaurs. She bought them just for him. Mrs. Johnson is a frustrated grandma. She doesn't get to see her grandchildren as much, they live across the country, so she spoils Max instead.

"Are you sure you'll be okay?" I ask.

"Yes, Rocky! We'll watch a movie together, and then I'll put him to bed."

"Not later than 9 p.m., otherwise he'll be grumpy in the morning."

"No problem. You know you can count on me."

"Thank you."

"Have you heard from your mother?" asks Mrs. Johnson.

I shake my head.

"I'm sure she'll come home eventually."

I shrug my shoulders. I'm sure of nothing when it comes to Rebecca Prescott.

"Now go have fun and forget about us, everything will be fine."

"All right. Max, are you coming to give me one last hug?"

I hear his little steps on the floor, and a second later he's in my arms, kissing me furiously on the cheek.

"Have fun, big guy! And no trouble, promise?"

"I promise."

I then warmly thank Mrs. Johnson, before giving her the last recommendations for the evening. She has to kick me out like always. I know I can trust her, but I feel guilty.

It takes me a few minutes to come to my senses in the car, then a few seconds to get the car started, and here I am on my way to campus. For a rare carefree night.

2

Rocky

When we arrive in front of the Kappa Omega house, there are so many students that the outdoor space is overrun. The people on the lawn or under the porch, in these freezing temperatures, can only mean two things: the partygoers are already drunk and no longer feel the cold, or the house is so crowded that it is better to be outside.

Despite this, the party looks promising. Isabella parks the car, and we trot to the entrance. The KO House is a huge Georgian-style mansion, like all of Brown's buildings, with its red brick facade and huge white columns at the entrance. It seems almost too majestic for the hip-hop music that is shaking the walls currently.

As soon as we cross the threshold, we are struck by the intense heat, the excessively loud music, and the different perfumes emanating from all these over-excited bodies. One of the guys from the brotherhood has installed turntables to the right of the huge staircase in front of a huge arched bay window that could've been in a cathedral. A banner that stands at the entrance so that no one can miss it catches my eye.

Save a horse, ride an athlete.

Subtle!

And I think some took the joke literally.

The dance floor is filled with muscular male bodies and chicks rubbing on them as if they were hoping to see a genie come out of a lamp. Far be it from me to judge them, it would be totally hypocritical of me, knowing that I am here for the same reason.

"Ha! Ha! That's good, I'm in the mood for a rodeo," says Isabella, pointing to the banner. "But first, we drink!"

"Good idea!" Alyson replies.

We cross the hall and then one of the living rooms, to reach the kitchen. In general, it's the rallying point for the thirsty people. We elbow our way to reach the central island. Alyson manages to grab three red cups, a marker, and a bottle of vodka. She writes our names on the cups. Well, it is what I think she is doing, but when she hands me the cup, I understand why her eyes light up with humor.

"Balboa? Really! What grade are you in? In K?" I say ironically.

"Don't complain! Balboa is better than Barbie," Isabella winces, turning her glass to me.

I can't help but smile because the nickname suits her well. Isabella is a Barbie, but she's a Barbie of the 21st-century who can combine culinary talent and genius IQ. She's taking film classes, because she sees herself in Hollywood in a few years, but she could just as easily be a researcher.

"Thank you for your support, Rocky," Isabella sighs, falsely annoyed.

Alyson turns around and shows us her goblet on which is written "Boss," then proudly says while raising her glass, "Tonight, we are the three Bs! And I hope that the three of us will bang!"

"Especially you, Rocky! How long has it been since you saw the wolf?" Isa asks.

"The wolf? You sound like my grandmother," Alyson chuckles.

"Well, since I don't have much time to walk around in the forest, I'd say three months."

"Who was the last one?" asks Isa.

"Gordon Taylor," I answer.

"Mr. Tongue!" they both exclaim, disgusted.

"Yes! He didn't steal his reputation. But honestly, I liked when he showed off his skills down south. As soon as he kissed me, it was too much. Mmmh. Yuck!"

"I think I just threw up in my mouth," Alyson says.

"Can't wait for your mother to come back from her business trip then, so you can get back in the saddle. Pun intended," concludes

Isabella.

My heart sinks for a moment at the mention of my mother. I have absolutely no idea where she is or if she will come back one day and in what condition. I don't even know if I want her to come back. I can take care of Maxwell alone. My only fear is that social services will come and take Max away. I'm under 21. I am a minor, responsible, but a minor. The moms at school are starting to ask lots of questions, and I know my future depends on one bad phone call.

"Cranberry vodka?" Alyson suggests, bringing me out of my gloomy thoughts.

Tonight, I'm here to have fun and forget about everything. I try to reason with my brain, which never stops thinking and imagining the worst.

"Please!" Isa replies. "And put a lot, because I'll need courage."

"What about you, Rocky?"

"No, thank you, I'll have a beer instead."

"There's no beer."

"Yes, there is, I saw a keg earlier at the entrance," I explain, at the same time as Isabella grabs my arm.

"He's here! He's here! He's here!"

"Where? Where? Where?" I say in the same tone to make fun of her.

"Alec! In the living room in front of us, on one of the couches. Tell me he's alone?!"

I glance over her shoulder and find Alec, the beautiful, the famous, the holy grail Alec. I've heard so much about him, I feel like I know him like the back of my hand. Sitting, wearing a sweatshirt with the image of his football team, as Alyson had predicted. He is really very attractive, there's no denying it: tall, with dark hair, gray-blue eyes, and a tortured gaze. He has the look of the broken guy that all girls dream to fix. To top it all off, he's really nice. But he made the fatal mistake of breaking my best friend's heart, and in solidarity, I will never be able to admit it.

"He's talking to some friends. But there is no girl in sight," I finally answer her.

"Great! How do I look?" Isa asks.

"Like a million dollars," we both say to boost her confidence.

"Well, I'm going to go see him! It's now or never, come on, girls!"

"You go ahead! You don't need us. We are good here next to the alcohol," replies Alyson.

"No, girls, please! If I show up alone, it's too desperate. On the other hand, with you, I'm the girl who has friends and who meets an old friend. Nothing more normal than that."

Alyson rolls her eyes.

"You and your bullshit stories... Can't you leave a little room for spontaneity?"

"Spontaneity is for losers. Do you think Elle Fanning got the role of her life by being spontaneous?"

We are both left speechless, because one: arguing with Isa is pointless, and two: who the hell is Elle Fanning?!

Without further explanation, she turns around, expecting us to follow her like the Beverly Hills princess that she is. Alyson follows, but I use the *I'm going to get a drink* card to buy some time. If I have to witness Isa's humiliation number five, I'd rather not be sober.

In a few minutes, I reach the entrance. Looks like the whole college got together in this house tonight. I finally see the keg appear like an oasis in the desert. I weave between people, trying to ignore the lustful gaze of some guys on the V-neck of my T-shirt. A ridiculous old reflex pushes me to readjust it, so that they see as little as possible. Next to some girls who wear short skirts or corsets, such as the pretty blonde in front of me, I'm dressed like a nun. She's talking to an athlete whose face I can't see. My eyes get lost on the curve of his muscular shoulders and the sexy jeans that give him an amazing ass. I understand the flirty smile she gives him.

I finally arrive at the Fountain of Youth, take a sip from my glass to give me courage before pushing through the crowd again. I haven't taken three steps, when a sudden movement makes me wobble and my body hits something hard. My hard-earned beer spills on me. I growl in frustration.

"Damn it! Can't you be more careful?" I yell at the idiot who just caused the accident.

My cup disappears from my hands.

"Hey! Help yourself!"

Those were the last words I managed to say, before my brain

stopped being able to form sentences. The wall I landed against is actually a torso, a hard, muscular torso. That hard, muscular torso belongs to the most attractive guy I've ever seen. Caramel eyes with green flecks stare at me. Casually styled brown hair frames an angel or demon face, I'm not sure. In any case, he's unreal. My gaze then rests on his lips, so pink, so appetizing. I feel the irrepressible desire to put mine there. The said lips are moving now. I think they are trying to communicate with me and when they break into a bright smile, I force myself not to die of dazzlement.

"Sorry for my idiot buddy…" he says before pausing to read my name on the cup, squinting. "Balboa?"

Damn it! Even his voice is sexy!

Deep and raspy. But what strikes me the most is his magnetic, electric presence. It's like the oxygen in the room has been sucked out. He raises an eyebrow, probably waiting for an answer. I swallow and nod. My brain having taken off, I don't correct him. This living god can call me whatever he wants. But I will make Alyson pay for his stupid joke!

"That idiot Adam spilled your beer all over you. Wait, I'll clean you up."

Clean me up? What does he mean exactly? And why are dirty pictures flashing in my brain?

I watch him wedge my cup between his teeth, unable or unwilling to protest. I'm like a deer caught in the headlights of a car. Unable to move, unable to think, and unable to say a coherent sentence.

And then he does something incomprehensible that does nothing to improve my state of hypnosis. He lifts his white T-shirt; abs of steel appear under pearly skin. I have time to see a brown birthmark which reminds me that he is human. He then grabs my left forearm and cleans the beer that has spilled there with the bottom of his T-shirt—I think I'm forgetting to breathe—then gently, slowly, he cleans my hand before replacing the cup. All the while, I can only admire his nimble fingers and feel the incredible warmth that this simple gesture gives me in all my favorite places. It feels like times has stopped. I no longer hear the music or the people around us, only my racing heart. I really need to get my act together.

He's just a guy!

A handsome guy, yes, but not enough to act like a complete idiot.

"There, that's better."

He lets go of my arm and I clear my throat which feels horribly dry.

"Thanks."

"You're welcome, Balboa!"

He winks at me and walks away, leaving me panting and thirsty as ever. I lose my blissful smile when I see him go back to the little blonde in the sexy corset that I saw earlier. As for me, all I have to do is fill my cup again and join my girlfriends.

✱✱✱

"Well, it took you a long time! What the fuck did you do?! Did you fall in the beer or what?" Alyson asks as soon as she sees me.

"If only you knew how right you are," I say, sitting down on the floor next to her.

Isa is in front on the couch, in the middle of a discussion with Alec. This room in the house is the only one that's somewhat quiet. There is a huge fireplace behind the couch, and the atmosphere is pleasantly dim. I silently thank Alec for coming to settle down here instead of in the kitchen or the hallway and allowing us to spend an evening away from the hustle and bustle, because Isa would have followed him even to the gates of hell.

"So, is she progressing?"

"He hasn't pushed her away yet, they've been talking for a while now. Things are looking good," answers Alyson.

But until when?

She didn't say it out loud, but I could practically hear her thinking it. We're both used to getting Isa being a mess, every time Alec blows her off, or worse, shoves his tongue down someone's throat, like on the last party. And it's been going on for months! No matter how hard we try to convince her to forget him and move on, nothing works! She has him under her skin. She is ready for all humiliations. Here is another proof, if I needed one, that love makes you stupid.

"Good for her," I say, watching them, relieved.

After a few sips of my beer, I finally relax. I let myself be lulled by the conversations around me. Alyson chats with Scott Pheris, a teammate of Alec. They're talking politics.

Several players from the football team as well as a few girls join in the conversation, and the jokes fly around our happy circle. The glasses are drying up and force the partygoers to go and refill. I wish them good luck. As for me, my journey earlier calmed me down. Anyway, I drink a little at parties. It's a new rule I've imposed on myself since I started taking care of Max. Speaking of my brother, I need to check that everything is going well for him. I text Mrs. Johnson.

> **How's my little man?**

> **He sleeps soundly. Playing with his dinosaurs has exhausted him.**

> **Poor thing! I hope he didn't tire you?**

> **Not at all. On the contrary, he brightened up my evening! And you, how is yours going? Have you met a handsome young man?**

I smile because Mrs. Johnson loves to ask me, *"When are you going to meet a handsome young man? A beautiful girl like you! Me, at your age, I wasn't so shy!"*

> **Very good, thank you. And no, still not!**

> **Okay, so stop texting your poor neighbor and focus on your party. I'll see you tomorrow morning.**

> **OK. Thank you for everything, Mrs. Johnson.**

I put my phone away and feel Alyson's hand slam down on my thigh, making me yelp in pain.

"Hey, what the hell?!"

"Damn, Rocky, did you see that handsome guy by the fireplace over there?"

I look up and see the guy from earlier. He's chatting with a member of the football team, and even from the side, he's gorgeous. Angled jawline, three-day-old beard, how come I never noticed that before? A such beautiful specimen!

As if he had felt my eyes on him, he turns around and our eyes lock for a few moments. The air suddenly seems electric to me, and I don't know what to do. I give a tiny smile, which could easily pass for a grimace, he answers it with a sexy wink before continuing his conversation.

"What was that? Do you know him, you sneaky little thing?"

"No, I don't!"

"Then why are you blushing?"

"Let's say we had an incident earlier, when I went to get a beer."

"An incident, what do you mean… Can you be more specific, please?"

"Well, I don't know, it's hard to explain, it was really furtive. In short, he cleaned me up."

"What?!" she yells, drawing the attention of the people around us.

This is the moment Scott Pheris chooses to come back with his beer. He sits down next to Alyson.

"What's going on? What did I miss?" asks Scott.

"Rocky was telling me she got cleaned up by Mr. Handsome over there."

He starts laughing.

"Mmh, I like dirty stories. But who are you talking about?" he asks, looking for the subject of our conversation with his eyes.

"The guy by the fireplace," Alyson replies.

"Ah, Jude!"

"It's his name?" I ask stupidly, with barely hidden excitement.

"Yes! Jude Hartnett. He just transferred from Harvard to play wide receiver on our team. He's gifted and already being courted by professional teams. Between him and Alec, we're sure to win the championship this year."

"Glad to hear how excited you are about this guy for your team, but let's go back to when Rocky was telling us how she got cleaned up by him. Did he, at least, use his tongue?" says Alyson.

"No! What the hell has gotten into your head?!"

"I do not know! Everything is possible with you. I knew you were gone way too long to get a beer. Well, spit it out, Rocky! And I want all the details," says Alyson.

Her eyes light up with mischief. She's expecting an epic story. She might be disappointed.

"Some jerk ran into me and spilled my beer. Handsome, here, cleaned me up with his T-shirt."

"That's all?" she asks.

"Yeah!"

Her eyes narrow. "No exchange of numbers or saliva?"

"Nope!"

"It's not much, but it's still sexy!"

"Yeah! Especially since I had a glimpse of what was under his T-shirt, and I can assure you that it's worth it."

"I believe you, given the build he has. No, but she's unbelievable, this Balboa! She comes out once every earthquake, but as soon as you leave her alone for five minutes, she hooks up with the best!" she says.

"Don't get carried away, Al! Nothing more happened. After that, he went back to chat with a hot chick who monopolized all his attention. If anyone is going to hook up with him, it's probably her."

"I don't see her anywhere. What I see is my girlfriend, Rocky, who hasn't had sex in three months, about to end the curse by fucking a stadium god!"

I literally choke. Alyson, in her great generosity, pats my back to help me come to my senses.

"What? Three months?" Scott asks.

"Yeah, you realize, we have to do something about that," says Alyson.

"Please say it louder, I don't think they heard you in Boston," I protest after spitting my lungs out on the floor.

"Oh, that's okay, Rocky! It's just us!"

As Scott says those words, I look up, praying that Mr. Handsome hasn't witnessed this moment of extreme elegance. No one can look sexy while choking. The universe definitely hates me, because his caramel eyes are definitely focused on me. He gives me a bright smile. I smile back at him, torn between embarrassment and excitement. Maybe I have a chance after all, if he smiles at me like that.

I pray inwardly that he will come and talk to me, but no. He looks away and focuses on his conversation again. Bummer! If I had drank more, I would go flirt with him, but I don't have the courage right now.

"If you want, Rocky, I can help you out," Scott offers, by playing with his eyebrows.

"You pervert!" says Alyson.

He takes a blow on the bicep which makes him wince in pain.

"Ouch! Alyson, you hurt me," he complains.

She rolls her eyes. "I barely touched you. You're quite a sissy for a football player! Isn't it your job to get hits so you don't let the ball pass?"

He responds with a nice middle finger.

"That's what I get for playing the altruist. I just wanted to make myself useful."

"If you really want to be useful, tell Jude to bring his pretty little ass over here," says Alyson.

"Nope! Don't do that! It's ridiculous! We are not in high school, stop." I panic.

But I don't have time to finish my sentence when Scott has already jumped to his feet and is on his way to the object of my desire.

3

Rocky

Before I understand what is happening to me, I'm in a pool game with Mr. Handsome and my two treacherous friends. In a very subtle way, Al and Scott suggested that Jude and I team-up. I'm mortified and barely dare look him in the eye. Why? Because I don't know what Scott has been telling him about me, hoping to set me up. Probably something embarrassing.

As a result, I can't focus on the game, or anything else to tell the truth.

Jude tries to help me by pointing out which balls I should aim at, or which angle I should be on, but every time he comes near me, I tense up like a string. So, I seem more unsympathetic than anything else. I'm not surprised if I can't get him…

My only party of the month, and it's going to end in me striking out. A lost game later, the boys offer to get us another drink and I find myself face to face with Alyson.

"He's really hot, this Jude!"

She whistles through her teeth and tilts her head, ostensibly watching their posteriors move away.

"And Scott's not bad either. I think I'm going to try again with him. What do you think?"

For all answers, I pinch her, bringing her back to reality.

"Ouch! What's wrong with you, Balboa?"

She rubs her arm excessively, frowning her perfect eyebrows.

"Stop calling me 'Balboa!'" I get annoyed.

"I think it suits you, and Jude thinks your name is 'Balboa.'"

She smiles. My irritation escalates.

"Surely that's not the only bullshit he thinks about me…"

"What do you mean?"

"Why did you open your big mouth with Scott? Now my chances of seducing Jude are definitely off!"

"Uh… I remind you that, without my intervention, you would still be drooling over him from a distance."

"Nope. Without your intervention, I would still have my dignity and I could have played the card of the inaccessible girl. You know, the one everyone loves, mysterious, secret," I say, lifting my chin. "I'd still be in the race, you know! Now, I must look pathetic, because knowing that asshole Scott, his attempt to approach was probably the dumbest."

I take a tired voice of a frat boy as well as a nonchalant posture, I only miss the cap upside down in order to imitate him as well as possible.

"'Hey, Jude! Do you want to fuck? Because my friend Rocky, she hasn't had sex in three months, and she wants you! Run, man!' I'm not romantic but now, this is bordering on the ridiculous!" I conclude.

She laughs, because she knows that I'm right.

"If being an architect doesn't work out, I strongly suggest a career in cinema, you rock my world."

She can't help but make the umpteenth pun with my first name.

"Stop it, I mean it. I haven't been able to say two words to him without stuttering because of your bullshit. He must take me for a real idiot," I sigh, annoyed.

"No need to think you're smart to introduce you to his cock."

I groan, and she laughs again.

"Rocky, relax! It's just a party, just a guy. Have fun and stop overthinking. You really need good dick right now."

I roll my eyes.

"Yes, and it's not going to happen tonight! Thank you very much."

"Stop it, you don't know that. The night is still young, and the possibilities are endless. You know what you need?"

"No?"

"A shot of tequila!"

"I already had a beer. I don't want to be sick tomorrow morning when I pick up Max. It doesn't seem like much but taking care of a 6-year-old boy takes energy. And a hangover is the last thing I need."

'You won't get sick if you just take a shot, and at least you'll stop behaving like you have a broom up your ass."

"First, I need a dick, then the broom in the ass! Friends of poetry, good evening!"

"What? It's true! It's time for your mother to come home so you can party like it's supposed to."

"Yeah…"

It may never happen.

"When is she coming back?"

I clear my throat.

"In two or three months. She's in Japan now."

She nods but stares at me curiously. I change the subject. "So, shots?"

"Yeah, wait, I'll text Scott to grab a bottle of tequila on the way."

The two boys return. I try to look in all directions except Jude's, but it's hard to ignore the sun when it's dazzling you with its beauty. My God! I have a huge crush on this guy! I need to pull myself together before I start writing poetry to him.

"Here."

Jude hands me my cup of soda.

"Thanks."

I smile at him shyly. He looks at me for a long time, his eyes are crazy, indescribable. A unique color and intensity that makes me want to drown in it or jump on him. Lucky me, he looks away before I do something humiliating.

In front of us, my two stupid friends seem to be comfortable. Maybe even a little too much.

"Tequila, huh? You're is in a festive mood," Scott laughs, undressing Al with his eyes.

"Maybe," she replies, staring at him defiantly.

Oh no! They're not going to hook up in front of us, on top of it!

I snatch the bottle from Scott's hands to break their flirtatious moment and take a sip straight from it. Not too much, just enough to burn my throat, awaken my senses and inhibit my fears.

We share the bottle and when Jude takes it with his big hands that I dream of seeing on my body, he takes a clean sip, wiggling his Adam's apple. My eyes linger on the drop that landed on his lower lip. He flicks his tongue for a second to make it disappear. My God! This, which I am probably the only one to notice, sends my blood pressure through the roof. I really, really want to sleep with this guy. And I must be terrible at hiding it because he smiles at me like he has access to all the dirty thoughts going through my brain right now.

"The pool table is free again, let's go," he suggests, clearing his throat.

"Yeah, let's go!" I say in a husky voice, as if he had just suggested that we have sex.

This time, thanks to the tequila, when we play, I'm completely relaxed, and I manage to score some points. Our duet is making winning shots, and it brings us closer. Between complicit glances and smiles of appreciation, the ice melts little by little between us. Besides, it's not just the ice that melts, my panties too, every time he brushes me or helps me to position myself...

Not that I need it, I'm an excellent pool player. Years spent in seedy places waiting for my mother has some advantages, I guess, but that he doesn't know. Screw my skills if that means more contact with this athletic body! Show me how we play, baby! Line your body with mine, please.

"The blue one in the corner," I announce proudly before leaning down to fulfill my wish.

And boom, it goes in! I raise both arms in the air and clap my hand with Jude, who seems as competitive as I am. I think my mojo is back.

"Great move, Balboa! Looks like you don't need my help anymore."

Of course I do, but on a different level, and I hope you're a great lay, I think as I polish my stick and glare at the others.

"The red one, front pocket."

"Okay, stop showing off, Balboa, and play," mocks Alyson

who is now in Scott's arms.

I ignore them and lean suggestively because scoring in pool is not my only goal!

"Go for it, beautiful! You're not going to miss," says Jude.

Beautiful!

His deep, slightly raspy voice saying that word puts me in a state of euphoria that should make me ashamed.

Come on, focus, Rocky!

My eyes visualize the trajectory even before hitting the ball, a sharp blow, and the red goes straight for the pocket.

Jude's cry of joy sounds like music in my ears.

It's his turn to play, and he takes his time. I watch him polish his stick, a circular, precise gesture that gives me ideas forbidden to children under sixteen. He bends over and, at this moment, I regret being in front, and not behind to admire the view. But what he offers me from the front is just as spectacular. His eyes narrow when he concentrates, his brown hair falls back on his forehead. His biceps tense. A flick of his wrist sends the yellow ball towards its abyss and my excitement to new heights.

Is it me or is it hot in here?

"Do you want to play the next move?" asks Jude.

I clear my throat, eyeing him.

"Sure, thanks!"

I score one point after another and snatch victory with undisguised pride. I turn to Al and Scott who don't care about the game anymore, because they're making out.

"Well done, Balboa!" Jude congratulates me as he stands in front of me.

His size makes me look up.

"Too bad they are too busy to see your exploits."

"You, at least, you noticed, that's all that matters."

His gaze lingers for a second on my sulky pout.

"Right," he answers.

"Well, we have to go! Uh… Scott wants to show me something in his room," Alyson announces while the latter is literally devouring her neck. "We'll be back in… thirty minutes."

"One hour," the latter grumbles without lifting his lips.

"Uh… OK! Well, see you then! Have fun!" I say.

"Yes, you too. Get to know each other," says Alyson, waving her hand.

"In the biblical sense of the word," Scott adds before turning on his heels, taking Al with him.

I growl in exasperation, once again mortified by their lack of discretion. They might as well stick a sign on my back: "Desperate girl who hasn't had sex in three months!" But luckily, Jude doesn't pay attention to their remarks.

"I think we lost them for the evening," he says, watching them walk away. "Looks like you're stuck with me, Balboa."

***

Jude looks at me again with his feline gaze. He's both gentle, dangerous, and incredibly sexy. He has the look of Clint Eastwood in *The Good, the Bad, and the Ugly*.

I hope he will show me his gun…

"What?" Jude asks.

"What?"

"You were talking about a gun?"

I blush instantly. I'm fantasizing out loud now.

You're crazy, Rocky!

"No, it's nothing, I was thinking of a movie I watched last night."

"Yeah, which one?"

"*The Good, the Bad, and the Ugly*."

He smiles.

"You know that one?" I ask.

"I love that movie. A classic."

I imitate Clint Eastwood's voice. "'There are two kinds of people in the world those with guns and those that dig.'"

"'You dig?'" he finishes for me.

He has no idea how well that phrase describes me.

"The end scene is iconic," Jude says

"Yes! When they look at each other for a long time before shooting?" I ask.

"Yeah. No dialogue, just eye contact with intense music. This director is a genius."

"Sergio Leone, the father of the spaghetti western."

"Sounds like you know a lot about it." Jude says.

I nod. "I love classic films, from *Breakfast at Tiffany's* to *Rebel Without a Cause*. In fact, I like everything old, ancient, books and buildings. I love anything with a story!" I explain enthusiastically.

Maybe it's because I don't know my own story, but I don't want to tell him that. Instead, I add, "Except men, of course."

His eyes widen.

"I mean, I have nothing against old people, but not for… You see, right?"

I make a ridiculous gesture that makes him raise an eyebrow.

I feel myself blushing with shame. Sometimes I have no idea how to shut the hell up.

"In short! I think I wasn't just born in the right era."

"I'm glad that you were born at this time and that you are here in front of me, Balboa."

I swallow because he has a way of looking at me when he says these words… As if every syllable counts, as if we were alone in the world. He gives me his full attention. And I really want to kiss him.

"Can I show you—"

"Your room?" I say without thinking.

"What?"

He arches an eyebrow, as my cheeks flush again.

"Uh, no, nothing. Pay no attention to me and my boiling hormones. You were saying?"

I drown my embarrassment in my soda. He smiles like the devil, telling me he heard what I dared to suggest. Damn it! If only I was drunk, I could blame my boldness on the alcohol. But no! I'm sober. The effect of tequila is now a distant memory. My attitude is linked to one thing, and one thing only: my libido has been frustrated for too long.

"Come on, I have a great place to show you."

I hope we end up naked in this place.

"Okay!"

He takes my hand inviting me to follow him. His touch on mine is an aphrodisiac. His skin is rough, typical of athletes. Years of training throwing the ball and lifting weights leave some marks. I wonder what kind of marks it could leave on my body…

Yes! I'm definitely hot like an oven.

We find ourselves after a few feet under a glass roof. The place is quiet, contrasting completely with the rest of the house. It's a little cold but, given my level of arousal, the cold is rather welcome. It will allow me to calm down and avoid throwing myself on him at the first opportunity. I don't promise anything at the second or third opportunity, though. We sit on a small sofa, there are plants everywhere, and some are hanging.

The greenhouse itself is magnificent, barely lit by the lanterns that litter the garden. We can smell the soil and the flowers. Through the tinted windows, you can see the courtyard and hear a few students talking and laughing.

"It's really pretty here."

I don't know why I'm whispering. Our proximity, the absence of noise, or the feeling that he shares a secret place with me.

"Why are you whispering?"

"I don't know."

We start laughing.

"Do you like it?" he asks, looking everywhere around him.

"It's wonderful. I have been to the Kappa Omega house several times and had never seen this place."

"I don't think the frats boys are very proud of it, it's not manly to admit that you like flowers and plants," he says.

"Do I have to conclude that you have no problem with that?" I ask.

"No, I have no problem with my virility. Did you doubt it?"

I don't know why my gaze lands on his crotch at this moment.

Who does this kind of thing except a sex-obsessed?

"Uh no…"

He smiles and shakes his head, obviously very amused by my perverse behavior.

"I often come here to recharge my batteries. It's the only place in the house where I can have some peace and quiet."

"You live here?" I ask.

"Yes, for about three weeks. I just transferred from Harvard to play on the football team."

"And you like it?"

"Brown is cool, but Harvard was my first choice."

"So why did you change?"

"I had no choice."

"Oh?"

His face darkens. I want to ask him a thousand questions, but I don't want to be intrusive, and since I don't tell anyone anything, I'd have a lot of nerve to ask him questions.

"Yeah, it's a long story. Still, I like to come to this greenhouse to escape the other members of the team. They're cool, but loud. Sometimes I need to be alone. Living in a fraternity has its advantages and disadvantages."

"And your room?"

"You seem very interested in my room!" he teases.

That's it, I'm blushing again. He smirks at me, a playful glint in his eyes, a dimple appears, and then I lose control. I hoist myself on my knees and literally climb on top of him. One leg on each side, my arms around his neck, his hands landing on my hips in reflex.

I move forward to kiss him. He moves back.

What?

I didn't expect him to reject me. I had the impression that he liked me, despite my clumsiness. Obviously, I got it all wrong. Three months of abstinence, and I can't read the signals anymore. My cheeks are on fire.

"Sorry, I thought you… that we… that you finally wanted us to…"

How could I say this without sounding pathetic?

"Never mind."

I choose to retreat and try to get out of the mess I knowingly got myself into by pulling myself out of his arms, but he holds me back.

I rest my forehead on his shoulder to hide. My hair provides the perfect camouflage.

"You thought I brought you here for sex?"

"Yes… and in case it wasn't clear, I wouldn't be offended if you decided to lay your hands on me," I mumble.

I'm screwed anyway, might as well be honest!

He starts to laugh, a frank and sincere laugh.

"Don't worry, it's pretty clear!"

He caresses my back like he would with a small kitten.

"You are a funny girl, Balboa."

"Is it a good or a bad thing?"

He forces me to face him, picking up my hair with his big hands.

"A good thing, a very good thing indeed. And I would really like to talk before anything happens between us."

Really? Who is this guy?

I think I just ran into the last gentleman on the planet. I literally throw myself on his cock and he wants to make conversation?

And all that in the Kappa Omega house? The devil's antechamber where there must have been more sex than in Hugh Hefner's Playboy mansion.

Caught a little off guard, I do what I know how to do best, which is to be silly.

"Okay, you want to talk? So, we're going to talk. I was born on the 21st of June around 6 p.m., apparently in cries and tears, but that, I believe, is universal—"

He laughs again.

"OK! OK! OK! I don't want you to go back that far. Just tell me something meaningful about yourself. For example, Balboa, your name, where does it come from? Are you Italian?"

"That's not really my name. And I don't know if I have Italian origins. My mom is all-American: blue-eyed blonde who loves fries and burgers, drives a Fords, and smokes Marlboros," I list, avoiding specifying the rest of the things she likes, such as alcohol and opiates. "As for my father, I never knew him."

"Oh, sorry."

"Don't worry! I had nineteen years to get over it."

And one irresponsible parent is enough for me, no need for a second.

"Why is it written 'Balboa' on your cup, then?" he says, pointing to it on the coffee table in front of us.

"Alyson wrote that to make fun of my real name."

"And what's your real name?"

"Scott didn't tell you?"

"No! He told me a lot of things, but not your name."

I grimace. "What did he say to you, that jerk?"

He smiles. "A real bro never reveals what a bro tells him. Bro Code!"

"Does this Bro Code really exist? Or do you make up rules that suit you depending on the circumstances?"

"A little of both," he laughs. "So, what's your first name?"

"Rock, my name is Rocky."

We look at each other for a moment, and he repeats it to himself, smiling as if trying to get used to it. And I don't know what makes me fall more, the sound of his voice or his smile. It's like the sun comes up when he smiles.

"It's pretty, Rocky, it looks good on you!"

I roll my eyes.

"It would look good on me if I was a dog or a stripper."

"Ha! Ha! You're crazy!"

"No, just lucid. You can't look serious when your name is Rocky. You can't get a job with responsibilities when your name is Rocky. My mother condemned me to mediocrity by giving me this name, and all that, and all to honor the bastard who knocked her up. My first name is like an old, faded tattoo on a lower back. That says a lot about my white trash origins, except that I didn't do it on a drunken night, and I can't hide it with a T-shirt."

I said a little too much about myself, and I immediately regret it. I look down and feel completely ridiculous for being on his lap, for throwing myself at him. I behave exactly like a Rocky, as my mother would have done in my place, and I will surely end up like her. No wonder he rejected me, he must be used to being around little princesses, polite, well-behaved, and reserved. Everything that I am not.

"Hey, look at me. I don't see you like that at all. On the contrary, you are… I like you a lot, Rocky!"

His comment makes me raise my head. My breathing catches when I see how intensely he is staring at me. His thumb caresses my cheek. And his lips are closer than ever.

"You are…"

"I am?" I repeat in a low voice.

"You're pretty."

He kisses me on the cheek, then lets his lips slide slowly before continuing.

"Funny..."

His nose caresses mine, I part my lips and hold my breath.

"Sexy..."

He grabs my hair with an intensity that contrasts completely with his initial softness.

"And honest!" he concludes before pressing his mouth against mine.

I am breathless. His lips are soft and firm just as I imagined them. He slides his tongue over my lower lip, and the moan that escapes me should shame me, but I'm too busy enjoying the invasion of his tongue to care. When it meets mine, my heart starts racing, and it becomes difficult to breathe. His mouth silently commands me to open more, and I do, savoring every touch, every bite.

I cling to his broad shoulders and begin to rub myself against him. He makes a noise in his throat and places one of his hands on my butt to accompany my movement, forcing me to slow down and press down even more. It's hot and steamy, and the friction sends an electric jolt through my spine.

"Rocky..." he breathes before kissing my neck.

His mouth trails down my collarbone to my cleavage, which he dots with wet kisses, lighting a fire on my skin.

"I bet you have the most beautiful breasts in the world."

"I don't know, but you'll find out soon enough," I gasp.

I grab my T-shirt and throw it over my head. My eagerness makes him smile but he loses that pretty smile when his eyes land on my breast. I have a moment of doubt. Is he disappointed? Maybe he expected bigger... He's an athlete, he must have seen hundreds of beautiful bodies, and I'm nothing special. He closes his eyes for a moment, and when he opens them again, a bestial glow of desire animates them. My God, this guy is hot!

"Can I kiss you here?" he asks me, gesturing toward my breasts.

I'm a little surprised by his chaste request.

Why does he ask my permission, when I've been rubbing myself on him for a while now? The signals are pretty clear, aren't they?

I just threw away my T-shirt. If that doesn't mean "touch me," then I don't understand anything anymore. This guy is confusing. He's got the looks and confidence of a stadium god, the status of a college star football player, which usually comes with machismo and an overinflated ego, and he's delicate, and caring. He must be—

"Are you a virgin? Do you really want to do it?"

My mouth spoke before I could stop it.

"What?"

His eyebrows furrow.

"No! Not at all! And can't you see how hard you make me?"

A thrust of the hips brings me to my senses. My God! I can't wait to see him naked, but that's not likely to happen if he asks me for written permission every step of the way. I'm for consent, but once I've said yes and know I can say no whenever I want, there's no need to do more.

"Yes, I do! But then why are you asking me questions instead of just taking me?"

He shakes his head laughing.

"I just want to make sure that's what you really want and that you're not doing it because you think that's what I want from you. I just want things to be clear between us and that there are no regrets afterwards."

Oh! He thinks I'm one of those girls who hangs out after sex or sleeps with a guy to please him. Noble of him to worry about that. But I don't fit either of those scenarios, and he's about to find out.

"Jude, I really, really, really want you. I'm not looking for a relationship. Even if I wanted to, I don't have time for that. I won't be looking to see you again or become your girlfriend, so you can relax. What I want is sex, no strings attached! That's all! Promise! There will be no embarrassed wake-up or requests asking for a second round. It's a one-shot deal, so give me all you've got."

I see his jaw clench and his nostrils move. He's holding back from jumping on me, that's obvious.

"Okay. But I want you to tell me if there's something you don't like or if you want me to stop. Okay?"

The look on his face could not be more serious.

"No problem. Do you want me to yell a safe word, *code red, code red*?'" I say, swaying my hips against him.

He shakes his head, amused, and pulls me firmly before whispering against my mouth in a hoarse and excited voice, "A simple *stop* will do."

He suddenly gets up, carrying me with him without any effort, then he puts me on the ground.

"Take off your clothes."

"I see we don't need a roadmap anymore." I laugh at his authoritative tone.

My attempt at humor falls completely flat when he pulls his T-shirt over his head.

Wow!

He is really well built. Even his muscles have muscles. I am speechless, and I've seen naked athletes before, but he beats all records. I'm glad I came tonight.

"Get rid of those jeans and sit on the couch with your legs apart.

"Yes, sir!"

I do so without hesitation because no proposal has ever sounded so good to me.

He gets rid of his jeans too, but stays in his underwear, and there, I discover the rest of the specimen: long muscular and powerful legs, a perfect ass, and this V-line that makes me salivate in advance. My God, he could pose for GQ magazine he's so handsome! And on the front page, please!

He notices my lustful gaze and gives me a flirtatious wink but doesn't show any more pride or arrogance than that. I think if I had his body, I would walk around naked all the time.

He leans over me and places a chaste kiss on my mouth, then one on my neck. He continues on his way lingering for a long time on my breasts, as if he understood what my weak point was. It must be said that my moans are a good GPS for those who know how to listen. Unfortunately, not all guys are so attentive.

He continues his way down to my most sensitive point. He kisses me above the embroidery of my thong. Pulls on it with his teeth. Which has the effect of making me shiver and feel a little guilty.

"You don't have to do this, it's way too intimate for a one-shot."

"You asked me to give it all, right? And that's just a bonus for me, I wanted to eat you up the minute I saw you."

The breath that escapes his mouth when he speaks close to my intimacy ignites my excitement, but I can't help but open my big mouth!

"Mmh, that wasn't that obvious to me."

He straightens up to look at me, forgetting what he was about to do. I think I heard my pussy protest.

"Really? Yet I noticed you as soon as you walked through the door with your two girlfriends."

He says this in a warm voice while sliding my panties down my legs. Unfazed.

"You hide your game well, then?"

"I'm a football player, Rocky. I'm trained never to reveal my game. Besides, how could I not notice you? You're a hottie! The kind of hottie you don't see very often."

He caresses my cheek as he says those words and then kisses me slowly, so slowly that his gentleness disturbs me, because I can hear my heartbeat racing. His hands wander down my body, then insert themselves between my legs, my pulse quickening at the thought of him touching me there.

"You are so wet, Rocky."

It seems to excite him.

"I think that's an understatement."

He swallows my answer with his hungry mouth, his tongue and fingers moving at the same time, slowly at first, then faster and faster. Frantic, insatiable, he caresses my clitoris, and I have to detach my lips from his to be able to express my pleasure loudly.

All my senses are on alert. He pushes my legs apart and slides two fingers in. I moan loudly, so loud that I must have been heard outside the greenhouse. Jude wraps a hand in my hair and holds me inches from his face. He watches me consume myself under the pressure of the comings and goings of his fingers, my mouth in an O-shape, gasping for breath. I let myself be overwhelmed by all these sensations. His eyelids wrinkle. Focused, he probes my reactions to adjust his gestures. He seems to understand the Rocky software quite well.

"Like this? Is it good?"

I nod, not finding the breath necessary to express myself more eloquently. His fingers bend and find that sensitive spot that only I know how to operate, and he rubs it over and over, encouraged by my moans and—oh, my God!—I think he is about to make me come. With his fingers!

How it is possible?

No one before has managed such a feat. Eyes wide, I throw my head back and gasp his name. He takes the opportunity to kiss my neck, my breasts, and that's too much. I take off like a rocket and I explode in the middle of the flight, shaken by uncontrolled tremors. My body arches and stretches like a bow, before falling back into a magnificent fullness.

I close my eyes to better savor the jolts of pleasure that continue to shake my body. My breath is taken away and my brain is numb. So numb that I don't notice I've collapsed on Jude's chest. When I finally come to my senses, I straighten up and he gives me a naughty smile. Half-excited, half-amused.

"Looks like you needed it?"

I nod frantically, still unable to formulate a sentence.

"It's been a while."

"I can see that. So, ready for what's next? I need a little more, Rocky, now that I had a taste."

He licks his fingers still shiny with my desire.

And it's so sexy that I blush.

Jude smirks at me like the devil, then reaches for a condom in his jeans pocket.

"I see you didn't come empty-handed. Isn't that a violation of the perfect gentleman's guide?"

I can't help but be a smart ass, even though I'm not doing so well right now. Impressed by him, his angelic smile, his steely muscles, and his magic fingers. My heart races as he unrolls the condom on his sex with a certain dexterity. I don't know why I suddenly feel vulnerable.

"Ready?" he asks me most seriously.

I nod. But I knew that wouldn't be enough for him. So, I provoke him, more to give me courage than anything else.

"Yes! Go ahead, Jude, fuck me hard, please."

Jude lifts me up and thrusts into me with one hard stroke. We both moan in pleasure and… with surprise. It's so good right now!

"Damn, Rocky, you're super tight!"

"And you, you are super wide!"

"Please, tell me it's not your first time?"

"No, it's not," I say, shaking my head.

Even if his size makes me feel like it's my first time.

He presses my hips and lifts his pelvis, stretching me deliciously, filling me with his cock. I move around him to get used to his presence. His imposing presence. One thing is certain, it can't be ignored, I feel it everywhere in my body. And I love the feeling it gives me. I contract my pussy to relax, he hisses a curse between his teeth.

"Your pussy is magic!"

"Thank you," I say, not quite sure what to say to that.

It takes me a while to calm my racing heart. I feel like I'm out of breath when we've barely started the serious stuff.

I lean on my knees, put my hands on his beautiful torso, and admire him as he slowly rises and falls inside me. His pectorals are full, finely drawn, and his abs, a work of art. I want to fuck his abs. He has that sexy V-line that goes down to his sex. It's a feast for the eyes, and for everything else, for that matter. Watching his body is definitely not the best way to calm my ardor. Neither touching him. His skin is soft as silk.

My gaze then falls on his face. I hope he makes one of those gross faces guys sometimes make during the action, just to gross me out a bit and keep me going longer. But no! Once again, I'm wrong. He's sexy as hell. He looks focused and serious, staring at the place where our two bodies meet as if it were an impossible equation to decipher. He sees that I'm watching him, and our eyes lock for a moment. His gaze of a young Clint Eastwood makes me completely smitten.

Calm down, Rocky!

"I ended up getting your gun," I say, breaking up that all-too-intense moment and bringing it back to where it belongs, to hookup status.

"What?"

"Earlier, remember when I was talking about a gun? I was referring to your cock."

He growls.

"Stop talking bullshit and give me your mouth, baby."

I freeze.

"I don't want you to give me a little name! It's way too intimate for a one-shot."

He frowns and tries to read things in me that I don't want to reveal, but in this position, I feel particularly vulnerable and more able to play the strong head who has everything under control.

He sits up, wraps his big hands around the back of my neck with his large hands, then whispers in my ear, "Keep telling yourself stories and making stupid rules, if it makes you feel any better, but you and I know very well that once won't be enough for us."

I'm about to protest but he punctuates his remarks with a thrust that makes me gasp.

"This is way too good to only do once."

He grabs my waist pressing me against him. Our lips connect and disconnect to the rhythm of his thrusts. His tongue licks mine. His hands dig into my hair, and he pulls. I don't know if we kiss or eat each other, but one thing is sure, it has the benefit of calming my fears and putting my brain on mute.

I move on him. He gives me a hungry look, then grabs my butt with his big hands, so tight I'm sure I'll have marks tomorrow morning. He contracts his abs and stands up to take me. My God! It's so deep like that that I think I'm losing my mind. I wrap my legs around him to take some of my weight off him, but he doesn't seem the least bit bothered by my hundred pounds.

He moves without any difficulty and puts me against one of the windows of the greenhouse. The cold freezes my back and multiplies tenfold my sensations. Caught between the heat of his body, and the cold of the glass, I start to moan loudly. He grips my ass, making me move up and down his cock at a painfully slow pace. It's so intense that I feel like I can feel it in my stomach. His caramel eyes have turned black, and he penetrates me. My heart starts to beat faster.

I bring my lips closer to his.

"Fuck me, Jude!"

He grunts, then kisses me wildly. His tongue makes wonders in my mouth. I'm surrounded, overwhelmed by all these sensations.

I need oxygen, but I can't bring myself to stop kissing him long enough to breathe.

I squeeze my thighs around him, already feeling the beginnings of my orgasm forming in my lower spine. He grits his teeth and picks up the pace. His thrusts become erratic and noisy. Our two gasping breaths join this joyous symphony, until I reach the point of no return.

"Yes, go ahead, baby, cum for me!"

And I obey him, I let myself go again. This time, my cries are so intense that I muffle them by biting his shoulder. It excites him. He growls, then hammers me with precision, fueling the shockwave that's already coursing through my body, making it last beyond bearable. My brain goes offline, and I start shaking so hard I can barely stay on top of him.

He squeezes me to keep me close to his chest. My mouth glued to his ear, I struggle to breathe, to think, I feel his cock pulsing inside, and he comes in turn in an animal growl.

I don't know how it all ended. All I know is that a few minutes later, when I open my eyes, I'm lying on the couch, on top of a naked and breathless Jude, the sound of rain pounding on the greenhouse.

Each drop seems to echo the beating of my body.

How long has it been raining? We stay there in silence, panting, enjoying the warmth of our two tangled bodies.

"Thank you, Harvard, for the transfer!" I say after an eternity.

The sound of my voice startles us both. He lowers his head as I raise mine.

Shit! He's so beautiful!

He gives me a tired smile, his eyelids are heavy, he looks like he is about to fall asleep. He caresses my back, my hair. I should get up and end this. Caresses after sex are not part of the "one-night stand" deal, but there is what I want and what I am able to do right now. He tilts his head and kisses me softly.

OK! That's too much!

"I'm going to have to write a letter to the headmaster of Harvard to thank him warmly. You are by far the best one-night stand I have ever had."

His face tenses for a moment, then he replies, "Really? Enough to do it again?"

"What? Right now?"

He chuckles.

"You're relentless. No tomorrow night, or tomorrow morning, if you change your mind and decide to sleep over."

For a moment, I want to say yes. Sleeping in his arms and waking up to doing again sounds like a great idea, except I can't. Tomorrow morning, I get Max back and resume my stressful life between classes, work, and bills to pay. Max is not at all a constraint, on the contrary, he is my ray of sunshine, the only thing that keeps me going when I give up. His smile and my determination to offer him a better life, better than anything I have ever known. That's what keeps me going, but that's also why I don't have room for anything else. Jude is an amazing fuck!! He made me see stars, but he must not become more than that. I need all my concentration, all my energy for Max and my classes.

Besides, once Jude finds out the kind of life I lead, he won't want to be stuck with me. A guy like Jude has too many opportunities to get attached to a particular girl, and that's exactly why I chose him. We had a great time! But we can't go further. Trying to prolong the pleasure will only make the fatal return to reality harder.

"You look like I just suggested you carry my future children," he says, tapping my chin. "So? What do you say?"

"No, Jude. It's tempting, but I told you, I never swim twice in the same pool. Although this pool is heated and has a spectacular view of a dream landscape."

He laughs at my metaphor.

"I have never been dumped by comparing me to a swimming pool."

"I'm sure you've never been dumped at all."

His cocky smile tells me I'm right.

"There is a first time for everything."

"You haven't dumped me yet, and I haven't said my last word."

"Honestly, you would be wasting your time."

"Maybe."

He challenges me with his eyes and slides his hand down my spine. My skin is covered with goosebumps.

"But something tells me that I still have a chance!" he says in a voice so sexy that the vibrations make my nipples shamefully hard.

One thing is for sure, my body loves him.

"That something is arrogance."

"Or determination."

Now his hand is on my ass, and I'm titillated again.

"In case you were wondering, the greenhouse windows are tinted. No one could see your cute little ass from the outside. I would never expose you like that."

"You didn't hear me complaining!"

"True, but I wanted you to know that."

"Thank you for caring about my virtue."

I smile and decide to tease him.

"I see that M. Gentleman is back."

He slaps my ass, and I squeal in surprise. Then he rolls me under him.

"I'll show you a gentleman!"

He kisses me breathless. When I feel him harden, I'm ready to lose myself in his arms again. One last banging to say goodbye, it can't hurt us. Can't it?

I know it's a mistake. I know it contradicts everything I've said, but it's like that last drink you can't help but down on a drunken night. I'll wake up tomorrow with a terrible hangover, but for now, I want to let myself be intoxicated by Jude Hartnett.

COSTA RICA

4

Jude

The training is brutal. Each of us pays for the excesses of the day before. The training session breaks down the last molecules of alcohol that were still slowing down our bodies.

Coach Callahan and his assistant are furious and make us pay by making us do wind sprints. After an hour of frantic running, I am literally coughing up my lungs on the grass.

A whistle brings us all together in the middle of the field. The coach is wearing a scowl. With his graying hair and bags under his eyes, he looks at us, a grimace of displeasure screwed to the corner of his lips.

I've only been part of the team for three weeks, but I quickly understood how he works. First, he yells, then explains his strategy. He is very stingy with compliments, and when they do come, they are truly deserved. The most important thing is that he is a great champion, the former Dallas Cowboys quarterback. They won two Super Bowls because of him. And that deserves respect.

"Alright, guys! It's not with this kind of attitude that we will beat Yale!" he thunders in his deep voice. "And you know what I think?"

"A season that starts badly is very difficult to make up for," finishes the whole team in unison.

He looks at his clipboard and reviews us one by one. Those who are still suffering from yesterday's party are having a bad time. None of us flinch. Then after burning out his anger and breaking his voice, he eventually softens and becomes more constructive in his criticism, "Alec, be more precise with your passes. You systematically pass to the right, it leaves too many opportunities for the opposing defense to anticipate your game."

"Yes, coach!"

"Scott, Adam, beef up your defense! It's too weak, too nice. The adversary must be afraid to mess with you."

The two giants nod in agreement.

"Jude! It's not bad, you're fast. On the other hand, focus, you missed some key catches today. During a game, that can hurt us."

I nod, too breathless to come up with an answer. Anyway, other than agreeing with him, there is nothing else I can do. He's right, I'm not focused today.

Coach Callahan continues to give advice to each member of the team. Some are raked over the coals, but none of us would dare to contradict him. Football is first and foremost a sport of discipline. One strategic mistake, and one of us can end up in a wheelchair. So, even if sometimes it's hard to be yelled at, we know that deep down, it's for our own good.

"Okay, back to the locker room now. And get some rest tonight. I don't want to get zombies in the morning."

We obey. As I grab my helmet left on the ground, Coach Callahan calls out to me.

"Jude! Can we meet in my office for five minutes?"

"Sure!"

I put my helmet under my arm and follow him under Alec's worried look. A real mother hen. I have known him for a short time, but I appreciate that he took me under his wing. My integration into the team and the fraternity went smoothly, and I owe Alec a lot.

I give him a reassuring smile, even though I have no idea what the coach wants from me.

We arrive at his office in dead silence. He seems tense, which doesn't make me feel any better. The last time I found myself in the office of a coach, it was to get fired from the team, a memory that I like to forget.

"Close the door, please."

I obey and settle into one of the old leather armchairs that sags under my weight. I watch him put away his clipboard, then type something on his computer for long, painful minutes.

To pass the time, I focus my attention on the various trophies that adorn the showcase behind him. There are a lot of them. It's impressive. I'd like to do my part. If we win the championship, it would be a great way to finish my degree, and it would open all the doors for me to the pros. My dream would finally come true, and I could take care of my mother who broke her ass to get me to practice bought all my equipment, drove me to all the games, all while juggling two jobs.

"Jude."

My attention snaps back to him at the sound of his voice.

"How's your integration into the team going?"

"Pretty good! The guys are nice, I get along with most of them. Alec is a great captain, he's been a good friend to me."

"Very good, very good."

He scratches his chin. The touch of his fingers on his three-day beard causes the same crackling sound as an out-of-tune radio static.

"Did you tell them why you transferred from Harvard?"

My blood freezes, like it does every time I think about that. *About her.*

"No…" I answer, pulling on an invisible thread of my pants.

"Good, I'd rather that they don't know. It would be better if they thought you had chosen us. It could weaken the balance of the team and jeopardize our chances of winning the championship if you tell them the truth."

"I understand! Either way, I don't want to dwell on it."

"I get it, son, what happened to you is a hell of a mess."

"Yeah."

"Anyway, we're glad to have you. Once you get settled in, you'll do wonders. I'm sure of it."

I scratch the back of my head, a little embarrassed. So far, I haven't managed to play at my best level and that frustrates me.

"Thank you, Coach! I won't let you down, I promise."

He waves his chin at me in a gesture of dismissal. I seize the opportunity and join my teammates. In the locker room, it's the usual mess. Heated conversations, laughter, and singing echo. The atmosphere is joyful, even though the coach gave us a lecture. But the party was crazy and successful for everyone, so there's a good mood going on. *The Pussy Effect*, as Scott would say.

I get rid of my gear and step into the shower. The feel of the hot water on my numb muscles feels great and I let out a long sigh of relief. I'm going to be fine here at Brown, I'm sure now. And my hopes of turning pro are back.

I soap myself up, run my hand over my shoulder and notice that I have a bruise. I can't help but smile.

Rocky.

Images of her biting my shoulder to muffle her screams, as she shook with pleasure in my arms, come into my mind and made me hard again. I haven't been like this for a girl since I was 15.

She makes the sexiest moans in the world when she fucks, and her body… A work of art! She's all curves and smooth skin. This girl is fire! And like fire, she's elusive. My cock wasn't yet dry before she was already barricading herself behind a wall. She wouldn't even give me her number.

The only thing I managed to get was to walk her to her car. A crappy old car that has trouble starting. My protective instinct took over. I offered to drive her home, just to make sure she got home safely, and didn't break down on a road in the middle of the night. From the look on her face, it looked like I was suggesting she sell her firstborn to the devil.

Arms crossed over her plump breasts, she lifted her chin and glared at me, "A one-night stand doesn't take you home, Jude."

How stubborn she is! And where does she get all these bullshit rules from? It almost seems as if she repeats them to herself to better believe them, to keep me at a distance. If I understood one thing about Rocky last night, it's that she has no problem giving 100% of herself sexually, but the rest is unavailable. I wonder why. In any case, I like her, I really like her, and not only physically. There is something in her that touches me and attracts me, a fragility, a sincerity, a depth that makes me want to know more. The fact that she is completely crazy, says exactly what's on her mind, and plays pool like no one else doesn't ruin her charm. I've never had so much fun with a girl. I like her natural, her outspokenness, her freshness, and I have every intention of seeing her again.

5

Rocky

"Rocky, that's not the way to do it!" The teacher said to add the baking soda first."

"OK! OK! I'll go get it. If the teacher says so, then it must be true!"

The teacher this! Teacher that! She always knows everything better than everyone, the teacher. And I suspect Max is using it as a catalyst to tell me what to do. The little opportunist!

I groan while rummaging in the cupboards, I can't find the baking soda. I may have stored it in the laundry room. I sometimes use it to remove stubborn stains from his white T-shirts. I look above the washing machine, on the shelf where all the products are lined up, but nothing.

However, I was sure I had bought some not so long ago. But like everything else, the baking soda was consumed at the speed of light. We'll have to go shopping again. We have almost nothing left to eat. Problem is, I'm broke. My account should show a total of one hundred dollars, and it's barely the fifteenth of the month. Usually, I manage my budget to the penny, but this month I had unexpected expenses, like buying Max new sneakers. He damaged them while playing football. Even if he insisted that he didn't need new ones, I didn't want him to go to school wearing tennis shoes with half a hole in them. I didn't want Max to be bullied the way I was at his age. Kids can be very cruel. I know something about it.

In addition, the other moms are keeping an eye on things. No detail escapes them. So, the sneakers with holes in them would have been the talk of the town for weeks. They keep asking questions about our situation. These gossipers who have nothing else to do but investigate people's lives.

"It' s been a long time since we've seen Rebecca?"

"Is she fine?"

"Her new job must be very demanding!"

"I hope she's not sick, at least?"

"Nooooo, everything is fine, but thank you for your concern. By the way, did you hear the Cummings are getting divorced?"

My strategy is always the same. Respond casually like I don't carry the weight of the world on my shoulders, then redirect their attention to other topics. It works every time! All they need is something juicy to ease their boredom. It must be nice to have time to be bored. Anyway! Now is not the time to philosophize, I need to find that damn baking soda.

After literally turning the house upside down, I return empty-handed to the kitchen as Max continues to refine his volcano. It's science week at school, and everyone has chosen a topic to study. Max chose volcanoes. I'm surprised he didn't take the dinosaurs. Maybe we are entering a new phase.

He's growing up so fast, and his own mother isn't here to see him. Besides, he asks more and more questions, about mom, about her absence. Each time, I come up with approximate answers, but he's too clever to be fooled. Soon, I'm going to have to tell him the awful truth: Mom is gone, Mom may never come back. How do you tell a 6-year-old that the most important person, the one who is supposed to defend you and love you against all odds, has turned her back on you?

Of all the shit she did to me in my childhood, abandonment was not yet on the list. I believe it's done. She definitely checked off all the boxes for the shittiest parent on the planet. The worst part is that I'm sure she's rebuilt her life somewhere in another city, in another state, and she doesn't care about us anymore. Rebecca Prescott always works the same way: if she loses a man, she finds another, and too bad for the collateral damage. Just thinking about it makes me angry and saddens me at the same time. This time, the collateral damage is a little 6-year-old who deserves better than that.

I take a deep breath to gather my wits and lean against the

door frame. Max is always busy painting his cardboard carefully. He is super serious, and like every time he is focused, he sticks his little tongue between his teeth. I sit down in front of him.

"How's it going, toad?"

"Great! Look, the paint is almost dry. All that's left is… didn't you find any baking soda?"

"No, sorry, but I was sure we had some."

"Okay, so what do we do?" he sulks. "It sucks, a volcano without an eruption."

"Well, we're going to buy some, my little man. I'm not going to let you go back to school with a half-done project."

"Yay! That way, we can also get a present for William. It's his birthday soon, and he loves the Avengers."

Damn, that slipped my mind! One more thing to buy!

My brain makes the strange sound of a cash register.

"And I love the Avengers too, you know," he says casually.

His mischievous eyes meet mine. He is the king of seduction when he wants to get something. If he is not heading for a career as a paleontologist, Max will have a great career as a lawyer ahead of him.

"But, it's not your birthday."

"Yes, but it's in six months. I could have a mid-birthday present."

"I love the concept, but no, my little love."

He sulks a bit for the sake of it, but I know exactly how to cheer him up.

"How about adding dinosaurs to the model to make it even more realistic?"

His big brown eyes meet mine, and a toothless smile revives his baby face.

"Yes! Yay!"

He gets down from his chair, then rushes to his room. He comes back with a box full of dinosaurs, places them all around the volcano, then explains to me what each eats. Which one is the ferocious, and why they disappeared. I listen to him religiously playing surprised at each piece of information, while he talks to me about it all the time and I could write an encyclopedia of dinosaurs if I heard him talk about them so much.

I like that he is passionate like that. At least when he's immersed in his world of tyrannosaurs, he doesn't think about our troubles.

Once again, the day flies by at lightning speed. It's already eight o'clock when Max goes to bed, and I haven't worked a second on my medieval architecture paper due tomorrow.

"Come on, my little man, it's time to sleep now."

"Nooooo, one more story!"

"Max, you're going to be tired tomorrow. It's late."

I put away the book *Jack and the Beanstalk* I just read to him in his little library.

"Rocky?"

"Yes, my baby."

"Stop, I already told you that I'm not a baby anymore," he pouts.

Yet, right now, in his superhero-colored pajamas, with his wild curls and his little red cheeks, he reminds me of when he was a baby, and wiggled around in his sleep sack. I'm keeping this information to myself because I don't want to upset him.

"Sorry, I meant *yes big man!*"

"You know?"

"No? But I'm sure you'll tell me."

I talk to him while picking up the dirty laundry.

"I don't like Jack!"

"Who is Jack? One of your friends that I don't know?"

For a moment, I imagine the worst. A stranger, a malicious person would have escaped my vigilance and would have hurt him. Life taught me to be suspicious of everyone. There are many more deranged people than we think.

"No, Jack in *Jack and the Beanstalk*!"

"Ah! Why not?"

"Well, because he's an idiot and a thief."

I sit next to him, curious to hear his explanations. He always has very interesting theories about the heroes of fairy tales, and he often makes me see things in a new light. And this time is no exception. He tells me in his adorable little voice in a serious way, "Well, first, he goes to the market, and he gets tricked into trading a cow for two beans, and that is really stupid. He could have negotiated at least ten."

"It makes sense!"

"Then, he steals the giant's treasure when he had done nothing to him! And that's mean."

I burst out laughing because his demonstration is unbeatable. Yeah, he'll definitely be a lawyer!

"I agree with you! Jack is a stupid thief, Snow White a naive submissive woman, and Cinderella should kick her stepmother out."

He nods and claps my hand. Max is as cynical as I am. And I don't know if that's a good or a bad thing.

"Come on! Now it's time to sleep."

He lies down, I arrange his blanket so that he is not cold and is as comfortable as possible. He sighs with relief.

"Well, you'll be fine, my little toad."

He just nods and opens his arms for me to hug him. I quickly go for it. It's my favorite moment of the day, when Max stops playing big and cuddles up to me like he did when he was little.

I kiss him hard. He clings to my neck and squeezes me so I can't escape.

"Maaax, I have to go now."

"What's the password?"

"Tyrex?"

"Nope!"

"Tyrannosaurus?"

"Nope."

"Polacanthus?"

"Nope!"

"Maaaaax!"

"Rooooooockyyyy!"

"Let go of me."

"I want the password first."

"Okay, you asked for it."

I tickle his ribs to get him to let me go. He burst into a giggle and started fidgeting all over the place. His bursts of laughter invade the room and warm my heart, so I redouble my fervor so that he laughs even more. At this precise moment, I forget all my fatigue, all my problems. He eventually calms down, but his eyes continue to sparkle with joy.

"Good night, toad. Sleep well."

I rub my nose against his.

"I love you," I add.

He nods, rolls over, grabs his blanket, and hugs it tightly, then falls asleep. I look at him tenderly for a moment before mentally slapping myself.

Back to work, Rocky!

I sigh with fatigue, it's going to be a long night.

I take out my medieval architecture book, highlight all the key ideas I want to put in my paper, before expanding my research on the Internet. My plan and introduction are already written when my phone lights up. This is a message from Isabella who writes to me in our chat group modestly called *Bitches are out*.

Isabella: Rocky!!! We miss you!

They send me a selfie, and from the blush on their cheeks, I can tell they're drunk.

Rocky: Thank you. I miss you too. How's the party going on?

Isabella: Top! We're at Shamrock, and there's a concert by an indie band, it's great! It's so crowded! Wait, I'll FaceTime you.

Isabella calls me, turns on herself so that I have a full view of the event.

"It looks great," I say.

"There's the football team, too. They won their game against Yale, so they decided to celebrate. You would see all the groupies around them, it's unbelievable!" Isabella complains. "Alec hasn't spoken to me all night. He's distant with me again."

"Sorry, Isa."

"By the way, Jude asked about you!"

My heart jumps and I try to calm my enthusiasm to avoid the girls from going back to their daily harassment since we met, *You should go out with him, he's great. Forget your ridiculous rule and live. Did you take a good look at him? Did you see how hot he is?* And the worst is when they go into their psychological delirium of *Rocky, you deserve to be loved, let love into your life*. There, I really want to scream.

"Oh yeah?"

"Yeah, he thought you were with us, and when he realized you weren't, he looked disappointed."

"Is that true?"

I smile despite myself. The thought of him still thinking about me warms my heart. It's been over a month since our sexual escapade and I have to admit that I've been thinking about him a lot, about his smile, his voice, and his body...

"Yeah, I don't know what you did to him, but he seems smitten."

"Don't exaggerate either!"

"I'm telling you, you should have seen his pretty little face break down."

"I'm sure he must have found something to console himself with since then."

"Maybe, but honestly, Rocky, I think you should review your one-night stand rule because a specimen like Jude doesn't grow on trees," adds Alyson. "And if I wasn't already with Scott, I think I'd be tempted."

"I'm single," Isabella says. "Maybe I should go hit on him. Besides, it would be the perfect revenge against Alec... What did you say? That was the best sex you ever had?"

"If you touch him, I'll strangle you," I say.

The two of them look at each other like the two punks they are and burst out laughing.

"Maybe you're not so detached after all," Isa mocks.

"I hate you."

"No, you love us," Isa replies.

"Well, in two weeks, are you going out with us?" Alyson adds.

"Yes, Max has a slumber party for the birthday of one of his friends, so I'll be available."

"And your mother, is she coming home soon?" asks Isa.

"No, uh, actually, she called today to say that... her business trip was extended by a few months. So, it looks like she won't be back for a while."

The sound of an electric guitar is heard, as well as the shouts of the crowd around the girls, completely covering my voice.

"Well, Rocky, we can't hear you anymore! We miss you. We give you a big kiss and see you tomorrow," yells Isa.

Both of them wave goodbye on the screen with enthusiasm, I do the same before hanging up. I sigh for a long time. I hate lying to my two best friends. They don't deserve to be led on like this. Maybe I should tell them everything. I'm sure they would understand. But I hate being pitied. Somehow, continuing to pretend that my life is normal allows me to deny reality and not crumble before the mountain of responsibility that comes with it. In my head, I keep telling myself: *So far, so good.*

6

Rocky

"Please! Please, please, please!! Start! Start! Start! Start!"

I turn the damn key in the damn ignition, and I get the same damn reaction again. Meaning, nothing! It's official, my car just quits on me. Damn it! That's not a good time!

I sigh in despair, before hitting my forehead against the steering wheel several times. I can already imagine the avalanche of shitty consequences that this will cause in my daily life. If my car won't start, how do I get to college every day? How do I do my grocery shopping? How to pay for the repairs? I'm going to have to sell some of my stuff, my computer, or something else? I don't own anything valuable, so it's going to be hard to collect the extravagant amount.

I could eventually ask for more hours in the cafeteria or ask for an advance on my paycheck, but that would mean missing even more classes and jeopardizing my school year. I didn't make all these efforts to finally fail. My life is like a house of cards, a gust of wind, and everything goes down the drain. Tears of bitterness, fatigue, and general annoyance threaten to surface, and I force myself not to let the emotion overwhelm me. I check my watch, Max finishes school in fifteen minutes. Even with a miracle, I won't be there in time. The bitches moms will drool again. I can hear them spitting their venom from here. Poor Max, I don't want him to wonder what I'm doing. Or if I'll even come.

In a burst of courage, I pull on the tab that opens the hood and exit into the autumnal sweetness. Fortunately, to my misfortune, the weather is sunny today. A gust of wind lifts my hair, and I shiver in spite of everything. I blow on my hands, rub them together to give myself courage. Facing my hood, I don't really know what to do, I don't know anything about mechanics. So, I start touching everything, shaking the battery, tapping on the motor. Anything and everything, as long as the miracle happens.

But of course, the car doesn't magically start.

I pull out my phone and look for a tutorial on YouTube. It may be naive as a solution, but the tutorials have often saved my ass, like the time the washing machine broke down, or when I had to make Max up as a zombie for Halloween. The internet is a gold mine. You can find everything there, it's crazy! I'm sure you can find tutorials on how to de-flesh your neighbor if you look hard enough. On the other hand, you have to have the patience and the desire to get into the cheesy staging of Internet users who think they are Spielberg.

After a few minutes of research, I find one that explains that two wires must be connected. I start looking for the two wires. The deafening sound of an approaching engine echoes behind me. I turn around suddenly and see a guy on a motorcycle. Given my posture, he must have an amazing view of my ass! The biker parks his bike, raises his visor. My heart misses a beat.

"Jude?"

He takes off his bike helmet, hangs it on the handlebars of his bike and walks towards me, looking worried.

"Is everything okay?"

"Yes, everything is fine! I was just telling a story to my engine," I quip.

Why do I say such stupid things? I could slap myself in the face, but I don't know, he confuses me and prevents me from behaving like the responsible adult that I normally am.

Luckily, he doesn't pay any attention to my childish behavior.

"It won't start?"

"No."

He glances under the hood, flicks a couple of things, looking intensely focused.

"Can I have your keys?"

"They're still in the ignition."

He walks around me and settles into the front seat, looking for a solution inside that he didn't find outside. A few seconds later, he comes back to me, a deep wrinkle has appeared on his forehead, and the sentence falls.

"Your starter is ruined."

"Oh no! I knew it, the mechanic had warned me."

I put both my hands on my face and growl, "Can you fix it?"

"Unfortunately, no. I could possibly get it started, but I would need a car for that, with battery cables. Do you want me to call a tow truck?"

"No, thank you, I'll be fine."

A tow truck! What am I going to pay him with?

I turn away from Jude, stamp my foot like an annoyed little girl, then look up at the sky to hide my annoyance. He places a comforting hand on my shoulder. A tear of bitterness escapes me, I make it disappear as quickly as possible with the back of my hand.

"Hey, don't worry, it's not a big deal, just a part to change."

He comes closer to me, turns me around, and hugs me when he sees how affected I am. For anyone else, a car breakdown is nothing, just a little hitch that makes you lose an afternoon, but for me, it's the extra grain of sand that breaks the already shaky machine of my existence.

Breathe, Rocky! This is not the end of the world.

I bite the inside of my cheek and remain impassive. I do everything not to break down. But when he presses a kiss to my temple, I let my sadness and frustration take over, and I cry my tears against his neck. He hugs me tighter, the smell of his spicy cologne and the warmth of his body are the perfect shelters for my sadness. He caresses my hair and helps me to get rid of my pain. He must be thinking that I'm crazy to cry for so little. I'm ashamed of myself and, at the same time, I feel so good in his arms that I stay there for a while. I end up coming to my senses and, with that, my distance.

"I have a mechanic buddy who lives in Warwick, I can ask him to come by and take a look at your car if you want?"

"Thank you, but it won't be necessary. Anyway, I don't have time to wait. I'll… I'll… find a solution. In the meantime, can I ask you a favor?"

"All you want!"

"Can you drop me off somewhere?"

"Sure."

I give him the address of Max's elementary school. He doesn't ask any more questions than that, and that's fine with me.

"Have you ever been on a bike?"

I shake my head no. He smiles.

"There's a first time for everything."

"I guess."

He offers me a helmet. This one, unlike his, doesn't have a visor and looks much more elegant. I manage to put it on without too much difficulty, but I stumble on the clasp.

"Come here."

His hands are busy closing my helmet with a disconcerting slowness, which allows me to admire him. My eyes land on his lips, which I long to feel on me again. The last time was so long ago that I feel like it didn't really happen. He clears his throat, and my eyes go up to his, they're filled with desire and tenderness too.

"Don't look at me like that if you want me to keep my distance."

I nod my head. Because I don't know what else to do. He turns around, gets on his bike, balances the bike before starting it up with a deafening noise. I do my best to sit behind him.

"Ready?"

"Yes!"

He grabs one of my hands, then wraps it around himself.

"You'll have to hold on tight, Rocky!"

I obey him without flinching, trying to ignore the butterflies that flutter in my stomach as my chest crashes against his back and my arms wrap around his steel abs. The smell of leather and his perfume invades my senses, I close my eyes to better savor it. Then we fly. For twenty minutes, there is only him, me, the autumnal smell of Rhode Island, the golden leaves that litter the ground and the noise of his motorcycle.

***

Jude

I drop Rocky off in front of what appears to be an elementary school. The motor stops under the impulse of my wrist. She gets off a little clumsily, almost staggers when she puts her foot on the ground. I don't know if it's the effect of the bike, but she looks completely disoriented.

"Well, thank you for… dropping me off."

She arranges her coat, then waves awkwardly to say goodbye or to order me to leave. Hard to know with her. I don't move. I get off my bike, take off my helmet and watch her walk away. It's been far too long since I've seen her to be satisfied with these few ridiculous minutes with her. Who knows when I will have the chance to see her again? I watch her tight little ass in her jeans walk away.

She really has a dream body! And having felt her against me all along the ride gave me a hell of a hard-on. Usually, I like to go fast, but this time, I rode slowly to keep her with me as long as possible. I only dream of one thing: to put her back in my bed and do all the things to her that I couldn't last time.

After a few meters, she turns around and looks at me over her shoulder.

"You can leave now!"

What a bossy chick!

"I would like to, but you still have my helmet."

She puts her hand on her head, surprised to have forgotten such an important detail.

"Oh, yes, that's right, sorry. I'm not thinking straight."

That's the least we can say! And I smile even more, because I have the feeling that I had something to do with it. She tries to get out of the helmet, but the clasp gives her a hard time again. I laugh when I see her struggle. Angry and impatient, she finally gave in and brought her sexy little ass back to me. Her big black eyes are on fire, her full lips form a thin line of displeasure, while her hair neatly frames her perfect face. It's crazy how beautiful she is! Of a fresh, natural beauty, she doesn't wear makeup. My eyes wander to the tiny beauty mark in the corner of her mouth.

I can't help but place a furtive kiss on her lips. She tenses up and glares at me.

"Don't do that!"

"Sorry, I—"

No time to finish my sentence when I hear a small voice behind us.

"Rocky! You are late."

She turns around, when I haven't had time to free her from the helmet yet.

"Sorry, my little toad, I had a car trouble."

She picks up a short blond boy with curly hair whom she kisses on the cheek.

Is it her son?

No! She is much too young to have a child of this age. I watch the little boy in her arms, he doesn't look like her at all. And then he called her *Rocky*, not *Mom*. She may be babysitting. The real question is How does she manage to focus on her studies while doing odd jobs? She must be in deep shit financially.

With my mother, we had enough money trouble that I recognize the signs. If I hadn't had a football scholarship, I wouldn't have been able to afford Brown or Harvard. That's why she started crying, because her car wouldn't start. Because she can't afford the repairs. And me, I suggested she calls a tow truck. How stupid can I be sometimes!

"Ha! Ha! You look funny with that on your head, you look like a Ninja Turtle."

"Always the first to make fun of me Maxwell!"

She puts him on the ground, then asks me softly, "Can you take the helmet off now, please?"

I do so, a little confused, as she holds her breath and looks in every direction but mine. I want to ask her a million questions, but I don't dare. Besides, I'm pretty sure she's going to tell me to fuck off.

"Rocky, who is this giant?"

"Uh, this giant…"

She looks at the little one, and her face fills with tenderness and love.

"He's a friend of mine."

The little boy looks at me a little shyly, so I kneel down to get to his level.

"My name is Jude! And you?"

"Maxwell, but everyone calls me Max."

"It's a champion's name."

"Thanks! Did you know that means *great* in Latin?

"No, I didn't know. Thank you, buddy, you taught me something today. Tell me, how old are you?" I ask

"I'm six!"

"6-years-old? And you already speak Latin?"

"Yes, Max is very advanced, the teacher says he's a little genius," Rocky answers for him.

I smile at him, and he smiles back. He's missing a few teeth, which makes him adorable. His gaze then lands on my bike.

"Do you like motorcycles?"

He nods shyly.

"Maybe I could take you for a ride one of these days? Well, if Rocky agrees."

I straighten up, thinking I have her approval, but instead she glares at me. What could I have done to make her angry?

"Your little brother is adorable."

I try to preach the false to get the truth and it works.

"Thanks."

So, it's not babysitting.

"Well, we have to go! Thanks again for dropping me off, and uh…see you next time."

"What about your car?" I ask.

She shrugs. Resigned.

"Well, it won't start anymore, so it won't go very far. I'll take care of it tomorrow, with a clear head."

"Okay," I say.

Rocky takes her little brother by the hand and crosses the road, towards the bus, I suppose. I watch them walk away, a little stunned. From time to time, Max turns around to see if I'm still there. I only move when they disappear around the corner. I reach into my jacket pocket to pull out my motorcycle keys and find with surprise that I have kept the ones from Rocky's car! Shit! I climb on the bike hoping it's not too late to give them back to her, because I have no idea where she lives, and I don't have her number.

7

Jude

Practice starts in an hour. I debate with myself. Missing training is something I've never done. I know it's not a good idea, especially since I'm new to the team and I still have to prove myself. But shit, there is something more important right now!

Rocky doesn't seem to have the time or the means to repair her car. I don't really know her family situation because she's as open as a prison door, but my gut tells me she needs help. Whether she wants to admit it or not. I pick up my phone to let Alec know I'll miss the practice.

> **Jude: Yo, captain! I won't be able to come to practice today!**

> **Alec: Okay, I hope you have a good reason.**

> **Jude_I have to help a friend who is in deep shit.**

> **Scott: Which friend? We're your only friends, and we're all here. Admit that you're having sex, and that it takes time, because you can't have a hard-on.**

I'm laughing. Scott really is the king of jerks.

Jude: Stop blaming your erection problems on me. I know a couple of blue pills that can fix your troubles.

Alec: You'll settle your kid stories somewhere other than the team chat. But just so you know, the coach hates no-shows. You risk not playing the game this weekend if you miss practice.

Jude_I know, but no choice.

Alec: OK... Nothing serious at least?

Jude: No, it's just something I can't put off.

Scott: She's good, I hope?

Jude: Seriously, Scott, a peach emoji?

Alec: Don't hesitate if you need help.

Jude: It's okay, man, I manage. Thanks.

Scott: Yes, don't hesitate!

He adds an eggplant emoji. I laugh and give him the middle finger.

Alec: OK, see you tonight at home.

Jude: Yes, mom!

Then I call Paul Sanchez, an old friend from high school. He still lives in Warwick, as do most of my buddies. I'm the only one who got out of the mud. Thanks to football!

"Hartnett! Long time no see. How are you, bro?"

"Good, good. Listen, I'm calling you, because I need a favor."

"Is your bike giving you trouble?"

"No, it's rolling great thanks to your talents."

"Ah! It's a great piece. Too bad you don't want to sell it to me."

"You know it's my baby, I could never do that."

My bike is the most precious thing I have. I spent an entire summer doing odd jobs to pay for it, and I wouldn't give it up for anything. Yet, as a football player, I'm not supposed to own one. The university is paying way too much to have me break my leg during the season. So, I have to keep a low profile and avoid being noticed. But today, the weather was too good for me to resist. I did the right thing, otherwise, I probably wouldn't have run into Rocky.

I have always loved motorcycles. It started when I found a picture of my dad in an old closet, buried under a pile of clothes. I had shown it to my mother, curious to know who the guy on the motorcycle was. In the photo, he and my mother were hugging and looked in love. From the age of four, I had already more or less guessed that he was the missing piece of the puzzle of my family. Instead of answering me, my mother got angry and snatched the picture from my hands, confirming my suspicions. That same evening, I snuck into her room to retrieve it. I've kept it ever since. We never talk about my father. All I know is that they met at a carnival, he knocked her up and broke her heart before disappearing.

Rocky and I obviously have something in common. Besides being super sexually compatible.

It was hard for my mother. Coming from a hyper-conservative Irish Catholic family, being an unmarried mother was worse than a crime, but she was strong and raised me like a master. Thanks to her, I never lacked anything.

"I know, I know! But damn, it's really a shame," finally answers Paul. "Well, what can I do for you, bro?"

"I'm in the southern suburbs of Providence, the car of one of my friends doesn't start. I'm pretty sure her starter needs to be replaced, could you come to take a look at it, please?"

"Yes, no problem. I was just leaving work. I grab my toolbox and head over."

"Great! I knew I could count on you. Thanks"

"You're welcome! Besides, it gives me an excuse not to go straight home. Lucia is driving me crazy right now."

An hour later, Paul is cleaning his greasy hands off his jeans. He fixed the starter and checked everything else. Apparently, the timing belt is about to fail as well. I would have to warn Rocky, but without her number, it's complicated.

"The problem is that I don't have her number or her address."

"But you have her keys."

"Yes, I'm waiting for her to figure that out and then try to find me."

He stares at me with that mocking look that I know him too well.

"Who's this girl who makes your head spin?"

"I told you, she's a friend."

"A girl you're skipping training for, something I've never seen you do since we've known each other, a friend for whom make me move from Warwick a friend whose contact details you don't even have?"

I answer with an embarrassed grimace.

"Either there's something you're not telling me, or you've lost your balls since you've been at Brown, bro!"

I run my hand through my hair.

"Look, it's complicated."

"I see that… Wait!"

In a few strides, he goes back to the car to rummage in the glove box, then pulls out a bill.

"Here we go! Rebecca Prescott lives at 6321 Hillcrest Wood Drive!"

"Rebecca? It must be her mother's name, thank you! I'll be able to bring her car home. That'll save her a bus ride in the morning."

"You're welcome, people are careless! You can't imagine how many things they leave lying around in their car. And this mysterious girl is no different from the others."

"Thank you, Paul! I think I owe you one."

"Don't worry, it's really not complicated to change a starter."

"How much do I owe you?"

"You don't owe me anything. With everything you've done for me, that's the least I can do."

"No, at least let me compensate you for the trip. Warwick is not next door."

I take out my wallet. He shakes his head.

"Listen, Hartnett! If you really want to pay me, offer me premium seats for one of your games."

"Deal! How is Lucia?"

"Good! Well physically, because mentally, she's gone crazy. Her pregnancy hormones are driving her crazy. Sometimes I feel like she's going to kill me if I open my mouth or shut it too long. I walk on eggshells. As soon as she sees me, she wants to talk about everything that I never do well enough for her."

"Ha, ha! I can imagine, it must be hell."

"I'm telling you! Ever since she got pregnant, she scares me! I sleep with one eye open in case she decides to carry out all the threats she makes to me during the day."

His phone starts to vibrate.

"Damn, it's her! To believe that she has antennas and that she knows exactly when I'm criticizing her. She's the Antichrist, that girl! I promise you. Well, I have to go man. Wish me good luck! And if you don't hear from me, call the FBI!"

The worst part is that he doesn't seem to be joking. He waves at me and disappears into his shiny, noisy Chevrolet Camaro. As for me, all I have to do now is bring that car back to Rocky.

***

I arrive in a typical residential neighborhood in the southern suburbs of Providence. I spot Rocky's house and park. It's pretty, modest in size, and well maintained.

It's not a big deal but is much less crappy than the apartment in Warwick in which I grew up.

I knock several times on the door, no one answers. I try to look through the window when I am stopped by an old lady.

"Excuse me, young man. Can I help you?"

The tone of her voice and the frown on her eyebrows contrast completely with the kindness of her request. What she would really like to say is, "You better have a damn good reason to snoop like you're doing right now!" She reminds me of my grandmother: sweet and kind on the outside, but a real pit bull on the inside.

I cleared my throat.

"I'm looking for a friend."

She crosses her arms and raises an eyebrow, inviting me to say more.

"Rocky Prescott! I'm one of her classmates from college, here to drop off her car."

I point to the vehicle to give more credit to my point. She turns around, and when she faces me again, her face has softened considerably.

"So, you're a friend of Rocky?"

"Yes."

"I've never seen you before."

"Let's say that our friendship is very recent."

"My name is Carol Johnson, nice to meet you."

"Jude Hartnett, the pleasure is mine."

"Rocky went to do some shopping. She shouldn't be long but come and wait for her at my house. I live just across the street and just made coffee."

I hesitate for a moment.

Isn't that how most horror movies start?

An innocent old lady offers you to go to her house, then once inside, she turns into a monster and kills you with an ice pick. I push these gory thoughts out of my head. I will never watch horror movies with that jerk Scott again.

"I always overdo it just in case I have company," she adds coaxing me. "Which doesn't happen often at my age."

I wonder if the lonely, desperate old lady card works every time, but so far, it's working because I find myself accepting without flinching.

She gives me a big, satisfied smile. I can see that she has something on her mind, but I couldn't possibly decline her invitation. My mother raised me better than that.

Her house is in fact just across the street and, as we cross the small path that leads to her driveway, I notice that her lawn would need to be mown.

Before I even open my mouth, she says to me, "My gardener is on vacation, I have no idea how to use the lawn mower."

She looks embarrassed.

"I can do it for you if you want."

"Oh, really?"

"Yes. When I was in high school, it was my main occupation to make pocket money."

It paid so well that with Paul, we even considered quitting school and starting our gardening business. Luckily my mom talked me out of it.

"Thanks! You're adorable, but I don't have enough to pay you right now."

"Oh no! I'll do it for free as a favor to you. It will only take me ten minutes at most."

"In that case, I gladly accept. Come and sit down for a coffee before."

A few minutes later, I'm sitting on a floral couch waiting for Mrs. Johnson or Carol, as she prefers me to call her, to bring me a coffee. Please don't let her put arsenic in it. This place could really serve as the setting for a horror movie.

I hear the sounds of dishes coming from the kitchen and look around me. There are knickknacks everywhere, old furniture and family photos. One, in particular, catches my attention on the fireplace: Rocky and her little brother. They are all smiles with cotton candy in their hands. Rocky looks at her brother who has his mouth full.

"She's beautiful, isn't she?"

I jump and turn around.

"Yes."

"And she's a good girl."

She tastes good! That's for sure!

I feel guilty for having salacious ideas in front of this lady who could be my grandmother.

"Would you like sugar and milk in your coffee?"

Thankfully, her more than pragmatic question brings me back to reality.

"Yes, please."

She pours the milk carefully before stirring it with the same delicacy. I feel like I'm witnessing a satanic ritual. For a moment, I wonder how I managed to land here instead of going to practice. Mrs. Johnson hands me the steaming coffee. I take a sip to give me courage.

"What kind of friend are you to Rocky?"

Her question takes me completely off guard and makes me cough loudly.

"Uh, excuse me?"

"Are you the kind of friend in love with her?" she asks bluntly.

"Uh, no… We're just… Uh, well, we barely know each other, and I…"

"You hardly know each other, yet you are there, talking with her old neighbor, waiting for her to come back?"

I don't know what to say to that, so I keep my mouth shut.

"Tell me a little about yourself."

"There's not much to say… I'm from Warwick, I'm a business major and I play football for the Brown University team."

"Ah, that's nice."

"Yes, it is."

There's a silent moment. I look around me as she stares at me. I suck at making conversation, so I say the most banal thing that pops into my head, "And you? Are you retired?"

No sooner do I say this than I realize how ridiculous it is.

Mrs. Johnson starts laughing, not helping my embarrassment. "Do I look that old?"

"No, that's not what I meant… I'm sorry if I offended you."

"Don't worry, I'm teasing you. I've never worked. Rob, my husband was in the Navy. We traveled a lot before ending up in Providence. I'm what is called a stay-at-home mom. All my life, I have taken care of my children. And now they're all gone."

Her tone becomes sad, and I hate myself for asking the question. If she starts crying, I might just run away. I have no idea how to comfort an old lady.

"Lucky for me, there is little Maxwell who sometimes brightens up my days."

"Maxwell, Rocky's little brother?"

"Yes, I babysit him from time to time to allow Rocky to breathe a little."

"And their parents?"

I understand that I have gone too far, because the old lady's face is veiled, she puts down her cup a little too quickly and says to me, "Well, I think it's time to mow the lawn, don't you? Before it gets dark and it's impossible to see anything."

"You're right!"

I finish my coffee in a few big gulps and get up, following Mrs. Johnson's lead.

"The mower is in the shed," she explains.

"Okay, I'll take care of it."

"Thank you, you are an angel fallen from heaven."

"Oh no, it's no big deal."

I get to work quickly. Her yard isn't very big, so I know I won't be long. After mowing the front yard, I start preparing the lawn mower to go back into the shed when I hear a familiar voice behind me. "What you're doing here?"

8

Rocky

"Can I have an ice cream when we get home?"

"No, Maxwell! Not before dinner, it will ruin your appetite."

"Why are you stopping?"

"No reason…"

"Isn't the boy who drove you mowing Mrs. Johnson's lawn?" my little brother asks shrewdly when he looks in the same direction as me.

"Yes, it's him."

"What is he doing there?"

That's the hundred-thousand-dollar question I'd love to find an answer to.

"I don't know. Well, come on! Let's get the groceries in."

We put the essentials on the kitchen table and put the fresh produce in the fridge. The task is quickly completed because there is not much. On foot, it was difficult for me to take everything I needed, anyway.

Through the window, I can still hear the whirring sound of the lawn mower. Damn Jude! I will strangle him! That'll teach him to follow me home. I would never have accepted his help if I had known he was a real snoop. I hate snoops!

"Max, can you start your homework? I'm going to see my friend. I need a minute."

Just long enough to rip his head off.

"Can I have an ice cream while waiting for you? I really, really, really want it."

"After dinner, sweetie."

"Oh! You're not funny."

"I love you too."

I wait for a second, making sure Max is doing what I'm asking, before opening the door. I rush into a football player, far too intrusive for my taste, who has improvised himself as a gardener to better spy on me.

I cross the street in less time than it takes to say it and by the time I reach his level, I'm a little out of breath. He doesn't see me. He's far too busy winding up the cord of his lawn mower. He lowers himself. I see a piece of tanned skin on his muscular back appear. How does he get a tan? In autumn? In Rhode Island? While the average person is as white as snow! Including me. See! Once again, he manages to distract me with his Apollo physique, but I quickly come to my senses. Sexy or not, I hate nosy people.

"What you're doing here?"

He turns abruptly.

"Rocky?"

He has the nerve to look surprised!

"Don't act surprised to see me. What the hell are you doing in my neighborhood, at MY neighbor's?"

"As you can see, I was mowing her lawn."

He gives me his most beautiful smile, the one he knows is irresistible. My irritation goes up a notch. I hate having my private space invaded, and that's exactly what he just did.

"I got that! I have eyes! But the real question is *why*? What the hell are you doing here, did you follow me? You are spying on me?"

"No, not at all! What are you going to imagine?"

"Look, Jude, I don't know what kind of sick game you're playing, but if you're think you're seducing me by invading my privacy, you're on the wrong track. I hate nosy people who snoop around and meddle in things that are none of their business."

His eyes darkened and his face hardened.

"I hate to burst your bubble, beauty. I was doing a favor for an old lady who asked me to. It has nothing to do with you!"

"You were doing a favor for an old lady? You've got to be kidding me! And by chance, this old lady turns out to be my neighbor?! How did you know where I live if you didn't follow me?"

"I appreciate your trust in me, but I'm not a psychopath! I don't usually follow people. If you want to know everything, I came here to bring you your car. I spent the afternoon trying to fix it. I had a buddy from Warwick come over specifically to help me. I didn't want you to have a hard time getting to college in the morning, so I figured the best thing to do was to bring your car to you. There was a bill in your glove box that had your address, and that's how I knew where to find you."

He did what?!

I turn around and notice for the first time that my car is parked a few feet from the house. How did I not see it? I was so obsessed with my anger at Jude that it obviously blurred my vision. Speechless, I turn to him.

"Why?"

"I think the word you are looking for is *thank you*!"

"Thank you! But why are you doing all this, Jude?"

He strokes his neck nervously and looks embarrassed.

"Because I don't know... Because I like you! Because we're friends, and I usually help my friends."

"We're not friends, we barely know each other. Just because we slept together once doesn't mean we're friends! What do you want in return?"

His eyebrows furrow. He watches me, puzzled.

"I don't want anything in return."

"Good, because I have no intention of going out with you or having sex with you a second time. Even though you did me a favor."

"Fourth."

"What?"

"If we sleep together again, it will be the fourth time. Since the first time, we got a three-time winner."

He's serious! He wants us to have a battle of numbers!

"That's not the point! It won't happen again!"

"Don't be so sure, Balboa."

He moves closer to me, towering over me. He places a hand under my chin, forcing me to look at him. His feline eyes dive into mine. The worst part is that I stand there, completely hypnotized by his gaze.

"I feel like you and I have something special," he whispers in his husky, sexy voice. "And the energy you put into lying to yourself tells me that you know it as much as I do."

I step back carefully, trying not to over-interpret the quickening of my heartbeat when he's so close to me. The distance helps me come to my senses.

"Are you always this cocky? Or is it something you reserve only for me?"

"I already told you! I'm not being cocky, I'm just stating the facts. You're going to dare to tell me that the night we spent together wasn't magical?"

I swallow with difficulty.

"Tell me you haven't thought about it since?"

Hot images flash through my head and prevent me from thinking rationally.

"I…"

"You're thinking about it now."

He comes close enough again to overwhelm my personal space with its amber scent. His smell is absolutely bewitching. My gaze is lost for a few seconds on his lips.

"Now, I can see that you want me to kiss you. So, why don't you stop giving us both a hard time and just let me invite you for dinner? We could get to know each other, find out if this energy between us is a flash in the pan or fireworks."

I close my eyes for a moment, not seeing him anymore helps me gather my courage, and I pull away from him again.

"Sorry, Don Juan! But with me, it's once, and once only. Thank you for your efforts, it's really flattering, but you can mow the lawn of all my neighbors, it will never happen between us again."

He remains silent for a moment, visibly resigned, and nods, his lips pressed into a thin line. He searches in his pocket.

"Here!"

I unclench my arms and accept my car keys. Then, without saying a word, I turn around and walk in a hurry and, I hope, confidently. I don't turn around, and he doesn't try to hold me or call me. Why would he? I was hateful! But he deserved it, didn't he?

Who does he think he is? I'm not a charity case, I don't need help. I know how to manage on my own.

He had no right to rummage through my glove box and follow me here. As my steps accelerate, my certainty of having reacted correctly slows down and makes me feel guilty.

I open my front door, close it quickly and lean against the wood. My heart is racing, and my blood is pounding against my veins. I am a whirlwind of emotions, and it takes me a few seconds to come to my senses. Luckily, a glance at the kitchen brings me straight back to reality. Maxwell is enjoying an ice cream with his guilty look that I know all too well. Instead of annoying me, this vision causes me to laugh, which attracts his attention.

"Rocky, I'm sorry, I really tried to resist but I wanted too much."

"That's okay, my little man."

I sit across from him. He has Rocky Road all over his face.

"Can I have a taste?"

"OK!"

I take several big bites. It's true that it's delicious, and it has the magical effect of calming my anger.

"Hey! You're going to eat it all."

I return the ice cream to my little brother and approach the sink to do the dishes. Through the window, I see Jude. He chats with Mrs. Johnson. What could they possibly be talking about? I know I can rely on Mrs. Johnson not to tell anyone intimate details of my life. But when it comes to Jude, I'm not sure. He seems like a good guy to me, and I'd be lying if I said he's not turning me on.

That's exactly why I have to keep my distance.

9

Rocky

"What did he do?!"

"It's crazy, right? I mean, who does this kind of thing? It's borderline psychopathic to follow me home, isn't it?" I say, shoving a large handful of chips in my mouth with the great class that characterizes me.

Tonight, the girls came over to spend the evening at home, like every Sunday, to watch *Game of Thrones*.

I finish swallowing and articulate, "Not to mention the mowing the neighbor's lawn."

"I think it's adorable! The guy is really addicted to doing all that: fixing your car, helping your neighbor. I don't see why you're upset!"

I roll my eyes because Isabella is an eternal lover, and she would find romance even in Charles Manson.

"Well, you, I'm not listening to you! You're hopeless case! Alyson, what do you think? Psychopath or big psychopath?"

"I'm thinking of Mrs. Johnson! She must have enjoyed seeing handsome Jude Hartnett working on her lawn. For once she can have some action, poor thing," Alyson replies from the kitchen where she searches the cupboards for a bottle of alcohol. "Maybe, she'll be the one taking advantage of him."

"Ew! I think I just threw up in my mouth just imagining it," I say.

"What? There are a lot of guys who like older women. Haven't you seen all those celebrities in Hollywood?" Isabella comments nonchalantly.

"No, but stop talking nonsense, both of you. Mrs. Johnson could be Jude's grandmother," I say.

"So what? The best jams are made in old jars!" laughs Alyson.

"Ew! You just gave me mental images that I can never erase from my brain!"

"You see? That's your problem, Rocky! You don't want Jude, but you don't want to share him with others either."

Isabella snatches the bowl of chips from my hand.

"Learn to share a little bit," Isa says.

"By *sharing with others*? You mean with my 60-year-old neighbor, my little brother's babysitter? Am I the only one who finds the turn of this discussion absurd?" I say, stifling a laugh.

"So what? Everyone deserves a piece of happiness. No matter how old they are," concludes Isa.

And I don't even try to reason with her anymore. Alyson comes back from the kitchen, looking disappointed.

"Damn it, Rocky, you're kidding, don't you even have a tequila somewhere?"

"I may have some wine in the pantry, but I promise you nothing."

I used to hide the booze when my mom was still around, and she drank whatever she could get her hands on. I straighten up to get the wine, and I take the opportunity to go for a little walk in Max's room to check that he is sleeping soundly.

No sooner have I pushed the door open than I notice a small light under his blanket. Max is still reading. I lift his blanket.

"Boo!"

He jumps.

"Rocky, you scared me."

"Sorry, my little love, but you should be asleep by now."

I gently take the book from him.

"No, I want to at least finish the chapter."

"Diary of a Wimpy Kid is not going to fly away. On the other hand, you, tomorrow, you will have a hard time waking up, and you're grumpy when you haven't slept enough."

"That's not true," he protests, pouting.

"Yes, it is, and you know it as well as I do. Come on, now, go to sleep!"

"Say, Rocky? Can I go say goodnight to the girls before I sleep?"

"But you already did, about an hour ago, when you promised me you were going to sleep, remember?"

"Please! I won't linger, I promise."

When Max gives me his pleading look, I can't refuse him anything. He is fully aware of it, and he uses and abuses it cheerfully.

"Alright, go! But you have five minutes, no more."

"Yes!"

My little man gets out of bed faster than a rocket and rushes to the living room where he is greeted by the girls' cries of joy. Considering all this excitement, I don't think he's going to sleep anytime soon.

I'm going to get the bottle of wine that I open in the kitchen, while listening to the nonsense that my two crazy girlfriends tell Max who loves to be cuddled and pampered by them. I even think he has a mega crush on Isabella. At any age, men prefer blondes, it's well known.

I return to the living room loaded with a tray that I place on the coffee table. Alyson doesn't waste a second before pouring herself a drink. She also hands me one, but fails to serve Isabella who is too busy cajoling Max.

"Alright! That's enough, little man! You said good night to everyone, it's time to go to bed now."

"Okay."

Maxwell unhooks himself from Isabella's arms with regret and trots towards his room. I follow him. He turns halfway and blows a kiss to Isabella who returns the favor. Always so flattered to receive the attention of a male.

"Come on, Don Juan, let's go."

We arrive at his room. Max slips under his blanket, grabbing his teddy, and curls up against him. I adjust the blanket under his chin before kissing him on the cheek and rubbing my nose against him like we always do.

"I love you, sweetie."

"I love you too, Rocky."

"Have sweet dreams!"

I stand up and go to turn off his little bedside lamp.

"Rocky?"

"Yes? You know, when I grow up, I'm going to marry Isabella."

His comment makes me laugh.

"Okay, Don Juan."

"And everyone will be at the wedding, even mom."

As soon as he says this sentence, my heart becomes heavier. He hadn't mentioned her in a long time.

"Will Mom be back from her trip soon?"

"Yes, sweetie, she'll be home soon. Go to sleep now."

"Why she has been gone so long?"

I take a deep breath to give myself courage. Facing Max's sad gaze kills me. I hate having to lie to him, but how do I tell him the truth? He's too young to understand. And I refuse to break his heart. He's already lost his dad, so admitting that mom may be gone for good is too much for a little kid his age.

However, I know that sooner or later I will have to face things. My life is a ticking time bomb that threatens to explode at any moment. My mother may never come back. And if she ever returns, God only knows in what condition. I'm the best at burying my problems and pretending nothing happened. I had years of training. And I wouldn't be so affected by the situation if it was just me. But this is also about Max. I take a deep breath and kneel down at his bedside.

"Listen, sweetie, you know she's working."

"Yes, but why can't I talk to her on the phone?"

"She must just be very busy, that's why."

My voice is just a whisper, and Max's eyes fill with tears.

"Tyler says it's weird that mom doesn't pick me up from school like other moms."

"Tyler is an idiot! You shouldn't listen to him."

I wipe away my little angel's tears by biting my lip, so I don't crack myself.

"I miss Mom."

"Me too, my baby, I miss her. But while waiting for her to come home, I'm here, and I love you more than anything in the world."

"I love you too."

He takes a deep breath and closes his eyes as if carrying the world on his shoulders. At this precise moment, I would do anything to erase all his sorrows. It is with a heavy heart that I leave Max's room. I lean against the hallway wall for a moment to collect myself. A thousand questions swirl in my head and threaten to overwhelm me. The bursts of laughter that emanate from the living room bring me out of my torpor. I take a deep breath and join my friends.

"Ah! She's finally here, we can start the *Game of Thrones* marathon," announces Isabella.

"Is everything fine?" Alyson asks as I sit down next to her. "You look a little preoccupied."

"Yes! Yes! I'm fine! Don't worry. I'm just preoccupied with a paper that I have to do in contemporary architecture."

"Oh, Rocky! I'm sure you'll kick ass like you always do. You're the best! If you need help, don't hesitate. It's law, my major, but I'm good at writing stuff."

"Thank you, girlfriend! It'll be fine, don't worry."

I display a smile that I hope is convincing, before taking the remote control in hand and announcing in a falsely playful tone, "Showtime!"

"Yes!"

10

Rocky

Today is one of those days when I run around like a chicken with its head cut off. After dropping Max off at school and spending forty-five minutes in traffic, I had to sprint across campus to catch my first class of the day, industrial design, my favorite. The only one where we don't spend our time listening to the teacher talk while logging on our keyboards so as not to miss a crumb. You never know, the lost crumb could just be the subject of the next exam. Sometimes, I have the impression that teachers choose the most boring detail of their course as an exam subject to teach us to stay focused no matter what, or to better exercise their power.

Industrial design is different! We are in the real world. We are asked to do, to express ourselves, to draw plans, to invent new building concepts—eco-friendly, anti-terrorist attacks—and I must admit that I am passionate about it.

Mr. Gravel is one of those dynamic teachers who is driven by what he teaches you and believes more in know-how than just knowledge. He is not satisfied with abstract theories. In fact, he has enrolled a few students in the class in an urban competition. The contest is to come up with a plan to renovate one of Providence's old buildings on Huntington Street.

It is an old shoe factory bought by a wealthy businessman who would like to transform it into high-tech offices while keeping the 18th-century appearance of the facade. Mixing history and modernity is my favorite thing. So, I was particularly flattered when Mr. Gravel nominated me. If my project is chosen among the hundred others, I can pocket a check for ten thousand dollars, which would allow me to cope for a little while. So, I better not miss out.

The class ends with Mr. Gravel reminding us that all projects are due before the Thanksgiving break. I still have three months, but I haven't made much progress. I promise myself that I will work on it for at least two hours tonight when Max goes to bed.

My inner voice is laughing at me because I've been wishing the same thing for weeks. I've been having a hard time concentrating lately. Besides the anxiety that twists my stomach every time I think of my mother, or the fatigue that overtakes me as soon as I lay my head on a pillow, there is something else: there is Jude. I can't stop thinking about him. I try to forget him, but I can't.

I've lost count of the number of times my brain has wandered off and played out erotic scenarios when it wasn't being stupidly romantic. Me, romantic? You wouldn't think so. Yet, he inspires all sorts of emotions that I find hard to ignore. And how to forget him? When we constantly hear about him, his team, their prowess in the field, the parties they organize among their fraternity.

Football players are treated like true heroes around campus. A ridiculous form of royalty that comes with privileges and courtesans. And even though I have no desire to be one of them, I can't help but read the comments and reports of their scores on Twitter.

So, I know Jude didn't play against Boston University and the team lost their fourth game of the season. Fans were furious with the manager's decision to keep Jude Hartnett on the bench. A strategic error, according to the comments.

They've since made up for it and won the next two games. Instead of studying I end up going through Twitter. As if I haven't had enough, I eye Jude's Instagram account. His victories, the parties he attends. The girls who always seem to be around him. How can you blame them? He is gorgeous! His smile, his eyes, and his body. When we made love against the greenhouse window, I felt like I was lighter than a feather. A feeling of abandonment, as if nothing around us existed. One thing is certain, I will never be able to look at a greenhouse in the same way again.

I growl in frustration. Here I go again with my fantasy! Damn it! I feel like he cast a spell on me! A spell with his cock. He sure did. Or I've become my mother. My worst nightmare. I'm drooling over a guy when I have a mountain of problems. Yet I always promised myself never to become Rebecca Prescott. Maybe, before she met her own Jude, she was a responsible adult, then one day… Boom! One night, one spectacular sex party, and she turned into a scatterbrain. My thoughts are driving me crazy.

Who would have thought that a simple hookup could take up so much space in my head? And yet, I don't have any space. My head is filled with important things, like taking care of Max, shopping, cleaning. Working so I don't fall behind in my classes, praying that my damn car doesn't break down again.

Last time, Jude did me a big favor, even though I blame him for snooping around in the glove compartment. But he still took a big chunk out of my life. I'll never tell him, of course! Either way, I'm not sure he'll ever talk to me again, given the way I yelled at him.

I haven't seen him since that story, about two weeks ago. I think he's avoiding me. And that's good! Not seeing him should help me forget him. The real question is, when will I get my mental faculties back?

I think the orgasms he gave me were so powerful that they fried some of my brain cells. I can't think of any other explanation. I shake my head to get him out of my thoughts. I have to go to the cafeteria to cut vegetables and get ready for the eleven o'clock service.

A bunch of students, whose only concern is to know if there will be nuggets or pizza on the menu today, will soon arrive for lunch. No room for my moods in these conditions.

I put my things away in the locker room and put on my kitchen uniform. I wave to my colleagues and quickly get to work. There are tons of vegetables to peel and chop. I became an expert with a knife by cutting and mincing. Plus, there is something relaxing about this activity.

At eleven o'clock, the doors open, and all the students rush in with a joyous hubbub. It's time for me to start the second phase of my job: distributing food in the lunch hall. This is the least glamorous part.

Most of the students are cordial and just smile at me when I serve them. Others, always the same, systematically ask for more and, when I repeat the same answer, they protest or clearly show me their disdain. As if I had something to do with it. This is the rule of the university. I'm just doing my job. The last thing I need is to be fired for giving preference to some.

I'm just explaining life to a tall redhead when I hear someone say my name. I immediately recognize this hoarse and broken voice, by the impact it has on my skin.

"Rocky?"

Jude stares at me like he can't believe his eyes. I do the same because he is breathtakingly beautiful. He's wearing a black and red jacket with the image of the Tigers, the university football team. Me, I wear my ridiculous kitchen outfit with my hairnet on my head. I haven't seen him in weeks. Of course, we had to meet again when I look like a nuclear mushroom and I'm threatening to knock a student out with my ladle.

Dear universe, why do you hate me so much?

"I didn't know you worked here!"

"Yes, I do, as you can see."

I smile at him, but I don't dare look him in the eye. Last time we saw each other, I was yelling at him. Not ideal for feeling comfortable now. Between that and my hairnet shame floods me.

"I come here for lunch every day. It's weird that we've never met before."

"I only do the eleven o'clock shift. Maybe you might come later."

"It's true. Usually, we eat at one o'clock with the team."

I turn my head and see Scott, Alec, and other Tigers members I know by sight, behind him. They all give a cordial wave to greet me, to which I respond with an odd ladle movement.

"Glad to hear that."

There's silence while we observe each other in the most awkward way. What are we supposed to say to each other after we've slept together and yelled at each other? *How have you been all this time?*

Thankfully, the mountain of muscles behind him shows their eagerness to fill their stomachs and force us out of our awkward silence.

"Okay, one second, Adam!" Jude says to calm his friend, then he turns to me again. "So, what's on the menu today, Rocky?"

He looks around at the different options available to him.

"As you can see: pizza or chicken with vegetables."

"I'll have the…"

He lets this sentence linger for what seems like an eternity, while looking at me intently, as if I was the one on the menu. He passes his tongue on his lips, the room's temperature seems to rise a few degrees. I think I'm blushing, and I think he's happy about it, because he gives me a knowing smile that shows one of his dimples.

"So, have you made your choice?" grumbles his colossal teammate.

"Yeah, I'll have the veggie chicken, please, Rocky."

"Finally! It's about time, I'm starving."

I cleared my throat.

"Very good choice."

I'm busy filling his plate. I feel his intense gaze burning my skin. I try not to shake or blush more. I have always been the queen of hiding my feelings out of survival instinct. With my stepfathers, the colder I was, the less they approached. But with Jude Hartnett, the walls I've spent years building don't seem to protect me anymore. He makes me feel things, things I don't want to feel.

"Here you go. Enjoy your lunch!"

I place the plate on his tray.

"Thanks!"

I expect him to leave, but he just stands there.

"I suppose I don't get any extra?"

From the little sparks that shine in his eyes, I understand that he is kidding and that he is referring to the altercation from earlier. I start laughing so hard that I catch the attention of everyone in line behind him.

"No, indeed, no extra, sorry!"

Jude is still not moving, and the line has grown.

"I think your buddy is going to kill you if you don't move."

"Adam? He barks more than he bites."

"If you want something else, the desserts and salads are a little further."

I explain the obvious as if it were his first lunch in this cafeteria.

"I want a lot of other things, babe, but that's a topic for another day."

He gives me a bright smile, my cheeks heat up, and the other parts of my body too. He bends his face towards mine, then whispers to my attention only, "Damn it, Rocky! Can you explain to me how you manage to be so beautiful with a hairnet on your head?"

I mechanically bring my hand to my hat. He doesn't give me time to answer and walks away, leaving me completely confused by his remark. I manage somehow to come to my senses and stop smiling like a fool each time his words replay their sweet symphony in my head.

The rest of the shift goes smoothly, I chat with Scott and Alec when it's their turn.

As I pick up the trays, clean the tables, and put away the chairs, I find myself looking for Jude with my eyes. I finally see him. He is sitting with his teammates. Some girls have joined them. One, in particular, caught my attention. I recognize her right away. She's the hottie he was talking to at the Kappa Omega party before we collided.

I observe him discreetly while cleaning a table. A flush of jealousy comes over me. Crap! Why does that make me mad? Maybe because she is very pretty, elegant and with a very pleasant face. From here, I can see that the clothes she wears are branded. She must live in a big house and vacation in the Bahamas with her perfect family every winter, like most Brown students. Me, if I can keep my fragile raft afloat until Christmas, I'll be happy.

I hate when I'm jealous. But beyond her undeniable beauty, what really upsets me is that she shares her lunch with Jude. I should look elsewhere, I should do my job, but impossible! I continue to spy on them. And all the preaching I do to myself doesn't change anything.

Jude seems hanging on her lips. Their complicity is undeniable. She must have said something very funny, because the whole table burst out laughing. She looks proud of herself! And when she caresses his forearm, I grit my teeth.

I must have pushed the chairs a little too hard, because several people are now staring at me like I've lost my mind. I suppress the urge to give them the middle finger. What's wrong with them? Let them eat their pizzas and leave me alone! With my spirits low, I put away the trays left by some negligent students, before sweeping up.

Fortunately, Jude's table is not in my area. The last thing I need is to turn into a Cinderella in front of him and his girlfriend. *Is she really his girlfriend?* says my little inner voice, which sometimes frustrates me because it is so naive.

Of course, she is. They're so perfect for each other that it's sickening. But why did he have to do his little act to me earlier if he already has a girlfriend? Not to mention the car! And at the Kappa Omega party, what's wrong with him? He slept with me while she was around. Unless they are an open couple?

Or that they are not a couple at all?

"Shut up!"

"Sorry?"

A student about to throw away her salad, and whom I was visibly blocking the way, looks at me, flabbergasted.

"Oh no, nothing… Sorry… I was talking to myself. It happens to me sometimes."

I give her the most innocent smile I have and she quickly walks away. I think she thought I was crazy.

I resume my task, and my thoughts inevitably return to Jude Hartnett. Fucking, Jude Hartnett! With his devastating smile and innocent look, he's actually a fucking player!

Finally, he is not the gentleman I thought. And if I had imagined myself for a nanosecond to go out with him, eventually, when my schedule would allow me, this stupid option is definitely out of the question now. I like clean booty calls, not those with a girlfriend. The whirlwind in my head brings me to one and the same conclusion: Jude Hartnett is to be put in the rank of assholes. It's time to move on. My sadness gives way to anger, it's progress. But what I really need is to not feel anything at all. No admiration, no sadness, no hate. Just to be serene and comfortable again.

The floor is finally clean. The cafeteria is ready to welcome the noon shift. My shift is over. Finally! I can have my lunch, I'm starving. I help myself to two slices of pizza and a salad, then I go to sit at one of the tables near the large windows that overlook a beautiful garden. It's a little setback from the rest of the cafeteria, and the view is breathtaking. The Rhode Island fall is particularly beautiful, cold too, but that doesn't bother me. I enjoy cold weather. Of all the states I traveled through with my mother as a child, this is by far the most beautiful. The trees have already started to change color and have donned their orange coats. My eyes get lost on the horizon. Nature has this incredible calming effect on me. At least that's what I think, until I see him appear in my field of vision again, the object of all my torments: Fucking Jude Hartnett!

11

Rocky

"Rocky? Can I sit with you?" Jude asks, hands in his pockets.

His caramel gaze probes mine. Oh, that innocent and sexy little look… One could think is an angel, when in fact, he is the devil incarnate. Why do I want to rip his head off? Objectively, he did nothing to me. Except for making me lose my mind, of course, but that was at my request. What the hell is my problem?! Am I angry with him for giving me an orgasm or for not being available? Or that he was never available? When I don't want him to be? Because I don't want a relationship. I must have become the queen of hypocrites for all of this to seem normal.

"Sure, if you want. But I'm warning you, I don't have time to small talk. I only have twenty-five minutes before my next class."

"It's better than nothing."

He turns over a chair and sits astride it, before giving me his best smile. And that smile—my God!—is a weapon of mass destruction. I already know all the ravages it can do, and I don't want to let myself be charmed again.

For weeks I've been trying to get him out of my head. Weeks of him invading my every thought. And the worst part is that we've seen each other… like… twice? It's not much when you think about it, but it had a huge impact on me. An irrational urge to flee grips me. Survival instinct, probably. All I would have to do is get up with my tray and head out with my head held high. And off I would go! Goodbye, Mr. Handsome with fiery eyes! But I can't do that.

It wouldn't be the first time you looked completely ridiculous, adds my inner voice.

"Shut up."

"What's that?"

"Uh, no, nothing! I was talking to myself. Sorry."

"You do that a lot, I think."

"What?"

"Talk to yourself. The night I met you, you did it."

"Yes, I do that sometimes."

An old habit that I developed when I was little. At the time, I had even created an imaginary friend to deceive my loneliness. But I avoid mentioning this detail to him because it's really pathetic. Instead, I take a big bite of pizza. My God! It's good! My taste buds are tingling. I wipe my mouth with a paper towel. Jude watches me carefully. His beautiful caramel-green eyes stare into mine.

"How's your car?" he finally asks.

"It's working fine so far."

"That's good. My friend told me it had a timing belt problem, so you know, if it gives you trouble, don't hesitate to call me. He's a great mechanic, and he'll take care of it."

"Thanks, but I'll figure it out."

"As you wish."

He seems disappointed in my dry tone, which makes me feel guilty, so I try to be nicer.

You can do it, Rocky!

"By the way! I wanted to thank you for helping me out and to apologize for my behavior the other day. I was a little on edge and shouldn't have yelled at you like I did. Not after everything you've done for me."

"No problem! I understand that you didn't appreciate me showing up in front of your house and going through your glove compartment. I'm sorry if I seemed intrusive, but my intentions were good."

"Apology accepted."

He gives me a sincere smile, and my heart skips a beat. I can't take my eyes off him. I could swear he's reading me like an open book.

I cleared my throat.

"You don't have to go to class or practice? A guy like you must be busy, right?"

"A guy like me?" he asks, laughing. "What's a guy like me?"

A terribly sexy, terribly talented, and terribly nice guy, to whom I again want to do terribly dirty things.

"Well, an athlete. You have to train… what… three times a day?"

"Two," he corrects. "Is that your polite way of asking me to go away?" he asks, amused.

I'm blushing. And I'm really not one to blush, but since Jude, that's all I do.

"No, not at all, I'm just trying to make conversation."

And now I'm on the defensive. I feel like I'm the horny teenager who can't corral their dirty thoughts in math class.

Stop thinking about his cock, Rocky!

"So, you want me to stay and tell myself that you can't stop thinking about me, right?"

"Pfff, come on! Sorry to disappoint your overinflated ego, but I had better things to do than think about you. I am a very busy girl."

And the Best Actress Oscar goes to… drum roll… Rocky Prescott!

"I saw that. Anyway, I missed you a lot. I couldn't get you out of my head. I don't know if anybody ever told you this, Rocky, but you're a great fuck. And shit, I'd be crazy not to want to do that again."

His honesty takes me completely by surprise. I thought we were going to play a little game of seduction but obviously, that's not Hartnett style. The style of Hartnett seems to be "I unpack everything on the porch and take what you want." He is incredibly straightforward, except that there are still a few details of the utmost importance that he forgets to mention. And that bothers me!

"I'm sure you'll be able to comfort yourself with… that… other girl."

As soon as I say this sentence, I immediately regret it.

His eyebrows furrow.

"Who are you talking about?"

"The pretty blonde you were having lunch with earlier and who was already by your side at the Kappa Omega party."

Why did you say that, Rocky! Damn it, my mouth deserves to die in agony.

"Victoria? She's just a friend, there's nothing between us."

"You seemed close though… at the table, it looked like she was your… girlfriend."

How can I make him believe after that I'm totally unaffected by his charm? The best thing for me is to put this pizza in my mouth and choke on it.

"Did you spy on us?"

He smiles like a cat that has just swallowed a canary.

I shake my head no and blush even more.

"So, how do you know we were close if you haven't been watching us? Stop lying to yourself, babe! You spied on us because you're jealous."

"Jealous? I'm not jealous! Why would I be jealous? No reason to be jealous. Jealousy is not my style at all."

"You're jealous."

He crosses his arms over his large muscular and tempting chest. My fingers itch, hesitating between caressing his pecs or slapping him to wipe away the satisfied grin he's wearing right now. I shrug my shoulders instead, feigning indifference, and focus my attention on my dripping cheese pizza.

"If you really want to know, Rocky, I don't have a girlfriend… Well, for now."

Now he's freaking me out again with his confident, penetrating stare.

"But I'm working on it."

I swallow, my throat feeling horribly dry.

"And you, are you still single?"

With my mouth full of pizza, I nod like an automaton, and the smile I receive in return is even more splendid than the autumnal spectacle through the window. I look away. After a brief silence, he adds, "It's a good sign that you're jealous, it means that you like me."

I don't say anything. Obviously, I have lost my tongue. My gaze wanders over his sculpted torso, his broad shoulders and move down on his arms. He took off his football team jacket and rolled up the sleeves of his polo shirt. He wears a stylish black leather watch. His hands are very neat for a sportsman. Yet, I remember them feeling rough on my skin, and that it gave me a lot of pleasure. I imagine them again browsing my—

"What are you thinking about?"

"The math assignment that I have to turn in later."

He gives me an incredulous look that tells me he doesn't believe a single word I've just said.

"Math? I thought you were studying architecture."

How does he know that?

"Did you research on me?"

"I plead guilty. I googled you and looked you up on the college website too. And if you ask me, the picture you put on your college profile doesn't live up to reality. You are much more beautiful in person."

"And you say that to me like it's normal. As if you hadn't just invaded my privacy again."

He raises his arms in surrender. "I wanted to see you again, I had to start somewhere. You're closed like a prison door. You didn't even give me your number after the explosive night we spent together."

"Explosive? Don't you think you're overreacting a little?"

He licks his lips and repeats in the sexiest tone, "Explosive, babe, and I'd be happy to refresh your memory if you'd stop running from me."

I bite the inside of my cheek to hide my arousal. I grab the bottle of water on the table, just to quench my thirst and calm my ardor.

"Besides, you never replied to my message."

"What message?"

"I sent you a message on your university e-mail box."

"I never use it."

"I figured it out."

"What did you write to me?"

"It doesn't matter anymore."

"Why didn't you just ask my girlfriends for my number? I know you have seen them many times."

"No way. If anyone is going to give me your number, it's going to be you. In case you're wondering, I'm still waiting for it."

He leans on his elbows, reaches out and tucks one of my locks behind my ear. His knuckles brush my cheekbone, and it makes me emotional. Suddenly, I realize that I'm still wearing my horrible hairnet on my head. I rip it off with such haste that it makes him laugh.

"Don't laugh at me or I'll kick you in the balls."

"It's a shame you took it off. I thought you looked hot with it."

"Pff, bullshit! I hate this thing. It makes me look like a mushroom."

The simile makes him smile more.

"It's a good thing I've always loved mushrooms. As a kid, I was a Mario Bros fan, and Toad was my favorite character."

Now I'm laughing.

"You suck at flirting."

"I'm great at flirting."

"No, you suck, you just compared me to Toad! That's the weirdest thing anyone's ever said to me to make me feel better about myself."

"Believe me! I'm not seducing you yet. But we're getting there."

His voice is much more serious this time. The mood has changed from joking to serious in less time than it takes to say it. I shut up immediately and realize that his thumb is drawing invisible circles on my wrist. I can feel the effect right down my spine. I withdraw my arm immediately. His caresses prevent me from keeping a clear head. He looks at me for a long time, then says, "Rocky, I'm going to be honest with you. I really like you and I want to see you again, to get to know you better. I'll wait until you're ready. I'm a patient and persistent guy."

"You don't take *no* for an answer?"

"Never!"

I laugh at his childish look.

"More seriously, I always respect a girl's *no*," he says in such a serious way that I can only believe it, "but you, Rocky, you don't say no, you hide behind rules meant to protect you. Am I wrong?"

Okay, in addition to being an athlete and a sexy gentleman, Jude is perceptive. Too perceptive.

Lucky for me, he checks his watch and seems surprised by what he reads there.

"Right now, I have to go."

"Okay."

Saved by the bell.

Even though I'm glad I don't have to answer his question, I'm disappointed to see him go so quickly, a disappointment that I try to hide as best I can.

"But we'll see each other again."

It's a promise, almost a threat.

12

Jude

A few days later...

Today, we are playing our sixth game of the season, and if I felt particularly ready and confident about the outcome of this game, I am disillusioned. But it's not for lack of training like crazy this week. After my last meeting with Rocky, I threw myself into training and weight training sessions, just to burn the energy that I dream of burning with her.

But no weightlifting has erased the obsession I have for this fucking chick. The more I force myself to stop thinking about her, the more I think about her. I'm even at the point where no other girl gives me a hard-on. I'm going crazy. There's something special about her. It's like an invisible thread connects me to her.

Still, overtraining or not, the match against Columbia is violent. But I'm used to taking hits. But now, I can't feel my ribs anymore because of all the tackles. The referee seems particularly careless. My buttocks have never landed so much on the ground as during this game. The four giants in charge of stopping me are not particularly fast, but they don't hesitate to hit me in an unauthorized way, even when I don't have the ball. Looks like they're here more to beat me up than to play football.

But no need to complain, if the refs don't throw a flag on the play, there is nothing to do except take it and get up. As a wide receiver, it's my job to position myself strategically to receive the ball and dodge the defense. So far, I haven't been particularly effective.

Our teams are still neck and neck in the last quarter. 14-14! A tie. The referee blows his whistle, and the ball goes to Columbia. If they get to our end zone, we're screwed. They must be blocked at all costs. The coach is tense. This is the sixth game of the season. If we lose, it will be four wins and two losses. Not a great score to start the season.

Football is a game where the mindset is very important. The Columbia Lions know that seeing our teammate Caldwell go out on a stretcher had a negative impact on team's motivation. And they're playing it up. Insults fly, tempers flare and tensions become dangerous.

"I'd rather die than let those assholes win! They don't play fair and don't deserve to crush us," Phillips spits when we are in a huddle.

Alec brings us together before the final kickoff and urges us not to let go.

"One minute left on the clock, guys! We've got to stop these losers! We can do it! This game is for us!"

"Are you ready to give it your all?"

"Yes, Captain!"

"I did not hear anything!"

"Yes, Captain!"

We make a war cry, and here we are all ready to play. The referee blows his whistle. The Columbia quarterback throws the ball more than thirty yards, but his receiver fails to catch it, blocked by Adam who's sticking to his heels. Scott caught the ball before it hits the ground. The entire stadium rises to its feet and holds its breath, because not only have we stopped them, but we now have a chance to score and definitely win the game. Damn it! This is our chance to put the finishing blow to them.

Scott runs eighteen yards, passes to Alec who yells "43-59!" then throws the ball in front of him. I understand right away and run as if my life depended on it. Alec's throws are so precise that I have no difficulty catching the ball. Now the hardest part is ahead. I have Columbia's entire defense rushing at me in the hope of stopping me. Fear and adrenaline pump through my veins, giving me wings. I dodge Parker, go around Douglas, feign to go right, taking the whole defense with me, to finally run to the left. I almost drop the ball several times, jostled by my opponents. I grit my teeth and accelerate. Speed is my special talent. I feel like I'm flying.

The referee still hasn't blown his whistle, so I run, until I reach the end zone of Columbia. There is no one in front of me, I throw the ball in a dramatic way, the buzz sounds, the crowd goes wild. The displays show "touchdown." The public and the cheerleaders are ecstatic, and my teammates rush on me to celebrate this unexpected point which ensures our victory. The game ended with a score of 21-14. The best feeling in the world!

Our exit from the field is widely acclaimed. Adrenaline is followed by the euphoria and the pride of victory. The coach has a word for each of us when we walk past him.

"Well done, my boy! You do two or three more actions like that, and I guarantee you that all the pro teams will be lining up to get you," he says to me.

"Thank you, Coach!"

Damn it! That's why I love this sport! You get beat up and we suffer for ninety minutes, but when we win, we feel like we are the kings of the world. When we arrive in the locker room, the atmosphere is festive. Scott plays us his hip-hop playlist and launches into a wild dance that he immortalizes on Insta. He manages to bring several of our teammates with him. In a towel or in an underwear, everyone dances, and the coach has to arrive to signal the end of our post-game party. Everyone sits on the bench to listen to the coach.

"Congratulations, guys, for tonight! You showed them how we play football!"

"How's Caldwell?" Alec asks.

"Nothing is broken, he's just a little shaken up and will be back tomorrow."

The news is met with applause from the team. Caldwell is one of the defenders, he threw himself into battle, saving us several times. Seeing him leave the field unconscious shook us a lot. It was yet another reminder, if any were needed, that this game is as exciting as it is dangerous: one bad fall, one collision, and it's a head trauma. Knowing that he is fine is a huge relief.

After the shower, we all get on the bus to go back to campus. This is when fatigue and pain start to surface. My ribs are bruised pretty bad, and every movement hurts like hell.

"Is everything fine?" Alec asks next to me when he sees me wince.

"Yeah, few bruises, nothing serious."

"I saw that they hadn't missed you."

"That's an understatement. During the first quarter, I thought I was the ball."

"They tried to break you down because they know you're dangerous. And tonight, you showed them just how much."

He gently shakes my shoulder. "That victory was epic, man! Alright, let's celebrate now."

"No, honestly, I'm exhausted. I'm going home."

"You've got to come with us, Jude! This victory, we owe it to you! And it's Friday night! No practice tomorrow."

"Did someone say party?" Scott asks, in front of us.

He straightens up and turns to face us. Adam does the same.

"Sorry, really, I'm done."

I only dream of one thing, lying on my bed with two ice packs on my ribs.

"Otherwise, we can invite people over. Everyone brings beers and pizzas. Something simple. You don't even have to go out. The party is coming to you, Jude!"

"Come on! Every time, your little parties end up being a fucking mess, and I have no desire to clean up tomorrow morning," I say.

"Worse than a girl, Hartnett!" Scott scoffs, earning him a middle finger from me.

"How about Shamrock?" offers the latter while looking at his phone

"Beer and burgers! You know how to convince me," Alec replies.

"Great!" says Scott.

Scott rubs his hands together.

He must already be imagining the number of chicks he's going to flirt with tonight. He and Alyson are in an open relationship. Which means they only sleep together if they can't find someone better. And that happens a lot these days, because I see her in the morning discreetly leaving the house with the clothes from the day before.

"Adam, you in?" asks Scott

"I don't know, is there any pussy?"

"Yeah, the girls are over there, apparently. Alyson just texted me," answers Scott.

"Girls? What girls?" I find myself asking.

"Ah, Jude is waking up," Alec comments, amused.

"If you want to know if your unicorn is coming, the answer is *yes*," Scott says

I straighten up hastily, which causes a jolt of electricity in my ribs.

"Rocky?" I ask.

"Yup!"

Damn, Rocky at a party!

It's as rare as seeing a shooting star. Fuck the pain, I can't miss it.

"Okay, I changed my mind. I'm coming."

It doesn't take much for my buddies to mess with me for the rest of the trip, but I don't care. The important thing is that I will see her again.

13

Rocky

Shamrock is really packed. And we are struggling to make our way through the crowd. It doesn't help that I'm wearing four-inch heels. The Crazy Dudes are playing tonight and, according to Alyson, this band is the Foo Fighters of the indie scene!

"I swear, girls! In a year, we'll have to fight and pay a fortune to be able to see them in concert!" Alyson continues to assert since we arrived.

Not that we question her judgment. Isabella and I don't know anything about it anyway, and both followed her here for far less noble reasons than finding a great band.

Apparently, Alyson isn't the only one who thinks they're awesome, hundreds of other people seem to think so too, turning my favorite pub into one of those trendy places where you have to wait in line to get in. It's crazy, it looks like all the young people of Providence are meeting here tonight.

All the youth of Providence, except the one person you dream of seeing again, my annoying little inner voice remarks.

And if I could, I'd gag its mouth with duct tape.

But it's not wrong. Since my last meeting with Jude, which was exactly five days, eleven hours, and forty-three minutes ago, I have dreamed of seeing him again, of feeling his lips on mine again, and I hate myself for that. I can't get him out of my head. What's new under the sun? He's in all my wet dreams and, as soon as I hear his name, I find myself getting butterflies in my stomach like a 15-year-old girl watching her favorite boy band on TV. I'm so pathetic I should I'd slap myself. That's why, tonight, I decided to take control of the situation. Do anything to detox me once and for all. And how do you get rid of an addiction? By finding a substitute. Something strong enough to take me away from my first source of addiction, but not enough to create another one. A kind of human nicotine patch. And for that, I brought out the heavy artillery.

Isabella was amazed when I asked her to lend me a dress. She's been dreaming of giving me a makeover for so long. This time, I let her take care of me, and I had it all: make-up, hairstyle, and cleavage. She may have gotten a little carried away, because I feel like a walking cliché with my short black dress and my hot red lipstick, but it takes what it takes.

Tonight, I came to hunt some men, and this pub packed with rock lovers seems like the perfect hunting ground. There are tattoos, beards, and testosterone everywhere I look. The *Forget Jude* operation can begin. Problem? No matter how much I play Judy Garland, I can't walk in heels, and going back and forth in the girls' room, runway style, is not going to change anything.

"Shit!"

I groan when I almost twist my ankle for the tenth time in less than an hour. I feel like a fawn taking its first steps, and—damn it!—I miss my Vans. I wonder who the pervert is who decided that perching young women on spikes was supposed to be sexy. It's a real torture, and when my butt finally lands on a bench, I let out a long sigh of relief.

"God, I thought we were never going to sit down. My feet are on the verge of a nervous breakdown."

"Yes, honey, you have to suffer to be beautiful," says Isabella.

"Bullshit," Alyson replies. "You don't have to hurt yourself at all to be beautiful, Rocky! And no one should have to bother with that either."

Here we go again! I love my two girlfriends, but they are so different and so complementary at the same time.

"It's another stupid injunction of this patriarchal society to better enslave us, us women. And as long as we play by its rules, we'll be exploited," continues Alyson.

"'And the last fight let us face,'" intones Isabella, her fist raised, to make fun of Alyson.

"That's 'The International,' a revolutionary song and the communist anthem, uneducated! It has nothing to do with what I am saying."

"It's the same. Anyway, it's too late for you to be giving us your feminist speeches, Alyson! Rocky and I are here to hook up, and we catch more flies with honey than with vinegar. Right, Rocky?"

She raises her hand for me to high-five it.

"Yep," I say, responding to her gesture.

Alyson rolls her eyes.

"You two are hopeless. Rocky, I thought you were on my side."

"Usually I am, but tonight I'm on a mission."

"Oh yes! Operation *Forget Jude*!"

"Exactly," I answer.

"Honestly, I think you're making a mistake. Jude is a great guy. He has a lot of qualities, and he likes you. Why don't you give him a chance? Instead of trying to hook up with some vulgar booty call who won't be a match for you. At least you know he knows how to use his cock," says Alyson.

"That's the problem. He knows too well how to use his dick. And since we slept together, I only have half a brain left."

"And that's a problem because…?"

"Because I can't afford to have such a distraction with my classes, my job, my little brother. I need all my mental faculties."

"Your mother will be home one day, and you'll have more time for yourself," Alyson says.

"Yeah," I say without conviction.

"Well, what does a girl have to do to get served here?" Alyson groans, trying to get the attention of the busy waiter chatting with the customers at the next table. "Looks like he's pretending not to see me."

"Let me do it!"

Isabella hardly raises her hand, as if she is hailing a taxi, when the waiter immediately spots her and comes back.

"Seriously?" Alyson gets annoyed.

"See, that's what cleavage powers are all about!" Isa says.

"Ladies! What can I do for you?" asks the waiter while

cleaning the table on which we are sitting.

He also clears away half-empty beer glasses.

"Margaritas for everyone?" asks Alyson.

"No, I'll take a cosmo to go with my Sex and the City look," I say.

"Good idea! Tonight, you're Carrie Bradshaw."

"I'd rather be Samantha Jones, the maneater. Like her, tonight, I would like to have a one-night stand with a complete stranger."

Maybe I shouldn't have said that out loud, because now the waiter is staring at me like I'm a prize. He takes our orders and gives me a naughty smile before turning on his heels.

"Anyway, we know who Miranda is, the bitter lawyer," laughs Isa, pointing to Alyson.

"Bitter? Me? I remind you that I'm the only one of us who's had plenty of orgasms in the last few weeks."

"With Scott?"

"Yes! Who knew? He's really...(she has that dreamy look that makes me immediately jealous) good at it. You know, everything they say about athletes is true! Power, endurance, and all that! This is happiness!"

I really can't argue with her. Jude has been the best fuck of my life. And the fact that he works out every day to play football and stay in shape probably has something to do with it.

And here I am thinking about Jude again! I'm hopeless. Luckily, the waiter returns with our drinks, giving my imagination a break.

"The cosmo is on me!" he says before giving me a wink.

"Mmm! He's flirting with you," Isabella comments, as soon as he leaves our table. "And he's kinda cute, don't you think?"

I watch him walk away with his long, brown hair that he has styled into a bun and his ripped jeans, but I don't feel for him.

"Yes, it's true, if you like the rocker style. He's a little trashy for me. I like them a little cleaner. You know, the kind that showers every week."

"You, you like them a little more like Jude," Alyson quips.

I shake my head, amused. She's right, but I just came here to forget about him, so I might as well ignore her comment and not think of a six-foot-tall handsome guy with abs of steel and a devastating smile.

Our conversations shift to less controversial topics. Alyson tells us about her week. Isabella complains about Alec's indifference. The last time they saw each other, he told her he just wanted to be friends. Apparently, he's still affected by a girl from his past and doesn't want anything serious. As for me, I tell them about the renovation project for the shoe factory on Huntington Street. We spend half an hour talking, when the lights go out and a clamor rises from the crowd gathered in front of the stage.

"Ah, here we go, the group is coming! We have to get closer," says Alyson.

I grab my cosmo, put my shoes back on, despite the pain in my toes—tomorrow I'm sure I'm going to have blisters—and then I follow in the girls' footsteps. We get as close as possible by elbowing people out of the way.

The band steps on stage, and immediately the fans show their appreciation with shouts and whistles. Four boys who look barely older than us and a girl with pink hair step into the light. The drummer beats three measures, and the atmosphere is electrified in no time. The sound of an electric guitar invades the room, then follows the deep and grungy voice of the singer who has a crazy charisma. What is surprising is that there is a huge cello that sits in the middle of the stage. The pink-haired girl is dancing her fingers over it, and the contrast between the different instruments is amazing.

"I told you they were awesome," Al says.

"You should have told me that the singer is really hot," answers Isabella. "He has a Kurt Cobain vibe."

"It's true," I say to her.

"Do you think he can see me from the top of the stage?" Isa asks.

"I don't think he can see much from where he is, because of the spotlights."

"But I feel like he's been watching me for a while now," Isa says.

"You always feel like everyone is watching you, girl."

"It's not wrong," Isa laughs.

After three songs, Isa and I are total fans and thank Alyson for bringing us here.

The fourth song is very catchy, and the three of us start dancing with our hands in the air. It's been a long time since I had this much fun, and it feels good not to think about anything. We dance like crazy. Isabella does her famous step where she lowers herself to the ground in a split that would make many burlesque dancers jealous. Proving that her years as a high school cheerleader were not for nothing. Alyson dances to the beat and sings the lyrics out loud as if she were part of the band. As for me, I close my eyes and let myself be carried away by the melody, my hands in my hair. I could almost forget my foot pain. I'm on my second free cosmo, and it helps inhibit the pain. Randall, the waiter, continued to supply me while hitting on me. I know that he is 23-years-old, that he is passionate about rock, and that he would very much like to take me for a ride after his shift.

I kindly declined his invitation, but that didn't seem to discourage him.

So, I'm on my third cosmo when I decide to go to the bathroom. As usual, the line of girls is endless while there is no one among the boys. After bouncing for ten minutes, I can't hold myself back any longer. The door to the boys' bathroom opens, I rush in. Screw the rules. They are individual toilets anyway, so I don't see where the problem is.

I do my little business, then take the opportunity to put on some gloss. The reflection in the mirror gives me the image of a girl I barely recognize. My eyes look huge with all the makeup Isabella put on me. I find myself pretty, different, but pretty. Rocky 2.0, I imagine. My rosy cheeks, however, leave no doubt as to my drunken state. Maybe I should have eaten something before going out. I was so busy with Max that eating was the least of my worries. Tonight, he's having a sleepover at his friend's house. I only get him back in the early afternoon, so I can afford a little excess.

I put my lip gloss back on, then come out of the bathroom. I come face to face with a tall rather sexy blond who looks at me as if I've just committed a crime.

"Sorry, I'm not the type to follow the rules," I answer his silent question.

He smiles at me. I do the same and walk away towards the bar. Despite my slightly spinning head, a fourth cosmo seems like a good idea. Tonight, I'll do what I want! But I need to relax, to think of nothing. A carefree night is all I want.

Randall spots me quickly and serves me before I even ask him for anything. When I turn around, I find myself face to face with the blond guy from the bathroom. He is so close to me that I jump.

"Hi!"

"Hi," he gives me a mischievous smile. "Can I buy you a drink?"

"No, thank you, I already have what I need."

"Shame."

I rest my lips on the rim of the glass while looking over his shoulder. My girlfriends are still dancing. I estimate the distance that separates me from them and how much I will have to suffer to walk there.

"What's your name?"

"Rocky."

"Nice to meet you, Rocky, I'm Christian."

He places a hand on the bar, creating a shield with his body between me and the rest of the world.

"Are you here by yourself?"

"No, my friends are by the stage over there. In fact, I should go join them."

He doesn't move to let me pass. Instead, he comes closer, penetrating my personal bubble, and I don't know if I like it or not. A mixture of both.

"Why are you in a hurry, beauty?"

Why am I in a hurry to get away? After all, I came here for this. Meet a guy and forget about Jude. This boy would be just perfect for that. I give myself a mental slap and force myself to consider the gorgeous specimen in front of me. He is tall, blond with blue eyes, with a well-defined square jaw and a determined gaze.

I think I just found my antidote!

14

Jude

Damn! If one more person collides with my ribs, I think I'm going to lose it. Going out was a bad idea. I shouldn't have listened to Scott. I'm sure he lied to me to make me follow him here. Obviously, Rocky is not here. After the longest ten minutes of my life, walking through that crowd of sweaty bodies, we managed to reach the girls. But of course, the girl I came all this way for is nowhere.

"Jude, I'm going to get some beers, do you want one?" Scott offers.

"No, thanks, man. I'll go."

"What, already?"

"Yeah, I didn't want to come in the first place, remember?"

I'm having a hard time hiding my irritation, but the pain and fatigue turn me into an impatient asshole.

"Have at least one drink. I'm sorry, man! I thought your unicorn was here. Alyson confirmed it to me by text message. You want me to ask her where she went?"

"No, it's okay. I've had enough of this bullshit."

I'm not going to spend my life chasing after a girl who doesn't want me.

"Don't worry. I'm just tired. See you at home."

"Wait, Jude."

I turn on my heels before he finishes his sentence and leaves Scott. I hear him calling my name, but I knowingly ignore him and continue on my way to the exit. I need all the patience in the world not to kick the latest fan who, too focused on his choreography, steps on my toes.

I'm in a terrible mood. I finally arrive outside, the wind whips my face, and it puts my ideas in place. Fucking Rocky! Once again, she succeeded in driving me crazy. And now, I've had enough. I order a taxi on an app and wait for it to arrive, leaning against the wall near the door.

The bouncer looks as blasé as me, facing the long line of people waiting to get in. We exchange a weary look. Strangely, I feel closer to him than to my friends tonight. And to think that I inflicted this to myself, for nothing.

My phone vibrates in my pocket, it's a message from Alec asking me where I am, I answer him quickly. And that's where I hear it. A squeak or muffled scream. Something barely noticeable that I could have completely ignored. The avenue is filled with drunken partygoers, and it could have been anything, but my instincts go on alert.

I look right and left, and this time I hear voices that sound like an argument. I think it's coming from the adjacent alley, where the pub's emergency exit is located. I take a look, there's nothing but the trash cans, but I could swear I heard something. I decide to venture there anyway, and I see her: Rocky. Pinned against a wall by a big asshole who is sticking to her. His face is buried in her neck. My jealous heart starts pounding loudly in my chest. There is something weird about this situation. For a moment, I hesitate. Maybe she's consenting, and they're just kissing.

I watch them silently, like a madman in the middle of the night. But no, this gesture, he cannot be consensual. She's clearly pushing his hand away as it works its way up her skirt, and Mr. Asshole doesn't seem to get the message. She ends up protesting verbally, I can hear it from here. My blood freezes in my veins, and I start sprinting towards them, "Let her go! You bastard!"

The tall blond turns to me, a little surprised. Rocky takes the opportunity to punch him in the face. Not a girl's punch, a real punch. A punch strong enough to throw him off balance. She then continues with a kick to the balls. The guy is bent over before I even have time to do anything. She continues to kick him. She seems to be furious. How can I blame her? I feel exactly the same. I grab her from behind, lift her away from him.

"Let me go! Let me go!"

She struggles with all her strength.

I realize that I must have scared her and put her down. When she turns to me, she has the look of a wild animal that has just been skinned.

"Jude?"

Her big black eyes widen, and she throws herself into my arms.

"Sorry, I didn't mean to scare you!"

"Jude? What are you doing here?" she says, pulling away from my embrace.

"I was going to ask you the same question."

I cup her face and watch every bit of her beautiful skin. If I see the slightest injury, I'm going to slaughter this asshole.

"Is everything fine? He didn't hurt you?"

"No…"

"Are you sure?"

My eyes rest on her body in search of a possible bruise. She wears a too short dress that shows off all her assets, and I feel the need to cover her. I take off my jacket and drape it over her shoulders. The asshole on the floor takes advantage of our inattention to get up and darts towards the club's entrance. I try to catch him, but Rocky holds me back.

"No, it's fine, let him go."

Her voice is almost inaudible, and her gaze, so often illuminated by an incandescent fire, seems completely extinguished.

"Rocky…"

I stroke her hair and she lets herself go limp against me, drained of all her energy.

"Why are you doing this to me, Jude?" she whispers against my neck.

"What am I doing to you?"

Before I can get an answer to my question, she starts throwing up everything she can on the ground and on my shoes.

"Shit!"

I grab her hair, lift it up so she doesn't get it everywhere. She pushes me away.

"No, leave me!"

She staggers, leans with one hand on the wall. I'm afraid

she'll fall apart, but I do what she asks and give her space. She finishes her business and returns, trembling and ashamed, to me.

"Feeling better?"

She nods looking at her shoes. I take a deep breath to calm myself and run my hand through my hair. I'm both happy and upset seeing her. What if something had happened to her? What if I hadn't checked? I want to yell at her, shake her and kiss her at the same time. It's a mess in my head. After a few seconds to come to my senses, I finally break the ice, "Come on! I'm taking you home."

"No, I don't want to be alone."

She said this sentence with such desperation that I want to hold her against me and not let her go, to protect her.

"Then, I'll take you home with me."

She hesitates for a moment.

"Don't worry, I have no bad intentions. Do you trust me?"

I hold out my hand to her.

She looks at it for a long time. Her eyelids crinkle. She blinks rapidly, as if she was thinking at full speed. My heart drums in my chest for what seems like an eternity, and then she finally grabs my hand.

"I trust you."

15

Rocky

I'm lying in Jude's bed, while he's in the shower. And the question I keep asking myself is, *how did I get here?* One thing is sure, it is that the operation "Forget Jude" is anything but a success. The goal was to get him out of my head, not get me into his bed. Well done, Rocky! Once again, you've failed.

Being here is a really bad idea. I should get up and leave. My hangover is just a distant memory. Tomorrow, we would forget the whole thing, pretend it never happened. I would forget the incident with Christian. And Jude would forget he saw me being groped against a wall and puking my guts out all over his shoes. Just another sordid university party like any other, nothing more, nothing less.

I should, but I don't, because there is what I want, and there is what I am able to do. Two things that are obviously totally incompatible. So, I stay lying in this incredibly comfortable bed whose sheets smell divine. I look around me, and oddly, I feel very comfortable here.

Jude's room is decorated in dark gray tones, with a minimalist touch. A few pictures above his desk, and a chest of drawers. In a corner, on a chair, there is also a guitar. I wonder if he uses it to get girls or if he really knows how to play it.

I hear the water stop flowing, then the bathroom door opens. And here he comes out in all his glory and manhood. A towel is wrapped around his waist, and his still wet hair is dripping down his shoulders. I swallow. He is truly handsome to die for. He goes to his dresser, pulls out a boxer shorts that he puts on under his towel.

If I was in my normal state, I would make a remark like, "There's nothing you're hiding that I haven't seen before." He'd laugh, drop the towel, and that good word would lead to a good sex. But now, I'm not in my normal state. I haven't said a word since we left that alley of hell.

I didn't open my lips in the cab. I didn't say anything when Jude forced me to take aspirin with orange juice. And I didn't protest when he suggested that I put on one of his football team T-shirts to spend the night, way too big for me, and so cliché. And now here I am, still silent, watching the countless muscles in his back tense as he lowers himself. He sits up, and our eyes meet.

"How do you feel?"

This is the tenth time he's asked me this question, and I always answer the same way, with a simple nod. He must think I've lost my tongue. My eyes drop to his chest, and I notice he has two huge bruises on his ribs.

"Oh my God, what happened to you?"

He doesn't seem to understand right away what I'm talking about.

"Your ribs? Did you get hit by a truck, or something?"

"Oh that? It's nothing just some injuries from the game. We played against Columbia tonight, and apparently the defense confused me with the ball."

He gives me his famous smile and acts as if those two huge bruises are just scratches.

"Are you sure nothing is broken? I mean, those bruises are really impressive!"

"Nothing two ice packs can't fix."

He touches them and grimaces slightly. I start to get out of bed.

"You should lie down," I say.

"Mmm! Looks like you're feeling better!"

Ignoring his attempt at humor, I push him toward the bed. He lies down without flinching and watches me walk towards the door.

"Hold on! Where are you going?"

"To look for some ice," I say.

"Are you going to go in that outfit?"

I look at my bare legs. Jude's T-shirt comes to my mid-thigh and hides the essentials.

"Uh, yes! What's the problem?"

"The problem is that there are half a dozen guys with no manners living in this house and you look incredibly hot in this outfit."

"Would you rather I put my sexy dress back on?" I provoke him.

He grimaces.

"So, relax, I'll only be a minute."

I cross the hallway and go down to the kitchen. I meet absolutely no one. Mr. Possessive should learn to calm down. I look for large ice packs in the freezer. There are about ten. Obviously, these players often need it. Then I run back upstairs. When I enter Jude's room again, he seems relieved.

"You didn't see anyone."

"No."

"Good. Rocky, Scott just called, and I told him you were here. He said he'd warn your girlfriends, because they're worried about you. Apparently, they've been trying to reach you for a while."

"Shit!"

"What, you didn't want them to know?"

"No, it's just that I feel bad for having worried them."

I look for my phone in my bag and indeed notice several missed calls. I text our WhatsApp chat group to reassure them.

> **Rocky: I'm sorry I didn't warn you.
> I'm doing well. I'm at Jude's.
> I'll tell you all about it later!**

I'm not waiting for them to answer me. I already know they're going to bombard me with questions, but that can wait until tomorrow. I grab the two ice packs.

"Ready?"

"Always, for you."

I put the ice on his ribs. Jude flinches, and deep wrinkles line his forehead. He closes his eyes.

"Is it painful?"

"No," he replies with a grimace, which makes me laugh.

"You don't have to play superhero in front of me, you know."

He opens one eye and answers honestly, this time, "In that case, I can tell you that it hurts like hell! And if you weren't here, I would surely be crying and calling my mom!"

"Don't overreact. I think you mostly need painkillers."

"I need a lot of things," he says, his eyes still closed, with a charming smile on the corner of his lips. "But I'll stick with the painkillers for now."

"Do you ever stop flirting?"

"Not when I have such a beautiful girl in my room."

"I'm sure it happens to you very often!"

"Not as often as you think."

I take two pills from the bottle he gave me earlier for my hangover and hand them to him, along with the rest of my orange juice. He thanks me, and I watch him swallow the pills, while I hold the ice packs to his ribs. He then gently takes over.

"Why did you go out tonight if you're like this, Jude? It really wasn't wise."

"I'm not used to being wise, babe. But if you want to know everything, I came out to see you. Alec told me you were in Shamrock, and when the unicorn shows up, you can't miss it."

"*The Unicorn*?"

"Yes! That's what Scott calls you."

"Why?"

"I don't know! I guess it's because it's very rare to see you at parties or because your beauty is legendary."

His intense gaze makes me blush. I look down.

"And in the end, I did well, didn't I?" he asks.

"Yes, once again, you saved me."

"Saved you? You kidding?! I remind you that you knocked that asshole out on your own. In true Lara Croft fashion. He didn't stand a chance against you. If I saved anyone, it's probably his ass, which you were kicking. Besides, I regret it, I should have let you take care of him. That motherfucker deserved a good lesson!"

"Lara Croft? You're crazy!"

"Even sexier than Angelina Jolie. And that punch! Wow! You really deserve your *Rocky Balboa* nickname."

"You're exaggerating!"

"Really, I'm not exaggerating! You looked like a ninja in heels. I've never seen a girl fight as well as you! Where did you learn that?"

"I took a few jujitsu classes in high school."

"You did?"

His face lights up with curiosity and invites me to tell him more.

"At the beginning, it was to defend myself." I was often afraid for my safety, but I kept that to myself. "And then I enjoyed it."

"That means you could kick my ass if you wanted to," he says with a smirk.

"Yes, but I'd still need a reason."

"You seemed to have a good one earlier," he says.

"What are you talking about?"

"Just before you threw up, you said, 'Why are you doing this to me, Jude?'"

"Oh, that!" I look down, a little embarrassed that he remembers that.

"Yes, that! What am I doing to you, Rocky?"

I take a deep breath. Should I be honest with him? After tonight, I believe the answer is *yes*.

"It might be a little embarrassing to explain, but after all, I do owe you an explanation, especially after throwing up on your shoes," I say.

"I think that's the least you can do."

"Tonight, I put on a super sexy dress and heels to flirt."

His eyebrows furrow, and I think I know him well enough to say he's jealous. And I like the idea that he is, I like it a lot.

"And the reason I did that and ended up in that alley with that stranger was because of you."

"I don't understand?"

"I was trying to forget you, Jude. To get you out of my head. I challenged myself tonight to sleep with any guy, as long as I could get your memory out of my head."

He flinched as if I just pressed on his wounds.

"Since we slept together, you're all I can think about. And I figured replacing your memory with another might be the solution. It's completely ridiculous, I know that, and it's also why I didn't want you to catch up with this guy when you had the chance. I turned him on, and I told him that I wanted to sleep with him and that we should go to this alley, and then all of a sudden, I changed my mind." I put my hands on my face. "I'm so ashamed of myself, I deserve everything that happened to me tonight."

"Hey, hey, hey! Don't say that Rocky. You absolutely don't deserve this at all. No guy has the right to force you into anything. Never! Do you hear me? No one has the right to hurt you."

He takes my hands away from my face so I can look at him. The depth and sincerity of his gaze pierces me and makes my heart beat a little faster. I want to kiss him so badly, but in this outfit, and on this bed, if I let myself go, I know I won't be able to stop. I look down first.

"I think we'd better get some sleep."

"Yes, you're right."

He gets up.

"Where are you going?"

"I'm going to sleep on the couch."

"Why?"

"Because I don't want you to think I brought you here to sleep with you. Not after what just happened to you, Rocky."

"I don't think that in the slightest, Jude. Come on, don't be ridiculous. You're not going to sleep on the couch with your bruises. Come here!" I say, patting the mattress.

"Are you sure?"

"Absolutely."

16

Rocky

Jude lies down next to me. We stay at a safe distance, listening to each other breathe. I try to focus on street noise or the heater, but his magnetic presence is impossible to ignore, even in the dark. He radiates such warmth that every pore of my skin tingles. The sexual tension is so thick you could cut it with a knife. I turn to face the wall. After a few minutes of silence, I hear him sigh deeply.

"Rocky?"

His voice is even raspier than usual. He sounds as aroused as me. With my heart pounding, I answer, "Yes?"

"Do you still do jujitsu?"

His question catches me completely off guard and makes me laugh.

"Why are you laughing?"

I turn to him, and he does the same.

"Because I didn't expect you to ask me that."

His face, barely perceptible in the dark, is inches from mine, and I can smell his cool, minty breath.

"What did you expect me to ask you?"

"I don't know… something about sex."

He arches an eyebrow. His eyes are now on my lips.

"I told you I could behave."

The real question is *do I know how to behave*? When he's so close and my heart is beating so fast, all the reasons I made up to keep him at arm's length feel pointless. He is pure temptation. And don't we say that the best way to resist temptation is to succumb to it? Here I am quoting Oscar Wilde to justify my irremediable attraction to Jude Hartnett! After this chaotic evening, it seems almost ironic to do poetry.

"So?" he asks, still waiting for an answer from me.

I clear my throat.

"No, I stopped."

"Why?"

"I don't have time anymore."

My eyes are used to the darkness now, and I can clearly make out his features, the line of his lips, the perfect structure of his nose, and his eyes, feline, intense, and soft at the same time. His hair falls in a happy mess on his forehead. His locks look so silky, and I have to resist the urge to run my hand through them.

"You don't have time anymore… for the same reasons that you don't have time for a relationship?"

I nod.

"Rocky? Can I ask you a question?"

"Sure…"

"You can tell me to fuck off if you consider this an intrusion."

"Or put you a jujitsu hold?" I joke.

"Even better!"

We laugh, then his face turns more serious, making me dread what's next.

"Are you taking care of your little brother alone?" he asks.

"What makes you think that?"

"That's the impression I had when I was at your neighbor's house."

My eyes widen.

"She didn't say anything to me, don't worry. It's just that I saw pictures of you and Max only, and then she told me about her babysitting. I've come to the conclusion that you were raising him alone."

I stay silent for a long time. I want to lie to him, to say what I've been telling everyone for months. It would be so much easier. But there is something about this moment that pushes me to be honest. I may regret it later, but whatever. In this darkness, with him so close, I feel like we're alone in the world and I can open up, for once.

"Yes… My stepfather died almost two years ago… and my mother… Let's just say she hasn't been able to get over it and she fell back into her bad habits. She has some problems with alcohol and drugs. After another argument where I begged her to stop destroying herself, she left, and I have no idea where she is now. Max only has me."

"I'm sorry, Rocky"

"Thanks."

"Do you think she'll come back?"

"I don't think she's coming back, no. She's probably across the country in the arms of a new lover, no longer caring about me or Max. When I was little, she took me all over the country like that. Going from state to state, from job to job, from guy to guy. It's the only thing that has always mattered to her, the love of a man. Luckily, this time she didn't take Max on her sordid escapades. Probably because she knows I can take better care of him."

"Have you tried going to the police? Surely there must be a way to locate her? A parent can't let go of responsibilities all of a sudden without being worried."

"I didn't want to tell them. I'm only a 19-year-old college student. I have no desire for Max to be taken away from me if they find out about our situation."

"Could they do that?"

"I don't know. I'm not sure that my profile is ideal. And I don't want to take any risks. And then do I really want her to come back? Her drunken behavior had become dangerous and toxic to Max. At least now, even though it's hard to do everything, I know he's safe. So, for the moment, I say nothing, even though I'm getting more and more questions in the neighborhood and at school."

"Does anyone know about this?"

"No one except Mrs. Johnson and you now."

"Alyson and Isabella?"

"No. They suspect something, obviously, but I have never confirmed it. Let's say I know they would definitely help me if I told them, but Max is my responsibility, and my responsibility only."

"Why are you telling me then?"

"Because…"

I take a deep breath and swallow the knot that has formed in my throat.

"I don't know... Because you kind of guessed it, because I'm tired of lying, and above all because deep down, I hope to scare you and keep you away from me for good. Because obviously, I can't do it."

I close my eyes and would rather stare at the ceiling than meet his gaze.

I feel him moving next to me.

"Look at me."

He caresses my cheek with his thumb, I find myself obeying him.

"It's not going to happen. There's no way you're going to discourage me, Rocky. I want you, with your problems and your imperfections."

"I don't understand, Jude! There are so many other girls in college willing to die to be with you, I mean, there's even a #JudeHartnett on Twitter where your college fan club is going wild. You're a future football star! You could have anyone! Why do you bother with problem girl like me?"

"You're a problem girl, maybe, but a very sexy problem girl."

He smiles, and his right dimple widens, melting my icy, recalcitrant little heart a little more. His determination and, above all, his perseverance move me. I kept pushing him away, and yet he's still there. It makes me feel like maybe I mean a little to him.

All my life, I didn't count for anyone. First, my father, who never wanted to know anything about me, and then my mother, who always put me after her boyfriends. I can't imagine mattering for anyone, especially not for a guy as popular as Jude. However, I want to listen to him, and I want to believe it. I don't know how he does it, but he manages to instill a little hope in me.

"Why me, Jude?"

His eyebrows furrow.

"The real question is: Why are you so surprised that I'm interested in you?"

"Well, first of all, because you barely know me."

"I know enough to want to know more! And then..." He runs a hand over my cheek. "I like challenges! When it's too easy, I don't care."

His retort stings me and brings all my biggest insecurities to the surface. Don't know what I was expecting, but I sure as hell wasn't expecting this!

"So, is that what I am to you, a challenge? A trophy? A prize for your ego? And what will happen once your goal is achieved? Will you find yourself another challenge? I don't have time for these stupid games, Jude!"

I jump out of bed under his puzzled gaze, hastily retrieve my things. I throw my dress in my purse, then put on my shoes. I need to get out of here as soon as possible before I burst into tears like the poor idiot that I am. What was I thinking confiding in him? What was I imagining? That he would comfort me? Understand? Fall in love with me? I may claim loud and clear that none of this interests me, I'm just lying to myself! I am pathetic! And it's time for me to stop ridiculing myself.

"Rocky! Where are you going? Wait!"

I hear Jude gets up, and I pick up the pace toward the exit. But he catches up with me in a few strides and crushes his palms on the door to keep it closed. Despite my efforts, I can't overcome his strength and open the door. He is right behind me. His body radiates incredible heat, and my panicked breathing makes me feel like I'm running out of oxygen.

"Let me go!" I whisper, my voice shaking.

"I'll let you go if that's really what you want, but please, at least listen to me until the end. That's not what I meant."

I swallow the knot that has formed in my throat, then turn to face him.

"So, what exactly did you mean, Jude?"

I wish my tone hadn't been so desperate. Unfortunately, the sadness took over the anger.

"What you mean to me, Rocky... I don't know! It's too early to tell. All I know is that I like you, I find you beautiful, natural, honest, strong, and brave. I know you're going to find this ridiculous, because we barely know each other, but I feel like an invisible thread connects me to you... I'm inevitably attracted to you. And I know it's mutual."

I nod. I can't deny the obvious, not anymore anyway.

His voice gets lower, and his intense gaze locks into mine.

"You tried to avoid me, to ignore me, fuck me, you put me through all the stages, but you can see that it doesn't work, you always think of me! If I believe what you confessed to me tonight. And I'm always thinking about you. So, what's left to do?"

"I don't know…"

"Sleep with other people?"

He says these words as if they taste like arsenic.

"I don't want to. You?"

"Don't want to, either."

"Good! So, the only thing left for us to do is try…"

"Try?"

"Try to be together! 'If you can't beat them, join them,' as the saying goes. The attraction we have for each other is too strong not to at least try to see where it can take us. I promise you I won't be a distraction to you and your brother. On the contrary, I want to be able to make myself useful, or if you prefer, to be discreet. I'll take the place you give me, Rocky. You decide! All these girls," he continues as if to give me the final blow, "that you mentioned on Twitter or elsewhere, none of them interest me. Not because they're too easy, but because they're not you. They don't have your sparkling, determined gaze, that mischievous glow when you smile, and that complex personality that makes me want to know more."

He brushes my hair back from my face. His eyes are now locked on my lips. I swallow. The urge to kiss him is almost unbearable, but I want to listen to him until the end, to know what he has to say to me. I have so many doubts and questions. And as if he had heard my inner request, he continues talking, "You thought you were scaring me by telling me about your situation, but you're wrong. On the contrary, it only confirms what I already knew: that you're a wonderful, strong girl! The love and devotion you have for your little brother is admirable. You don't hesitate to put your life in the background while keeping a smile, when half the girls your age would have collapsed. Do you know a lot of great women like that? Personally, I don't. So, I'd be crazy to miss my chance with you!"

I smile, and my heart is on the verge of exploding. All the dams of my will are about to give way under the weight of his devastating charm.

And this time, I'm not going to hold them back.

17

Rocky

Jude barely finished his speech when I threw myself at him. My mouth collides with his. He steps back, surprised, but quickly takes note of the situation and presses me against the door. It's almost painful.

His tongue doesn't waste a second invading my mouth, and I welcome it like a hungry, thirsty, demanding baby bird. It's the kind of kiss that goes from zero to a hundred in a split second. He grabs my hair and forces me to tilt my head to better impose the assaults of his tongue. A merciless struggle begins.

My hands slide from his hair to his neck, then to his broad, muscular shoulders. I continue my joyous exploration across his back to the elastic of his boxers, which I pull on.

But Jude suddenly breaks the kiss and grabs my hands in his to keep me from reaching my target.

"If you touch me there, I won't be able to stop myself, Rocky," he says, his eyes closed as if looking at me was too painful for him.

"I don't want you to stop."

His chest rises and falls in an uneven rhythm. His heart seems completely distraught, as well as mine. I'm scared! I don't know if I'm making the right decision, but I think I have no choice! My heart leaves me no choice. Eyes still closed and forehead pressed against mine, he adds, "Does this mean you're okay with giving us a chance?"

I nod, but obviously that's not enough for him.

"Say it loud and clear."

He steps back, his eyes finally open, and my heart skips a beat. They are so intense, expressive, and at this moment, I read only one thing: pure and primary desire.

"Yes, I want to try."

"You know, Rocky, that I didn't bring you here to sleep with you, right?"

"I know, don't worry about it. Nobody is forcing me to do anything right now. I want you. Damn, I've never wanted someone so much in my life."

To completely erase the guilt, I read on his face, and to prove my point to him, I pull my T-shirt over my head. Luckily, I'm wearing my best lingerie. I had a plan tonight! It didn't exactly go as planned, but I like this new plan even more. I reach behind my back and undo my bra under his hungry gaze. Jude shakes his head slowly and bites his lip. He's as sexy as hell.

"Fuck, Rocky! Do you know how beautiful you are? And how you make me feel? How many times have I thought about your body, your pussy, and how it felt to be inside you? Good thing I got hurt, otherwise I would have fucked you so hard you couldn't walk straight."

Wow! I can feel my pulse between my legs! Who says that kind of thing? Damn it! The temperature in the room just skyrocketed, and it's getting hard to breathe.

Jude caresses himself slowly above his boxer shorts, and I see an impressive erection taking shape. I remember it was wide, I remember it hurt, but I've never felt so full, literally or figuratively. Suddenly, I can't stand the distance between us anymore, and I grab his hands to put them on my breast. He bites his lip and caresses my breasts hard. I moan, and this time it's him who doesn't wait a second before kissing me passionately. He spins me around and brings me by the bed without ever stopping to kiss me. In a split second, I find myself lying with the man of all my fantasies leaning over me.

A devastating kiss later, my body vibrates with pleasure and demands more. Encouraged by my moans, Jude attacks my neck eagerly, impatiently. He nibbles on that sensitive little spot just below my ear. And my God, if his goal is to show me that every part of my body is his slave, then, he's succeeded!

My nipples harden while waiting to be honored. Jude is quick to reward them. He places tender kisses along my collarbone in the valley of my breasts, then wraps his tongue around one of my nipples and sucks it. My back arches in appreciation. He then takes care of the other, while giving me dirty, evil looks. I must be red as a tomato, and I keep moaning every time his tongue darts and licks my tips. He sucks them, nibbles them for a long time, patiently. I think I could cum, I think I might cum, even though we're only in the foreplay.

"Do you like having your breasts kissed?" he whispers against my skin, which has turned pink from the contact with his five o'clock shadow.

"Hmm… hmmm…" I say, my brain too foggy to formulate a coherent sentence.

Looking satisfied, he continues his assault for a few moments, before deciding that other parts deserve his attention.

Torn between arousal and frustration, I squirm under his kisses. He gets to my belly button, then grabs my thong. I help him remove it by lifting my butt and legs. He laughs at my eagerness. I shut him up as I get on my knees and grab his member through his boxers. His abs twitch in surprise. I take out his cock and caress it without mercy, while challenging him with my eyes. So, we laugh less now! His velvet skin slips through my fingers, and Jude forgets where he lives for a moment. He tilts his head back, it's the perfect moment to take him in my mouth.

"Shit, Rocky!"

The strangled sound that escapes his lips as I wrap my tongue around his shiny head is the reward I've been looking for. He strokes my hair and brushes it away from my face, watching me as if the secret of the universe is at the tip of my tongue. He is beautiful when he's vulnerable. His eyebrows arch and his eyelids crinkle, while his mouth forms an O.

"Fuck, yes, babe, suck it!"

I take his cock out of my mouth and look at him, satisfied and playful, before taking him back again. This time, I try to get him deep inside. It's not easy, because he's wide, but I don't get discouraged and I'm rewarded for my efforts with an animal growl. I suck him like I did before. The muscles of his abs are even more prominent and those of his thighs jerk. I think he's struggling not to cum. One more lick, and he'll be done.

"Rocky!"

He pulls on my hair to force me to let go. His strangled voice and his authoritative tone titillate me even more. I love being in this position of power. I pretend not to understand and take it again, twice, he tastes like heaven. I'm addicted to the warmth of his soft, firm cock in my mouth. My hand covers what I can't get in.

"Babe, stop it now!"

He pulls me off his cock before exploding. When our eyes meet again, his are crazy. He digs his hands into my hair and kisses me passionately, hard, breathtaking, our teeth chattering. Our exchange becomes torrid, animal, an emergency, a battlefield. I scream when he puts me on my back and, then spreads my legs with a sharp movement. Looks like I woke the beast! His mouth devours me, to punish me, to reward me, I have no idea. All I know is that I like the primal, sexual feeling that emanates from him, as if he were urgent to make love to me. He kisses my entire body down to my most sensitive spot, leaving me gasping with desire.

When his tongue makes contact with my clitoris, I think I see stars and I clutch at the sheet. I scream a little too loud, before remembering that I'm in a fraternity house and that the rooms next door are probably occupied. I put my hand over my mouth to stifle my moans! But damn, he's good with his tongue! He licks and squeezes, then makes circular motions, devouring me. My hips rise in spite of myself, and I rub myself against him.

I pull on his hair, he pulls on my tips in retaliation, and the pleasure is only tenfold. He sits up, lips shining with my desire.

"Babe, your pussy is beautiful, and your taste, I could lick you until dawn."

He places two fingers in my mouth, an electric shock runs through my spine as he brings them back into me. Satisfied, he disappears again between my legs, except this time the assault is double, and at the limit of the bearable. He nibbles my clitoris, then sucks it. The oxygen seems to have left my lungs, and my breathing becomes jerky. I feel like I'm suffocating with warmth, desire, happiness. His tongue, his fingers, it's too much! I arch my back, close my eyes, squirm under his grip, and beg him not to stop.

"Jude! Yes!"

He pumps inside me, slowly at first, then faster and faster. He hooks his fingers and reaches that sensitive, magical place.

"Oh, my God, Jude!"

I close my eyes to try to calm the volcanic eruption that is born inside me. But I can't, I can't control anything, not even the volume of my screams. My brain is short-circuiting. He keeps pressing that magic button until the explosion is inevitable. The shock wave travels through my entire body, silencing me and making my legs shake. Jude continues to lick me, ignoring my spasms, until I block his head with my hands. He is trying to kill me. I know it for sure now.

"Oh, my God, that was… that was…"

No words come to me to describe what I felt. Jude lies down in front of me, while I'm limp, drained of all my energy. He caresses my back covered in a film of sweat. His caramel eyes have a particular glow, which I can't understand.

"Where the fuck did you come from?" Jude breathes.

My heart races, and I kiss him tenderly. It takes me a few seconds to recover from my orgasm and realize that his erection is pressing against my thigh and demanding attention. I get rid of his underwear, determined to make him come in my turn. His ribs are hurting, so I'll take the lead.

"Do you have condoms?"

Without answering me, he turns around, opens his bedside drawer, and takes out what we need. I take him from his hands, straddle him, kiss his dick and roll the condom over his gorgeous cock, then lean down to kiss his bluish ribs.

"Does it still hurt?"

"Yes, but that's not what I want to think about right now. Not when you're this sexy and naked in my bed. Come here!"

He intertwines his fingers in my hair and brings my mouth where he wants it, which is against his. He opens my lips and pushes his tongue in, eager to taste me. I can taste myself through him, it's disturbing and arousing at the same time. With each caress of his hot tongue, my arousal soars. It's the hottest kiss on earth, and I try to ease my arousal by moving my hips. His cock slides against my wetness, without penetrating me. I wonder how long he can resist like this, before entering me. He is the most patient lover I have ever had. And I'm the first to give in.

"Jude, if you don't fuck me right now, I think I'm going to die."

He smiles against my lips.

"Take what you want, Rocky."

With these words, I position myself so that he can enter me. I slide down on him and we are propelled into heaven. I close my eyes to savor this first intrusion and to get used to his presence, and when I open them, I see him looking at me with admiration.

"What's the matter?"

"You're beautiful," he breathes.

"Thanks."

I can feel my cheeks heating up.

"And I forgot how tight you are. I'm not sure I'll last very long."

"Am I dealing with a premature ejaculator?" I scoff.

His pride seems wounded at my teasing and he sits up to face me.

"That would be a first."

This position makes me feel him even more deeply, and I moan with pleasure. He swallows my moans and starts moving inside me. Damn, this is too good! His thrusts are slow, controlled. He places his hands on my hips to lift me up and control the pace, watching my reactions. Our lips are a few inches apart, but they don't touch each other. I feel like I belong to him more and more. With each thrust, he becomes mine and I become his.

When the pleasure becomes unbearable, I close my eyes and throw my head back. He takes the opportunity to kiss my neck, then my breasts. His hands leave my hips and grab my breasts to knead them, before bringing them to his mouth one after the other. It drives me crazy. I know my orgasm is imminent. I push him down, and I work against him, until my breathing becomes erratic, and I reach the point of no return.

"Yes, babe, fuck me! Give me everything you got."

And I obey him, picking up the pace. We are nothing but movements, moans, and pleasure. He looks at me seriously, his jaw clenched. A few drops of sweat appear on his forehead. He is beautiful like a god! I clench my teeth so as not to come too quickly, but once again, I have no control whatsoever. The depth of his penetrations, his beauty and the desire in his eyes create a sensory overload and propel me back into a trance state. The orgasm seizes me this time like a whirlwind. Intense, inevitable, and devastating.

I suddenly stop and collapse on his chest, deprived of all energy, my body sweating and my hair covering my face. But he is not done with me and hugs me against him while penetrating me with force and precision, making the pleasure last an immeasurable amount of time. And what happened next, I don't remember. It's a blur. I don't know when he came, if he came. I just know I've never felt better lying there, on his sweaty body. His heart beats against my ear at an insane rate. We're both out of breath, and I'm floating on a cloud of bliss.

I don't want to run away from him like the last time, on the contrary, I could fall asleep there and—I don't know if it's a good or a bad thing—in his arms, listening to him catch his breath. I don't want to be anywhere else.

18

Jude

Rocky is lying on top of me. I'm caressing her back and hear her purring. I don't know if she is aware of it, but she makes the sexiest noises in the world. I can't help but touch her pearly skin. My hand moves back and forth, down her spine to her lower back, where there are two adorable little dimples. Thankfully, the sheet covers the rest, because her beautiful round ass is worthy of all my fantasies. She has this amazing arch!

I hope she really meant what she said earlier, about giving us a chance, because there's no way I'm going back. I like her. I like her a lot and, if I listened to myself, I would fuck her again. However, I'm dead tired. I played all four quarters in the game, not to mention my ribs are screaming. But Rocky has the kind of beauty that would wake the dead. Brunette and glowing. The type of girl who doesn't need makeup to be beautiful. Her skin, her smile, and her freshness are enough. I feel her slip away from my grip, so I squeeze her even tighter.

"Hey, where are you going? Don't tell me you're panicking again."

"No."

"Good, because three rejections are too much for one man."

"I didn't give you three rejections."

She speaks into my neck, her voice almost sleepy, and her breath gives me chills.

"Let me refresh your memory, baby! Rejection number 1: After our first time."

I kiss her earlobe.

"Rejection number 2: when I walked you to your home."

This time I kiss her temple

"And rejection number 3: in the cafeteria."

She glances up and her guilty look makes me laugh softly. I take this opportunity to steal a kiss.

"Oh, I didn't realize! But now, I promise you that I didn't want to get out, just give you space. Don't you guys like space?"

His big black eyes are quizzical.

"Who told you that?"

"Nobody! But that's what I thought. At the same time, what would I know? I never stayed after sex."

"Ever? Why?"

"I don't know. Maybe it's too intimate. It's something you do with your boyfriend. And I never had a boyfriend."

"Never?"

"No"

"Not even in high school?"

She shakes her head. Her hair caresses my chest.

"Why?"

She shrugs. I don't think I will have more information on the subject for tonight, but I can always tease her a little.

"Does that mean you consider me like your boyfriend?"

Her whole body freezes, and she tries again to push me away. It's so easy to make her react. It's not just in sex that she's reactive. Rocky is a passionate girl, and I like that.

"Just kidding, Balboa. I'm not at that point either, I reassure you, but I appreciate being treated like a privileged person."

I force her to lie on top of me, wrapping her arm around my chest and her leg over mine.

She caresses my huge bruise with her fingertips.

"What about your ribs? Am I hurting you?"

"A little late to think about that, after fucking me like a horny Amazon."

I thought I would make her blush, but it's quite the opposite. She gives me the hottest look in the world.

"That's what you get when you're too sexy."

And that's how all my efforts to contain myself are undone.

I grab her chin between my fingers and kiss her again. The taste of her lips, the warmth of her tongue drives me crazy and makes me hard again.

"I think I should get you more ice anyway," she says against my lips.

"Are you breaking the mood on purpose?"

"Excuse me for worrying about you," she says.

"If you really want to worry, you should be worrying about something other than my ribs."

I put her hand on my cock, squeeze it so she can feel how excited she makes me.

"Hello, you!" she says in the direction of my member that I rub subtly against her belly.

"You're not tired?"

This time she's talking to me.

"No."

I lie, I'm exhausted.

"You?"

"No," she says, caressing my face and devouring my lips with her eyes.

Her voice has dropped a few octaves, she plants a first chaste kiss on my lips, then a second, lips half-open, languorous, then a third with just the right amount of tongue. I roll over her and wince in pain.

"Jude! You're not going to get better if you're not careful."

"Forget my ribs, woman. I'm a real man, a buffalo hunter."

She laughs, while I already kiss her neck.

"That's not what you were saying earlier. I think I heard you talking about calling your mom."

I smile against her skin and lick the sensitive little spot just below her ear, the one that makes her shiver and hardens her nipples. She moans and relaxes completely under me.

"I would have done anything for you to touch me, babe. I was this close to pretending my dick was broken."

"Seriously?"

I'm now at the level of her collarbone which I cover with kisses.

"But I didn't have to get that far."

"You lied?"

"You'll never know."

I overlook her breasts. They are perfect, neither too big nor too small. They hug the palms of my hands like they were made for me. Their pink tips point and call to my mouth. I circle them with my tongue. She moans for a long time, forgetting all her repartee. I already know that I will love to silence her by making her die of pleasure. I spotted her weaknesses, and her breasts are at the top of my list.

I go back to her mouth, and after making sure she's ready for me, I take another condom, penetrate her again. We moan loudly. And the feeling of fullness is almost immediate. Damn. She is just perfect. And that pussy! I'm not sure I can ever do without it. It wraps around me like a tight, warm glove. Heaven.

This time, we make love slowly, tenderly, looking in each other's eyes, the urgency of the release having passed. We even succeed the feat of cumming at the same time. And that just confirms that we are very, very sexually compatible. To think that she wanted to pass on all that. Exhausted, Rocky collapses on the bed, and I, on her. I get up to get rid of the condom and lie down next to her again. I stick to her pretty little ass and wrap my arms around her stomach. I place kisses on the back of her neck and pass a possessive leg over hers. I'm about to fall asleep, but before that, I want to make sure we're on the same page. And that once the sexual excitement is over, she's not going to run away. Like the last time.

"Rocky?"

"Mmm…"

"So, are you still willing to try? To be together, I mean."

She turns to face me, nods in agreement, but stays quiet as she chews on the inside of her cheek. Even in the dark, I sense the discomfort. I could have done with it, but I can see that something is wrong.

"What's going on? Do you regret it? Are you not sure of yourself anymore?"

"No… I'm not sorry, but it's just that…"

"*That what*?"

"Do you understand that you won't see me often?"

"Yes, Rocky! And that's fine with me. I'm a college football player, remember? On top of all my classes so I'm very busy too. You won't always have me in your way all the time. I promise you. Just enough to make you cum and laugh."

She smiles.

"For that, I know I can trust you."

The end of her sentence is overshadowed by a yawn.

"Tired?"

"Exhausted."

"Sleep now, I intend to wake you up at dawn to fuck you again. Just to seal our deal."

"Can't wait for tomorrow morning, then."

The atmosphere seems to relax again. She nestles against me. Our two bodies fit together perfectly. My chin on top of her head, I've never felt better. There could be a nuclear attack outside and I wouldn't notice. Silence fills the room.

"There is something else I'd like to tell you."

She turns to look me in the eye. I tuck a lock of hair behind her ear, to encourage her to speak.

"There is Max."

"I know."

"He is and always will be my priority."

This time, she's dead serious. His determined gaze proves it to me.

"Of course, babe."

"I'll never be like my mother. I'll never put him on the back burner. He deserves better than that."

"And that's admirable. I expect nothing less from you. And if I can help, I want you to know that I'm here. Max is very lucky to have you. You're a wonderful big sister," I say, caressing her cheek with my thumb.

"Thanks. He hasn't had an easy start to life so far, with the loss of his dad and now mum gone, so I'm doing what I can. There are so many things missing. Above all, I don't want him to go through the same horrors as I did at his age. Kids can be so cruel."

"You didn't have an easy childhood?"

"It's the least we can say. I changed schools faster than my shadow. So, at school, I was either the new a little weird, or the girl without friends, or the little slut, depending on the year. And

I think I deserved all those labels. The truth is that I was trying to build myself, and my mother was not really a model that I wanted to identify with. So, I went through all the possible and imaginable phases: short hair, long hair, blue hair, piercings and clothes that were too sexy or too baggy; kleptomania… Not to mention all the school difficulties. Anyway, I don't know why I'm telling you all this. Usually, I don't like to talk about it."

She plays nervously with an invisible thread on the pillow and looks horribly embarrassed.

"And look at yourself today," I say, taking her hand and bringing it to my lips. "You're at Brown, one of the most prestigious universities in the country. You study architecture and you are by far the smartest, most interesting, funny, and most beautiful person I know."

She smiled again. Victory!

"What wouldn't you say just to put a girl in your bed, Jude Hartnett?"

"Ha! Ha! That's true, but in general, don't usually have to say much! My natural charm is enough."

"Pretentious!"

"I'm not pretentious, more like sure of myself. You need at least that when you play football, otherwise you can get knocked down pretty quickly. But you, Rocky Prescott, you're not good for my ego. I have never struggled so much to convince a girl to go out with me."

"You know what they say, challenge makes you grow."

"In that case, I must be at least ten feet tall. Do you know how long I spent in this room thinking about you and playing with myself?"

"And to think that I thought you were a very busy guy."

"Never too busy for that. And now that I have you on hand, you're going to have to fulfill all my fantasies and baptize every corner of this room."

"I'm a willing victim."

She kisses me for a long time before retreating.

"Okay, so what about you, what's your story? Wait! Don't tell me. Let me guess. You grew up in a big, beautiful house with a close-knit family. You always knew what you wanted to do, and you succeeded in everything from the beginning. I bet you were already Mr. Popular in high school, the kind of guy who bullied me back then."

"It's almost like that, except for the 'big house and close-knit family' part. My mother and I lived in a crappy apartment in Warwick. She worked like crazy to allow me to focus on school and football. I have no siblings, and I never knew my father."

"No?"

"No! For the rest, you are right. I was very popular in high school. I was even elected prom king three times in a row."

"That deserves respect! I have never been to a school dance."

"None at all?"

She confirms with a nod.

"Never?"

"No… I was never invited. In middle school I never stayed long enough to make friends, in high school I was just not interested. A girl with blue hair cannot afford this kind of frivolity. It would ruin her reputation."

"You must have been sexy with blue hair. If I had known you in high school, I'm sure I would have fallen in love with you."

"I doubt that. You would never have looked at me. I was in my bubble. I didn't speak to many people, and I wore clothes three times too big for me. I didn't assume my femininity."

"Were you a rebel?"

"No, I was an outcast."

"We have to fix that," I say.

"Fix what?"

"The fact that you never went to prom."

"What? Are you going to take me to a ball, like Cinderella? I'm warning you that is not my thing."

"Why not? I'll do it right, with limo and suit."

"No, thanks! Besides, I hate wearing dresses," she says.

"That's a shame! It looks divine on you. Your long legs are just amazing," I say, stroking her thighs.

She moans and moves closer to kiss me. Her warm tongue meets mine, and a few minutes later I find myself inside her again, her heart pounding against mine, exactly where I want to be, in heaven. In my new heaven.

19

Jude

In the morning, I am awakened by loud voices and laughter emanating from the floor below. The guys are already up and energic. A real miracle when you know what time they got home last night. And given the noise they were making at three in the morning, they must have been drinking gallons to celebrate the victory. Thankfully, there is no practice today. I will be able to enjoy my morning and the hottie that shares my bed.

Last night we didn't stop making love. It could have been enough for me, but it's not, I still want her. We talked a lot too. She told me about her troubled past with her irresponsible mother. Imagining her sleeping in the car, not being sure she had enough to eat, broke my heart. I feel like I know her better, and more importantly, I understand her reluctance and fears better. She didn't have an easy life, and everyone around her kept disappointing her. No need to be Freud to understand that she has a hard time trusting people and has horrible abandonment anxiety. But I'm determined to prove to her that not all human beings are bastards and that she can count on me.

I roll over onto my stomach, trying to scratch out a few more minutes of sleep.

My hand goes in search of Rocky's skin. I need to feel her. I swallow the smile that has appeared on my face, because there's obviously no one in the fucking bed but me. Talk about a cold shower. I groan in frustration, both fists pressing against my forehead. I scan the room with my eyes and listen for any sign of someone in the bathroom, but it's clear: Rocky is not there, and neither is her stuff. She must have slipped away discreetly at the first light of day. Just as I feared. We can't really call that a progress. Once again, she left me. I'm good for sex, but more? She's just not interested. Images of me doing the same thing to many girls race through my head. Rocky, this is my fucking karma payback. I turn over on my back, my erection remembering last night.

The feeling of incomprehension that overwhelms me is powerful. At what point did I go wrong? I was sure that this time... she had opened up to me. She had agreed to give me a chance, it was almost too simple. I growl at my own stupidity. In a fit of anger, I pull myself out of bed. A jolt of pain in the ribs calls me to order. I decide to take a shower to calm down before joining the guys in the kitchen. No need to stay here moping, it won't make her come back.

I go down the huge staircase, cross the main living room, then arrive at the kitchen. The guys better not be fucking with me this morning, because I'm not in the mood to stand for their bullshit right now. I push the swinging doors. Fuck! My heart starts beating faster. If this isn't the most beautiful sight I've ever seen.

Rocky is there, making pancakes.

She's still wearing my T-shirt and a pair of my shorts that she has rolled up at the waist. She has also tied her hair, which reveals her delicate neck. She looks so beautiful in this outfit! And my primal male side loves seeing her wearing number twenty-two, my number. An implicit way of saying that she belongs to me.

I approach and hug her from behind, before kissing her neck tenderly. She freezes, a little embarrassed. It must be said that we're not alone and that the others are already whistling and shouting at us to find a room, but I don't care. I invite her to turn around and I kiss her deeply, to show her all my appreciation. She stayed.

"Hi," she says against my lips.

Her cheeks are slightly pink, her eyes are filled with tenderness.

"Hi! Did you sleep well?"

"Like a baby. And you?"

"The same."

She clears her throat and adds, "I made pancakes. You want some?"

"I'd love some. I'm starving."

I grab two plates, for her and for me, which I fill before joining the guys on the kitchen island that we use as a table, and I can't help but smile like a virgin after his first time. Besides, I'm not the only one smiling. Scott, Adam, Alec, and Alyson wear the same silly smile as me. They're going to ask me a thousand questions soon, but I don't care. They can do it. Since last night, I feel like I'm walking on water.

"Was the evening good?" Alec asks.

I don't answer and just dip my nose into my awful cup of coffee. Apparently, Scott made the coffee, but nothing can spoil my good mood this morning.

"I'll take that as a yes!" says Alec.

"Touchdown!" mimes Scott with the delicacy that characterizes him.

Alyson taps him on the shoulder but winks at me.

Their 3-year-old jokes last a few minutes, and I let them get it out of their systems. Rocky joins us and sits next to me. I place a possessive hand on her thigh, and she smiles at me before taking a sip of coffee. Of course, like the rest of us, she winces.

"Yuck, it looks like sock juice. Who made this coffee?"

"It's Scott," we all answer at the same time, blasé.

"We keep asking him to stay away from the coffee pot, but he has the memory of a goldfish," Alec scoffs.

"Pfft! For once I wanted to make myself useful, that'll teach me. I do, I get yelled at. I don't, I get yelled at. I can never win with you."

"Scott! If you want to be useful, do the dishes, sweep once in a while, don't leave your shit all over the house, and above all— above all, don't touch the fucking coffee maker."

The four of us say this last sentence at the same time, which ends up finishing Scott off.

"Fuck you guys!"

"Don't be offended, man! But damn it's not complicated to make coffee. How do you systematically screw it up?"

"It takes talent and dedication!" he ironizes.

"Does he have trouble with the proportion?" asks Alyson.

"That's not what you said last night," he replies to her.

"It's because he often falls on his head," Adam interjects.

"Look, Scott, that's three spoons, and that's two," he says pointing out his fingers as if he were in kindergarten.

"Me, don't understand!" Scott replies.

And everyone is laughing.

"Thank goodness, there are Rocky's pancakes to raise the level. It's delicious, Balboa," I say, stroking her back.

"You already got her into bed, Jude, no need to be cheesy," says Scott.

We both ignore his remark. This morning, it's only her and I who count.

"Thanks."

She turns her head, smiles at me, and I take the opportunity to steal a kiss. She tastes like maple syrup. Immediately, my mind wanders, and I imagine her naked with syrup on her—

"Hello, Earth to Jude."

"Huh, What?"

"Did you see all those comments on Twitter about yesterday's game?"

Alec holds his phone in his hands.

"No."

"This is crazy, man! The image of your last run to the end zone went viral. It has been retweeted over 1,200 times. Check that! And it goes beyond the campus."

I take his iPhone and whistle through my teeth. There are hundreds of comments and thousands of likes.

Damn, it's crazy!

Rocky looks over my shoulder, and her scent has a direct effect on my cock. What is it about this girl that makes me hard at the slightest touch?

"Wow! Is that you running here?" she asks.

"Yes," I say, I'm proud to confirm that.

"Well, you're really fast!"

"That's what they say!"

"The real question is 'Is he as fast in bed?'" Scott says before laughing and clapping Adam's hand.

I give them both the middle finger.

This bastard, he doesn't miss a beat. Good thing I can count on Alec to stay serious.

"Keep it up, Jude, and you'll soon have the biggest NFL teams knocking on your door."

It's about time, because it's my last year, so my last chance, and I wasted all of last year staying on the bench at Harvard. Football is my whole life. I've dreamed of playing pro since I was a kid and I don't plan to do anything else, no plan B for me. However, I have the impression that if I get carried away too quickly, I risk jinxing myself. It's my Irish side, I'm superstitious, and spots are expensive.

"Don't get carried away, Captain, it was just a game. An action where I got lucky. I will need much more than a mini buzz on the web to join the NFL."

"I say you've got what it takes. Your stats are among the best in the country."

"We'll see."

Conversations turn to last night's party, and allusions are made to our disappearance. Alyson keeps talking about the band and she ends up getting Scott's jealousy. We have the right once again to their fake argument.

"Say it if you want to fuck that stupid singer! Go ahead, I'm not holding you back."

"Scott, I know you often fall on your head and find it hard to understand, but—"

"Here we go!" comments Alec while refilling coffee.

"Is it always like that between them?" laughs Rocky.

"Always. They love to hate each other. But usually, it does not last, and it ends with them making out. Wait a minute," says Alec.

"5-4-3-2-1!"

And just as I predicted, here they are, licking each other's tonsils.

Rocky holds back a laugh, which makes her eyes shine. Damn, how I love her eyes.

I must have stared at her too long, because she looks at me strangely.

"What's the matter?" she asks.

"Nothing, I'm just glad you stayed."

"Thanks."

We look into each other's eyes, until yet another heavy joke from my buddies breaks the moment. Rocky spends the rest of breakfast talking to Alyson, and I spend my time touching her, wishing she were naked and stayed in my bed longer this morning. I can't get enough of her, and with each grain of skin that I touch, my libido spikes. Any hope of spending more time with her vanishes when I see her get up and ask Alyson to walk her to her car.

"I can take you if you want?"

"No, it's okay, Jude. It's on my way, and Rocky and I have a lot to talk about."

"Okay," I say resignedly.

I walk them both to the door. Alyson understands that she is in the way when she sees us hugging.

"Hey, take it easy, cowboy. Well, Rocky, I'll be waiting for you in the car."

Rocky answers with a wave of her hand, her mouth too busy devouring mine to speak. I force my tongue past her lips, and damn, the moan she lets out makes my balls quiver.

"Are you sure you have to go already? I had hoped that we could replay the scene from the greenhouse."

I place light kisses on her neck. She leans back, pressing her lower abdomen against mine, and I already feel myself getting hard. I think she's trying to kill me.

"Mmh, it's tempting, but no, I don't want to be late. I have to go get Max."

She said the magic word, I definitely can't argue against that. Besides, she made it clear yesterday that he's her one and only priority, and I can only respect that.

"Okay, babe, in that case, I won't hold you back any longer."

I release her with regret and let her leave without insisting.

She walks away, staggering slightly, confused. She turns around and gives me one last look before disappearing into Alyson's car.

As for me, all I have to do is go for a run to burn off all the energy I want to burn with her.

20

Rocky

"Damn it, Rocky, I want all the details!" says Alyson, and I barely have time to close the car door.

I knew she was holding back earlier at breakfast not to expose me, but now that it's just the two of us, she lets go, and that makes me laugh.

"What do you want to know?" I ask.

"All! Absolutely everything. From the size of his cock to his endurance, not to mention how you ended up in his bed, when you loudly proclaimed that you wanted nothing to do with him. And if you miss any detail, I'll knock you out with my purse."

"OK! OK! OK! But stop screaming. You're going to put a hole in my eardrum."

My face is buried in my hands and it's hard to realize what's happening to me. My cheeks are burning. I feel like I can still feel his presence and his lips all over my skin, not to mention that my panties are soaked. A consequence of the last hot kiss he gave me.

"Well, where to start?"

"With the main thing. His dick."

"Haven't we had this conversation before?"

"No. You just told us it was the best sex you ever had and didn't go on about it. Apparently talking about it kept you from forgetting it. Now that you've done it again, I don't want to hear anymore lame excuses. I want the most graphic details. So, I repeat, his dick?"

She finally starts the car, and I laugh before answering her, "Perfect."

Obviously, my answer doesn't satisfy her, because she throws me one of those looks of which she has the secret, the one which wants to say, "Are you fucking kidding me?"

"Rocky, I'm warning you that if you don't do better than that, I'll call Isabella, and you know very well that to her, you won't have any choice but to spit it all out."

She holds up her phone like a threat. A car passes us, honking. We've been moving like snails for the past few minutes.

"OK! OK! But focus on the road, psycho! What do you want to know, exactly?"

"Are you doing it on purpose or what? Its size? Its circumference?"

"Ah yes, you want that level of detail?"

"You're sleeping with the hottest guy on campus, I have the right to a few juicy details. I'm privileged to be your friend. Maybe one day he'll be famous, and I can sell this story to the press. So, is it more of a cucumber or a cup of yogurt?"

I burst out laughing.

"No dick can look like a cup of yogurt!"

"Oh, believe me, there's everything in this world, even peppers."

I laugh and shake my head. Alyson's got a knack for bullshit.

"If you really want me to compare it to a vegetable, then it would be a zucchini instead."

"You're kidding!"

"No, I'm telling you. It's perfect, large enough to make you feel amazing."

"I hate you. And the rest? Performance? Endurance? Ability to put the cover back?"

"Mmh… How do I say this?"

Images of his torso glowing above me, in front of me, behind me flash through my head, and I have to squeeze my thighs together to calm the heat that is building up dangerously there.

"You have that look!"

"What look?"

"The look of the girl who discovered the secrets of the universe."

"Ha! Ha! He's good, he's really good. I think if I had to summarize, I would say that he plays football like he fucks."

"Uh, do you realize he's known for his speed? So there, you just gave me the image of a jackhammer."

To punctuate her words, she taps on the dashboard at a frantic pace, once again causing me to laugh. Another car passes us, honking. This girl is completely crazy.

"No, on the contrary, he's patient, strategic, waiting for the perfect opportunity to move forward on the field. He builds his game, and when it's time for a touchdown, you only have your lungs to scream victory."

"That's the sexiest metaphor I've ever heard. You should write it on Twitter: *Jude Hartnett plays football like he fucks*. It would be sensational."

"And that would attract all the wrath of his fans. I'm not suicidal."

"But wait a minute, have you ever seen him play?" she asks.

I fidget in my seat, a little embarrassed, I feel like my fingers have been caught in the jam jar.

"I may have watched some of his performances online."

"Ah, sneaky one! And to think that all this time, you made me, and Isabella think you didn't want to hear about him."

"True, but I couldn't help but spy on him. What else is social media for, if not to spy on others?"

"I plead guilty. I do the same with Scott."

"By the way, you two seem to be getting pretty serious, from what I could see this morning."

"No, we're just good friends."

"Are you guys exclusive?"

"No, not really, but it's true that I haven't been looking elsewhere lately. I don't know about him; I don't ask him any questions."

"Yet it seemed to me to be more than that. You fight like an old couple."

"It's just our way of communicating. Either we yell at each other, or we climb on each other," she winks at me. "But don't try to change the subject, Rock my world! Back to God of the Stadium! How did you end up in his bed last night?"

I bury my face in my hands.

"I really didn't mean to."

"I know you didn't! I was there when you were going on and on about the thousands of reasons to Not. Go. Back to bed. With him. So, allow me to be confused."

"Long story short, operation "Forget Jude" almost went horribly wrong. I met a guy on the way to the bathroom, Christian, he seemed to me to be the perfect antidote to Jude: handsome, interested, with conversation. After a few minutes of chatting, I offered to take him down the aisle to… you know what! And once the fateful moment arrived, I couldn't. Christian didn't appreciate me pushing him away and started being a little pushy."

"The bastard! Are you okay? He didn't hurt you?"

She looks at me with concern.

"No, because Jude showed up."

"And he kicked his ass?"

"No, I took care of that."

She giggles, while turning in the parking lot of her dorm where my car is, which I left the day before, just before the makeover session.

"That's my Rocky! Girl power! Did you give him a karate grip that you know how to do?"

"Jujitsu."

"Jude must have been hallucinating."

"A little yes! Anyway, I was still a little shaken by it all, and when Jude asked me to come to his house, I accepted. Ah yes, I also threw up on his shoes, but that's a story for another day."

"So, you slept together?"

"Yes."

"What are you going to do? It's a simple relapse, like 'Oops! Excuse me, I slipped on your dick,' or do you plan to meet again?"

"I think we'll see each other again," I say in a very small voice, still a little shocked by the words coming out of my own mouth.

Me, the high priestess of unattached sex.

Alyson glances at me, her eyes shining with excitement and a satisfied smile blooming on her face.

"In a booty call or more serious?"

"No, serious," I say under my breath.

"I'm sorry, what? I did not hear you."

"Serious," I say, louder, but still in a whisper.

"I still do not understand. Articulate, you can do it, Rocky! Go ahead, say it clearly. The universe is listening to you."

What a brat!

"Serious. There, are you happy?"

"Yes, I'm happy. But like, are you his new girlfriend?"

"Huh no! Let's not get carried away either. We just said we'd take it as it comes and see where it goes. Well, he said it, because I just nodded silently."

With her hand over her heart, Alyson gave me a look worthy of a movie star who had just received an Oscar, too moved to make her speech.

"Oh, my little Rocky! She's all grown up. She's ready to enter the adult world and have a real relationship. Maybe her heart isn't made of ice after all."

"Oh, shut up, Alyson!"

She laughs, then asks, "So, when's the next date? Can I come and watch you? I promise you that I will be super discreet. I feel like a mom dropping her kid off at preschool for the first time."

"Can you be serious for five minutes?"

"Yes, sorry. So, when?"

"I don't know, he talked about taking me to dinner next Saturday, but I said no."

She rolls her eyes.

"Well, that's not a good start. You know that, for this to work, you're going to have to agree to see him again, Rocky?" she mocks.

"I know, but Saturday is bad timing. I have Max. I can't ask Mrs. Johnson to keep him again. And I don't like him sleeping out of his bed more than once a month. I know Max doesn't mind, he loves going to Mrs. Johnson's, but on principle, I don't want to."

"Isabella and I can babysit if you want?"

"I don't know—"

"Come on, say yes! We love Max, and he'll be delighted to spend time with Isabella, he's absolutely madly in love with her. And then, I really want to make it work with you and Jude!"

"Why?"

"Because he's a good guy like few others. He's not macho and seems to like you a lot. You would see the number of chicks who come to the Kappa Omega house half-naked and try to get his attention, you would be hallucinating. And yet, every time I saw him, he remained unmoved, while most guys would have taken advantage of it."

"If you think you're reassuring me by telling me that, you're on the wrong track."

"All I'm saying is he's spoiled for choice, and yet he chose you. Rocky, I've never seen him look at a girl the way he looked at you this morning. And you, you may not be convinced, but you deserve happiness."

"Don't start with your existential conversations."

"Okay, I'm quiet, but on one condition," Alyson says.

"And that is?"

"That you accept his date on Saturday."

"Fine."

"Yeeesss!"

21

Rocky

If I was worried about being stalked by Jude, I was on the wrong track. The guy is busier than a minister. When he's not in class, he's at practice. And when he's not at practice, he travels the state with his team for games. So much so that I barely saw him this week. And besides a few torrid FaceTime's and a visit to the cafeteria where I work, we barely run into each other. Luckily, it's Saturday night, and the opportunity to see him again is finally here.

I'm in the bathroom trying to put on makeup to look decent. I straightened my hair for the occasion and took out my prettiest dress, as well as my prettiest underwear. But this time, no question of me perching on heels! Booties will do the trick.

The doorbell rings and makes me jump, as I'm trying to put on that damn eyeliner. Wipe off. Redo. Again.

"I'll get it!" Max yells.

My little brother rushes out of his room to open the door. He knows Isabella and Alyson are going to babysit him tonight, and he's been in a tizzy ever since I told him the news. I even got him to clean his room by using the Isabella argument. If I had known how powerful his desire to please her was, I would have used her before.

I step out of the bathroom and whistle through my fingers to stop him in his tracks.

"Max! First, ask who it is before opening."

He slips on his socks and stops right outside the door.

"Isabella, is that you?"

I hear my friends' laughter echoing through the door.

"Yes!"

"And I'm here too," grumbles Alyson.

But Max doesn't care. He opens the door and throws himself into Isabella's arms, who welcomes him with great pleasure.

After a long hug, she puts him back on the ground.

"Do I at least have the right to a hello, little toad?" protests Alyson.

"Of course."

Alyson kneels down and hugs my little brother in turn before ruffling his hair.

"Look what I brought?"

"Yes, popcorn!"

Max jumps for joy.

"And you know what we're going to watch tonight?" asks Alyson.

"What"

"*Jurassic Park*!"

My little brother is gloating with happiness and excitement.

"So, who's your favorite babysitter, huh?"

Max looks at Isabella, then Alyson, not knowing who to choose, between his love for blondes or dinosaurs. I arrive just in time to save him from this drastic choice.

"Stop torturing my poor little brother. Come in, girls," I say, taking the popcorn off them and putting it on the kitchen table where Max's drawings serve as a tablecloth.

"Toad, can you tidy up, please? You wouldn't want Isabella to think you are a messy boy, would you?"

"Right away."

He rushes to his sheets and colored pencils scattered all over the kitchen to pick them up and bring them to his room. I watch him do it, in disbelief. Usually, I would have had to repeat it at least ten times before he would get to work, but I said the magic word.

"So, Stadium God hasn't arrived yet?" Allison asks.

I look at my watch: seven forty-five. I only have a few minutes left. And my makeup is still in the construction stage.

"No, and fortunately, I'm not ready yet."

I head for the bathroom, Alyson, and Isabella following me. They settle as they can, one on the edge of the tub, and the other, leaning against the wall in front of me. I lean over to the mirror to try and evenly apply that damn eyeliner that doesn't seem to want to comply tonight.

"Wait, let me do it."

Isabella takes it from my hands and, like the Superwoman that she is, achieves in seconds what I have been trying to accomplish for almost ten minutes. When I grow up, I'll be like Isabella. Which means, a real woman who knows how to do women's things.

"*Voilà!*"

"Thanks."

"This dress is very pretty!" remarks Alyson.

"Yes? It's not too girly?"

"Yes, but I remind you that it's what you are, Rocky, a girl," says Isa a hint of sarcasm coloring her tone.

"Very funny! You know what I mean. I don't look disguised? Do I still look like me?"

The doubt in my voice is impossible to ignore. My two girlfriends exchange a knowing look, amused.

"Damn, I didn't think that one day I would hear you talking about clothes to please a boy," Alyson mocks. "Who are you? And where is Rocky Prescott? The tomboy with three pairs of jeans in her closet. Jude must really be making an impression on you."

I shrug my shoulders and look at myself in the mirror, having trouble recognizing myself. This dress was Isabella's idea. I was going for my usual jeans and T-shirt look, but she managed to convince me by playing on my heartstring: jealousy. On Instagram, she scrolled through all the profiles of the girls who follow Jude, each one more beautiful and sexier than the next. And as pathetic as it sounds, that was enough to convince me. I hate being vulnerable, sensitive, and jealous, but sadly, I'm all of those things when it comes to Jude Hartnett.

"You are beautiful," Isa reassures me. "This dress is neither too short nor too low-cut. It just highlights your dreamy curves. It's Jude who's going to have a hard time keeping it in his pants."

I make eyes at Isabella, but she tells me that Max is in his room. The bell rings again. And my heart starts pounding in my chest. The three of us stare at each other with different expressions.

"I think your Prince Charming has arrived."

I swallow, take one last look at myself in the mirror before heading to Max's room to say goodbye.

As I cross the hallway, I give the girls their final recommendations.

"Max can't go to bed after nine o'clock."

"Got it!"

"He can eat popcorn, but not too much either!"

"Okay."

"And make sure he brushes his teeth before going to bed!"

"No problem."

"And for *Jurassic Park*, if you could skip the scary parts... I wouldn't want him to have nightmares, he's way ahead of his age, but deep down he's still a baby and—"

"Stop, Rocky! Trust us. We'll take good care of him. You, focus on the beautiful specimen waiting for you behind the door."

I bite my lip trying to ignore the butterflies dancing the limbo in my stomach. The reason I'm so nervous about this date is a good indicator of how inexperienced I am in this area. If we had nothing to say to each other? What if our chemistry had disappeared? What if he changed his mind and decided I wasn't worth it after all?

I take a deep breath and open the door. My heart skips a beat, and all my doubts disappear when I find myself facing Jude's caramel-green eyes.

"Hi!"

"Hi!"

"You brought me flowers? You didn't have to," I say accepting the bouquet.

"It's our first date, I didn't want to do things halfway."

He caresses the back of his neck, a little embarrassed.

"Come in for a second, I'm going to put them in a vase."

I open the door again and we catch my two friends, their ears glued to it. And the worst part is that they don't even pretend to be sorry that they were caught spying.

"Hi, Jude!"

They stare at him eyebrows arched.

"Hi! How are you?"

"Great. And you?"

"Great."

"I'll be right back," I say.

I hesitate to leave him in the clutches of these two pests, and I'm right to be wary, because as soon as I turn my heels, they start to cook him.

"So, Mr. Handsome? Where are you planning to take our little Rocky?"

"Don't answer their questions, Jude," I shout from the kitchen, filling the vase with water.

"You know if you want to keep her all night, you can. You have our full trust and permission."

I growl in frustration. These two little pests really have no limits.

"Indeed, she needs to relax, she has been under a lot of stress lately. College, her job, her car issues. An oil change is strongly recommended, and I'm not talking about her car," explains Alyson.

"I'm sure, Jude, you'll find the perfect way to release all the tension that's been built up under her body," Isabella adds.

I hear Jude laughing, and I rush to his side to prevent my two crazy girlfriends from continuing their show.

"Don't you have any babysitting to do?" I ask.

"But that's what we do!"

And as if he heard us, Max emerges from his room. He looks a little intimidated when he sees Jude by my side. My heart tightens. I don't know what he is thinking at this moment. I met my mother's various boyfriends so often, and most of them were complete losers who saw me as either a little pain in the ass or as prey, that my stomach couldn't help but knot up. But all my worries vanish when a big smile appears on Max's face.

"Do you remember my friend Jude?"

"Yes, he's the giant who drops you off with your Ninja Turtle head."

My two friends burst out laughing.

"I love this kid," Alyson says.

"And that's who you're having dinner with tonight?"

"That's right."

"Thanks, Jude," Max says.

"You're welcome, man, but why are you thanking me?"

"Because, thanks to you, I'm going to spend a *Jurassic Park* evening with my future wife, Isabella."

"Your future wife, no less?"

"Yeah! I'm sure one day we'll get married."

"You're right, big boy! In life, there's nothing like determination to make your dreams come true," smiles Jude, giving me a look that made me blush slightly.

"And I still count for nothing," Alyson retorts, falsely offended, ruffling Max's hair.

"Okay, kids! Have fun and, above all, do lots of silly things," says Isabella, before pushing us outside and closing the door behind us.

"I'm sorry. They're completely crazy."

"No, they're funny and, above all, they seem to adore you," Jude says.

"Yes, I'm very lucky to have them."

I'm a horrible girlfriend who keeps lying to them. I need to tell them about Mom, especially since Jude knows now. Which makes me feel like the worst traitor the earth has ever borne. No time to get lost in my head when Jude pulls me to him with a sudden gesture and takes my face in his hands before crushing his lips against mine. I welcome him with a hiccup of surprise, which allows him to introduce his tongue. The kiss is short, but wild, like a prelude, the lightning that announces the storm. When he lets go of me, I mechanically bring my fingers to my lips, a little stunned. Jude gives me his famous charming smile. One day, that smile will be worth millions of dollars, I'm sure. He already earned him thousands of fans among the female population, including me.

Above all, don't think about it, Rocky! The other girls don't count. Maybe if I tell myself that enough, my anxieties about not being good enough for him will go away. Maybe Santa Claus exists, too?

"Sorry, I couldn't wait any longer!"

"You're excused!"

"You look stunning tonight."

"Thank you, you're not bad either."

By "not bad either," I mean he's sexy as hell. He's wearing an impeccably ironed white shirt that shows off his muscles. He's left a few buttons open, and I see his delicious, tanned skin appear, his pecs already making my mouth water. If it were up to me, we'd cut dinner short and go straight to bed. But Mr. Gentleman here wants to make it right, with flowers, dinner, and the works.

Jude grabs my hand, brings it to his lips before walking over to a dark gray Jeep Wrangler parked right in front of the house. He opens the door for me.

"After you."

"Thanks! Is this your car?"

The only time I've ever seen him drive, he was on a motorcycle.

"Yeah! Gift from a sponsor."

"You're sponsored?"

"Yeah."

"That's awesome! I didn't realize that playing football in college had such benefits. Does everyone on the team have a sponsor?"

"No, just Alec and me."

"You must be proud?"

"Yes and no, my real goal is to be selected by a great team, not to be sponsored. I know I sound like an asshole when I say that."

"Sure, you do."

He's laughing, I think he's getting used to my lame sense of humor.

"But you have to understand that I have been playing football and dreaming of becoming a pro since I was old enough to walk. I won't settle for a simple advertising contract."

"That's already a good start, no?"

"It would be if I were a freshman or sophomore, but now I only have a few months to get noticed." His face darkens. "I don't really have a plan B if football doesn't work for me."

"I'm sure it will happen. The whole campus is raving about your prowess on the field."

"It's a lot of pressure. Spots are tough to get. And I wasted an entire season warming the bench," he says.

"Why? Did you hurt yourself?"

"No… It's a long story."

His jaw clenches, and I sense that it's a topic he doesn't want to talk about, so I don't insist. He drives in silence for a moment, merges onto the highway, and that piques my curiosity.

"Where are you taking me? Hold on! Let me guess, a large gourmet restaurant where you need a survival guide to know in what order to use the cutlery."

"Not at all!"

"No? Yet, it's the perfect first date for the perfect gentleman."

"I'm not a gentleman, Rocky. I think I proved it to you the night I fucked you against that glass window."

I blush when I think back to this hot moment that will forever be engraved in my memory.

"You brought me flowers tonight. I don't think it's been done since the 19th-century. Nowadays, the trend is more towards dick picks. So, I say you're romantic, and a gentleman. But that's a compliment. You're a rare endangered species, Jude Hartnett."

Intrigued, he turns to me. "Have you received any dick pics?"

"Dozens of them. It's the new trendy thing. Sometimes you zoom right in on the object, sometimes, with questionable lighting, it can be really disgusting."

"I can imagine. It's like, 'Hi, my name is John, and this is my dick.'"

"Exactly! That's the new way to introduce yourself. No pun intended, of course."

I burst out laughing and catch him looking at me intently.

"It must not be easy being a girl, but I promise if I send you a picture of my cock, I'll fix the lighting."

"Thank you, see, I told you: gen-tle-man!"

He puts his hand on my thigh and pushes my skirt up to the limit of indecency.

"Stop provoking me, Rocky! Otherwise, I'll stop this car and show you how wrong you are about me."

His voice, which has dropped a few octaves, and his wild eyes make me shiver. I want to take him up on it, but I tell myself that the longer I wait, the better. Besides, I'm starving.

"Okay, so where are we going to eat? I'm starving."

"At Petes!"

"Pete? The restaurant on the harbor?"

"Correct."

"You're taking me for a burger? I thought you were more adventurous than that!"

"I'm not taking you for a simple burger. I'm taking you to eat the best, oldest, and most authentic burger in all of Providence. Weren't you the one who told me you liked old things?"

"You remembered?"

"I remember everything about you. The way you blush when you come, the small hollows in your lower back, and your fascination with things that have a story."

He gives me a corner smile that hollows out one of his dimples, while remaining focused on the road. I take the opportunity to observe his profile. He is absolutely gorgeous. A well-defined jawline, almond-shaped eyes whose color is always mysterious to me, sometimes green, sometimes caramel, with golden sparkles. His emerging beard, which I know does wonders between my legs, and his dark brown hair, which he often runs his hand through, complete his Greek god physique perfectly. When he turns to me, I pretend to look at the landscape.

"Do you like what you see?"

"Yes, the ocean coast of Rhode Island is beautiful."

"Not as gorgeous as you in that dress."

His hand is still resting on my thigh, and he caresses it slowly, sending electric shocks up my spine.

"I thought you hated wearing skirts?"

"It's true, but I wanted to make an effort for you! Also, I wanted Isabella to stop bothering me. But don't get used to it too quickly, because it won't happen often. So, enjoy while it lasts."

"Oh, I appreciate it, I even appreciate it too much."

A few minutes later, we are both seated on a colorful bench, with equally colorful menus in front of our eyes. Pete's is the kind of place that seems suspended in time. The walls and decor haven't changed since the fifties: black and white tiles, a counter where regulars sit, drinking a coffee or tasting a homemade pie, comfortable benches. This is the last authentic place in the harbor. It's resisting and doesn't want to give way to one of these new chic industrial places that seem to have invaded the street.

The waitress, a friendly 50-year-old named Suzanne, recommends the double cheeseburger, their specialty. We follow her advice.

"I really like this place," I say, looking around.

"I knew you'd like it, but you've never been here before?"

"No. I just knew the name."

"Glad to introduce you to a new place, then."

The waitress comes back with our drinks: beer for Jude and Coke for me.

"Who are you playing against next weekend?"

"You don't know the schedule of the Tigers?" Jude says, looking falsely offended.

"Who do you think I am? A groupie? Sorry to disappoint you, but some of us have other things to do than keep up with the football team's schedule."

I lie. I'm absolutely aware of their every move. I have their schedule hanging on my fridge and I participate in discussions on Twitter concerning them, under a nickname of course. Some of the girls' comments about Jude make me cringe, but who am I to argue with them?

"We're playing against Briar! Return match. We'll probably spend the night in Connecticut."

"Another busy weekend?"

I try to hide my disappointment as best I can. I know I said I will have very little time for him, blah-blah-blah. But I was far from imagining that he would be the one who would have very little time for me, and above all, that it would piss me off so much. But I'd rather have my fingernails pulled out with tweezers than admit it out loud.

"Saturday night, I'm free."

"You are?"

Fucking desperate voice! How can I maintain my blasé, detached girl image when my vocal cords refuse to play their part?

"No big legendary party at your fraternity if you win?" I ask.

"Yes, there is! But I'd rather party between your thighs."

I spit out a sip of soda in a typically feminine gesture. Typical me. But damn it! He has a way of going from sweet to hot, in no time, causing me to have variations in body heat that I'm sure are dangerous to my health.

"I mean if you're available of course?"

"I'll see what I can do... Maybe you could come over to the house. Maybe we could watch a movie or something after Max goes

SONIA BIRDY — 173

to bed?"

That's the lamest plan ever. I'm well aware of that, but I can't offer him better. I have responsibilities. I hold my breath waiting for his answer.

"I'd love it!"

"Great!"

I try to force the blissful smile that appears on my face at the thought of spending my Saturday night with Jude, with fucking Jude Hartnett. Why he'd rather hang out with me doing boring stuff, than attend his team's legendary parties, is still beyond me, but I try not to think about it too much.

I decided to follow Alyson's advice: enjoy it while it lasts. He'll finish university this year, then he'll surely be chosen by a team on the other side of the country, and that will be the end. He'll fly towards his destiny as a football star. And I'll come back to my golden rule: no boyfriend. No distractions! I refuse to follow in my mother's footsteps. Jude is an exception. A delicious exception, a very gifted exception, and very easy to appreciate. An exception that fits into my schedule without disturbing it. An exception that will be leaving soon, anyway.

So, there are a few months left. Thinking like this, knowing that there is an end date to our relationship, allows me to temper my anxiety and keep my heart at bay. And let's be honest, I have years of experience with restricting feelings.

When our food arrives, I throw myself on my double cheeseburger. The first bite makes me hungry. I watch Jude mix his mayonnaise and ketchup before dipping a fry into the unsavory pinkish mixture. Then his eyes meet mine. Green with a tint of caramel, or caramel with a tint of green. Either way, his irises are fascinating. Like those works of art that never offer the same perspective each time you dive into them. A walk in the forest, a dip in the ocean. The promise of an adventure, dangerous, inevitable.

He smiles at me, fully aware that I'm staring at him like he's part of my meal, and tries to hand me a fry.

"You want some of this?"

"Ew. No thanks, I don't want your yucky sauce."

"That's not what you said last time!" he says, giving me a wink.

He then shoves the fries stained with mayochup, which was previously intended for me, into his mouth.

"You don't like ketchup?"

"I love it," I say.

"And the mayo?"

"The same," I respond.

"But both at the same time are a problem for you?"

"Go figure! I'm a woman full of contradictions."

"Indeed, based on my experience, you made me feel more like the kind of girl who doesn't say no to double stimulation," he says.

I stifle a laugh. "Two crude jokes in less than a minute. You're in good shape Jude Hartnett, and then it's me who only thinks about sex?"

"On that, Rocky, I think you beat me."

"I doubt that," I say.

He arches an eyebrow and shows me the last text I sent him. I'm blushing. Sometimes I may be a little over the top. But the thing is, I have no problem declaring my intentions when it comes to sex, but for the rest, it's a little more complicated.

"Okay! I give in."

I continue to devour the best burger in the history of burgers while moaning with pleasure.

"Mmmh, I think I want to make love and have children at this burger."

"Yeah?"

I nod my head. "Lots and lots and lots of kids."

He looks at me for a long time—his sandwich is already a distant memory—and drops a bomb on me that I wasn't expecting at all.

"Speaking of kids? How many do you want?"

What?

I choke on my huge mouthful of burger and do my best not to spit it all out on the table. I finally get the crisis under control. When I have recovered the use of speech and my lungs, I retort, "Seriously? What kind of question is that? Don't you think you're going a little fast? It's our first date, and you're already talking about kids? What's the next step? Talking about a retirement plan?"

Irony. Guilt. My two favorite strategies for shutting down the opponent. Except Jude doesn't care. He seems straightforward, comfortable with all subjects, he doesn't fall into the trap that I set for him and firmly expects an answer.

"Relax! It's just a good way to get to know each other, I didn't say I wanted to have kids with YOU."

He takes a sip of beer.

"Talking about climate change, favorite color or interests, that's a normal conversation to get to know each other. Talk about starting a family, not really. Even I, who have the social skills of a Post-it, know that."

"You don't have to answer if you're scared," he says.

"I'm not scared of anything, I do jujitsu."

He starts laughing. "You're the biggest coward I know."

"I'm not a coward at all." I cross my arms in front of my chest, well aware that I'm acting like a 5-year-old kid in a playground.

"Prove it!" he says, challenging me with his eyes.

I roll my eyes. "You know that's the kind of psychological manipulation I use with my little brother to force him to finish his dinner?"

"Does it work?"

"No, because in my family, we're stubborn."

He just smiles. He pulls off that smile. The one that gives it this nonchalant air and which, I am convinced, contributes to accelerating the melting of the ice of the North Pole. He says nothing and finishes his fries, letting the silence make me feel guilty.

"Okay! Okay! Mr. Big Questions! I'm going to pretend this conversation isn't weird at all and answer anyway. Let's just say I never really thought about it. I'm only nineteen, so it's not in my priorities."

"Of course, it's not in my priorities either, Rocky Prescott. In five years? In ten years?"

I think for a long time while drinking my glass of water. "I'm not sure I want some, no."

My answer makes him frown. "Why?"

"Let's just say I didn't have the best of mothers, and I'm too afraid of being as bad as her and screwing up the life of my future child. Who knows, maybe being a shitty parent is in the genes? And in my case, both my parents are irresponsible. The chance that I lost in the genetics lottery is way too high. So, I can't take that risk."

His forehead wrinkles under the appalled expression he's wearing.

"You should stop defining yourself by her or by them. You're your own person, Rocky. I'm sure you would make an excellent mother. You're gentle, kind, full of empathy and consideration for others. Besides, you're already taking wonderful care of Max. I know you'll freak out again if I tell you this, but I'd love for you to carry my kids someday."

He laughs. At this point, it has become a game between us. He provokes me by playing the guy who moves too fast, and I piss him off by playing the chick who slows down.

"Okay, psychopath! Pack up your gametes. We've known each other for two minutes. And as far as I'm concerned, you're just my new favorite hobby. Nothing more. So don't get carried away."

"In two weeks, you'll be madly in love with me."

"Not a chance, I don't have a heart."

He laughs shaking his head. "We'll see about that."

"Dream on, Hartnett! Dream on. So, what about you? I would be curious to know—"

"I want four."

I widen my eyes. "Four?"

"Yes, four! I always wanted to have a big family. Growing up, it was just my mother and me, and I often dreamed of big noisy gatherings around the table where we remake the world passing dishes."

Me too. Except that I also dreamed of having a stable roof over my head.

"It's a beautiful image. But damn, four? Four children of a footballer who is six feet tall. Have you thought about your future wife's uterus?"

"Six feet three inches! And at the same time, if she's able to take me, she'll be able to carry four kids."

He bursts out laughing. Smile, dimples, charming eyes, he would be able to sell hell to a saint.

"Besides, I'll be able to make up for all the inconvenience caused."

A sexy gleam in his eyes, he wets his lips.

"Honestly, no amount of sex could convince me to carry four kids."

"See, you're already projecting."

Just as he utters this improbable sentence, Suzanne reappears to ask us if we need anything else. His amused look is hard to ignore. We order dessert, trying not to giggle, but burst out as soon as her back is turned.

We finish our dinner talking about college, our plans, and our respective pasts.

I spoke to him for a long time about the renovation project of the Huntington Street building proposed by Mr. Gravel.

"Ten thousand dollars is a damn good price."

"Yes, and it would help me buy a new car. I really need one," I say.

"Does your car still give you trouble?"

"Yes."

"I can lend you my car if you want, I don't use it much. I'd rather ride my motorcycle," he says.

"No, thanks."

"Why are you so stubborn, Rocky Prescott? Take the help I'm offering."

"Why are you so insistent, Jude Hartnett? I can take care of myself," I say in the same tone.

The waitress brings the bill, Jude grabs it before I can even react. I'm a little embarrassed, because I don't like feeling indebted, but he flatly refuses to split the bill with me, which leads us to a heated discussion about gender equality. I still managed to pay the tip, much to his dismay.

"Don't you ever give up?" Jude sighs.

"Never."

He shakes his head, amused, before moving on to the thousand and one things we want to say to each other tonight. The topics of conversation never seem to dry up. It's so easy to be with him, so natural.

And when the evening comes to an end, we have remade the world, laughed, and shared memories so much that I didn't see the time passing, and unfortunately, it's already eleven o'clock, my curfew.

We are now parked in front of my house, and I have no desire to leave him.

"I had a great time with you, Jude."

"Me too, Rocky."

He says this as he takes my face in his hands and kisses me slowly, tenderly. His lips taste like the strawberry milkshake we just shared. By sharing, I mean that we fought to make sure everyone could eat as much as possible. Obviously, we could have ordered two, but that would have been much less fun. No, instead, we placed ridiculous bets on who was going to eat the one and only strawberry on top of the whipped cream, proving that Jude Hartnett isn't just competitive on the field. I ended up getting the last word and the strawberry, and I feel like he is claiming his due by devouring my mouth.

What was meant to be a chaste kiss to say goodbye becomes hot and intense in less time than it takes to say it. Jude digs his hands into my hair to pull me to him, I pivot and get on my knees. In my haste, I bang my head on the ceiling of his car. We half laugh as we continue to kiss. He puts his hand behind my thighs and helps me sit on top of him. Within seconds, I find myself wedged between the steering wheel and his hard, firm body, my skirt pulled up over my thighs and my hips seeking contact. The heat he gives off is incredible. His scent invades all my senses. And my heart starts beating so hard that I feel like he can hear it. His nose buries itself in my cleavage, he places open kisses all over my skin which is covered with goose bumps. He moves his lips from the birth of my chest to my collarbone and along my jawline.

"Rocky… what am I going to do with you?" he says.

"Unfortunately, nothing, I have to free Alyson and Isabella."

"I have to let you go, then?" He says without conviction while continuing to kiss me on the neck.

"Yeah."

His eyes rise and he looks at me for a long time, intensely, with an almost serious air.

"What's the matter?"

"I'll give you two weeks."

"For what?"

"To fall in love with me."

His arrogant smile dazzles and exasperates me at the same time.

"In your dreams, Hartnett," I say, straightening up and pushing my skirt back into place.

I comb my hair with my fingers. No need to fuel the girls' imagination. I already know that they will throw me with questions as soon as I get home.

"Goodbye, Balboa."

"Bye, Jude."

"Don't think too much of me tonight."

"What's your first name again?"

He laughs as I close the door, but doesn't leave right away, and I feel his eyes on me, like lasers, as I walk away. I try to walk straight. To be dignified. As dignified as one can be with tangled hair and soaked panties. When I still don't hear him leave, I turn around and ask him to go. He does, but not before giving me the peace sign with his fingers through the window. I shake my head in amusement, then give him the most blasé look I can muster.

But at the rate my heart is beating, I'm afraid he's the one who's right.

22

Rocky

I spend the rest of the weekend working on my project. Max and I do our homework together. He loves that. For some reason, the thought of me having homework like him makes him laugh out loud. He must imagine me in a classroom like his with markers and puzzles. He talks at breakneck speed, as usual, and goes from topic to topic. And his new obsession is Halloween. We have already chosen his costume: he will be a T-Rex, of course. And to please him, I'll be one too.

Unlike the rest of the girls my age, I won't be a sexy nurse, or a sexy referee, or a sexy pumpkin. But if it makes Max laugh and feel like he belongs to a real family, I couldn't be happier to look like a Michelin Man.

Lately, Max hasn't talked about Mom at all. I don't know if I should be happy or worried. I know he is thinking about her because he keeps putting her in his drawings. But that's it. I feel guilty. I know I have to have this horrible conversation with him at some point. The horrible conversation where I tell him he's an orphan. And break his heart. The thought of stealing a piece of his innocence drives me crazy. I'd rather have my arm cut off than destroy his sincere, beaming smile. I hate having to do this. There will be a before and an after this moment in his life, I know that. He will never be so happy, so enthusiastic, so optimistic again.

Clearing these horrible thoughts from my brain, I cook dinner. Being busy allows me to forget. We share our dinner by discussing everything and nothing, then comes bath time, and finally bedtime.

Today, it's him who reads me a story. He is growing up. He reads better and better, and it reassures me. At his age, I was not even able to name the letters of the alphabet. My education suffered because of my mother's irresponsibility. I was uneducated, tossed from place to place, sleeping in the car, or seedy motels, or the trailer of a new boyfriend. Instability is the enemy of learning. At least I can be proud of myself. Max may not have everything he needs, but I make sure he has at least that: stability and love. Lots of love!

Besides, my nose is buried in his neck while he takes pleasure in doing the voices of the different characters, it makes me laugh. I tuck him in, kiss him, then leave him to go to my own room and move forward with my project. The ten thousand dollars is mine. I'm gonna make sure I win this fucking contest. I need it. For my car, for my bills, to give Max a great Christmas. Maybe I can take him on vacation for a few days. After hours of hard work, I get tired and fall asleep on my book.

***

It's cold! I'm hungry.

"Mom, where are you?"

I'm shaking all over. I try to fall asleep, but hunger pangs keep me from dozing off. I look again in the glove box. Maybe there's something left of our last stop at a gas station. Chips, candies, anything, as long as I have something to eat. I search for a long time, looking in the trunk to see if there's anything left either.

All our belongings are stored there. Blankets, clothes. Some memories of our thousand and one lives. I sigh, then look out the window, which is covered with frost. We're parked in front of an old house where Mom disappeared a few hours ago. Rock music emanates from the place, and loud adults come and go regularly. Every time the door opens, I hope to see Mom's frail, tired figure.

Maybe she will come back with some money, as she sometimes does. Maybe we can go sleep somewhere warm. In those places where there is a breakfast. I salivate imagining bacon and eggs… The door opens. A new hope is born in my chest and immediately dies when I see two bodies appear, screaming and not walking very straight. They are arguing. The guy pushes the woman whose body bangs against the car, making me jump.

I'm scared! But I'm not crying. I never cry. Mom doesn't like it when I cry.

I want to get out, to get into this house, to beg mom to come home, to take me somewhere where I'll be safe. But the last time I had the nerve to follow her and interrupt her adult activities, she was very angry. I don't want her to be angry. I want her to love me. That's why I don't cry because I know she doesn't like me crying. However, she often cries, in general, because of men.

Mom is sweet and kind most of the time. She tries to make me laugh. She's just not good at feeding or protecting me. And then, when she's in love, she wants me to make myself very small. Adults don't like children. Well, the adults she hangs out with, anyway. That's not a problem. I'm great at disappearing and taking up as little space as possible. But now, I'm really hungry and I'm starting to worry about her. What if something had happened to her? I gather my courage, remove the three blankets I have on me, grab my coat and get out of the car. The cold has made all my limbs numb. I feel like a rusty robot. I walk up to the porch. The music gets louder as I approach. There are bursts of voices and laughter. Nobody notices me when I push the door open. The room is dark and smoky, there are empty beer bottles, and I don't know what else on the floor.

I look for Mom in the middle of all these bodies dancing, talking, or doing even weirder things in the corners. My small size allows me to sneak around easily. A smell of pizza comes from the kitchen, I can't help but follow it. There are people here too. My eyes fall on the slice of pizza that a red-haired lady is shoving into her mouth. I swallow. Our eyes lock. She shows me the slice of pizza and silently asks me if I want some. I nod, and she steps down from the dirty counter where she was sitting to bring it to me. I make it disappear in a few bites. She offers me another one, I accept. The second slice suffers the same fate as the previous one.

"What's your name?"

Her voice is hoarse, and she coughs in the middle of her sentence.

"Rocky."

"What are you doing here? This is no place for a little girl. My God, this is not even a place for a stray dog!"

She laughs and takes a drag on her cigarette. I shrug.

"I'm looking for my mom."

"What's her name?"

"Rebecca Prescott."

"Oh, the little blonde who just moved to town?"

I don't answer anything.

"Come on, I'll help you find her."

I follow her, and she takes me to the living room where she asks questions to people who all answer with the same blasé look. Their eyes are too bright and sometimes move strangely. Like mom's when she takes those funny pills and doesn't sleep for days. A bearded, tattooed, and dirty guy shows her the floor. I go up with her, and we find Mom lying on her stomach, half-naked and unconscious.

I throw myself on her and scream, "Mom, Mom, wake up! Mom, please wake up!"

She's not moving, I'm scared she's dead. I keep screaming, shaking her. She doesn't move, doesn't answer.

"MOM!"

"Rocky, wake up!"

I open my eyes and find myself face to face with my little brother. He has climbed into my bed and is holding his blanket to his chest. He looks scared, and I feel bad for waking him up.

"Why are you screaming like that? I don't understand anything you're saying, either. You're scaring me."

Shit!

I grab him in my arms and hug him desperately. His curls tickle my nose and his smell of kid's soap mends my broken soul.

"Sorry, my little man. I didn't mean to wake you up. I had a nightmare."

"You know that monsters don't exist. You told me that yourself."

I smile and wipe the tears from my face.

"You're right, little man."

"Do you want me to sleep with you?"

"Yes, come here."

He lays down next to me, and I hug him so tightly I'm afraid I'll break him. He gives me an Eskimo kiss before putting his blanket to his nose and falling asleep. I look at him for a long time, caressing his hair and his little red cheek. He is innocence itself, an angel, and doesn't deserve this shitty life without parents that fate has imposed on him. I think back to what he said to me and fall asleep with the idea that, unfortunately, monsters exist, and that a strange intuition tells me that they are about to come out of the closet.

23

Rocky

This week, I'm depressed. Still a little shaken by the nightmare I had on Sunday. So, when our work group gets together, and Emma shows me how well she's done with her project and how much Mr. Gravel has loved her ideas, I suppress the urge to scream in frustration.

I'm happy for her, but it reminds me that I was unable to focus and make a sketch. All my problems of anxiety and frustration hover over me like vultures around a carcass in the desert. This is the gloomy state I'm in as I walk down the hallway of building B on my way to the cafeteria to take my shift.

I walk hastily, turn right and see Jude, leaning against a wall, talking with four or five girls, all looking at him with doe eyes and eating up his words as if he were the eighth wonder of the world.

Immediately, a surge of jealousy attacks my stomach.

Breathe, Rocky!

I hate the effect he has on me. I watch him being the playboy, flashing his dimpled smile, and feel my blood boil in my veins. That's probably why he didn't answer my text. He was too busy using his charms to seduce his next victims.

I knew something was wrong. Usually, he is rather reactive, I barely have time to finish writing to him that I see the famous three dots dancing. Except when he's playing football. But I know his training schedule, and it's been two hours since he finished. Plenty of time to answer me. A whirlwind of questions swirls through my head: What the hell is he doing here? He doesn't have any classes in this building, it is reserved for architecture and industrial design students. Why is he not replying to my text? Why is he flirting with all those chicks right in front of me? While he claims loud and clear to want to be with me?

Maybe he's had enough? And that the first signs of weariness are showing? He got what he wanted, and now he's moving on. A tragically banal story. It pisses me off because I didn't ask him anything. Or rather, I specifically asked him to leave me alone. I should have listened to myself and not engaged in something that was going to make me so vulnerable. With a heavy heart, I decide to turn around and go through the back door. No desire to see him. I don't want him to see me. In this state, I don't trust my reactions or what I might say.

"Rocky!"

Shit!

I quicken my pace, pretending I didn't hear Jude's voice calling me. I place my headphones over my ears in case he needs further justification for my escape. I turn up the volume to Train's, "Drops of Jupiter" and continue on my way. A hand lands on my shoulder and spins me around before I reach the exit. I look up to meet Jude's puzzled gaze. He says something to me, but I don't hear him. He pulls the headphones out of my ears, somewhat exasperated.

"Rocky, are you avoiding me or something?"

"Not at all. I was just going to the cafeteria to start my shift. It's not all about you, as crazy as that sounds."

He runs a hand through his hair, a little confused. "Can I go with you?"

"No."

At his reaction, I feel like my answer just slapped him in the face. With my arms crossed over my chest, I must look as comely to him as a prison door.

"Why?"

"Because I'm sure you have better things to do, like talking to those girls."

I'm not proud of what I just said to him, which is exactly why I'm looking at my shoes instead of his perfect face. This perfection that I want to hate today. This perfection for which I should never have succumbed and which I will never live up to.

"What are you talking about, Rocky? I came here to see you."

"Well, you saw me, now you can go back where you came from. Playing pretty boy with whoever wants to pay attention to you."

I don't know why I'm acting like a 6-year-old kid. I don't know what I'm looking for. Maybe push him back? Maybe to provoke him? Maybe I want him to hold me back? All I know is that I hate I can't control my feelings since I first laid eyes on him. It's official, I have become my mother. My worst nightmare. And I have to end this roller coaster before it's too late.

"Can I know what's wrong with you?"

"What's wrong is that I'm tired of you."

"Will you tell me why?"

"No! That would take too long to explain and not at all interesting. What you have to remember, however, is what's going on between us…"

I wave my hands frantically between the two of us to punctuate what I'm saying, in case he didn't understand.

"It's time for this to stop. It was fun while it lasted, but I got tired of it and prefer to end it before it gets really boring. Besides, it will allow you to focus on football and your—bitch fans."

His eyebrows suddenly furrow, and his face turns dark, his jaw clenches so hard that I can see the muscles moving. He doesn't answer, grabs my elbow, and pulls me behind him. When I give more resistance, he stops, leans forward, and throws me over his shoulders as if I were a bulky bag of flour.

"Hey, what are you doing? Put me down right now!"

My bag falls to the floor, he kneels down to pick it up and tucks it under his arm, then effortlessly continues on his way, ignoring my protests. The few people in the hallways all look amused. Some people even greet him, as if the fact that he has a hysterical girl screaming on his shoulder is absolutely normal.

"Let me go, you freak!"

Silence.

"Do you know what that's called?" I shout.

"An intervention?"

"No, asshole! Kidnapping!"

"Really?"

I see his smirk in his reply, and it pisses me off.

"Really! Let me down right now if you don't want me to crush your balls, asshole."

He stifles a laugh. "It's getting better and better, Balboa! Better and better."

I wiggle for him to let go, but his grip is firm. The idea of biting his butt crosses my mind for a moment, but before doing that, I continue to negotiate.

"Are you an idiot? I know you're not a genius, but there's a difference between a woman and a football, fucking wide receiver!"

He continues to advance, unfazed, and I keep insulting him, tireless.

"Oh, that big mouth. The fact that you're able to talk so much upside down with no trouble breathing gives me so many sex ideas, babe."

"Don't call me *babe*, and you're making your case worse! I'll add sexual harassment to kidnapping. It's going to cost you, Hartnett!"

He laughs at my comment. "It's totally worth it."

"Help! Somebody call security!"

Nobody reacts. If I needed one more proof that the university is at his feet, well, here it is!

I smack him on the butt and wiggle to get him to let go. He tightens his grip and slaps me on the ass in return. I yelp in pain and squeeze my thighs, because this pain makes me feel strangely good and turns me on a little.

What's wrong with me?!

He opens a door and finally drops me on the floor before all my blood has migrated to my brain. It takes me a few seconds to realize we're in a broom closet. I punch his chest with all the rage I've built up.

"What the fuck is your problem, Jude?"

"You're my fucking problem, Rocky! What's wrong with you? Why are you giving me this bullshit? I thought we were past the game of cat and mouse!"

"Because I… I… because I hate you!" I push him again. "You drive me crazy! Why don't you answer my texts and why do you flirt with everything that moves?"

He looks at his phone and seems to discover my texts. He

answers them, playing his fingers on his keyboard, the light from the screen illuminating his still closed face. Mine lights up when a small ringtone sounds.

"Done, I answered you."

"Fuck you, Jude!"

"I'd love to, but the person I want to fuck with spends her time blowing hot and cold."

"That's not what I do."

I pull at my hair, confused, and completely lost. My reaction is disproportionate, I know that, but his is not good either. Throw myself on his shoulders like a caveman. I think on the crazy scale, we both break the record.

"That's exactly what you're doing, Rocky! One day you're hot and begging me to fuck you everywhere and in every position. The next day, you pass me in a hallway and completely ignore me. I'm having a hard time keeping up with you. I gave you the space you told me you needed. And now you're making a scene for me not answering your texts fast enough," he spits, clearly irritated this time.

I run my hand over my face. I hate him! I hate that he's right. I hate that he's so insightful and that my feelings for him grow so fast. That he is the first person I think of in the morning and the last person I think of at night. I hate that his absence is the worst of presences. And that the hours spent without him seem like an eternity. I'm completely losing my mind. He gave me two weeks, but it took me much less than that to fall in love with him, and I know it's going to be a rough landing.

All my anxieties take me by the throat. I'm not good enough. I can't do it. He's going to leave me like everyone else who was supposed to love me. And I'll be just a shadow of myself, a zombie unable to care for anything but my broken heart, unable to care for Max, and I can't... I don't want to... become my mother.

"Look, Jude, I think the two of us was a really bad idea."

He growls in frustration and presses his lips to mine with such force that I topple back. He holds me back with his big hands, thrusting his tongue into my mouth, choking off the rain of insults I had in store and turning them into moans of pleasure and abandonment. We back up until my back hits what appears to be a locker.

"I won't let you dump me again, Rocky! We have already passed that point! I won't go back," he threatens between two devastating kisses that make me whole and remind me who the boss is.

"I hate you," I say, panting against his lips.

"You don't hate me. You want me as much as I want you."

I bite his lip for an answer. He flexes, turns me over with a sharp movement, places a possessive hand between my legs, his erection rubs against my back. He passes his hand under my sweater and forcefully slips his hand under my bra. He pinches one of my nipples. I moan in pain. He yanks my hair and kisses my neck, biting my skin in the process. I'm sure I'm going to get bruises on my neck, but strangely, this troubling feeling clarifies the confusion in my brain. I hate him, but I want him. I hate him, but I need him. I hate him, but he's the only one who can fill the void I feel in my chest. We rub against each other. His hard and firm body seems to want to soak into mine. I don't know if I want to do him good or bad things, but I want to feel him inside me.

His tongue wanders all over my neck, my earlobe, and my lips, lighting a fire with each touch.

"Rocky, I'm about to fuck you until your brain is incapable of thinking. Till your mouth can't say all that shit anymore. You are mine, Rocky! Mine!"

"Jude!"

"Say it!"

"I'm yours."

"You want this as much as I do. It's not over between us. It's just started!"

He squeezes my chest even tighter, his voice husky and warm in my ear.

"It's… not over between us, say it!"

"It's not over, Jude."

"If you don't want me to fuck you right now, it's now or never to say it!"

"I do! Fuck me, Jude!"

With an animal grunt, he lifts my sweater and pulls it over my head. My bra quickly joins it. I think he's ripped it off, judging by the tingles I feel on my arms. He grabs my breasts and kneads them hard, I gasp harder, my heart and everything else on the verge of exploding. His fingers go around my waist and unbutton my jeans. He lowers them violently with a sudden gesture, taking my panties with him, and slips one of his fingers into my slit to collect the fruit of my excitement.

"You're wet, Rocky! Wanna see how wet you are?"

I nod frantically, with the odd feeling that if he asked me to damn myself, I would respond with the same devotion.

He grabs one of my hands and places it above my entrance, then draws circles over my swollen clitoris, forcing me to caress myself. It's raw, it's dirty, but it's so erotic it makes my head spin. We hear people walking past the door. For a moment, I wonder if he took the time to lock it before ripping off my clothes. But my thoughts are immediately drowned in the divine sensation of our intertwined fingers over my most sensitive area. I don't know who does what anymore, where his fingers end and mine begin, but this confusion is delicious.

He forces me to arch my back.

"Oh, you have a fucking ass, Rocky. You drive me crazy. One day I'll take you there, too. This ass, like the rest, is mine."

He kneels behind me, and a second later I feel his tongue enter my slit. He sucks, licks, nibbles, spreads my butt for better access. I hesitate, because no one has ever done it to me from this angle, but it's so good, so raw that I give in to this incredible sensation, forgetting my vulnerability, forgetting that I'm naked and that he's fully dressed. He ventures his tongue where no one has ever been before him, where I never imagined letting anyone go, but it seems that Jude Hartnett is able to make all my certainties, physical or emotional, go away. He tastes me inside like I'm a juicy passion fruit. I lean on the locker in front of me when the pressure gets too intense.

"No, keep caressing you, babe."

Doing my best to stay balanced, I place a hand over my clitoris and self-stimulate until the sensation becomes too overwhelming, incredible, explosive.

My legs are shaking, and a violent, rapid orgasm makes me scream his name at the top of my lungs. Jude straightens up and pulls me to his chest, still wearing his sweatshirt. I wonder how he doesn't die of the heat. I'm about to turn into a human torch and the only way to bring my temperature down is to moan like crazy. He places a hand over my mouth to stifle my screams, as the last jolts continue to go through me. I smell my scent all over his lips, on his fingers, on mine.

"Shush, babe! You don't want the whole building B to hear how hard you're being fucked."

I let my head roll over his shoulder, drunk on his dirty words and his brutal caresses. I hear him undo his belt, then I feel his cock against my ass. The sensation of his velvet skin against my butt feels outrageously forbidden. He searches his pocket for a condom and unrolls it over his cock.

"Ready?"

I nod, biting my lip. And he enters inside me in one thrust, growling obscenities that I have trouble understanding. He pulls out almost completely and thrusts in again brutally, my chest pressing against the cold locker. My nipples are so hard that they are likely to leave a mark. His imperial cock lights my walls on fire, pulling me apart, making my synapses burn.

"You feel that Rocky? Do you feel how good it is between us?"

"Yes."

"That's why it's not over."

He pulls out again and thrusts to the hilt, this time snatching a guttural cry from me. He rotates his pelvis and I think I see stars. He stays there, against me, torturing me. I shake my ass to get him moving, to relieve the burning passion that has built up in my belly. Short of breath, heart burning, I look at him sideways.

"What are you doing?"

"I'm waiting for you to beg me to fuck you, Rocky," he growls. "I'm waiting for you to admit that you want that. That I'm not the only one dying of desire for you."

He keeps my hips against him.

"I want it too," I whisper.

A thrust.

"I didn't hear you."

"I want it too!"

Another thrust!

"No more bullshit! No more going back."

A thrust.

I nod.

"You're mine. Say it!"

"I'm yours!"

He growls, then speeds up his back and forth, one hand wrapped in my hair to hold me as he wishes and the other pressing on my hips.

And just like that, he's thrusting into me at a frantic pace, making me promise not to back down again. I tell him everything he wants to hear. I am ready to promise him everything. He takes me with fury, with determination. I feel in each of his thrusts, a threat, an affirmation, a promise of eternity. I rock forward and hold on to the locker in front of me, then cum without restraint, panting and sweating. Jude continues to thrust for a few more minutes, then his breathing becomes erratic, his movements rough and confused. He penetrates me once, twice, three times before exploding inside me and hugging me very tightly against him. His sweaty forehead on my shoulder.

"It is not over."

"It's not over…" I repeat before turning my face to him.

His eyes are as serious as ever. Eyelids heavy, he kisses me, while he is still deep inside me. He ends up withdrawing, tearing from me a grimace in the process. He ties a knot in the condom that he places at the bottom of the pocket of his football jacket. *A gesture he must have made a thousand times*, can't help noticing my asshole brain. I choose to ignore it and pick up my clothes to get dressed.

"Sorry, I don't think you'll be able to use it anymore."

Jude holds my bra which is now a shred at his fingertips, a smile on his face.

"No big deal. Usually, I don't wear one. So…" I shrug my shoulders. And as if I had just said the most erotic thing to him, Jude straightens up, takes a step towards me, wraps me in his arms, lifts my chin, and kisses me slowly, tenderly.

"Do you know what I'm going to think about all day?"

"No?"

"To you, without a bra. Your breasts stimulated and irritated by the folds of your wool sweater."

He caresses me over my sweater, reigniting a desire that I thought was completely tamed.

"And I'm going to be very jealous, because only I have the right to stimulate you like this. And it's going to be very difficult for me to concentrate on anything other than sucking your breasts, until they are able to cut glass. And tonight, when Max is in bed, I'm going to come see you. I'm gonna climb out your bedroom window while you sleep and make you pay for all the mental images you've been putting in my brain all day. You see, I'm jealous too, Rocky, jealous of the guys who cross your path, who work with you on your architecture project, jealous of those who fight for you to serve them in the cafeteria and jealous of this fucking wool sweater. But when it happens to me, I go to you."

He moistens his lips. Lips that I have been staring at for a while.

"I'm not rejecting you. So, the next time you feel doubts, frustrations, or jealousy, you come to me, and I'll fuck you."

He squints his eyelids.

"I will fuck all the fears out of your system. I will kiss all your anxieties away. I'll fuck up anything that's stopping you from opening up to me and admitting that you like me, that we both have something special that we haven't finished exploring."

He raises an eyebrow, as if to say "Understood?" I nod my head, half-excited, half-confused by the most disturbing and compelling speech I've ever heard.

I have plenty of sharp, ironic remarks to make about him, and the old Rocky would have a field day with them. But I don't, because yes, I have to admit, he is magic. Before he took me to this broom closet, I was ready to stop everything and rebuild my fortresses. And now I am ready to take the risk of being with him again. Maybe I'm bipolar? Or maybe he's really good? Really convincing, really irresistible. It's the only thing that allows me to explain what comes out of my mouth afterwards.

"Are you really going to come tonight? No, because if you are, you can go through the door. We're not high school kids anymore."

He shakes his head, amused. "Is that all you remembered from what I just said?"

"Yeah."

He laughs, leans his forehead against mine. "You drive me crazy, Rocky Prescott."

"I know, I'm sorry and… thank you," I say shyly.

"Thank you for what? For the orgasm?"

"No… For being there, to bear my craziness and, above all, or not running away, because I can be unbearable sometimes."

I look down at my feet and fidget my hands so as not to face his gaze. He grabs my fingers and brings them to his lips.

"I told you, Balboa! I'm here to stay."

Then he kisses me slowly, tenderly, just enough to make my head spin.

And that night, he kept his promise. As he did every night after that.

24

Rocky

"Damn it, Rocky! What the hell was that?"

"I promise you that if you don't tell us everything, we'll strangle you."

"Shh!"

A little redhead with glasses sitting directly across from our table looks up from her laptop and glares at us.

We are at the library in building B. I had two hours to work on my project and I took refuge with the intention of moving forward this time. Thanksgiving is fast approaching, I have to get moving to complete my paper, but that was without counting on Isabella and Alyson who rushed in like two furies, a few minutes after my arrival, to throws questions at me. I still don't understand what they are so excited about, because they are both talking at the same time, waving their arms, while I am trying to decipher the important information in the middle of the screams and laughter. I feel like I'm in front of Max when he's too excited to talk and gets confused.

"Calm down, girls! I don't understand anything," I say.

"Oh, is she doing it on purpose?!" Isabella asks.

"The best thing is that you show her, Isa! The proof by the image, there is nothing better," says Alyson dramatically.

I observe them, impatient, my gaze goes back and forth between them like a ping-pong ball. Isabella pulls out her cell phone to put it in front of me.

"Jude Hartnett plays fireman with a mysterious brunette! Is that you, Rocky? Head upside down, on Jude's shoulder, right? "Al asks. "No, because if it's not you, we have a six-foot-tall football player to castrate. But if it's you, you have some explanations to give us, because I've been making a lot of scenarios since I saw this photo, and all of them are prohibited for those under 18."

My eyes lock on the picture she finally stops wiggling and—oh, my God!—I think I forget to breathe.

"Damn it! It can't be true!"

I put my hand over my mouth because I just screamed.

"Shh!" says the redhead again, this time even louder.

"Shush yourself!" Alyson retorts.

"We're in a library here! Not in a coffee place. Go argue somewhere else, groupies."

"Is it to me she's talking like that?" Alyson gets carried away.

Knowing she's New Yorker and hot-blooded, I intervene before my study session turns into a wrestling match and be permanently banned from the library.

"Sorry, we'll keep it down, I promise."

I give her the most angelic smile I have in stock, wait for her to calm down and refocus on her computer to shout-whisper to my friends, "Where did you see that?"

"It's all over Instagram and Twitter! You hadn't seen it?"

"No."

I soak up every detail of the photo and feel my face heat up. I am ashamed to be in this position, posted on social media. Not to mention that the photo is far from being to my advantage. I quickly go through the comments. Some are nice, some are mocking, and what is mainly mocked is the size of my ass.

Seriously, I'm a size small! And I often skip meals, not out of coquetry, but out of necessity. So, what the hell is their problem? You have to be a size zero to meet their stupid standard! And why does that piss me off so much?

I'm not the type to diet or worry about what people think of me. I'm pretty comfortable in my own skin, but it's hard to remain unmoved in the face of this avalanche of public insults. Every comment I read makes me sick.

"Jude is in love?" "Frankly, he could do better!" "There's really nothing special about this girl." "Is that cellulite I see? Yuck! Jude, you disappoint me!" "A diet is essential!" "In ten years from now this ass will be as big as the state of Massachusetts."

I feel a kind hand land on my shoulder.

"Nobody can look glamorous from this angle, Rocky!" Isabella reassures me, when she sees that my eyebrows are furrowed in the face of the cruelty of people. "And don't worry, I experienced the same hatred when I was dating Alec. You're the new girl to beat. They'll get over it."

"Yeah," I say, shrugging my shoulders, feigning indifference, although my ego is stung. "Well, that explain why everyone greets me in the hallways and why no one bothers me with an extra potion in the cafeteria."

"So, Rocky, are you going to tell us? I'm dying to know how you ended up perched on his shoulder in broad daylight in the middle of Building B."

The redhead in front of us huffs, then slams her computer before putting away her things with much more energy than necessary, to show us her displeasure. I feel bad to have disturbed her, but this is not at all the case of Alyson who rolls her eyes, gives her a cheerful smile, before telling her ironically to have a good day. She gives her the middle finger, and I have to stop Al from jumping on her.

"No, but you saw this?"

"Admit that we deserve it a little," Isabella reasons.

"Honestly, we barely spoke loudly! What a brat! Good riddance!" says Alyson.

The three of us watch her go away, and when she is far enough away, my two friends turn to me, "Okay, back to Jude!"

I smile, because just hearing his name puts me in a state, and I tell them the whole story, as well as the episode of the broom closet, keeping the raw details for me, like his tongue in my—

"It's even better than I thought it would be," Isabella concludes, her eyes dreamy.

"Yeah, it's hot, but stop me if I'm wrong, basically, this pretentious Jude offers you to solve your fear of commitment, with... what? His dick? That's his plan?" asks Alyson.

Isabella and I giggle because we hadn't thought of it that way.

"Yep, that's exactly that," I say, laughing.

"Honestly, isn't he going a bit far?! I don't mind him being gifted, but this is bordering on megalomania."

"Honestly, he's not just good. He's ma-gic! And I don't say that lightly."

My two best friends are howling like wolves, attracting the attention of the whole library, and I almost get kicked out this time.

After Alyson and Isabella's departure, I try somehow to focus on my project. But all the comments I read earlier keep spinning in my head, making my self-confidence melt away like snow in the sun. Maybe I should go on a diet after all? But what am I saying? I mentally slap myself and force myself to think about something else. Like the thousands of sketches, I have to draw for the Huntington Street renovation project, for example. But nothing helps, not the Michelle Obama-like motivational speeches I like to repeat to myself nor the threats to smash my skull against this table if my brain refuses to comply. My thoughts migrate again and irretrievably to their favorite subject: Jude.

I wonder if he knows about this? if he saw this picture? Probably not. He would have told me about it during his many nocturnal visits over the past three weeks, or even on Halloween, when he surprised me by coming in dressed as a dinosaur. I had vaguely told him about our plans with Max and I hadn't even dared to invite him for fear that he would refuse. The Kappa Omega has a legendary party every year for Halloween, and my candy hunt and horror movie plan were no match for the party. He showed up with his arms full of candy for Max, then walked the streets with us to collect even more, a big smile on his face, like it was the coolest thing in the world.

Why is this photo popping up now? When the thing happened a long time ago. I wonder if I can report it. Anyway, I hope he didn't see it because it's super humiliating. I already know that I'm no match for him, that I'm average girl, rather pretty, but average, not at Jude's "Stadium God" level. But seeing it written in black and white kills me. I groan in frustration and lay my forehead on the wood of the table.

When it seems obvious to me that I won't achieve anything with my project, I decide to do something useful: go get some books to borrow for tonight, in case I miraculously find inspiration after this long exhausting day. A girl has the right to dream. So, I head to the contemporary architecture section and run my fingers over the various books. I take the one by Robert Mallet, go through it briefly, put it back. I continue my quest. Strangely enough, my focus has returned. The smell of books and the calm of the place, there is nobody here but me and it has the effect of calming my turmoil. So, I am completely immersed in a book when I feel two big arms hugging me, a familiar smell capable of melting my panties on its own, and a warmth enveloping me from the outside, but especially from the inside. My brain is fuzzy for a moment and I have tell to myself that I will definitely not be able to study anything today.

25

Jude

"Babe… I missed you!"

I press myself against Rocky's ass and hug her from behind. She smells so fucking good, and she's so soft. Her typical smell is a mixture of perfume, shower gel, and Rocky. Her thick, shoulder-length hair tickles my nostrils when I dip my nose into it. I press her against the shelf of books she was browsing, and she lets herself do it, then places a hand around the back of my neck, arching her back more, before turning her pretty face to mine.

"Me too," she breathes.

My heart races and I smile like a kid in front of his Christmas present. I know I look like a puppy dog, it's not my habit to skip an hour of class to go see my girl. But since Rocky, my habits have changed. Adam sent me a WhatsApp text to let me know he spotted the unicorn at the library. My friends keep calling her that, and I didn't hesitate for a second to skip biology class to see her. I fucking missed her. And the word is fucking weak.

It's crazy! I saw her last night. However, we watched an old classic movie in her room: *Breakfast at Tiffany's*. Crap that she loves and that I managed to find by using my connections at the university. We can't deny to the Tigers' wide receiver anything, not even a VHS player which is no longer sold since *Stranger Things* era. It took me some time and energy, and more importantly, cost me a few remarks from Scott who thinks I've lost my balls since I've been with Rocky. But honestly, seeing my girl's eyes light up in front of my find is worth all the fuss in the world. So, he can go fuck himself with his bullshit mockery.

Besides, what this asshole doesn't understand is that my balls have never felt better. Rocky takes the greatest care of them and doesn't shy away from any sexual prowess to satisfy them. Just this morning, she thanked them with the kind of sucking that only she can do. I say it and I repeat it: this girl is fire! I run my tongue over her neck, her earlobe, and whisper how beautiful she is, before turning her back to me and devouring her. Her mouth melts like candy against mine, and when she moans against my lips, I have to hold back my hard-on. Unfortunately, I can't do it very well and she notices it too. Because of our height difference, my cock hardens against her belly.

"I think we have a visitor."

"What's new under the sun?" she mocks.

I lean forward and rest my forehead against her, in a vain attempt to calm myself down. To slow down the blood flow that migrated to the southern part of my body.

"Seriously, babe! I feel like I'm thirteen again when I'm with you. All I can think about is you, about us, all I can think about is being inside you every fucking second of the day. It's driving me crazy! I skipped a biology class to come to see you."

"It's not like you really need to go to class. The teachers will be happy to give you an A+ on the exams so that you can continue to defend Brown's colors on the field."

"What the fuck are these cliches is that?"

"Dare to tell me that it's not true."

"That's not true, Balboa! All my grades, I earned them."

"Pfft!"

She rolls her eyes as she often does. "I never see you working."

"That's because I'm a genius."

"Or a liar."

"Why does it give me a hard-on when you insult me?" he asks.

"Because everything gives you a hard-on."

"Everything? No! You? Yes!"

I press my cock against her belly, in an absolutely not heavy attempt to titillate her. She laughs.

"You need to go get therapy, Jude Hartnett."

"I have a better solution. A more efficient and faster way."

"Oh yes, which one?"

Her gaze becomes playful. She knows exactly what I'm going to suggest, but she wants me to spell it out for her. One thing I've noticed about Rocky is that she loves sex, and unlike some others, she doesn't hide it. She knows what she wants, and what's refreshing is that she doesn't hesitate to come and take it. Playing with my cock, like it was her favorite instrument.

She likes that I'm a little brutal too, that I bite her breasts or slap her ass, but most of all she likes me to talk dirty, that I tell her what I'm going to do to her. And I give it my all, using the dirtiest terms I can think of. Someone has to do something to satisfy this hottie. And I'm happy to do the job.

I whisper my intentions in her ear. She laughs and shakes her head.

"It's tempting! Really tempting! But I have work to do."

"It will only take me a few minutes, just enough time to…"

I try to unbutton her jeans. She abruptly pulls my hand away.

"Jude! We're in a library."

So what? is my first reaction. This wouldn't be the first public place I've had sex in. Of course, I avoid telling her that. She already takes me for a walking cliché, a star football player in college with the parade of groupies and one-night stands that goes with it.

"There's no one around! Besides, no student is going to come and venture into this boring department. Except you. Most people use Google these days. All these books have yellowed pages and dust for a reason, Rocky. Nobody uses them. It took me three hours to find you, so if we're quiet and discreet, we'll go unnoticed."

I bury my face into her neck and nibble on her sensitive little spot just below her ear. She gasps but continues to argue. Stubborn as she is.

"As discreet as a six-foot-tall football star can be, whose every move is watched by all the groupies? Have you ever heard of the expression 'a bull in a china shop?'"

"And have you ever heard of the bull in my boxes that is about to explode?"

She giggles. I take advantage of this little moment of relaxation to stick my tongue into her mouth and explore every corner of it. I bite her bottom lip and pull on it, then suck on her tongue while rubbing against her. I grab her ass and lift her to align my cock with her pussy. And apply the pressure that I know will bring her down. She moans into my mouth. A good indication of my impending victory.

"Babe, I really want you!"

"Me too."

Fuck yes!

"But we can't do it here."

Fuck no!

"Let's go to my room, then?"

"It's on the other side of campus, I will barely have time to get there before I have to leave."

"Climb on my back, I'll sprint over there. They don't call me *Flash* in the field for nothing."

She laughs again and punches my shoulder. The worst part is that I'm serious. I'm ready to do anything to get inside her right now, and that's what I'm trying to explain to her.

"Uh… no! You're crazy! Not to mention the rumors that would spark."

"Who cares?"

I kiss her, or rather, I devour her like a wolf that hasn't eaten in days.

"I care. I don't want to be dragged through the mud again."

"What are you talking about?"

"Nothing."

Her eyes darken, and she bites the inside of her cheek as she does when something is bothering her. This directly calms my ardor, and I put her down on the floor. She looks at her shoes. Yeah. There is something wrong.

"What's going on, Rocky? Who dragged you through the mud?"

"It's nothing, really… nothing at all."

"Really, nothing? I can tell you're upset, so talk to me, babe."

I'm now caressing her cheek. Any trace of sexual urgency has left my body to give way to my protective side. Someone is messing with my Balboa and better get out of the state of Rhode Island before I catch them.

"It's really nothing! Jude, I don't want to bother you with this, it's ridiculous. I'm not even sad… just a little… how to say… disturbed."

Why do her eyes tell me otherwise, then? I hate to see her pretty mouth droop.

"Please talk to me."

She looks down again and takes a deep breath.

"Okay. It's just… just on Twitter and Instagram, on the #JudeHartnett."

I frown, expecting the worst. The #JudeHartnett was created by fans, or rather female fans, of the Tigers when I joined the team. Apparently, it's a tradition at Brown. All team members have one. The fans are virulent. And if most of the time, it's about chronicling my athletic exploits, sometimes it's used for less glorious purposes. We had a laugh with Alec when we discovered a romance written on Tumblr about the two of us. We're supposedly a secret couple, and our every move on the stadium is spied on to further this theory. Usually, I don't give a fuck about these crazies, but this time, it affects Rocky. And This is something else. She won't take her eyes off her feet the entire time she's recounting what Isabella and Alyson showed her.

"Rocky, look at me."

I pat her chin.

"Don't listen to all that bullshit, it's crap. Your ass is gorgeous! You're gorgeous, and anyone who thinks or says otherwise is an asshole. If I listened to everything they say about me, I'd go crazy."

"Everyone compliments you all the time," she says.

"They praise me when I win, but as soon as we lose, I get insults. That's the game, that's how it is. And it won't get better if I turn pro. I'm sorry you had to be involved in this, babe. You didn't choose this path."

"I chose to be with you…"

And I hope this shit doesn't bring it all back into question again.

With Rocky, I feel like I'm playing a dangerous game where I can't control the rules. I always feel like she's slipping away from me, or that she doesn't open up completely. And that turns me on as much as it scares me.

"How do you not get affected?" she finally asks, snapping me out of my thoughts.

"I don't look at what they say, simple as that. It's bad for me and for my focus on the field. And you should do the same, Balboa."

"Okay."

She smiles and relaxes in my arms. I hug her tight, kiss the top of her head. We are interrupted by a vibration. Her phone. She grabs it, and her face turns serious.

"It's Max's school!"

She turns around to take the call. The tone of her voice could not be more serious and judging by the wrinkles of anguish that dig her forehead, this is not good news. I stay at a safe distance, but I listen.

"What? It can't be! Max wouldn't hurt a fly. Sure. Thank you for letting me know. I'll come and get him right away. Thanks for calling me."

She hangs up and runs a hand through her hair before gasping in desperation. I reach out to hug her, but she backs away.

"I have to go. It's Max, he's been in a fight! I have to go get him."

"Do you want a ride?"

"No, I'm good. I have my car."

She looks completely confused.

I let her go and watch her walk away, her shoulders hunched and her gait unsure. I don't know exactly what she was told on the phone, but it was enough for her to rebuild this fucking fortress meant to keep me at bay.

26

Rocky

"You must understand that this kind of behavior is serious and that we cannot tolerate it in our school."

I listen to the principal explain to me what Max did. He hit one of his classmates with a rock in a fit of anger that I didn't know he was capable of. My little brother is sitting in the chair next to me, his little body curled up and his cheeks flushed with shame and grief. Lots of questions come to me, and the most glaring is *Why?* The problem, Mrs. Langton is too busy talking to me about the consequences to give me any explanation.

"I assure you that won't happen again, miss."

"I hope so because Tyler's family is furious. He could have ended up in the hospital if the stone had hit his eye."

"I'm really sorry about that. I'm going to have a chat with Max and make sure he understands. He's not violent, never has been. Tyler must have done or said something that put him in this state."

"That's it!"

She throws her hands in front of her to show her exasperation.

"You're already trying to find excuses for him! That's not how we're going to move forward."

"That's not what I'm doing! But I'm just trying to figure out why my little brother, who is gentle as a lamb, throws himself on one of his classmates and tries to hit him with a stone? There must be a reason. Did you at least ask him the question before you suspended him for the day?"

"Of course, I got nothing but a shrug and tears."

I turn to my little brother who hides his face in his lap.

"Miss Prescott, I know that Max is an adorable little boy. But what he did is serious enough to catch my attention. Let me be clear with you, Miss Prescott, a lot of people are wondering about you. It's been a very long time since we've seen your mother, and there's a lot of talk about that. Until now, I didn't worry about it more than that, because it had no impact on Max. But now, I can't pretend that it's not happening. Where is your mother? I would like to talk to her."

"She's working, she's on a business trip."

She raises a suspicious eyebrow and crosse her hands over her desk. I swallow the knot that has formed in my throat, trying to keep a straight face.

"On the information sheet filled out at the beginning of Max's schooling, she was a simple saleswoman. Stop me if I'm wrong, we don't do a lot of business trips in this area."

"She's changed jobs in the meantime, she's in marketing now. But I don't quite understand what that has to do with the situation."

"Maybe if she was around more, Max wouldn't behave like this. Look, Rocky, I know you're doing your best in your parents' absence, but you're young and still a student. Raising a child alone is a big responsibility. Maybe you need help? Let us help you."

By us, what does she mean exactly? Child Protective Services?

A cold sweat runs down my neck as I imagine my worst nightmare might come true. They could take Max away from me! A vision of him struggling as he is dragged away sends shivers down my spine. I swallow the bile that has risen from my stomach and answer, trying not to show my dismay, "I tell you again that I'm not alone! My mom will be home soon, and thanks for your advice, but we'll manage. And as I told you before, it will never happen again. You have my word."

"I hope so, Miss Prescott, because otherwise the punishment will be more severe."

I nod, my lips pursed to keep from screaming, and straighten up with all the calm I have left. I take Max by the hand and head for the exit. He's been suspended today and can't return to class. I buckle him into his car seat in dead silence. I'm mad at him for drawing attention to our family like this, for letting Jude distract me when my little brother is obviously not well, and mad at my mom for even remotely causing me problems.

"Go to your room, Max! You're grounded," I tell him, as soon as we crossed the threshold of the house.

I know I should talk to him first. Trying to understand his behavior but, right now, I'm unable to do so without yelling at him. The prospect of losing him if Mrs. Langton calls family services terrifies me.

I watch my little man walk away up the stairs while I slump on the couch trying to collect my thoughts. I rub my face for a long time, as if trying to tear my own skin off. I need Rebecca Prescott to grow up, get sober and get ready to be a mother, I need a fucking miracle!

I look up and see my little Max staring at me from the top of the stairs, his face flushed, and his eyes filled with tears.

"I hate you, Rocky!" he says, his voice full of sobs.

Shit!

Immediately, I rush towards him, but he turns his back on me and runs to his room where he locks himself.

"Max, please open the door."

"No! Go away!"

"Max, please. I'm sorry I acted so stupidly. My baby, open the door for me."

"No! I don't want to be with you anymore. I want Mom!"

And then I hear him sobbing loudly. Suddenly, he becomes the 6-year-old boy he is, vulnerable, whom life has not spared. My heart has time to break a thousand times before I find the key that opens his door. And when I finally make it into his room, he's just a shivering ball, curled up under the blanket. I lift it and lie behind him, grabbing him and hugging him tightly. His small frame seems even more frail and fragile than usual.

"Hush, my baby! Stop crying, I'm here."

He turns to me, and his big hazel eyes meet mine. The sadness and despair I see there makes me want to scream.

"Rocky, I'm sorry I hit Tyler."

"I know, my little angel."

"But he said things to me that hurt me."

"What exactly did he say to you?"

"That mom died like dad, and that's why she stopped picking me up from school." He swallows. "He said I was an orphan and would end up like Oliver Twist."

"What a little jerk!" I can't help but say.

And it has the advantage of making him smile a little.

"Is it true? Is Mom dead?"

"No, honey, that's not true. She's not dead. She's…"

He looks at me with a glimmer of hope in his eyes and I hate having to shatter all his illusions. But I can't lie to him anymore. I realize in that moment that it's time for me to tell him the truth. He's too young to understand, I know that, but lying is worse. It leaves the door open to the worst scenario, much worse than the sad reality. So, I take my courage in both hands and say, "Mom is gone. She left to try to find herself. She's sick. Her head tells her to do things that aren't always fair to us. But she can't help it. And we can't do anything about it either. She likes us. She's just unable to stay with us like all the other moms."

He nods and plays with the necklace around my neck. A long silence settles between us while I caress his back and he looks at my necklace as if it were the most fascinating object in the world.

"Will she ever come back?" he whispers in an insecure voice.

"Yes, she will, but I don't know when, honey."

He seems to be thinking. "So, she's not dead, she's just gone, but she'll be back."

The fact that this sad shitty option gives him hope breaks me. Max is like me, he is satisfied with the crumbs. Of the little love we want to give him.

"Yes, sweetie. She'll come back when she's better. I don't know how long it will take, but she'll be back."

"Rocky, do you still love me, even though I was mean?"

"Of course, I love you, baby! I'll always love you no matter what you do. I'll never stop loving you, and above all, I'll never go anywhere. I'll always be there for you."

"Promise?"

The fact that he doubts it, that he needs reassurance tells me that my mother's irresponsibility has already taken its toll on him. And I hate her with all my heart for damaging his beautiful soul.

"I promise."

I give my pinky to him as we often do to seal pacts between us. A slight smile appears on his lips. He grabs my pinky with his and we kiss our fists.

"You and me, it's for life, sweetie."

"Rocky?"

"Yes, my baby!"

"I'm hungry."

"That's good, because I was planning to make you strawberry pancakes, with real strawberries." His eyes widen.

"And whipped cream?"

"Lots and lots of whipped cream."

"Does that mean I'm not grounded anymore?"

"No, sweetie. But I don't want you to hit Tyler, or anyone else, even when he deserves it. And that little jerk deserved it."

He giggles.

"You've already said two bad words. That's two dollars in the pot of forbidden words."

"Totally worth it! Come on! You're coming to help me make the pancakes."

"Yes!"

Max leaps from his bed, his enthusiasm visibly restored. I'm not fooled. I know it will take more than whipped cream to heal his wounds, but I'll be there every step of the way. To pick him up when he falls, to wipe away his tears when he cries, and to mend his heart when he breaks.

That night, after putting Max to bed, I'm completely distraught and have a hard time getting to sleep. I'll have to talk to Mrs. Langton to reassure her, to prevent her from calling family services. Maybe I'm being a little dramatic, and she's not thinking about it, but she looked really alarmed, and I can't take the risk.

I have too much to lose. I could possibly volunteer for one of the field trips, to get into her good graces and show her that I am involved in my little brother's education. The problem is *when*? I can't keep missing classes. It's the end of the semester, and there are lots of exams. I haven't made as much progress on the Huntington project as I hoped, and I'm not sure I'll be able to turn it in on time. Goodbye great Christmas presents! Once again, I'm letting down my little brother.

I keep turning and turning, but I can't seem to calm the storm that is raging under my skull.

Think positive stuff, Rocky!

Eating ice cream with Max, sharing a giggle with my friends, Jude's lips on mine.

Plop! Plop! Plop! Something knocks on the window. I straighten up, put my glasses on my nose and approach the window. Plop, plop.

I open the window and find myself face to face with Jude. His face wet, he grabs my neck and kisses me. I let myself go to this tender kiss. The raindrops that bead on his face slide on me too, and I shiver.

"Come inside. You'll catch a cold."

He steps over the window. I grab a towel from the bathroom and throw it to him. He reaches to catch it, but it crashes into his beautiful face. I stifle a laugh.

"And he calls himself a college football star."

"I have to say that I have quite a distraction in front of me."

My cheeks heat up in front of his fiery gaze.

"Did you forget to unlock the window for me tonight?"

"Sorry!"

I keep staring at him as he dries off with the towel. His hair is a mess on his head, and of course, that makes him even hotter. He gives me his sly smile the one he often gives me when he notices that I'm drooling over him.

"Come here, babe."

His hoarse, drawling voice turns my knees to jelly. I stagger toward him. He takes me in his arms. He's still wearing his soaked jacket, while I'm only in shorts and a T-shirt. He's cold and wet. But despite the discomfort he gives me on the outside, I feel much better on the inside. He has this power over me. It's exhilarating and scary at the same time. Scary, because he will eventually leave. Everyone always ends up leaving.

"I love it when you wear your glasses. It gives you a sexy nerd vibe," he says, kissing me on the nose.

This tender little gesture melts my poor heart even more.

Don't get attached, stupid heart!

"Do you want me to keep them for sex?"

"That's my Rocky! Action oriented."

He kisses me once again. His tongue caressing mine tenderly before withdrawing and taking on a more serious look, "Is everything fine? I mean, I called you at least twenty times and you didn't answer. I got worried."

"Yes, sorry, I've just been very busy."

"And is Max okay?"

"Yes! He got into a fight at school. But nothing serious."

I unhook myself from his arms, because he's getting too intrusive, and go back to bed. He takes off his jacket, his shoes, then follows me. He sits next to me.

"You want to talk about it?"

I shrug my shoulders.

"You should. It would do you good to let things out, babe."

He caresses my cheek. I'm more in the habit of burying them in a dark hole and covering it up as quickly as possible.

"What would make me feel better is for you to fuck me. Take your clothes off, Jude."

He doesn't do it. I straddle him and begin to unbutton his jeans.

He frowns, not quite the reaction I was expecting. He takes my hands out of his fly and brings them to his lips. I look at him like he just slapped me. And somehow, that's the impression I get. What's wrong with him? He doesn't want me anymore? Is it the picture on social media? All the negative comments from people on the internet have convinced him that I'm not good enough for him? Shit, my expiration date came way earlier than expected apparently.

"Don't you want to talk? I feel like you need to."

"Since when did you become a therapist? What I need is your cock, right now."

I crush my mouth hard against his and suck his lip. He moans, kisses me back, before entwining his hands in my hair to keep me away. His caramel-green eyes probe mine.

"What happened with Max, Rocky?"

"It's none of your business."

I lean over and kiss him on the neck.

"Why did he fight?" he insists, making my irritation soar.

I don't fucking want to talk! He doesn't understand, or what?

Change of strategy. I take off my T-shirt and push him back, then kiss his chest. He lets himself go for a moment, then resumes, "Baby, talk to me, I want to be able to help you."

"You're already helping me."

I take out his cock and start jerking him off. He is hard with pleasure.

"Rocky…"

I take him in my mouth, he falls on his back, grunts, and places his palms over his eyes.

Victory!

"Fuck!" he growls, before blocking my head and forcing me to withdraw.

The look on his face when our two eyes meet tells me that he has just made a superhuman effort.

"Jude! What the fuck is your problem? Don't you want me anymore?"

I straighten up and jump out of bed in rage. I must look crazy with my messy hair and swollen lips. He sits and watches me pace, then straightens up, walks over, and cups my face in his palms.

"Rocky, I really want you! I always want you. You know I do! But I can give you more than a few orgasms. I can also listen to you, comfort you, and offer you my help."

"Oh yeah? Do you think you can help me?"

He nods.

"In that case, do you know where my irresponsible mother is?" I push him violently, but he barely moves. "How do I get her to come back? How? Do you know how?"

I push him again.

"And above all, how to make her come to her senses? How do I get her to behave like a real fucking mother?"

I scream with rage and push him, but he always comes back each time, towering over me with his powerful body, his crazy energy. With his presence. Reassuring. Exasperating.

"You see? You can't do any of these things! Then you can't help me, Jude! No one can help me."

I push him violently once again; he comes back and takes me in his arms.

"No! get away! Go home!"

He hugs me tight as I struggle. A fit of anger comes over me, and I take it out on Jude. I pound on his chest with my fists.

"Go away! Get out! I don't need you! I don't need anyone."

I don't know why I'm doing this, but I can't seem to stop. And the worst part is that he takes the blows without flinching. He remains silent while I say a bunch of horrible things to him, my face twisted and flushed with anger. I must not be pretty, but I don't care. I feel the sobs compressing my throat, preventing me from breathing. I refuse to let out my tears, I'm afraid they will overwhelm me, drown me. I end up exhausting myself and pressing my forehead against his chest.

"Do you know how to put back together the heart of a 6-year-old boy who doesn't deserve all the crap that's happening to him?" I whisper, out of breath.

"Babe... I'm sorry."

He wraps me in his arms. I breathe in his scent, letting his warmth, his softness, wash over me, and burst into tears like the poor idiot I am. Let all the sadness that weight on me out. I cry for long minutes. Unable to stop myself. Unable to reason with myself. All the while, Jude strokes my back, kisses the top of my head, but remains silent.

He must think I'm crazy, clinging to his shirt like a leech, cleaning my snot off of him. He probably came to have a good time. This is what I offer him, tears and snot. Not sure if this was the type of fluid he was expecting. Yet, I can't stop despite my best efforts to pull myself together. I never cry, always keep everything inside safe, for fear that once it comes out it will take me away.

My legs suddenly leave the ground. Jude carries me like a bride and lays me on my bed. I curl up and continue to cry. He disappears into the bathroom for a few minutes. Then I feel the mattress sag and his body wrap around mine. He hugs me tightly, protects me, fills me with his warmth, his positive energy, and all this without saying a word. My tears finally dry up and sleep takes me away.

***

My footsteps echo in the street. It's winter. It's cold. Snow is falling, and my coat is soaked. I shiver, my feet are frozen. Yet, I don't want to go home. I've been pacing in front of this damn house that I hate for thirty minutes.

From the outside, it looks quite normal. Modest like the rest of the houses in the neighborhood, a sagging porch and a crack in the wooden staircase that leads to the entrance. Nothing a little consideration and hard work couldn't fix. But seen from the inside, it's chaos.

John Flinstons, worker, and notorious hunter in his spare time, is the owner. And recently, he got himself a girlfriend. A talkative and lively blonde he met at his favorite diner. She was new in town, pretty to look at and very pleasant, especially when she was looking for favors. Their relationship quickly evolved from little counter flirtation to true love. Well, that's what my mom told me.

A few weeks later, we moved out of the motel on the side of the highway in which we had just taken up residence, to live with this respectable man, newly divorced, who was sorely lacking in love. "It will be different this time!" Again, my mother's words. What she didn't know, or pretended not to see, was that he wasn't lacking love, but rather humanity. He didn't seem to appreciate Mom having a second mouth to feed, someone to keep them from frolicking as they wished, and never missed a chance to remind me of that.

If I have the misfortune to open a box of cookies before he has had time to do it himself, I am in for a scandal. I cut the pastrami slices carefully, making sure the edges stay parallel so he can't notice I've been serving myself in his absence. I quickly understood the unspoken rules of this house of misfortune. Eat as little as possible, only during meals, no extra snacks. Shower quickly and avoid leaving the light on for too long in the evening in my bedroom. Oh yes! I have a bedroom! It's rare enough to be mentioned, so as much to say that I have no reason to complain. Otherwise, it would make me "ungrateful!" Again, my mother's words.

So far, nothing too serious. Since little, I go from place to place, and I'm used to adapting to other people's rules and being forgotten. So that's not why I'd rather freeze my ass outside than go home to warm up and finish my homework. No! The reason is much more disturbing. Just thinking about it makes me want to vomit.

Last week, when I was taking the fastest shower in the history of showers, being careful to turn off the water as I shampooed, my stepfather came into the bathroom to yell, that once again, I was taking advantage of his generosity. And when his bloodshot eyes landed on my, barely formed body, they stayed there far longer than decency would allow. Long enough for me to have the reflex to hide behind my tiny hands and for my last meal to go up my throat.

He didn't say anything, didn't do anything more, didn't tell my mother. When I wanted to tell her, she simply replied that I was just a child, that there was nothing to watch, and that he saw me as his own daughter. I wanted to believe her. I wanted it to be true, for my fears to be unwarranted, just a figment of a prepubescent 12-year-old kid's imagination.

Yet I could feel it, his gaze on me, everywhere, like a parasite pushing me to hate myself, to hide myself, to be ashamed, his persistent and perverse gaze. A silent threat that grabs you in the gut, but no one else seems to notice. Like a curse waiting, lurking in the shadows, for the right moment to attack.

I won't give him that opportunity. Never! I refuse to be alone with him again. So, I spend my time hanging out after school until Mom gets home from work. It's a miracle she's been able to keep him this long! But for once, I wish she had lost him, that she was always there, to protect me. The front door opens, and I hide behind one of the trees across the street. My stepfather staggers out and gets into his old car which is as tired as he is. He starts the car, reverses it. I move, change my angles, so he can't see me in his rearview mirror. God knows what he would do to me if he saw that I was hiding.

He's a scary man. He never came to blows with me, but just the sound of his voice makes me imagine the worst. And his eyes, I hate his eyes. He has a weasel look and big disgusting hands that I watch as he cleans his gun. Sometimes I scream in the night imagining his big disgusting hands on me. The only day I feel somewhat safe is Sunday. Hunting day for him, day of peace for me. I wish all days of the week were Sundays. I wish he would go hunting one day and never come back. I wish my mother would finally open her eyes we would go back on the road. Even sleeping in the car seems more attractive to me than being under this cursed roof.

My stepfather's Thunderbird disappears down the street, and I breathe again. It's a bit risky to go back now because I don't know how long he'll be gone. But I'm freezing to death, and I really want to go to the bathroom. I take a sprint, use my key and go into the house to go relieve myself, then I immediately stick myself in front of the fireplace to warm my hands.

My eyes keep going back and forth between the flames and the window. I'm on the lookout, for the slightest noise, the slightest movement. Ready at any moment to run away, go out by the back or lock myself in my room. But I never imagined that the danger would come precisely through the back door. And when I hear that horrible gravelly voice coming from behind me, I freeze in fear.

"Rocky! Rocky! Rocky! I didn't see you were there! For once you come home early from school, we'll take advantage of it together…"

27

Jude

"No... no... no!"

I hear Rocky stirring in her sleep. She's shaking. I open my eyes and hug her a little tighter, thinking to reassure her, but she continues to move, to turn her head in all directions, as if trying to escape from something. Shit! She's having a nightmare!

I sit up and turn on the bedside lamp. Her pretty face is tense, taut, haunted by a thousand and one terrors. And seeing her like that is fucking torture.

"No... Leave me... I don't want to... No!"

"Rocky, wake up!"

"No..."

It's not to me that she answers, but to the ghosts that torment her.

"No... no... no!"

I shake her a little more vigorously, no longer able to bear to see her in agony. She finally opens her eyes. Two large black holes haunted by fear. I am so disturbed to have access to the depth of her soul, without her having invited me, that I remain motionless. She finally blinks, releasing a few tears with this gesture. And the worst part is that I don't know if they are tears from yesterday or his fucking nightmare. So many monsters I would fight for her, if only she would let me!

She wipes away her tears, sits up, takes the bottle of water from her bedside, and downs a good half of it.

"You okay?"

It's the only thing I can think of to break the ice.

"Yes."

She rubs her eyes and ties her hair in a messy bun.

"I had a nightmare," she says, as if it's obvious.

I nod.

"Did I scream?"

"No, you didn't scream, but you were fighting. And you kept repeating 'No…'"

She bites her lip, shakes her head, and new tears stream down her cheeks. I erase them immediately and take her in my arms. She lets herself go and lays her head on my chest. I caress her hair, her back, I know she loves it, that it relaxes her, and I will do everything in my power, right now, to make her relax. We stay like that for a long time. I don't know what to say. I would like to ask her a thousand questions: What was she dreaming about? Does she often have nightmares? Does it have something to do with her mother's absence? But I'm afraid of the answers.

And I feel like a loser. Useless. To be exactly what she feared. Unable to understand and unable to help. I've been waiting for her to open up to me for so long, to show me her weaknesses. This moment finally arrives. And me, what am I doing? Spoiler Alert! Absolutely nothing. The problem is that my mind is screaming at me to get out, that this story is doomed to fail. Too complicated. That I have better things to do than try to get a girlfriend. I have to deal with her mountain of problems, while I'm just touching my dream with my fingertips. That I need all my focus and energy to make the tryouts. May the headhunters start looking for the next big shot. That the one from Chicago came to see several practices and that his team is seriously interested in me. That there is also San Diego, Dallas, and New York. That I haven't told Rocky yet, because I prefer to tell her when it'll be real. Despite all this, everything that should make me walk away, I can't. And the reason has nothing to do with it.

"Sorry, Jude…"

Her broken voice pulls me out of my introspection.

"'Sorry?' What are you apologizing for, babe?"

"For all this! For bumping into you yesterday and preventing you from sleeping now. I'm the world's worst booty call."

There she goes with that again! I groan, unable to hide my irritation. "Rocky! You're not my fucking booty call! You're much more than that! OK?! Get that in your head! I'm not used to seeing my booty call every day, helping them study, watching movies with them, taking them to dinner or sleeping with them, spending time with their best friends and mine. Whether you want to accept it or not, we're past the point of no strings attached sex! You're my girl! And as a boyfriend, I command you to unload everything on me. And babe, when I say everything, I'm talking about the good and the bad. From the exciting, sexy, explosive, but also what is ugly, sad, and hard, I want it all! I don't guarantee that I'll always be able to face everything, but I'll try, for you, for me, for us."

"Aren't those the lyrics to a Lady Gaga song?"

Damn, is she fucking kidding?!

She raises her head to me, her still red eyes now laughing, and I can't help but put my lips on hers. After devouring her mouth, I say, "Rocky, stop running away. What I mean by my clumsy speech is that I can be so much more than a dick to you. And that you can trust me."

"You're right," she says serious tone. "And I know I can count on you, but I just have a hard time opening up sometimes. But I'm working on it, and I thank you for your patience."

She closes her eyes like she's about to add something deep, then suppresses a smile. I feel that she is going to throw some bullshit at me.

"Besides… you're so much more than a dick. You also have the most beautiful pair of balls I've ever seen."

She starts to laugh, and it feels good to find this lightness with her. Even though I know she laughs because she's modest, she laughs because she doesn't want me to go too far, so I play her game.

"And you, the most beautiful ass in the world."

I slap her on the butt, and she squeals in surprise.

"That's not what your fans think!"

"Do I look like I care what anyone thinks?"

"No! Thankfully. Anyway, I'm really sorry I woke you up. You have practice tomorrow, and you have to get up in exactly three hours."

"Don't worry, babe! I usually don't sleep much anyway."

"You don't?"

"Six hours a night. Always been like that. When I was little, my mother worried because she always found me in my room playing in the middle of the night. After dragging me to several doctors, they all concluded that it was my deep nature. Don't need much sleep to be in shape."

"And with two hours less than us, poor mortals, you managed to become a top athlete?! At what point do I tell you I hate you?" she laughs.

"At what point do I tell you that I love you?"

She jerks her head up, and our eyes lock. Her black eyes, so luminous, so expressive, are as round as saucers. Mine too, to tell the truth. Since these words completely escaped me.

"What did you say?"

OK, too late to go back out now. Even though I know she's going to freak out completely.

"I love you, Rocky! I love you with all my heart. I didn't plan this, it just happened. But now I can't deny it anymore and I want you to know. I love you."

"But why?" she asks.

"Why what? Why do I love you?"

She swallows and nods.

"Do you need a reason?"

She nods as I scratch my temple to explain my feelings to her.

"I don't know... You have become as essential to me as my oxygen, you're in my every thought and you seem to speak the secret language of my cock like nobody else."

She rolls her eyes.

"That's not difficult!"

She tries to look as unaffected as possible, but by the gleam that shines in her eyes, by the blush on her cheeks, I know she's moved.

"I know you think I'm a sex addict and think I've slept with thousands of chicks. You're wrong. Girls have never interested me more than that. One fuck, why not? More? No thanks! I've had a few girlfriends, but I've always preferred the company of my buddies, and satisfying my cock has never been a problem or an obsession. Well, that was before you, Rocky. You changed me. I always want to be inside you, with you, to see you, to hear you laugh, to breathe, to moan, to touch you, to feel you, to make you lose your mind, to remake the world with you, to argue about the most insignificant things, to watch movies, to watch you study, to watch you think, chew on your pencil, to listen to you laugh. Just being with you."

I finish breathless as she looks at me, her eyes filled with tears.

"But you can't love me!"

"Why not?" I ask.

"Because I don't have anything to offer you but trouble."

"Everything you say is true, but I don't give a fuck. I love you, Rocky Prescott. And you don't have to be perfect for me to love you, you just have to be you."

She looks at me between tears she's trying to hold back, and I force her to straddle me.

"I love you, Rocky!" I repeat so she can get it into her head.

She closes her eyes, as if to escape my words. OK, that's not the reaction I was expecting.

"Stop saying you love me, Jude, please. What you like is the feeling that my body gives you."

She sits up, takes my hands, and places them on her breasts.

"I'm a great fuck, it can cloud the mind a little."

"Oh, yeah?" I ask.

"Yeah."

She thinks she's got me by the sex again, but I'm not going to let go this time.

"What I love, Rocky, is what you have here."

I put my index finger on her sex.

"What you have here."

I place my index finger on her temple.

"And especially what you have here."

I place my index finger on her heart, which is beating a thousand miles an hour. She closes her eyes once more, then looks at the ceiling. Her lips and chin quiver. Shit, I didn't mean to make her cry.

"Babe…"

I force her to lean towards me, her hair loose and caressing my face, her emotional and sad eyes penetrating me, as they have never penetrated me before.

"Jude, you can't love me. I'm broken inside," she whispers in a dull voice.

She says these cruel words to me with such sincerity that my throat closes.

"You're not broken, Rocky."

"I am. And you'll realize it sooner or later."

I kiss her, slowly, tenderly. Her lips barely move.

"I don't care, I'll pick up all the pieces one after the other, even if it takes my life."

"Thanks..."

She puts her face in my neck and, without my asking anything, tells me about her nightmare. I clench my fists as she explains what her stepfather tried to do to her.

"Fortunately, my mother arrived in time before he could..."

She swallowed.

"Anyway... She saw that he was in my room, she saw that I was terrified, but she didn't do anything."

"And that son of a bitch tried to corner you again after that?"

"No. I didn't give him the chance anymore and I think Mom knew, so she wasn't leaving me alone with him anymore."

"She stayed with that motherfucker anyway?"

"Yes. She was in love. And I always came after those romances. She ended up leaving him, but for some reason that has nothing to do with me. I no longer know what it was. All I know is that that day was the happiest of my life."

"Rocky, I'm sorry to tell you that your mother is a fucking asshole."

She laughs, while on my side, I want to smash something, like the face of her fucking ex-stepfather for example, and all the other assholes who made her suffer too. I have never hit a woman, but at this precise moment, I'm not against the idea.

Without another word, Rocky turns around and places her body against mine for me to wrap around her. I do so with great pleasure, like an armor. After a few minutes of silence, she whispers, "Don't hurt me, Jude."

"Never in a million years, Rocky."

"Good night."

"Good night, babe, I love you."

She doesn't say anything back, but I feel her body relax and settle against mine. She's surrendering, she really surrendering, and it's a feeling even more enjoyable than sex. At this precise moment, I know that we are bound for life.

I just have to convince her.

28

Rocky

"Rocky…"

"Mmmmm…"

"Rocky, wake up! I'm hungry."

"Uh…"

"Can you make me some pancakes?"

"Yes, of course, sweetie."

I answer Max like an automaton, without even opening my eyes, my voice and my brain clouded by sleep. What time is it? How long have I slept? And what is this hard thing against my butt?

It takes me a few minutes to realize that this hard thing is an erection, and that erection belongs to Jude. Which means he didn't wake up at dawn, as usual, to leave before Max got up. And that I'm in the deep—

"Shit!"

I jump out of bed like a devil out of a box, definitely awake this time. I pull the covers over Jude as fast as I can, cursing him. Mr. I-only-sleep-six-hours-a-night. My ass!

"You said a bad word again, Rocky!"

"I know, sweetie. I'm sorry."

I don't know if Max noticed anything, in any case, he says nothing and follows me to the kitchen, as usual. He sits in his chair and plays with his dinosaur while I work on making pancakes. I'm silently cursing Jude, the alarm clock that didn't ring, and the entire universe that obviously decided to settle some scores with me this week.

"Do you want some orange juice, sweetie?"

"Yes, thanks."

I serve him, then kiss the top of his curly little head. He curls up against me, as usual. So far, no disturbing signs.

"Did you sleep well?"

"Yes, I did."

He continues to play with his dinosaur making growling noises. I wonder if I should tell him about Jude, explain to him why he was in my bed this morning, but I don't dare, the timing is just too crappy. Yesterday, my little brother learned that his mother might never come back, and today, that? Well done, Rocky. Mrs. Langton is right, you are the worst parent the earth has ever born. I pour myself a cup of coffee to calm myself down, and above all, to think about what I should do to avoid making the situation worse. My strategy, as often, is to act as if nothing had happened!

Brave, states my conscience.

The pancakes ready, I place them on the table and sit in front of my little brother. I watch him take huge bites and devour his breakfast like a glutton. At least he hasn't lost his appetite, and that cheers me up. He can't be that bad if he's eating. Maybe he hasn't seen Jude and I'm worrying for nothing. He finishes his plate and I serve him again immediately. I promise, I'm not trying to buy his silence by flattering his stomach.

"Will you have more maple syrup?"

"You're giving me all this?!" Max looks at me with his big brown eyes.

"And you, you don't want it?" he asks.

"Not very hungry this morning, my angel."

"And Jude, he won't want it?"

I choke on a sip of coffee I had just swallowed.

Well, there you have your answer, Rocky!

"Erm, I think he's a little tired. Not sure he's coming to eat."

"Why? Did you play too much last night?"

Second sip that gets stuck and makes me cough. Embarrassed, I nod my head.

"We can say that, yes…"

"Me too, when I have sleepovers, we go to bed very late, and in the morning, we are always tired. Don't tell William's mom, but the last time, on his birthday, we played and laughed so much that I don't think we fell asleep before midnight," Max explains to me in a confidential tone.

"Really, midnight?"

"Yes, well, I think," he says, looking mischievous. "Anyway, it was late because his parents were already in bed. It was too much fun. I love sleepovers! Could I have another soon?"

"Of course, sweetie."

There's nothing I could say no to him, right now, for a lot of reasons, but guilt tops my list of parenting failures.

"Maybe I could invite Tyler over to make up for hurting him yesterday."

"It's a very good idea."

I want to ask him how he is. About the previous day's conversation, about Mom. But I'd rather not shake him too much and take his enthusiasm as tangible proof that he is fine. Add guilt to cowardice and you have my shittiest parenting survival guide on earth. I'm sure it could be a bestseller.

I finish my coffee listening to Max tell me everything he wants to do today.

Apparently, we're going to play football, eat pizza and ice cream for dessert, ride a bike and organize his collection of dinosaurs. But first, he gets his thirty minutes of cartoons. I validate the program of the day. Max rushes into the living room to watch TV. And it's time for me to wake up Mr. I-only-sleep-six-hours-a-night!

I climb the stairs in a hurry, open my bedroom door, and deliberately slam it hard. Jude jumps and looks at me like I just slapped him. He sits up, rubs his face, and shows off his steely abs. Well, hello to me. If Jude is handsome, usually in the morning, his beauty reaches such a level that he should be forbidden to exist. It's a good thing he usually bolts before I even open my eyes, because I think I can keep him trapped between my thighs all day. That sleepy little look, his narrowed eyes, his silky brown hair that falls perfectly, his angular jaw, his three-day beard, and that full mouth are a call for damnation. I would almost forget that his presence puts me in a delicate position and that he must return home as soon as possible. That has nothing to do with what he confessed to me last night, of course. I'm not trying to avoid him, not at all. That would be completely immature and beneath me.

"Why are you looking at me like you're hesitating between jumping on my balls or ripping them off?"

"Because that's exactly what I want to do."

"I don't know what I did to you, but I offer you the first option. And keep the rage, it's always explosive when you fuck me like you hate me. Come here, babe."

He spreads his arms, his sly smile, destroyer of panties, plastered on his lips. And I need all the self-control in the world not to obey him like a sex slave blinded by his aura. Instead, I cross my arms over my chest.

"Do you have any idea what time it is, Jude?"

"No."

He takes his cell phone.

"Fuck! Nine o'clock! Damn it! I missed practice. Coach Callahan is going to kill me."

He runs a hand through his hair, his biceps winking at me. Okay, now is not the time to check him out, but I can't help it. It must be said that we didn't have sex last night, and that he said very nice things to me despite the fact that I still behaved like a crazy person. The worst part is that I really want to believe him. Our relationship is a mixture of explosive sex, an impossible future, and anxieties of all kinds. The perfect recipe for disaster, for chaos, I'm the first to admit it, but yet, I woke up this morning with less weight on my chest, a lightness that gives me hope.

Hope, one of the worst vices in Pandora's box. It arrives when you least expect it, makes you dream, before exploding in full flight. I am fully aware of that. I'm afraid! I'm even terrified. But I think I just realized that my love for Jude is stronger than my fear.

Of course, I can't admit it to him. To say those three words he kept repeating to me last night. By embarrassment? Maybe! By superstition? Certainly! As if confessing my feelings out loud could break the subtle balance of our relationship. But nothing prevents me from showing my affection to him in other ways. And what better way to show him than by...

My waking fantasy is accentuated when he gets up and turns his back to me, this back so wide so muscular. OK! I give myself a mental slap. I have to pull myself together. My little brother is downstairs, and if I want to snatch the first prize in the shitty parent contest from my mom, I'm continuing on my wonderful path. Since yesterday, I think I scored a few points. I watch Jude search for a number in his phone.

"Hello, Coach Callahan, it's Hartnett!"

"Jude, don't talk so loud, Max is in the living room."

He gestures for me to be quiet. You've got to be kidding me.

"No, coach, I'm really sick."

He coughs falsely.

"That's not a girl's voice you heard. It's… uh, it's the TV!"

He gives me big eyes. It's funny to see him so sheepish in front of his coach. And if I was a demon, I would kneel before him, just to disturb him further. As if reading my mind and having access to my wildest fantasies, he raises a defiant eyebrow. I bite my lip to suppress a smile and approach him, with an irrepressible desire to piss him off. He pivots to avoid me. I try to slap his ass, but in a ninja-like move, he grabs my hands with one of his and traps them, then presses me against his chest. And all this while holding his cell phone to his ear. No matter how hard I try to struggle. Nothing works, he is imperturbable. As if I were a fly facing a colossus. He rubs his morning erection against my back and quietly finishes his conversation. My subconscious can't help noticing how easy it is for him to lie.

"Alec didn't know about it either. I went back to Warwick to see my mother. I must have caught a cold… OK, I will. Tomorrow? Yes, I think I will be there. Okay got it! Again, sorry for not calling ahead."

He hangs up, throws his phone on the bed and turns me to him with a quick gesture.

"You're a bad girl! You deserve to be punished."

He kisses me, and I forget why I was mad at him. His lips leave my mouth to rest on my neck, and my body melts completely against his, following him to the bed where he lays me down to make me lose my mind.

"Jude! Jude! Stop! We're not alone. Max is downstairs."

"He's up already?"

Obviously, he didn't hear me warn him earlier.

"Yes, and he came into the bedroom this morning to wake me up."

"You're kidding. Shit! He saw me?! Damn, I'm sorry, babe, I screwed up badly."

"You sure did."

"What was his reaction?"

"He thinks you came for a sleepover. He didn't seem to overinterpret the situation."

Jude chews the inside of his cheek. "That's good! Can you imagine if we were—"

I put my hand over his mouth. "Shut up! I don't even want to imagine it."

I lay my forehead on his chest and mumble, "It's my fault too. I usually lock the door when you're here, just in case, but yesterday I don't know what happened. Let's say that I wasn't thinking straight."

He clears his throat and caresses my cheek. I look up.

"That's the least we can say. Are you feeling better this morning?"

"Yes… thanks to you."

"Happy to be useful."

He kisses me tenderly. My heart is beating at a different pace this morning. As if it was excited and calmed at the same time. It's a strange and reassuring feeling.

"Do you want me to go now?"

"Yes!"

"Okay!"

He seems disappointed. Maybe he wanted me to ask him to stay? It's Saturday. He obviously missed his practice already, maybe it wouldn't be so bad if he spent the day with Max and me. But what am I saying? He probably has other a thousand times more interesting things to do today. Besides, he didn't ask me if he could stay. Max might not be ready for that, and I don't want to rush him. Jude kisses me again before straightening up and going to the bathroom. He comes out a few minutes later, dressed and smelling divine. He hasn't left yet, and I already miss him. I watch him walk to the window.

"No, wait!"

He turns to me, surprised.

"You can go through the door."

"What about Max?"

"He knows you're here, so might as well say hello to him, it'll be less weird. Besides, it's daytime, and my neighbors have a bad tendency to snoop on things that aren't their business. If they see you coming through the window, God knows what they'll think."

"Okay."

We both head downstairs. Max is staring at the screen when we arrive and is nibbling on his dinosaur's paw."

"Hi, man," Jude says casually.

"You're leaving already?"

"Yes."

"Oh, too bad! I wanted to play football with you."

Jude's eyes widen so much I think they're going to pop out of their sockets. As for me, I'm just as surprised as he is.

"I'd love to, buddy, but we will have to see if your sister agrees."

"Please, Rocky! Can he stay? I need someone who knows how to throw the ball! You're not very good."

I ignore my little brother's harsh remark and stare at Jude, looking for any doubt in his eyes. I don't want him to feel obligated to anything.

"Aren't you busy today?"

"Not really. I missed practice, so if you're ok with me staying, I can."

"Do you want to?"

"I'd love it."

"Then stay," I whisper, struggling to believe the words coming out of my own mouth.

"Yes!" shouts Max, jumping up from the sofa.

And that's exactly what my heart is screaming too.

"I'm going to get my ball. Follow me, Jude."

And Max disappears into the yard.

"Are you sure you don't have something better to do?"

He takes me in his arms, kisses me, then whispers against my lips, "Better things to do than spend time with my girlfriend whom I love, and her adorable little brother? Absolutely not!"

The day has passed in such harmony that I can't believe what is happening to me.

After a wild game of football, Jude taught Max how to throw the ball like a real quarterback would. I watched them from the kitchen window, oscillating between bursts of laughter and a tight throat. I tried not to let my heart notice too much how Max's eyes were shining, or how delicately and enthusiastically Jude encouraged him and explained the basics to him. To see my brother so happy, especially after yesterday's episode, is unexpected. Max is over the moon. So happy to be able to play with a guy.

I often noticed him watching our neighbors with envy as they played with their father. Of course, my little brother is not one to complain. He is like me on this level and has never made even the slightest comment. But it's a big sister's job to pay attention to these things. So, I redoubled my efforts to play with him. I'm a tomboy: climbing trees or throwing a ball isn't a problem. I'm not the type to be afraid of getting dirty or breaking a nail. But seeing Max's bright eyes when he look at Jude, I understand that was exactly what he needed. Of a male figure to identify with, if only for the time of a game of football. A presence that he sorely misses since the death of his father.

After football, Jude took Max for a ride on his motorcycle. Not very far, to the end of the street, with a helmet of course, and driving very slowly, but that was enough to make him his new hero. It was then impossible to keep my little brother quiet during lunch. He wanted to know everything about Jude and asked him lots of questions while devouring his pizza. Jude answered everything, and I forced my heart not to race seeing my two favorite people in the world get along so well. We then rode our bikes, and then Jude got caught up with Mrs. Johnson. From casual conversation to mowing the lawn, obviously, there is only one step. Mrs. Johnson knows how to use her charms, and poor Jude didn't stand a chance against her lonely, grieving widow speech.

To thank him, she invited us to dinner. This is how I found myself in Mrs. Johnson's kitchen chopping vegetables for her famous *pot-au-feu*. From all the questions she asks me, it's not just her favorite recipe she's planning to cook tonight.

"You and Jude seem to have become very close."

"You could say that."

I bite my lip as I peel the carrots.

"He really is a handsome young man! If I was your age, I would be in love with him too," she says.

"I never said I was in love with him. We spend time together, that's all."

"Really? So why are you blushing? Why are you looking at him like he invented light? You see, Rocky, you don't teach the old dog new tricks. I know how to recognize love when I see it. You might not say it with your words, but your eyes and everything else scream it. Anyhow, there's nothing wrong with being in love."

"No… Except that I don't know how it could work between us."

"It's already working. Just look at the two of you," she says.

"Right, but for how long? He'll probably be recruited by a pro team by the end of the year, and then he'll fly off to his glorious destiny while I stay here… So, there's no need for me to get too attached."

Jude and Max's laughter can be heard echoing from the living room where they are playing with the dinosaur collection Mrs. Johnson bought for my little brother.

"And I shouldn't let Max get attached to him, either."

"You know, Rocky, if there's one thing in life you can't stop, it's love. It grows even in the most unlikely places, even where it's not supposed to bloom."

"You're right," I say.

Anyway, it's already too late for my heart to get out of the way.

"Of course, I'm right, and in the meantime, enjoy life, Rocky, the beautiful opportunities it gives you, even if they are fleeting. They are worth living. Take this advice from an old lady who is full of regrets."

"What regrets? You had a wonderful life. You seem to have achieved everything," I say.

"Beware of appearances, my child. I may have missed out on my Jude, because of my parents, because of what society demanded of young women in my time. We were much less free than you, but that's a story for another day."

"Your Jude?! I want to know! I thought you had always been in love with your husband."

"I did love him, yes. I eventually learned to love him. He was a loving man, a wonderful father. We had a happy and quiet marriage, but I missed out on that love." She waves her hand between me and the living room where Jude is. "The one that keeps you from breathing when he's away. The one that makes you feel invincible, painted in color when the rest of the world is gray. True love, passion, the one that inspires poets."

I'm speechless as I watch her peel the potatoes, my eyes unfocused. Obviously, she still hasn't forgotten her first love.

"What was his name?"

"Who?"

"This man, the one you are still in love with."

"It does not matter! Besides, a woman doesn't reveal all her secrets. What I can advise you is to listen to your heart! We never regret what we did, but always what we have not done! Maybe this story that seems impossible to you today can work. Who knows? But if you don't try and stay closed like an oyster, it won't work, that's for sure."

"I don't see how."

She puts her hand on mine to comfort me.

"Have faith. The future has more imagination than you, Rocky!"

I meditate on these good words, which seem to resonate in me like a revelation, and repeat to myself, like a mantra: "The future has more imagination than me."

"Mmm, it smells divine in here. I'm starving," Jude interrupts, followed closely by Max.

And my body's first reaction is to get up and curl up against him. Of course, I don't, because first, I have my dignity, and second, it would contradict everything I just explained to Mrs. Johnson.

"That's a good thing! We've cooked enough to feed a regiment. In fact, you should invite your friends! I've really made a lot tonight, and I don't want all that food to go to waste. Rocky, don't you want to invite your two girlfriends?"

"Isa and Alyson?"

"Yeeess!" Max shouts. "I want to see Isabella."

"Okay, but are you sure you don't mind? I mean, it's going to be crowded."

"I love having company and being around young people makes me feel young too."

"But you are, Mrs. Johnson! Still young and glowing."

Her eyes light up, and she blushes slightly. The Hartnett charm has struck again. And I have to admit, that bothers me a little. Am I seriously jealous of my 70-year-old neighbor?

"What a charmer, this Jude! Ah, if I was your age, Rocky wouldn't stand a chance."

"Mrs. Johnson! Are you flirting with my boyfriend?"

As I say these words, Jude looks at me, his eyebrows raised, as if to say, "Am I your boyfriend now?" I choose to ignore his self-satisfied smile to better focus on my carrots.

"It's possible! Jude, you can also invite friends. The recipe for a good dinner is good food and gender balance. Of course, if they're as handsome and muscular as you, that can only be a plus!"

"Mrs. Johnson," I chuckle again.

"What?! An old lady has the right to treat herself once in a while," she says.

The four of us laugh and continue to cook, because there is plenty to do! Alyson and Isa said yes to the invitation, and what's even crazier is that Alec and Scott also agreed to come. And I thought the football team was spending Saturday night in the devil's antechamber trying to break into the Guinness Book of World Records for fucking. I was far from imagining that they would accept to come and eat at my neighbor's house, in a residential district of Providence. Once again, I was wrong. Not only did they come, but we spent a wonderful evening, between laughter and animated conversations.

Maybe Mrs. Johnson is right! The future has more imagination than I do.

29

Jude

Rocky is lying on my stomach, exhausted and languid. We just had sex in the shower, then against the sink. She was trying to dry her hair, her robe sagged, and that was enough to turn me on. Then we ended up on this bed, and I don't have a drop of cum left to share. She drained me.

She drives me crazy. I am absolutely, completely, totally crazy about this girl and I don't think I've ever been so happy in my life. I play with her hair as she strokes my abs and places a few kisses on my pecs. A pretty smile blooms on her angelic face. Her black eyes light up, and this feeling in my chest comes back to life.

"Why are you laughing?"

"I'm thinking back to earlier. The Trivial Pursuit game… It was hilarious to see Mrs. Johnson teasing Scott."

"It's so easy to mess with that jerk. And what a fucking sore loser! I thought he was going to flip the tables on us every time he got the answers wrong."

She laughs.

"Your friend is not bad at cheating either," I say.

"Alyson? She's the worst! She's not headed for a career as a lawyer for nothing," she confirms, chuckling. "She hates losing and would kill her father and mother to score points."

"They found each other then?"

I nod.

"They're perfect for each other."

She runs her index finger over my abs. The hairs on my forearms stand up at the simple touch. A silence follows, and I bring my lips to her ear, "And we found each other too, baby."

She raises her pretty face to mine, her gaze shines brightly, a feeling of warmth invades my chest. She brings her lips to mine and brushes them gently before saying, "I think that too."

I caress her cheek and kiss her slowly, tenderly, she returns my kiss with the same intensity, it's soft, warm, and damn, I feel so close to her, at this very moment. It's like all her fucking barriers are breaking down.

"I love you," I whisper.

She lowers her eyes. Maybe not all of her barriers. She places her hand on my racing heart with an emotion in her eyes, a vulnerability that drives me crazy. I want to take care of this girl. I want to protect her. I want her to trust me. I want her to be able to tell me that she loves me without feeling like she's selling her soul to the devil. And I know for that, I have to take it slow.

I take the hand she has placed on my heart and bring it to my lips. I kiss each of her knuckles and the inside of her wrist. She looks at me with her mouth half open, her breath short.

"Do you know what I liked best about today?" I say looking at our intertwined hands. "It's that you finally admitted that I'm your fucking boyfriend. To what do I owe the honor of this new promotion? I thought I was your improvised hookup?"

"Did I say that?" she asks, a mischievous gleam in her irises. "I have no memory of it."

I groan and roll on top of her, raising her hands above her head.

"No? No memory, are you sure?"

I nibble her neck.

"Ha! Ha!" she replies laughing. "No! No!"

"I know an excellent way to make you recover your memory," I say.

"You do?"

"Yes."

I put both her hands in one of mine and use the other to tickle her ribs. The laughter and screams that emanate from her tiny body nearly burst my eardrums. She struggles like crazy, her hair spread all over her face as she turns her head from left to right. I stare at her, amazed by her beauty. She is unable to hold back her bursts of laughter.

"Okay! Okay! Stop! It comes back to me!"

I stop tickling her, she is out of breath. Her cheeks are red. I sweep her hair to clear her face.

"So? Did you get your memory back?"

She thinks, with smiling eyes. She is such a stubborn person.

"I'm warning you, Rocky, I'm not going to let up until you confess."

She raises an eyebrow. Her delicious mouth breaks into a huge smile and she whispers, "Never."

"Okay, you asked for it."

"No!"

I redouble my effort, to make her go crazy. She laughs and struggles like a tigress, and suddenly she screams in pain and freezes. I freeze myself and release her immediately.

"Shit! Sorry, Balboa, I didn't mean to hurt you. Sometimes I don't measure my strength."

She opens her eyes, gives me a devilish grin, then she locks my legs with hers and turns me in a quick stealthy motion to sit over me, trapping my hands in turn above my head. I am a prisoner of a goddess, and I love it. A few millimeters from my lips, she announces triumphantly, "I got you."

"Cheater!"

"And you forgot that I did jujitsu."

She's on top of me, beautiful as an angel, her brown hair forming a silk curtain between us. I free myself from her grip and pull her to me, unable to resist her. She immediately rubs her pelvis against mine, and here we go again.

I grab her mouth and let her do what she wants with my body. She is on me. I devour her breasts. She gets aroused, moves, and slides on my cock. I bite her shoulder, she pulls on my hair, I slap her ass, turn her around and pull on her hips so that she offers me her ass, her splendid ass. She crashes with a cry of surprise, face, and chest on the bed, pulling at the sheets. I lick her. Her pussy is soaked, she gasps with pleasure. I play with her ass and lick it there, too. Damn, I so want to take that part of her. But it's not something you improvise. I grab the last condom I have from my jeans pocket, then thrust into her without warning, groaning. My balls thump loudly against her ass, again, and again, and again. Then I let myself go to the frenzy which seizes me. I can't stop, completely crazy about her. I pound her hard, fuck her, possess her furiously, to tell her she's mine, today, now, forever, to crush that she could one day belong to someone other than me.

She moans my name while trying to muffle her cries in the mattress. The most beautiful symphony. Her mouth runs out of air and her back is covered in a film of sweat. She is beautiful! A hottie, and I'm crazy about her. I fuck her hard and clench my teeth. She takes me like a champ and moves her hips to impose her own pace. She's absolutely not passive, ever. She moans louder and louder. I yank on her hair to pull her towards me. She is close, so close to cumming. I feel her vagina contract, and she lets go. This time, her orgasm is so powerful that she has trouble staying on my cock. This sensual vision finishes me off and I explode in turn, then collapse on her, completely drained and totally in love.

30

Jude

The months that followed can be summarized in two words: happiness and sex. I spend all my free time with Rocky, with her or in her, depending on the circumstances. She does her homework by my side, I make her review her lessons, sometimes dressed, sometimes naked. She comes to encourage me with Max during my home games, we go on motorcycle rides, parties with friends, and we watch all the old movies that I manage to dig up, in her room or in mine. It's paradise, and I'm falling more and more in love with her each passing day.

So, in love that the idea of having to leave her to join the Chicago Bears in a few weeks is killing me. I haven't talked to her about it yet, and I've asked the others to keep their mouths shut too. So far, no one has let it slip. I am surprised that trolls on social media have not dug up the information yet. It came together much faster than I thought it would. The team manager came to see my last game, the one we played against Harvard. I excelled during this game, determined to prove to my previous coach that he made a big mistake by letting me go.

The tension was at its peak. There was a lot of name-calling and pushing and shoving, but I kept up the pressure, scored three touchdowns, including an acrobatic one, and I was offered a contract which I signed on the spot. The salary is insane: tens of millions of dollars, in the first year. Impossible to say no to. I'll be able to buy the house that I have always dreamed of giving to my mother. I'll be able to buy her ten fucking houses with this money.

She cried when I told her on the phone. And that made me proud. It's my turn to spoil her to thank her for all the sacrifices she made for me. My mother never hesitated to sacrifice herself and to encourage me to believe in myself. Now it's normal that she is the first to take advantage of my new status as a professional football player in the NFL. Damn, it's good to repeat that to me! The little boy from Warwick who dreamed in front of these posters succeeded in the challenge. The only problem is that I won't be able to finish my year at Brown, and therefore not graduate. I tried to negotiate, but it was impossible. There are six months of intensive training camp before the season officially begins. Which means I have to leave in December.

I should be gloating at the thought of realizing my dream, but there is still one shadow: Rocky. I don't want to lose her. I know I need to talk to her. But what the fuck am I going to say to her?! *Leave with me?! Take Max! Drop out of architecture school, drop out of your life, and follow me.* I know she won't. She's got too much responsibility, and besides, what am I offering her? To be my groupie. To wait patiently for me to come home from training or games. I know she's going to refuse my proposition, she's already having a hard time confessing her feelings to me, so leaving everything for me...

The few times we talked about the future, she explained to me that she did not want a long-distance relationship. Her fucking lack of trust again. Fear of being consumed by thoughts and jealousy. For her, it's clear, our relationship has an expiration date. The day I leave to play football, we end our story. And I'm not ready to lose her.

"What kind of music do you want to listen to?"

Rocky's voice brings me out of my thoughts. She's sitting in the passenger seat of my Jeep and wearing her best dress. Her hair is arranged in one of those complicated buns that she took three hours to do by following a tutorial on YouTube. My girl and her tutorials. It's quite a story. We laugh every time she tries to solve the most incredible domestic problems with a tutorial.

"Why are you looking at me like that?"

"Because I love you and think you're beautiful."

She blushes and thanks me. Rocky has dressed up to impress my mom, and she's stunningly beautiful as always. I take her hand in mine and kiss the inside of her wrist.

"Well, you didn't answer me. What do you want to listen to?"

"Whatever you want, babe."

"Um…"

She bites the inside of her cheek and searches for a song on her phone's playlist. "Then it will be Kings of Leon."

"Perfect."

The voice of Caleb Followill emerges from the speakers, and my Rocky begins to hum absently, while munching Twizzlers that she offers to Max in the back. The latter has his nose buried in a book and barely answers her.

She turns around again, sighs, and lowers the mirror to do her hair again. I recognize the deep wrinkle she has on her forehead. She's nervous because she's worried. She is afraid my mother won't like her. No matter how much I tell her that it's impossible, that everyone who knows her loves her. So why should it be different with my mother? But this stubborn woman won't listen to me. How does she manage to be so perfect and feel so unworthy? She literally cried when I told her I wanted her to have Thanksgiving at my house in Warwick.

"You want me to meet your mother? Why? I'm not the kind of girl that mothers like," she told me, before giving me all the possible and imaginable reasons why it's the worst idea in the world.

I just stared at her, hugging her around the waist. I begin to know her, and when she's like that, in this state of doubt, I must not talk, just be there, present. Her face went through all the emotions, then she finally admitted to me that she was scared. I reassured her as best I could with my words and my kisses, she finally accepted, and here we are.

"We're almost here."

She swallows when she sees the *Warwick* sign appear.

"Everything will be fine, Balboa!"

I take her hand in mine before we get off the highway. We're driving through my town. Rocky looks out the window. There is not much to see, it's a rather modest city devastated by de-industrialization. When we arrive in the street that I grew up on. I park the car. Rocky collects the pecan pie she made for the occasion while I help Max down. We enter the building.

"My mother lives on the third floor," I announce. "We will avoid taking the elevator. Half the time it gets stuck."

Rocky grabs her little brother's hand and follows me up the stairs in tense silence. When we arrive in front of the door, I pass a hand on Rocky's back to help her relax, I kiss her temple before whispering in her ear, "Don't worry, babe! My mom will love you."

Rocky

His mother hates me!

I knew it the minute I shook her hand. She looks at me as if I was a fly she'd like to swat with her shoe. There's nothing I can say or do that will find favor in her eyes. I barely had time to walk through the door when I was already judged, condemned to the rank of "not good enough for my son." And the contempt I see in her eyes only confirms it.

This meeting was a very bad idea. I didn't want to come here. It was Jude who insisted. And as usual, he always gets what he wants. Originally, it was to cheer me up. I didn't win Mr. Gravel's competition. So, I didn't win the ten thousand dollars I needed so badly. I had planned to leave for a few days with Max. There is no one to blame, except me and my lack of commitment.

"You and Max could come with me to Warwick! I want to do Thanksgiving with the two women in my life," he told me after an explosive sex session.

He knows that I don't have all my neurons after the multiple orgasms he gives me. So, like the good strategist that he is, he announces the boring stuff at that moment. When I'm out of breath, and I don't know my name anymore. And it worked. I let myself be fooled. So here I am, in Mrs. Hartnett's living room, with the most conservative dress Isabella has helped me find at a thrift store, my poor pecan pie, and my little brother hiding behind my legs.

Mrs. Hartnett is beautiful, very beautiful. A tall brunette with blue eyes, who looks younger than her age. I understand where Jude's beauty comes from. But the comparison stops there because she is as cold as her son is boiling hot.

Don't think about that now, it's indecent.

I blushed as she throws questions at me, and obviously I'm still giving the wrong answers, because the line of displeasure on her forehead keeps deepening with every answer, I give her. First of all, I'm not Irish. And she doesn't like that. Only a true Irish woman can understand her son. Second, I'm not a Catholic. Judging by all the crosses in the apartment, that's also a problem. She hates my first name too.

"*Rocky*? Is your name really *Rocky*? It's not short for *Roxanna* or *Rochelle*?"

"No, that's really my first name."

"Erm… That's interesting!"

By *interesting*, she means white trash.

"And can you cook, Rocky? My son loves to eat."

Is she serious?! What question is that? I have thousands of things to answer to that. We're not in the 18th-century anymore, that her son has two arms and two hands, in addition to a dick, and that he can use it to feed himself. But of course, I don't say any of this out loud. I want her to like me too much, so the words that come out of my mouth make the feminist in me cry.

"Yes, I can cook."

"Very good, my boy needs a girl who is good in the kitchen. He loves to eat. And he doesn't have time with his classes and training."

And me, I have time?! I scream in my head.

I purse my lips not to reply, not to let my fiery temper override my desire to please Mrs. Hartnett, because I really, really want to please her. Thankfully, Jude comes to my rescue.

"Stop your interrogation, Mom! You're making Rocky uncomfortable."

He hugs me from behind and rests his chin on the top of my head.

"Is that right? Am I making you uncomfortable?" she asks, looking at me like an IRA terrorist.

"No, not at all."

I smile at her. She smiles back at me, but her smile doesn't reach her eyes.

She looks away to Max, still hiding behind my legs.

"And who is this little boy?"

"This is Maxwell, my little brother."

I don't know if Jude has explained my situation to her or not, but she doesn't ask me any questions and gives Max a huge, sincere smile. Apparently, her dislike is only for me.

"Now that you've arrived, I'll show you your room!"

"Our bedroom?"

"Yes, well, this is Jude's room. But he's going to sleep on the sofa, because you can do what you want at home, but here, we don't fornicate before marriage."

Forni... What? We're going to spend the night here? That's news to me.

"Mom, we only came for dinner, we're not going to stay," Jude objects.

"There's no way you're going on the road tonight. It's not safe."

"We didn't bring any clothes for tonight. Rocky doesn't have pajamas, neither does Max."

"I'll lend them something, of course. Are you questioning your mother's hospitality?"

Clearly, Mrs. Hartnett is not the type to take no for an answer. And she'll uses everything to get her way.

"We're going home, Mom."

"No way, it's too far," she says firmly.

Jude runs a hand through his hair and sighs. "Providence is half an hour away by car, no need to act like you're from Connecticut."

She caresses his arm.

"In that case, why don't you come visit your poor mother more often? If it's next door?"

She is tough! Obviously, recklessness and determination run in the blood of the Hartnett family.

"I'm a very busy boy."

"Too much, actually!" she says, giving me a sideways look that makes me uncomfortable. "Besides, you're going to celebrate your success with your friends, I invited them. They can't wait to see you. And we all know you can't drink in moderation."

Celebrate his success? What is she talking about?

I watch Jude scratch the back of his neck, a gesture he does when he's embarrassed or hiding something. I don't pay too much attention to it because I'm realizing that we're going to spend the night here and that I haven't been asked my opinion.

The idea of ordering an Uber crosses my mind, but Warwick is half an hour from Providence, and I'm broke.

Jude turns to me and takes my hands in his.

"Rocky, do you mind sleeping here?"

He seems sorry for putting me in front of a *fait accompli*. What am I supposed to say to that? Especially with the Gestapo watching me and waiting for me to give her a good reason to hate me.

"No! Actually, I would love to spend more time with your mother."

Like the good girl that I am. I hope she sees that I'm making an effort.

She approves of me being accommodating.

We follow Elena to Jude's room, and there, I enter his childhood. His bedroom is classically masculine. A queen-size bed covered in a blue checkered comforter, a dartboard and darts on the door, posters of Tom Brady and other NFL legends on the walls, and multiple trophies on his desk.

Above is a corkboard with pictures hanging on it. I smile when I find one of Jude wearing braces. I wouldn't have imagined it. In each of these photos, he is surrounded by friends, and he is often in football gear of different colors. Looks like he learned to play before he learned to walk.

"Don't judge me," he says while I'm already thinking of the many jokes I can make later.

Max seems fascinated by his trophies, and Jude kneels down to explain where each is from, I love the way they are together. They've gotten to the point where they don't even need me in the room to have fun. Jude shares his passion for football with Max, and Max shares his passion for dinosaurs with Jude. They have become very close, and that delights me as much as it scares me.

Mrs. Hartnett returns with clean linens which she puts on the bed.

"Here, this should be enough for the night."

"Thanks."

I continue my joyful exploration, and it's clear that at any age, Jude was a handsome kid. He is confident, smiling, the center of attention in every picture. Quite the opposite of me. Suddenly, I realize that I don't have any pictures of myself as a child or teenager, and the thought saddens me.

"Jude has always liked blondes," his mother says when she notices me staring at a picture of him smiling with a princess on his arm.

They've obviously just been crowned prom king and queen.

I can't help but run a hand through my hair.

"He must have changed his style."

I don't know how to take that remark, so I don't say anything.

"Well, that's not all, but dinner is in less than an hour, and I'm far from done, so I'll let you get settled."

"Do you need a hand?"

She seems surprised by my offer.

"I'd appreciate the help."

I kiss Jude and follow his mother into the kitchen. She gives me a red and white apron that I hastily wrap around my waist. She then asks me to prepare mashed sweet potatoes. When she reads the confusion on my face, she laughs and tells me to boil them first.

We cook in silence for a while. She tells me what to do and I obey without flinching, hoping that my submission and my effort will help her to appreciate me better. And I think it does. Every gesture seems to bring us closer. Her face relaxes, becomes warmer. And derogatory remarks are less frequent. She asks me questions about my studies, about what my future plans are.

"Architect."

"That's great. Why architect?"

I remember Jude asking me the same question. They both have the same curiosity, the same desire to understand what inhabits and fascinates the other.

"I have always been fascinated by things that have a history, and buildings through the ages remain the best witness to each era. Besides, I love to draw. It was one of my teachers, in high school, who suggested this path to me. I wasn't really planning on it."

In fact, the real reason, the one I put in my entrance essay to Brown, and which got me a scholarship, is more embarrassing. As a kid, when I slept in my mother's car or wherever we landed, I dreamed of having a house of my own. And I spent my time drawing it. A house with a garden where I could play. A house with several bedrooms where my imaginary brothers and sisters would sleep. A huge kitchen where we would share our meals, and a living room with a fireplace where we could all gather by the fire. I added more and more details as time went by.

"That's interesting," Mrs. Hartnett replies, pulling me out of my thoughts. "Not an easy path."

"No, but I am determined to succeed."

"I can see that."

She glares at me again, and I'm not sure I understand her tone and what it implies.

"And my son, where did you meet him?"

"At a party organized by his brotherhood."

"And did he seduce you?"

"At first, it is rather me who seduced him."

She smiles at me with that smile that again doesn't reach her eyes and answers curtly.

"Of course, you did. He's a catch, a future NFL champion."

A long silence follows. I cut, mince, she cooks, browns and fries. She compliments me on my ease with a knife. I explain to her that I work in the cafeteria on campus and that's where I learned to use one. She seems to appreciate the fact that I work. And once again, the atmosphere is heating up between us.

"And your little brother? You're raising him alone, right? Jude explained to me."

"Yes."

I cleared my throat not knowing whether to elaborate on my answer or not.

"And you rely on Jude to help you?"

"What? No!"

I frown, a little surprised.

"Jude would do anything for his friends. He seems to be crazy about you and that little boy. But he doesn't have time to play dad. He needs to focus on his career. He's a very generous boy, too much so. It's easy to mistake his kindness for weakness," she says dryly.

Her comment hits me like a ton of bricks, and I drop the knife in my hand. I pick it up, a little confused, and apologize. I can't find the words to answer her. She doesn't expect an answer from me anyway, because she's already busy taking the turkey out of the oven as if nothing had happened.

"Well, everything is ready, we will soon be able to eat."

I swallowed, torn between wanting to scream or cry. An all-too-familiar feeling grips my throat. I feel illegitimate. Not in my place, not good enough. Jude had managed to make me believe otherwise for a moment, but his mother, she sees clearly. She knows I'm not good enough. She knows I'm not up to it. And how to blame her? She wants what is best for her son.

The rest of the evening passes as if in a fog. I meet Jude's friends. They all seem nice and happy to meet me. I try to listen to the conversations, to participate in the exchanges, but my heart is not in it. Jude asks me fifteen times what's wrong. But every time I try to talk to him, everything gets stuck in my throat. The fact that his mother is glaring at me, waiting for me to ruin Thanksgiving for everyone, doesn't help me relax.

Once dinner is over, the dishes are done and the kitchen is scrubbed, I carry Max, who has fallen asleep on the couch, into the bedroom. I tuck him in, kiss him and go back, still feeling down, to the living room, where laughter can be heard. Jude looks so happy here among his friends. When he sees me, he smiles at me, "Come here, babe."

I sit next to him and listen to their stories of youth. Jude and his buddies offer to join the rest of the gang at The Logan. Obviously, this is where they hang out most of the time. I refuse, because I want to stay with Max, but everyone insists, and Elena offers to keep him. I hate this idea, but facing the general insistence, I capitulate.

31

Rocky

"Jude, who's that hottie on your arm?" shouts a dark-haired Mexican man, as soon as we cross the threshold of the pub.

"Rocky Prescott, this is Paul Sanchez."

"Ah! Are you the famous Rocky?"

"*Famous*? What do you mean?"

"Because Jude was so eager to impress you that he had me come from Warwick to fix your car. The worst part is that he didn't have your address or your number at the time. It was the first time I had seen him so depressed. Usually, it's the chicks who run after him. But you, my dear, you're the one who made him run."

I look at Jude who caresses the back of his neck, a little embarrassed.

"She gave me a hard time, it's true, but it was totally worth it."

He hugs me from behind like he loves to do and rests his chin on top of my head, while I thank his friend for doing me a favor.

Paul is short in stature, especially next to Jude, but he has the most infectious smile I've ever seen. And just being in his presence relaxes me. There are some people you just feel comfortable with right away. Paul is one of them. The two friends exchange news while I observe the pub with its dark and cozy decor.

The Logan is small and smells strongly of beer. It has a solid wood counter and screens showing hockey, football, and basketball games. It is the most typical and friendly place in town. A tattooed giant stands behind the bar and chats warmly with the customers. They all seem to be regulars and friends of Jude's, who came mainly to see him. He must have been pretty popular in high school, because there are at least thirty people who greet him, pat him on the shoulder, comment on his latest exploits on the field. I'm introduced to dozens of smiling faces, so much that I have trouble remembering the first names. Jude doesn't let go of me and leads me to a bench at the back of the room where other of his friends are gathered. Apparently, the inner circle, his high school football team of which he was captain. We are barely seated when pints of dark beer are pushed in our direction.

"I hope you like Irish beer," he says before taking a long sip of his Guinness.

I take a look at his Adam's apple, his lips, and his strong arms.

"I love everything Irish."

He places the glass on the table and offers me his best smile.

"It's a good thing I'm all about authenticity."

He grabs my face and kisses me passionately. I'm a little surprised by his fervor, especially in front of this audience, but I let myself kiss him and pull on his polo shirt as if I wanted to tear it off. His lips, his warmth, his scent so masculine, so bewitching, are the perfect antidote to my gloomy mood.

"I love you, babe, and I'm so glad you agreed to come. To meet all the people I care about."

"The pleasure is mine. Really."

I try to smile, but Jude reads me like an open book.

"Hey… are you okay? You've been weird since earlier."

"Yes, I'm fine."

My voice quivered slightly, and it didn't escape him. He caresses my cheek, as he often does, with his thumb on my lower lip and his caramel green gaze that has the ability to see through my soul. He sighs.

"I know my mom can be tough sometimes. I'm sorry about all the bullshit she said about your name."

"That's okay."

She's said worse, if he knew…

"Listen, she may seem unfriendly, but you have to understand that she is extremely protective. For years, it was just her and me, so she has a little trouble sharing me. And no one can ever live up to her son."

He rolls his eyes, a little embarrassed. "When I was a teenager, she scared away all my girlfriends."

"Did she?"

The fact that I am not the only one who does not find grace in her eyes reassures me a little. I understand, at this moment, that it is not particularly me that she hates, but all the girls who have the misfortune to approach Jude.

"Oh yes!"

He takes a long sip of his beer.

"All your blonde girlfriends, you mean?"

"Did my mom tell you that?"

"Yes, apparently, you had an obsession in high school," I say.

"Nonsense. It's pure coincidence. I was mostly banging cheerleaders back then, and it turns out they all had the same profile."

"The captain of the football team who fucks cheerleaders," I say, rolling my eyes. "So, cliché. You disappoint me, Jude Hartnett."

He gives me a half-playful, half-sorry smile. "I wanted to verify that the rumor was true."

"What rumor?"

"That flexibility was a plus in bed."

I spit out the sip of beer I just swallowed.

"What a pervert!"

"I don't pretend otherwise. But I was a teenager back then. The only thing that interested me was to win my games and keep my cock warm."

I burst out laughing at his honesty.

"Nothing has really changed when you think about it."

He grabs my face, slides his lips against mine, and whispers, "Except that now I'm in love with a jujitsu champion. And you know what? She proved to me that the rumor was true."

He presses his mouth to mine, pulling a sigh of pleasure from me. His tongue makes its way sensually and explores the inside of my mouth. He tastes like beer and Jude. I've missed him. I spent too much time trying to impress his mother, not enough with him. And I intend to fix it, and immediately. I deepen the kiss, savor it like we're alone in the world, and when he releases me, we're both panting with desire.

"Is it talking about my exes that turns you on? Or my mother? Because, in this case, it's really weird, Rocky."

I stifle a laugh.

"No, it's being with you that makes me happy."

"Yeah?"

"Yes!"

We stare at each other for a long time before being interrupted by Paul.

"Jude, when you're done swallowing your girlfriend's face, you can come play pool with us."

He raises an eyebrow and steals another kiss.

"Would you like a play pool?"

"Yes, definitely!"

***

"That's my Rocky!" shouts Jude, carrying me in his arms when I sink the last balls into the pockets, earning us a third straight win.

We then play a game of darts, and I impress everyone with my skills. Jude is so proud of me that he spends his time kissing and hugging me. We make a great team. The glasses of beer follow one another, and the shots too. Paul and I get along wonderfully. This guy is super nice and has a great sense of humor. He tells me the stupid things they did during their childhood. I learn that Jude was a thug in his spare time, and that he didn't hesitate to make small deals to pay for his equipment.

"So, you were dealing pot in high school? It's absolutely against the gentleman's guide," I say, wrapping my arms around his neck.

"I have absolutely no idea what you're talking about, officer," he replies, raising both arms in the air and pretending to be innocent.

I laugh and kiss him on the neck. He slides his hands over my butt, not at all embarrassed that there are all those eyes around us.

A voice rings out on the improvised mini-stage, and Hugh, the bartender, declares the karaoke open. Everyone screams, between joy and displeasure.

"Karaoke? I love karaoke!" I say.

"Do you want to sing?"

"Yes, why not?"

"How many beers have you had, Rocky?"

"I don't know, maybe three," I answer.

"And how many shots?"

"Um… Two! What is your point?"

"I think you're drunk, and the last thing you want to do is bawl into a mic."

"Bawl? me?! I'm gonna pretend you didn't just insult my wonderful singing skills."

"Babe, you have a lot of skills. But singing is really not your thing. I've heard you sing enough in the shower to know that."

"We see about that!"

With a determined look on my face, I step away from him and step onto the tiny stage. I whisper into Hugh's ear, and he nods. In a few seconds, the first notes of "Shallow" are heard. I look at Jude, who is torn between amazement and amusement. I sign to him to come closer. He shakes his head no. I insist. My drunken state gives me courage. I get the crowd to chant "Jude! Jude! Jude!" with me. The latter ends up giving in to social pressure, and when he stands in front of me, he looks amused and embarrassed. I sing the first lyrics.

"*Tell me something, boy…*"

And the whistles in the bar rise.

Surely because I'm out of tune.

Jude shakes his head and whispers something incomprehensible. I shrug my shoulders, approach him and hold the mic under his nose when it's his turn to sing. He refuses at first, which triggers reactions in the audience that I accentuate by waving them on.

"Damn it, Rocky, I'm going to kill you! What are you making me do?"

"Come on! You're not going to tell me that the tall, handsome Jude Hartnett is afraid of a tiny humiliation."

"OK, but you're going to pay for it!"

And just like that, he grabs the mic and sings Bradley Cooper's part.

He doesn't even have to follow the screen with his eyes, because I've made him listen to this song enough since he declared his love to me by paraphrasing Lady Gaga so that he knows the lyrics by heart.

He sings out of tune of course, but his raspy voice still gives me chills, and his natural charisma does the rest. The room is completely conquered by our poor performance. We sing! We sing out of tune and overplay the emotion, while adding sexy gestures. It's who will make the audience scream the loudest. We finish the song by making out under the laughter and the clamors.

"OK! OK! OK! Get a room," Hugh scoffs, picking up the microphone.

After that, everyone felt like doing the show, and the evening ended with improvisations on old raps and typical bar songs.

***

"Shhhhh!" Jude says with his index finger over his mouth, telling me to keep it down.

And I don't know why this vision makes me laugh, but I try to contain my laughter. The thing is, he's the one making a hell of a noise and he's having a hell of a time finding the keyhole. He ends up dropping the keychain on the ground. He turns back to me, a lazy smile on his lips.

"Fuck it! We're going to sleep here."

"No way! We can't do that! Let me try. Move over."

"Mmh… I like it when you give me orders," he says, pulling me brutally towards him, which makes us lose our balance.

Luckily, we catch up in extremis but that doesn't prevent us from bursting out laughing.

He looks at me smiling like the devil.

"You're pretty? I love you. Will you marry me?"

I laugh for my answer. Anyway, after all I drank tonight, the whole universe feels like a big joke. I bend down to pick up the keys and miraculously manage to open the door.

I turn back to Jude who is busy kissing my neck and rubbing his pelvis against mine, once again igniting that glowing fire in my insides that never seems to go out when he's around.

"Girl power."

"Dick power," he replies before pressing his lips to mine and kissing me as he pulls me forward.

I don't know how you land on the couch, but before you know it, his mouth closes on one of my nipples and his hands end up gripping my ass. I moan as he twirls his tongue over my extra-sensitive tips.

A light comes on, and Jude hides my semi-nudity by pressing me against his chest. Tucked up against him, I'm vaguely aware that his mother, the person who is far from my number one fan, is standing in the living room doorway glaring at us.

"I think it's time for bed, young people. Rocky, I'm not showing you your room…"

"No, I'm fine, thank you. I… uh… I'll… erm…"

"Get dressed and go find your little brother."

"Yes, ma'am!"

She finally turns on her heels, after the most embarrassing moment of my life.

And like the two idiots that we are, we burst out laughing.

"It's official, she hates me!"

CECIL HARDY

32

Jude

"You should talk to her about it as soon as possible. Secrets always blow up in your face, I know something about that," Alec breathes, pushing the 300-pound barbell up.

He looks pensive. I'm standing over him in case he lets go.

I'm not sure what he's referring to exactly, but I guess it's related to the mysterious girl he loved in the past who broke his heart. The one that prevents him from being interested in anyone.

"Yeah," confirms Scott who is busy building up his lower body muscles. "Besides, it's pretty good news. I don't see why you're keeping it from her."

"You're right, but the thing is, things are going so well between us right now that I don't want to ruin everything."

"Sooner or later, it's gonna come out"

"Yeah, bro! You're lucky the news hasn't already leaked on Twitter."

"Besides, knowing Rocky, she'll be super happy and proud of you."

"I don't doubt it, but…"

What I doubt is the future of our relationship. She'll probably want to end it as soon as she hears the news, and as naive as it sounds, I want to be able to use the few weeks I have left to convince her to stay with me, wait for me, or follow me. I'm so crazy about this girl that I will comply with all her conditions. Of course, I have no desire to admit that to my friends. They already take me for a puppy dog, so I respond with the empty and universal phrase, "Forget it, it's too complicated."

"Ah, girls' stories!" laughs Adam. "When I hear you talk, feel like you've had a vagina implanted. It's pathetic, guys."

"Adam, you don't have to talk about ass, muscles, and MMA fights to prove that you're a real guy," Alec retorts, motioning me to sit on the table in turn.

He takes a position above me, securing my workout. The perfect metaphor for our friendship. No need to talk to each other to understand each other. We look out for each other, on the field and elsewhere. I will miss this bastard very much. He hasn't been picked by a team yet, but I'm sure he'll catch the eye of a coach and we'll end up on an NFL field. He is a great champion, his stats prove it, and I have plenty of videos of his performances on my laptop to prove it. I won't hesitate, once I leave, to show them to my future coach, in case he is looking for a new quarterback.

The conversations still end up drifting to more manly topics, much to Adam's delight. Talking about feelings is still not our thing. After an intense session of weightlifting and CrossFit, we leave the gym exhausted.

"You guys want to go to Shamrock for pizza?" Scott asks when we find ourselves in the parking lot.

"No, I've got plans with my girl," I answer.

Earlier today, Rocky sent me a selfie, naked with a bowl of cereal, as she has done since the beginning of our relationship. Her selfies are subtle, and her nudity is just sketched out, she adds a semi-poetic, semi-erotic comment to which I answer with a lot of improbable emojis. I promised her to come after practice. Tonight, we're watching *Rebel Without a Cause*. I love meeting her in her room, slipping into her sheets after games or training. Sometimes she pretends to be asleep so that I wake her up with my kisses, and it always ends in an explosive sex session. It's driving me crazy to think that this is all going to end soon.

"We don't see you anymore," Scott grumbles, snapping me out of my fantasy.

"We just spent two hours sweating together."

"No, but I mean, for less boring stuff. Like I don't know, having a beer with friends. Jude, you're going to be leaving soon, and I don't know, it does something to me," he whines exaggeratedly, putting a hand on his heart.

This earned him a growl from the ill-bred bear named Adam.

I know Scott well enough to know he's half-kidding me, but I know he means it too, so that warms my heart. Alec, Scott, and I have developed a form of *bromance* over the past five months. Of the whole team, they are the ones with whom I get along the best. And I'm a little sad to be leaving them. They made me feel very welcome after I was forced to transfer from Harvard, they didn't ask me any questions, they didn't try to test me either, there was no unhealthy competition between us, and I will be eternally grateful to them.

"Okay, let me text my girl and I'll meet you at Shamrock!"

"Great, you're a real bro! Adam, are you in?"

"That depends! Are we going to talk rags and feelings?"

"Oh, shut up!"

Alec grabs him by the shoulder, and he complies, laughing. Everyone heads to their cars, and I take the opportunity to text Rocky to let her know,

> Hey Babe, I'm going to go have a beer with the friends and then I'll come over.

Okay, enjoy!
I'll try to study for the approaching finals.

> I'm sure you'll rock it!

Thanks!

> Do you need anything?
> A pizza? My help? Or my dick?

No, no, and yeeess! But later.
Now, I need to focus! Have fun! Say hi to Alec and Scott!

> I will! I love you!

She responds with a heart emoji. I'm so focused on my phone that I only vaguely notice that someone is leaning against my Jeep. A voice from my past calls out to me and my blood freezes in my veins. My eyes slowly lift from my screen and rest on the one I thought I would never see again.

"Beverly?"

33

Rocky

I wake up the next morning, face half glued to my medieval architecture class homework, and the first thing I notice is that Jude isn't by my side. An unpleasant feeling clogs my throat. Where is he? He never stands me up. The horrible idea that something happened to him, a motorcycle accident, or whatever, invades my mind and makes me shiver.

I fumble for my cell phone on the nightstand, rub my sleep-hazy face, and see with relief that I have several messages, including one from Jude. I read it immediately, the light from the screen making me squint.

Sorry, babe, something came up. I'll explain later.

Sent at midnight. A bit late! But I guess he let himself be carried away by his evening and his friends.

Relieved, I get out of my sheets, take a quick shower, before waking up Max and going on with the marathon of my day.

I arrive at building B where my first class of the day is with the strange feeling that everyone is looking at me and whispering. I must have become completely paranoid. Since I found my buttocks exposed on Instagram, I have the impression of being constantly spied on. But I'm sure it's in my head. Still, that doesn't stop me from looking at my outfit to make sure it's spotless, or from running a hand through my hair to brush it back into place. It wouldn't be the first time I forgot to do my hair in my morning race against the clock.

One time I was so messed up that I put my sweater on backwards. Luckily, I can count on my little brother to notice this kind of thing and make fun of me. Otherwise, I was good at showing up like that in college. I can't even imagine what people would say about me on the #JudeHartnett. *Jude's girlfriend not only has a whale ass but is a slut. What does he see in her?* Bla-bla-bla!

I walk through the hallway, which seems endless and hostile. And when I finally arrive in the amphitheater, I see one of my classmates, Emma, waving at me. There is a seat right next to her. Perfect!

I rush up the stairs and I can swear that once again all eyes are on me. Some people even shake their heads, looking sorry. What's the hell is going on? I have something on my nose, or what? I finally join Emma and sit down with a sigh of exhaustion.

"I've been studying all night. I'm exhausted! But I'm ready for tomorrow's final," I say, taking out my laptop.

For once I'm up to date with my studies, I'm quite proud of myself. And tonight, I'm going to be able to enjoy it with my Jude. I missed him so much yesterday.

"It's really good that you managed to focus despite the circumstances."

"Despite the circumstances? Um, what circumstances are you talking about? Someone died, and I don't know about it?" I joke, a bit confused.

Emma's face paled.

"Erm, I'm sorry, Rocky. I didn't mean to make you feel bad, but you don't have to talk about it if you're not ready."

OK, now, she's totally freaking me out!

"Emma, what are you talking about? I don't understand you at all."

She widens her eyes, looking really annoyed, and clears her throat before speaking in confidence voice.

"I'm talking about Jude."

"About Jude?"

"Yes, you're not together anymore, aren't you? He's back with his ex?"

"What?!"

"Sorry, I know it's none of my business, but it's all over social media. That's why I said something."

For a moment, I don't quite understand what she's telling me. It's as if my brain refuses to process the information, or that I've switched to another dimension where nothing makes sense anymore.

"Wait, let me show you," I hear her explain. "These photos are from last night."

My heart skips a beat and the walls of the amphitheater seem to close in on me. I hardly dare to look at the horrors she's putting in front of me. Jude is in an Italian restaurant with a tall skinny blonde. They eat, staring into each other's eyes, and then there's another photo where he helps her put on her coat, and finally another, a last one, that almost rips my heart out, well, rips out the pieces I have left. Jude is passionately kissing this girl. This vision hits me like a ton of bricks, and I can barely breathe. But I still find the energy to read the post that comes with the photo, and it's the *coup de grace*: *Spotted last night, Jude Hartnett in good company. He's finally reunited with his first love, Beverly Cooper, the daughter of his Harvard coach. Aren't they too cute? #LoveIsReal#PowerCouple#Juderly.*

I drop Emma's cell phone, which falls on my legs. I try to calm my heart which beats in my ears and my lungs which refuse to supply me with oxygen. I think I'm on the verge of hyperventilating.

"I'm so sorry, Rocky," Emma says, patting me on my back, because I've been hunched over like someone just punched me in the stomach.

The people sitting in the previous row turn around, alerted by my feverish state.

"Are you okay, Rocky? You're scaring me."

"Yes, yes, I'll be fine. I just need to get out of here."

The urges to scream, cry and vomit all grip me. In a surge of survival, I grab my things and run down the stairs as if I had death on my heels, completely ignoring the protests of the professor or the astonishment of the students.

I run through the hallways. My footsteps echo on the tiled floor, I run breathlessly to the exit door, and when the cold hits my face and takes my breath away, I slide against one of the brick walls.

Why, Jude? Why did you do this to me?

Trying to come to my senses and calm the tears that flood my face, I see the photos replaying in my mind, tearing my bruised soul even more. Beverly? His first love? The Harvard coach's daughter?

He has always been very secretive about his transfer. I understand why now. And like the idiot that I am, I opened all the doors of my life to him, shared with him my secrets, even the most embarrassing. And him, he always kept me in the shadows, taking advantage of me until the return of his beloved, his only true love. I let my face fall on to my knees and cry for a long time until I am dry of tears and my sadness turns to anger.

34

Jude

Screams and whistles echo from the locker room. The guys are always loud, messing around, making stupid jokes after practice. It's our way of letting off steam after being ordered around and tortured by Coach Callahan. But this time, the screams I hear are not the usual ruckus. No, there they look both surprised and excited and amused, and I really want to know what's going on. I get out of the shower, wrap a towel around my waist, and head towards the source of the clamor. And damn, if I expected that!

All my teammates are grouped together, half-naked. Some have their shit hidden behind their helmets or hands, and in front of all those asses is Rocky, My Rocky, hiding her eyes like a little girl would.

"Where's Jude?! I want to see Jude!" she cries.

What the hell is she doing here? In the locker room? She never came to see me in training, so in the locker room? What the fuck is going on? I hope nothing serious has happened. I whistle between my fingers, which has the effect of bringing everyone to silence. All eyes are on me, Rocky's too. But she changes her mind when she notices the degree of nudity surrounding her. I make my way to her.

"OK! OK! Get the hell out of here, guys, and get dressed, damn it!"

In a general hubbub, my teammates comply. I approach my girlfriend who is red-faced with anger, shame, I don't really know. I make sure everyone is dressed decently before telling her to open her eyes, which she does. And damn! If eyes could kill, I would already be dead!

"Rocky, what the hell are you doing here?" I say, clearly irritated.

The urge to throw her over my shoulder and take her away from all those naked guys is way too hard to contain. But my protective instinct takes over.

"Is everything fine? Is Max okay?"

She looks a little stunned, challenged by my question. She shakes her head.

"Yes, well, no! Max is fine, don't worry. But I didn't come to talk about him."

I give her a puzzled look. "No?"

"No! I came here to tell you that you're a fucking asshole, Jude."

My stupid friends all start screaming as if we were in a boxing battle and that I had just taken an uppercut in the face that knocked me down.

I turn back to this bunch of assholes, my eyes filled with the promises of murder.

"You have two minutes to get dressed and get out!"

Alec, who has just come out of the shower, takes note of the situation and also intervenes before things get out of hand.

"Well, guys, the show is over! Give them privacy! Let's get out of here! Who wants pizza?"

"At ten in the morning?" Adam replies.

"Never too early for pizza," retorts Scott who looks very amused by the situation.

I know he's going to bust my balls later with this story, make fun of me and that I'm going to get it, but for now, he's in solidarity.

With his characteristic authority and Scott's help, Alec manages to make them all leave, and I silently thank them. I finally find myself face to face with Rocky. To say I'm angry with her is an understatement. But I try to contain myself because she's just as upset as I am. And the question is *why*?

"Why are you telling me all this crap, Rocky?"

"Where were you last night, Jude?"

What?!

"Is that why you came all the way here? Because I didn't come to see you last night?! I told you, something came up. I was going to explain everything to you today over coffee, not naked in the middle of a locker room full of my idiot teammates."

"A something called *Beverly*?"

Shit! How does she know that? Another indiscretion of these fucking social media people. I'm not a motherfucker. I obviously intended to tell her about my meeting with Beverly. But not here, not like this, not in the middle of the locker room, and I barely have time to finish my sentence when we are interrupted by the hoarse and gravelly voice of Coach Callahan. Damn, it's getting worse!

"Hartnett! I hope I'm getting old; my vision is playing tricks on me and you're not fooling around with your girlfriend in MY locker room?"

His stern gaze lands on both of us. Rocky has her arms folded across her chest, flushed cheeks, and glaring eyes, not at all impressed, while I'm still half-naked with a simple towel wrapped around my waist. Not the best way to prove to him that what he imagines is wrong.

"Coach! I can explain everything to you."

He pinches the bridge of his nose and takes a deep breath. "I'm listening."

"Rocky had something very important to tell me. She had an emergency… an emergency… a family emergency."

"And she couldn't call you or wait for you to wear, I don't know, pants?"

I nod, aware that my level of credibility is a little low. But if I have learned one thing from football, it is that self-confidence is the key to victory. And once again, I play this card.

"Trust me! It's not what you think."

He takes a deep breath, looks at the ceiling.

"Okay, Jude! I want to believe that you weren't about to do something stupid with your girlfriend and risk getting suspended and jeopardizing your future. So, I'm going to close my eyes to what I just saw. I'll give you two minutes to clear the floor. And, son, you should stop putting yourself in situations because of girls."

His remark makes me wince, but I am careful not to react.

"Thank you, Coach!"

He turns around and screams as he leaves, "Two minutes!"

"Rocky? Would you mind waiting in front of my car while I get dressed and come and explain everything to you?"

Against all odds, my girlfriend, who is the most stubborn person I know, agrees. She just nods and does as I ask. As I get dressed, I think about what I'm going to say to her. I rehearse my speech in my head, put on my coat, and grab my gym bag. When I arrive in front of my car, I let out a sigh of relief. Rocky is there, leaning against the door. I approach her, try to wrap my arms around her, but she keeps me away.

"Don't touch me! I didn't come for that! I came to yell at you, possibly listen to your explanations, but it will be difficult to explain this!"

She slams her phone on my chest. I grab it before it crashes to the ground. My eyes narrow when I see a picture of me and Beverly kissing. Now I understand better why she's angry.

"Listen, Rocky! It's not what you think."

This sentence seems so lame, so hollow, but at least it gives me time to elaborate my explanations. She raises an eyebrow. Her irritation is palpable and radiates from her whole body. She's about to turn into a human torch if I don't put out the fire of her thoughts right now.

"Really? Because what I think, or rather what I see, is my so-called boyfriend kissing another girl."

Her face is both hard and sad.

"I didn't kiss her, at least not willingly. We were saying goodbye and she kissed me, I immediately pushed her away. But of course, the motherfucker who took this photo failed to capture it."

She thinks, biting the inside of her cheek. I take the opportunity to get closer to her and put my hands on her shoulders.

"Rocky, you know that these Internet users are talking nonsense!"

"Yes, but this photo? And what the hell were you doing with her, when you were supposed to be having a drink with your teammates?"

"This photo is compromising, it's true, but I can find you a dozen others that involve me with other girls. I can even find you some that involve me with Alec. And all of them are bullshit. Rocky, you have to believe me. You know I'm crazy about you. I haven't spent the last five months chasing after you to then cheating on you with the first girl I saw."

"Apparently, it's not the first girl that you saw, it's your ex-girlfriend!"

She raises her eyes towards me. Her deep black irises pierce me.

"Your one true love," she adds faintly. "And on top of that, she's blonde!"

She throws her arms in the air, exasperated. I'm torn between wanting to laugh or yell at her, she's so cute when she doubts.

"Rocky! I'm crazy about you! You know I am! Why would I do such a thing?"

"I don't know."

She waves her hands in front of her.

"Because you're a guy! Because you are all idiots who always think with your dicks. Because you got tired of me…"

She suddenly shuts up and lowers her head, looking dejected.

I move forward more, lean my forehead against her. Her mouth is inches from mine. I want to kiss her so badly to erase all her doubts, but I don't. Too afraid she'll bite me.

"Rocky, look at me," she does what I ask of her. "You know I love you."

She nods.

"Then trust me. I'll explain everything to you. But not here, not in the cold in the middle of this parking lot. Let's go to my room instead."

I press my key to unlock the car, and Rocky stares at me guiltily, biting her lip.

"I'm sorry, Jude."

"Why are you apologizing? You have nothing to apologize for. I'm the one who's screwing up…"

She steps aside, and I immediately shut up. The reason for her apology is right in front of my eyes: all four of my tires were slashed. Shocked, I look at her.

"Did you do that?"

She confirms while looking at her shoes.

"Sorry, I got a little carried away by my anger."

"That's the least we can say!" I say, half-irritated, half-amused.

"But you have to understand that five minutes ago, I was convinced that you had cheated on me. This picture is really convincing and—"

"Don't you think so anymore?" I interrupt her.

She shakes her head no.

"Not really. I still need to understand what you were doing with her. And why did you lie to me?"

I stoop down to check the condition of the tires and assess the extent of the damage.

"Jude, I'm sorry about your tires and ruining the paint."

"What? Did you scratch the paint too?"

"Just a little… but I'll pay for the repairs."

She's still looking at her shoes and flinches when I burst out laughing.

"Why are you laughing?"

I take her in my arms and kiss the top of her head.

"Because, Rocky Prescott, you really did everything to me! How did you do it?"

"With a Swiss army knife, I always have a Swiss army knife in my bag just in case."

I laugh more.

This girl is crazy, and that's why I love her so much.

Rocky

A few minutes later, we find ourselves in Jude's room. We took my car, and I kept apologizing for my immature behavior. I know Jude didn't cheat on me, I knew that the minute I saw him rush into the locker room, his eyes wide like saucers. He didn't look guilty at all. And unless he's a poker player and I'm a complete idiot, there's really no way he intentionally kissed Beverly.

I'm sitting cross-legged on his bed instead of in class, while he's leaning against the wall opposite me, arms crossed, making it a point of honor to explain everything to me, "I met Beverly when I was at Harvard. We shared a few classes together. She fell in love with me and never missed an opportunity to let me know. She was also my coach's daughter, and I knew sleeping with her was a really bad idea. But Beverly isn't the kind of girl who would take no for an answer. She wanted me, she would eventually get me. She'd told me several times, but I never really took her seriously, until one night, she slipped into my bed. We had just celebrated a victory, and I had been drinking a little too much. I had gone to bed before everyone else, and she took advantage of it."

"She raped you?!" I say, my heart pounding in my chest.

"No! I was still aware of what I was doing. She rubbed herself against me, instinct taking over, I did what any other guy would do if a pretty naked girl was moving against him horizontally. So, we had sex, and after that, she had me by the balls. She kept asking me to do it again, threatening to tell her father if I didn't comply. And in football, there are plenty of rules to follow. Not fucking the coach's daughter is one. I let her take advantage of that for a moment. I really didn't want to ruin my chances of going pro because of a booty call, but when she got too clingy and started choosing the names of our future children, I decided to end this masquerade. And then she told her father everything. Coach Cooper called me in, furious, and literally assured me that I could say goodbye to my career."

"What?! But that's unfair!"

"Yes, but I had just touched his precious princess who, of course, was careful not to tell him the truth. She made everyone believe that I was a bastard, that I had used her. Even my teammates were mad at me for compromising the team's cohesiveness. My coach did everything he could to prevent me from playing. I spent months riding the bench. Once no one considered me a good player anymore, he decided to cut me. I was sure that my career was over and that my dreams were behind me. Luckily, Brown happened. They had just lost their wide receiver, and the rest, you know. After that, I told myself that I was never going to take sex lightly again. That's why, the first time with you, I was hesitant. I wanted to make sure you were emotionally balanced and knew exactly what you wanted.

"I see. But what I don't understand is why you agreed to see her again last night, after all the trouble she caused you? If I were you, I wouldn't have given her a second. It almost cost you your career."

"Yes, but last night she came to apologize."

"A little late, isn't it?!

"It's never too late to do the right thing, Rocky."

"Are you going to see her again?"

"Of course not! The only reason I agreed to see her was because I felt so guilty. You see, after I left, I found out from one of my previous teammates that she had attempted suicide and was confined to a hospital for months. I'm not saying that I was the cause of her act. She had other issues that had nothing to do with me. But I'm not a motherfucker, and seeing her last night, smiling and healthy, was a relief. Plus, her apologies were sincere. They were recommended to her by her psychiatrist to help her in her recovery. So, I wasn't going to tell her to fuck off. That's not how I work."

I smile because he's really cute, that I love him with all my heart, and after thinking I was losing him for a moment, I finally feel ready to confess my feelings to him.

"You really are a good person, Jude Hartnett. Some would say you're a gentleman."

He rolls his eyes because he hates that I think of him as a gentleman, but that's what he is: a good, honest and reliable person.

"And the kiss?"

"Ah yes, the kiss!"

He closes his eyes, looking sorry.

"As we were leaving, as I was helping her put on her coat, she turned to me and said that she wanted to do one last thing to really put an end to our story. She walked over and kissed me. I was caught off guard, but I didn't kiss her back. I'm sorry, babe. I know that seeing this photo must have hurt you a lot. But if it can reassure you, I spent my evening feeling guilty and I hardly slept a wink all night. I obviously intended to tell you everything today before the assholes of the internet stepped in and did their own thing. Unfortunately, I didn't have the time. I hope you forgive me, Balboa."

I stand up and walk towards him, looking determined.

"Not only do I forgive you, but I also believe that I love you."

His eyes widen, and to say he's shocked would be an understatement.

"You love me?"

"Yes, I'm madly in love with you and I think I've always

loved you, but I was too stubborn to admit it."

He lowers his pretty face to mine and gives me a bright smile. I wrap my arms around his neck, stand on my tiptoes, and kiss him passionately. His mouth opens, and when he slides his tongue against mine, it's like he's pouring honey on my soul and heart. It's soft, warm, and sweet. I pull on his polo shirt. He grabs my ass and pulls me back. We end up horizontally, and he continues to kiss me until my lips are swollen, then releases me so I can breathe. I take a deep breath and savor the feel of his tongue on my neck. I feel him smile against my skin.

"You love me? Fuck, Rocky! You're not telling me that because you feel bad about my car?" he jokes.

I tap him on the shoulder and turn him around to straddle him.

"Stop being silly! Although, yes, I do feel bad about your car. But I have another way to make up for it."

35

Jude

Lying on her back, I watch my girl make my cock disappear into her mouth. Damn, that feels good! And I fucking love her.

I wrap her hair in my fist to allow her better access and enjoy the show. Her cheeks hollow out, and I have to concentrate on not dropping everything into her mouth before I even have a chance to take it. Her tongue curls around my tip, and Rocky makes the sexiest little noises in the world. She plays with my balls too and leaves no inch of my anatomy unexplored. My hips begin to move mechanically with the desire to fuck her mouth.

"Yes, that's it, babe! Suck!"

She takes me several times like a champion, then releases me to catch her breath. Her hungry eyes meet mine, making me a thousand erotic promises. She smiles as if she had a diabolical idea in mind. Whatever she decides to do, I'm happy to serve as her guinea pig. She lowers herself again and slides my cock between her breasts, sucking the tip every time it pops under her chin. I can't take it anymore! I sit up with a groan, kiss her swollen, insolent mouth, before turning her around and pulling her to lay her gorgeous pussy on my face. She screams in surprise, nearly falls over, but catches herself by clinging to me. She repeats my name like a prayer when my tongue meets her clitoris. She's delicious, I literally devour her. She is soaked, juicy, and her cum tastes like desire.

"Jude, oh, my God! Don't stop, I beg you, it's so good!"

She bends down again to take me in her mouth, and it's grunts against gasps, sucks against sucks. A frantic race for pleasure. It's who gets the other one to lose their minds first. Her moans vibrate against my cock and make me want to devour her even more. I spread her butt and thrust my tongue inside her. I could do this all day, Rocky has a gorgeous, pink, delicate pussy.

I straighten her up, she's now literally sitting on my face, and I couldn't be happier. She moves her hips, choosing the friction that feels best. I suck and tickle her clitoris until she freezes. A sign, if there is one, of her imminent orgasm. I lick her one last time before massaging her breasts hard. That's all it takes for her to start shaking frantically, then sprawling on the mattress.

I take the opportunity to take a condom from my wallet. Rocky is lying on her stomach, languid, catching her breath. Her messy hair and her satin skin covered in a film of sweat are a sight I will never get tired of. I have to tell her about my contract, I have to tell her everything. She finally told me she loves me today, so maybe she'll agree to follow me.

"What are you waiting for?" she says, putting herself on her back. "Come!"

"Impatient Balboa."

"Always."

I shake my head, amused, and lie on top of her, supporting my weight with my forearms. I look at her intensely, kissing her nose, her mouth, and her forehead. I let my lips slide against her skin to her ear,

"I love you, Rocky."

"I love you too, Jude," she whispers back.

I look into her eyes.

"Yeah?"

"Yes, with all my heart."

"Then say it again."

Her eyes flicker and light up in a way I've never seen before.

"I love you, Jude Hartnett."

She blushes, and it's the cutest thing I've ever seen. I know that confessing her feelings to me is hard for her. She's spent so much time building fortresses around herself that putting herself in that position makes her vulnerable. I know that better than anyone, but I have no intention of hurting her and I think she finally understands that.

I kiss her slowly, tenderly, and she kisses me back. This kiss is sweet and seems even more intimate than what we just did. I feel her heart beating hard against mine. She slides a hand down my back and takes a deep breath. Her gaze couldn't be more serious and so intense. I read a lot of emotions: fear, vulnerability, but also hope, and love.

"Again."

"I love you!"

I'll never get tired of hearing her say those words to me.

"One more time, baby."

She stifles a laugh, and her espresso-colored eyes light up like fireworks.

"I love you!" she manages to articulate, while my mouth is already on hers.

I smile, satisfied, spread her legs with my knee, straighten her hips and sink into her all at once. She gasps, and I take the opportunity to deepen our kiss. We make love slowly, tenderly, as if we had all the time in the world, as if we were alone in the world. With each thrust, she moans, and I swallow her moans, inhaling the air she exhales. She doesn't take her eyes off me. I don't know how long this moment lasts. An eternity. A second. But every time I insert myself into her warmth, I feel like I'm swollen with love. It's a moment of grace, of fullness, of pure fusion. I know at that moment that I will never be able to separate myself from her. She's mine.

I feel I'm close, so I speed up the thrust. She clings to my shoulders as I pound into her with all my might, holding back my orgasm. I want her to come with me. And I know exactly how to do it. I straighten up, place a hand where our bodies meet, and stimulate her most sensitive spot. She moans loudly.

Then I feel her pussy contracting around me. Her eyes close and her mouth forms an O. She cums silently, giving me the green light. I do not need to be asked and let go of all the pressure that has accumulated at the bottom of my spine, before collapsing on top of her. We find ourselves face to face, eye to eye, breathless. I place a long kiss on her lips and wrap her in my arms to enjoy her body's warmth for a few more minutes, before our two busy schedules take over and put an end to this enchanted moment. After a few minutes, Rocky breaks the silence, "Jude?"

"Yes."

"Do you forgive me for your car?"

She says these words in a low voice, a little ashamed, while walking her hand on my chest.

"I promise you that I'll pay you back for the repairs. I don't know what possessed me to do this! I was so angry."

"Don't worry about it! It doesn't matter. Paul will take care of it for nothing."

And I want to add that money is not, or rather *no longer*, an issue. But to do that, I have to tell her that I just signed the biggest contract in the NFL. Seventeen million dollars for the first year. Such a crazy contract for a rookie is proof that they trust my talent. The number makes my head spin just thinking about it.

"Rocky, I have to tell you something."

She raises her beautiful face and graces me with her dark gaze. Her eyes are so deep that you can easily get lost in them.

"If you want to do it again," she says, eyebrows arched, "the answer is *no*! You're super sexy, Jude. A sex god. But right now, I have to go to my shift in the cafeteria. Tonight, come by the house, and we'll pick up where we left off. I can't wait to see *Rebel Without a Cause*."

She kisses my jaw and straightens up to go into the bathroom. I let out a sigh and rub my face. I guess I could talk to her tonight. In any case, I have to do it as soon as possible, before someone else does. Don't want to repeat the disaster of this morning.

Rocky comes out of the bathroom in her underwear. My cock is the first to notice how beautiful she is. And the worst part is that she doesn't know it. She doesn't parade in front of me. She's just fresh and natural, comfortable with her body, without overdoing it.

"I used your shower gel! I hope you don't mind."

"No, baby, treat yourself!"

"Good, because I love the way you smell," she admits, looking a little embarrassed. "I feel like you're with me all day."

I smile, and she grimaces.

"Is it me or we're getting sickeningly romantic?"

She shakes her head as if disgusted by her own remark. She dresses while my eyes devour her, regretting every square inch of skin she hides under a layer of clothing. I want her naked. I want her against me, if possible forever, and that's exactly why I need to talk to her tonight.

"Okay, Jude, I have to go."

"I got it, don't need to say it twice."

"Are you going to stay here? You don't have class? Oh, yes, I forgot," she says, leaning down to kiss me. "No need to go to class when you're an athlete."

She laughs, and I catch her before she slips away.

"Damn it! You're not going to do this again! The reason I'm not getting up is to keep you from seeing this."

I grab her hips and make her feel my erection.

She bursts out laughing.

"Seriously, Jude, are you still hard?"

"Half hard! But if you'd stayed half-naked in front of me for another minute, I would be totally hard."

"I don't know if I should be flattered or horrified."

"Both. Flattered by the effect you have on me. Horrified if you knew everything going through my head right now."

"Jude Hartnett, you're an animal."

I growl to punctuate her words, and it makes her laugh.

She leans down to kiss me. Again.

"Well, I'm leaving."

But she doesn't. She continues to move her lips against mine.

"I mean it, I have to go."

"Yeah," I say, sticking my tongue in her mouth.

She immediately melts against me and asks for more.

"Jude, I'm really late."

"I know, you should go."

"Yes, I should go."

Her sentence is punctuated with feverish kisses, and her hips are already undulating against me. My hands go under the sweater she has just put on. My little pervert helps me by raising her arms.

"Lucky I'm not the employee of the year," she purrs against my lips.

But I barely have time to register the information when her phone vibrates in her back pocket, causing her to jump back to reality. I groan at the sudden loss of her attention.

She frees herself from my arms as soon as she sees the name of the person calling her and sits on the bed. Like the fucker that I am, I get behind her and continue kissing her. Her neck, her shoulders… I stop immediately when she suddenly stands up and her tone becomes serious.

"Mrs. Johnson, I don't understand anything. Max? My mother? You saw Max with my mom?"

She remains silent for a moment, pacing and listening to Mrs. Johnson's story. From here, I can hear the panic in her old neighbor's voice, and that's enough to put me on high alert.

Rocky runs a hand through her hair as if to tear it out. Her complexion turns waxy, and his eyes widen in terror. She puts a hand to her mouth to stifle a sob. I'm on her heels, trying to understand the situation. The hairs on my forearms stand on end when I hear her say this sentence that chills my bones, "She left with Max?! Call the police Mrs. Johnson. I'll be right there."

36

Rocky

The horror has happened. My worst nightmare has just come true.

My mother is back! Not only has my mother returned, but she has taken my little brother. Just saying that sentence makes me want to collapse.

Don't panic, Rocky! She might have just taken him for ice cream, I try to reassure myself. My heart is on the verge of exploding and my head is spinning. The worst thing is not knowing. I couldn't get much information out of Mrs. Johnson who was in tears.

I take a deep breath to try to calm myself down, like they teach us in jujitsu, to clear my head, but these fucking relaxation exercises never work on me! I'm on the verge of fainting. And thousands of questions are running in my head. My mother? Back? How is it possible? Why did she come back? Why didn't the school tell me that she had taken Max out of class? And why did she come back in the house?

The school doesn't know that she is a public menace. And it's all my fault and my need to keep up appearances.

Mrs. Johnson told me she looked agitated, looked like she was on drugs and my little brother was completely terrified by her side. She took him. She took him in a car to who knows where. She's either on drugs or alcohol and she's driving. The terrible thought that she could have an accident and that I could lose my little brother forever terrifies me.

I let out a sob that was stuck deep in my throat, and it alerts Jude. A protective hand comes to rest on mine as I sit in the passenger seat of my own car. Jude is driving fast down the highway and trying to comfort me at the same time. Thank goodness he was there to take charge because I literally collapsed after hearing the news. Unable to drive, I was shaking so much. A ball of anxiety has lodged in my chest and prevents me from acting and thinking rationally. But this is not the time to lose my footing. I must be strong. I have to find my little brother, before it's too late and she takes him away from me forever.

I call my mother's number for the umpteenth time, but she doesn't answer. She hasn't answered for months. Since she left. I'm not even sure that number is still working. But I still persist, just in case. I don't know what else to do and doing nothing is driving me crazy.

The drive home seems endless and consumes what little patience I have left. My nails are gone from biting them, and my feet are pounding on the floor of the car.

"Hurry, hurry, hurry, Jude! I'm begging you."

The latter runs all the lights until he arrives at his destination. As soon as he parks the car in front of the house, I jump out of the vehicle to join Mrs. Johnson. She is busy talking with a police officer.

"Rocky, I'm so sorry. I tried to hold her back. I did everything in my power. But she didn't listen to me," she explains, shaking.

"Did she tell you where she was going?"

"No! But she really wasn't in her normal state. Her eyes were unable to focus on anything."

"God knows what she took! Oh, my God, my little brother…"

I put a hand in front of my eyes. I don't want to imagine the worst. I can't.

"Are you Maxwell Adams' sister?"

I turn to the police officer who is taking notes. The fact that he remains there, unmoved, instead of turning over every inch of the place, irritates me to no end.

"Yes!" I say, jumping up and down with impatience.

"And you are his legal guardian?"

"No."

His eyes widen in surprise.

"So, who is his legal guardian?!"

"It's my mother."

The police officer looks at me, puzzled. His bushy eyebrows furrow.

"Then you're asking me to look for a little boy who went on an errand with his mother?"

"No... I... My mother, You... You can't count on her. She hasn't seen Max in months and—"

"Where was she all this time?"

"I don't know!" I yell.

"Did you notify the police for abandonment of a minor?"

"No!"

I pull at my hair in despair.

"But you don't understand that is not the fucking problem! While we chat quietly and you take your precious notes, she may have already left the state."

"I'm sorry, miss, but I can't do anything for you. Your mother has done nothing illegal."

I step back, as if he's just punched me in the stomach, and close my eyes to escape this reality. My mother just kidnapped my brother. My world is falling apart, and this jerk is telling me there's nothing he can do!

"So, you're just going to let her go?!" I say, my voice full of venom.

"I'm afraid I don't have the authority to do anything else."

Jude puts a hand on my lower back to reassure me and steps in, "Officer, I'm sure you can patrol, try to spot the vehicle and stop it for a simple ID check. If she's on drugs, you can arrest her."

"Yes," confirms Mrs. Johnson. "She must have taken something, considering the way she behaved earlier. Please, Officer! Think about this little boy."

The officer thinks for a moment while I pray inwardly for him to accept. He finally nods his head.

"Give me a detailed description of the vehicle, as well as a photo of her and Maxwell. I'll see what I can do."

"Thank you!"

I immediately run to Max's room to look for a recent photo. There are plenty in his office. I push open the door and see that his closet is upside down and some of his things are missing, I realize then that my mother has taken him away for good. She's probably already far away and I'll never see him again.

This sudden realization hits me like a ton of bricks and makes me lose all hope. I burst into tears and felt the ground crumble under my feet.

Jude

I find Rocky curled up in a ball and in tears, snuggled up against some of Max's clothes. Seeing her like this hurts me like hell and I don't know what to do to comfort her. I sit on the floor next to her and stroke her back, she cries for a long time. I grit my teeth with an urge to smash my fist into the wall, but I mustn't let myself get angry. I have to be there for her. She needs me.

"Babe, I am sorry. I promise you we'll find him."

She finally wipes away her tears, as if she were ashamed of them. Her face is red and swollen from crying too much.

"Yeah…"

Her voice is unrecognizable, scratchy with pain and sobbing. But she's strong, she's a warrior, my Rocky, so she takes a deep breath and straightens up.

"You're right. I have to pull myself together."

She grabs the photos of Max from her desk, along with one of her mother, and slips them into her jeans pocket. Before she leaves the room, I grab her by the arm, turn her around and put my hands on her shoulders, "Rocky, be brave. For Max. We'll find him, I promise. But you have to believe it. Don't despair. Do you trust me?"

She nods and sniffles like a little girl would. A gleam of courage and determination comes back into her eyes.

"I trust you."

"We'll find him!"

"We'll find him!"

I hug her one last time to recharge her batteries, but also mine. We are going to need all the energy in the world to face this mountain. I'm just as worried as she is, but right now I mustn't show her that I'm doubtful and don't know where to start.

Rocky gives the photos to the police officer who assures us to give us news as soon as possible. On our side, we decide to check all the places where they could have gone. Mrs. Johnson offers to stay at Rocky's in case they decide to come back.

In the car, Rocky downloads the map of Providence and its surroundings. She huffs in despair and frowns.

"There're so many places where he could be! It's like looking for a needle in a haystack."

"I know, but we have to start somewhere, babe."

"Pfft! But how do we know if they went north, south, east, or west?" she says, exasperated. "We're playing the lottery here with my little brother's life. We have no clue. No way of knowing."

"The best would be to divide the map into four and cover all areas at the same time."

"How do we do that? I don't have the gift of ubiquity yet, neither do you!" she gets angry.

"By asking for help, Rocky."

"To whom?"

"To our friends! But it also means telling them everything."

She doesn't think about it for a second before agreeing.

Isa, Alyson, Scott, and Alec immediately agreed. I briefly explained the situation to them on the phone and sent the description of Rocky's mother's car, the license plate, as well as several photos. None of them asked any questions or hesitated to offer help, yet I know how busy they are. Alec explained the situation to Coach Callahan who assured him not to worry about training and even offered his help.

Rocky and I cover the north and the others share the south.

After a frantic search that lasted all day where we scoured all the sleazy bars, motels, diners, and gas stations without success, exhausted from always asking the same question and always receiving the same answer, we're on the way back. No one has seen them, they seem to have disappeared from the face of the earth. Of course, I am careful not to share this reflection with my girlfriend who is already really down.

We arrive at Rocky's house, drained and more desperate than ever. I had to argue for long minutes to convince her to go home to rest and resume the search tomorrow. If it were up to her, we would still be driving and, with fatigue getting the better of us, it was getting dangerous.

It's after midnight when we arrive. Mrs. Johnson is still awake despite her age. Her features are as drawn as Rocky's. She loves Max as if he were her own grandson. The others are home too, but no one has the desire to go to bed, so everyone is gathered in the living room. Mrs. Johnson offers us coffee which we all gladly accept. Drowning our sorrows in a strong drink will help us get through the night.

"Did the police officer call?" Rocky asks Mrs. Johnson for the umpteenth time.

"No, sorry."

She sighs in despair and hides behind her hands. I caress her back and kiss her temple, "Don't lose hope, babe."

She answers me with a stifled sob.

"The police don't give a damn about this kind of thing," Alyson intervenes, earning the wrath of everyone for her brutal honesty.

"What? It's true. What we need is a private detective. My father is a lawyer. He works with a detective who's very good! I could call him. He could help us."

"And are you saying this now?! Couldn't you have done it before?" Isabella asks.

"Sorry, but I didn't think of that. He lives in New York. I'm gonna call him."

"Please, there's not a minute to lose. Statistics prove that the best chance of finding a missing person is in the first twenty-four hours. After that, it's almost impossible," adds this idiot Scott.

Rocky bursts into tears and Scott gets a punch in the shoulder from me and a slap on the head from Alec.

"Ouch! What the fuck!"

He realizes he spoke too quickly as he sees Rocky break down and immediately shuts up.

"Don't listen to what he says, Rocky. We'll find him. Tomorrow, we'll resume the search, and this time, we get the whole football team on it. That'll give us more area to cover," suggest Alec.

"There's no point anymore. Scott is right. She probably left the state by now."

This time, tears of sadness and bitterness shake my Balboa's body, and I immediately hug her to my chest, glaring at my bastard friend. We fall into an eerie, heavy silence. When Rocky's phone starts vibrating on the table, it seems almost unreal to us.

"Hello!" Rocky says her face tense.

Immediately, tears poured down her cheeks and my fists clenched mechanically. A great relief takes hold of us all when she pronounces these magic words, "Max, is that you?"

37

Rocky

"Max?! Where are you, my little man?"

He's crying. He sounds panicked, so the joy of hearing his voice doesn't last very long and quickly gives way to anxiety.

"Rocky, it's... Mom! She doesn't move anymore. I don't know what's wrong with her. I took her phone to call you, I'm scared."

"Calm down, my love. Tell me where you are, and I'll be right there."

"I don't know. We are in a hotel by the side of the road."

"Can you tell me the name of this hotel?"

"No..."

"See if there are cups or napkins with something written on them."

I hear my little brother searching, then he says to me,

"Yes!"

"Can you read me what it says?"

"Motel Attleboro Inn," he says with some hesitation.

Without me having to tell him anything, Jude takes notes on his cell phone, and my other friends are already looking up the location on the Internet.

"Sweetie, you are going to do one last thing for me: you are going to open the door and look at the room number."

"Okay."

He does it, I hear the wind and the noise of traffic, and a few seconds later, he announces to me in his adorable little voice, "There's a four, a five, and a three."

"Great, sweetie. I'll come to pick you up. Don't move!"

"Okay."

"Mrs. Johnson, can you stay on the phone to reassure him until we get there?"

"Yes of course!"

"There are three Attleboro Inn motels around Providence," Isabella announces.

We divide up the addresses to act as quickly as possible, but this time, I'm driven by adrenaline and hope. The knocks on the door echo with the rhythm of my heart, which is beating so hard that I feel like it's going to burst out of my chest.

"Who's here?"

"Max! It's me, open up!"

The latch unlocks after painful seconds, and I finally see my little brother appear. I immediately carry him in my arms and hug him with all my strength. The oxygen finally seems to be returning to my lungs. My God, I thought I'd lose him forever. My nose in his neck, I breathe him in, touch his hair, his face, a little hysterically, and make sure he isn't hurt. Everything seems to be fine, at least from the outside. But his expression tells me another story.

"Are you all right, sweetie?"

He nods and snuggles against me again.

"Oh, my love! I'm so sorry. I'll never leave you alone again," I say, hugging him tighter.

"Rocky!"

Jude's voice snaps me out of my torpor, and I run to the bathroom to find him. I see my mother lying on the floor with a needle stuck in her arm, her face waxy, and her mouth blue. A vision I've had far too many times in my childhood. Bile rises in my throat. I want to yell at her, shake her, ask her why she's doing all this to us. But for now, I just exchange a worried look with Jude, who is kneeling beside my mother's inert body, his hand on her pulse. He reassures me with a nod of his head, and I understand that she is still breathing.

"Her pulse is very weak," he told me.

Max, in my arms, sucks his thumb, something he hasn't done for years, and watches the scene.

Jude calls for help. They ask him to do CPR until they get there. As for me, I take Max away from this tragic vision, sit on the bed, with him on my lap, and try to reassure him as best I can. He is awfully quiet as I rock him and wrap him in love. I'd rather he cries, express his fears, his sadness, or even his anger, but nothing. He's like me, he takes the horrors of life without flinching. I caress his curls while singing his favorite songs. He doesn't listen to me; his eyes are elsewhere.

The ambulance arrived and the paramedics rush to the bathroom. Jude explains the situation to them, then the voices of the paramedics scream at my mother to wake up. She doesn't answer. A few minutes later, they carry her out on a stretcher, and Max curls up more against me. The paramedics talk to me, but I don't understand what they are telling me. It's as if I was no longer in my body and witnessed the scene from afar. They are talking in slow motion, yelling at me. I don't react. It's a very strange feeling, almost pleasant. I'm here without really being here, stuck inside my head.

Jude takes Max in his arms and grabs my elbow to straighten me out. He looks me in the eye, worried. He's talking to me. His lips move, his eyebrows furrow. He takes my hands in his.

"Babe, are you okay?!"

Eventually, the sound comes back

"Yes…"

"I think you're in shock, you're shaking like a leaf."

"No, I'm fine."

"Where are they taking my mom?"

"Baylor emergency room."

"Come on! We have to go there."

***

We're all gathered in the waiting room, freaking out over someone who doesn't deserve it. My mother is in the ICU, after overdosing. Apparently, the doctors pumped her stomach. She also took antidepressants, and the drug cocktail took effect. She would have died if we hadn't gotten there in time, according to the doctors. They don't know if she will make it or if she will have brain damage.

I hate her! I hate her for her irresponsibility and her selfishness that has plagued my life forever, I hate her for what she's doing to me and to Max, but I don't want her to die. So, I find myself praying. Something I never do. I have no religious education, never set foot in a church, but desperate situations, call for drastic remedies. I improvise a prayer that consists of closing my eyes and imploring the sky, the earth, the stars, the entire universe to save my mother.

I pray with Max who is lying on the chair next to me, his head on my lap. I pray as I stroke his hair. I pray as I feel Jude's hand moving over my back. Every once in a while, he slips words of encouragement into my ear and kisses the top of my head. How does he know she's going to be okay? Nobody knows anything. And I know that life can do the worst to you when you least expect it. When I see the doctor approaching in the distance, my heart skips a beat.

May the news be good! I sit up, taking care not to wake Max. I refused to let Mrs. Johnson take him home earlier. It was, however, the most rational thing to do. But I'd rather have him with me. After what happened today, I don't think I'll ever let him out of my sight again. The idea of keeping him from going back to school doesn't seem completely excessive to me. I observe the doctor in his blue uniform. He removes his hat before speaking to me.

"Miss Prescott, your mom is a fighter. She'll be fine."

A long sigh of relief escapes me, and I jump on his neck. The poor man in his fifties doesn't know what is happening to him and freezes.

"Thank you for saving her!"

"You're welcome, Miss."

"Can I see her?"

The question almost escaped me. In fact, I don't know if I want to see her, if I want to talk to her. The fear of losing her gone, anger and hatred take over again.

"She's resting now. She'll probably be conscious tomorrow morning. In the meantime, you should go home and rest. You all look exhausted."

I turn around to see my friends' faces. And yes, they look cooked. Alyson has her head resting on Scott's shoulder, Isabella is holding Mrs. Johnson's hand, while Alec drowning his thoughts in his coffee grounds.

It's after four in the morning, and they're all still here. For me and my little brother. All my life, I felt alone, with the feeling of not being able to count on anyone, but I must admit that I was wrong. I didn't have an ideal family, that's for sure! But friends are a family we create. And after today's ordeal, I think we've reached family status.

As for Jude, he's by my side right now, solid as a rock, holding my hand and reassuring me whenever I was losing hope. I don't think I've ever loved anyone so much. I was wrong not to believe it. Love exists and his name is Jude.

Jude smiles at me when he sees that I am watching him. That dimpled smile that never fails to turn me on.

"What's wrong?"

"Nothing. I just love you."

He smiles again, then wraps me in his arms. My nose crashes against his steel pecs, and I breathe his smell.

"I love you too," he whispers, hugging me tightly.

"Come on, let's go home."

38

Rocky

"Babe, can we go to bed? I'm exhausted."

Jude's voice snaps me out of my contemplation. I'm sitting next to Max's bed, watching him sleep soundly ever since we got home. I can't take my eyes off his delicate, innocent little face. When he sleeps, he looks even younger than his age, more vulnerable. He sleeps with his mouth open and snores lightly. His curls, a happy mess, cover a part of his baby face. My little brother, the apple of my eye, he has just been through hell, and I hope what he saw tonight won't impact him for life. Whatever happens, I will be with him, by his side, to heal his wounds. Jude holds out his hand and I take it. He helps me stand up, then we head to the bedroom.

"I'm going to take a shower," I tell him, while he's already yawning and rubbing his face, obviously exhausted.

A few minutes later, I slip under the covers next to him. He turns around as soon as he feels my presence and wraps me in his strong arms. His warmth and smell immediately make me feel safe, like I'm exactly where I need to be. I place a kiss on his chest. He returns the favor by kissing the top of my head.

"Thank you, Jude... For everything you did today for me, for us."

"You're welcome, babe, of course. Besides, I did nothing. You were the one who was strong."

His voice is even deeper than usual, I think he had fallen asleep. It must be after six in the morning.

"Are you going to visit your mother tomorrow morning? Well, I guess in the afternoon, considering the time. I can watch Max if you want? Unless you want to take him with you."

"What about training? You'll get in trouble if you miss it again."

"It doesn't matter anymore."

"Why doesn't it matter? Football is your whole life, and I would hate for you to miss out on the opportunity to go pro because of me and my damn problems."

He takes a deep breath, doesn't say anything for a little while, and I think he's dozed off, but when I look up, I see his eyes are focused on the ceiling, and that his jaw is clenched, and his face is grim. That's enough to make me worry.

"Jude, are you okay? I feel like you're hiding something from me."

He clears his throat and rubs his face like he did earlier.

"I'm fine..." he says without conviction. "I'm just tired. Don't worry about me."

He turns around, places a kiss on my lips as a distraction or to shut me up.

I don't really know, but I don't let myself be distracted, at least not for very long.

"Jude, I can almost hear you thinking. There's something on your mind, and I want to know what it is."

"Balboa, now is not the time, believe me. Not after such a trying day. You need to rest, get your strength back. Tomorrow, you're facing your mother, and the last thing I want is s put another layer of problems on you."

"So, there is a problem?!"

This time my desire to sleep is completely gone. I'm wide awake. I turn on the bedside lamp by my side, then turn back to Jude who has his arm over his eyes, blocking out the sudden blinding light.

"Jude! If you don't tell me what's going on right now, I'm going to explode. You've already told me too much or not enough! And the suspense is about to kill me."

He takes a long breath.

"I swear, you can be so stubborn!"

He straightens up in turn, the sheet falls and reveals his muscular chest. But I don't have the strength to fantasize right now. He runs a hand through his hair as if he was going to tear it out, keeps both hands behind his head, then gives me a painful look, and then I swallow, because I feel that what he is going to say to me is not going to please me at all.

"Please stop torturing me and tell me what's going on."

"Alright! You know I made myself available for the pro team draft this year."

I nod.

"Well, I got picked by the Chicago Bears."

I remain silent for a moment, waiting for him to elaborate on the negative part of the story, but when nothing comes up, I give him a puzzled look.

"That's great, Jude! This is great news! Why are you acting like this is big deal? This is what you've always wanted, what you have been training for."

"It's true but…"

"But what?"

"I have to leave in two weeks."

"What? But why so soon?"

I don't know anything about football. I had understood that if he was picked up by a team, it would be after graduation, which would be this summer or fall.

I was ready to see him go in June, but not right now. My throat tightens as I try not to look too affected.

"It's part of their process. They want to send me to a training camp six months before the start of next season."

"Oh!" I try to process the news. "And you've known this for a long time?"

My voice is so low that I can hardly hear myself.

"A few weeks."

"Weeks? And why didn't you tell me?"

He shrugs a shoulder. "I don't know, I never found the right moment," he says, looking tortured.

"Jude, we've spent the last few weeks together. Almost every day. You've had more than one opportunity to tell me about it, and I—"

"I'm sorry, okay! I screwed up! I'm a fucking coward. And if you want to use this pretext to leave, fine, so be it. I would have deserved it. But we were so happy, I didn't want to ruin everything. I was afraid that if I told you about it, you'd decide to cut our relationship short. And that…"

He swallows.

"… forget about it. Hate me, hit me, yell at me, but stay."

"You're the one leaving, Jude."

My voice breaks.

People always leave in the end.

That's exactly why I didn't want this relationship in the first place. I close my eyes and bite my lip, doing my best not to let the tears escape and flood my face. Total failure.

"Rocky, please don't cry."

I sniffle and wipe my tears away with the back of my hand. I'm fucking selfish! I can't do this to him and ruin his moment. I have to be happy for him, celebrate him, because he worked his ass off to make his dreams come true. Because he's an amazing person who has stood by me like nobody else Because I love with all my heart. And that's what you do when you love someone. You support them even if it means letting him go. So, I have to put on my big girl pants and act like the responsible adult that I'm not.

"I'm happy for you, Jude. This is an incredible opportunity. You're going to go pro. It's a childhood dream come true."

I try to smile, but again I fail miserably.

"Come here," he orders me, his arms wide open.

I nestle again in his arms. I breathe in that smell that I love so much with the strange impression that it's already slipping away from me. He hugs me tightly, then forces me to look into his eyes.

"Rocky, I don't want things to end between us."

"Neither do I, but I don't believe in long-distance relationships."

"You already didn't believe in relationships, at all, and look at us. So, we're not going to listen to your point of view, okay?"

I remain silent, still a little stunned by the news.

"I'll tell you what we're going to do, we'll take it one day at a time. Tomorrow, you're going to see your mom, I want you to focus on that, and only that. Max is probably going to need you a lot in the next few days, and that's the most important thing."

I nod my head as I listen religiously to his plan.

"On our side, we'll try to spend the most beautiful moments before my departure."

"But there are only two weeks left!"

"Two weeks in paradise with you is better than a lifetime without ever having met you."

I can't help but laugh. It's better than sobbing again. Even if, right now, if I listened to myself, I would curl up in a ball and cry until I no longer had a tear in my body.

"Do you realize that what you just said is completely cheesy?"

He smiles back. "It may be cheesy, but it's entirely sincere, Rocky. I love you with all my heart! I've never loved anyone like I love you. And neither time nor distance can spoil that."

"You don't know that Jude! You say that to me today, while you're in the warmth of my arms, but once you leave, once you get in Chicago, you're going to meet people. You'll meet gorgeous girls, and you'll forget me. I don't blame you. I was prepared for it. I knew that sooner or later our story would have to end. But I didn't know it would happen so quickly, nor that it would hurt so much. You taught me something essential. You taught me to love and to trust. And for that, I'll always be grateful."

"Stop talking like that! Stop talking like it's over between us."

"That's not what I'm doing."

"That's exactly what you're doing! As always, you're scared, and you're running away!"

"What other options do I have? You're leaving, and I'm staying. The equation is simple. You leave to follow your dreams, and there's no room for me in those dreams."

"Why wouldn't there be?"

"Because you're going to live another life away from me in another city! Because you'll have so many girls around you, so many opportunities that you'd be stupid not to take advantage of them."

He growls and his gaze pierces me. "I have no desire to be with any other girl but you."

"Sooner or later, the temptation will be too strong."

"Damn it, Rocky, you're driving me insane! Stop telling me what I'm going to do, what I'm not going to do. I love you! Do you hear me? I love you! That counts!" he says, beating his chest. "And I want to live this dream with you. I was planning to ask you to follow me to Chicago at the end of the year, with Max of course!"

"You can see that it's not possible! I don't even know if I'll be able to get custody of Max. I don't know what state my mother will be in tomorrow. I'm just a whirlwind of problems, Jude! You saw that today. My problems have problems, and you deserve better than that. You deserve better than me."

Once again, my voice breaks.

"Stop repeating this crap! I thought we were past that. I thought you understood that we were a team, that your problems are my problems."

"Yes, but you are leaving, and I'm staying."

A silence ensues, and an uneasiness hangs over us like a rain cloud. Jude stares at the ceiling and thinks for a long time while I try not to drown in my despair. Two weeks. Two weekends! This is horrible! How am I going to do without him? I swallow the knot that has formed in my throat and dig my nails into the palms of my hands so hard I must be bleeding. It's a nice distraction from the abysmal pain I feel inside. The one I can't reach. The one I can't make go away. After what seems like an eternity, Jude's raspy voice snaps me out of my torpor.

"Let me prove you wrong once again, Balboa. Let me prove to you that even from a distance it can work."

39

Rocky

The next two weeks passed like a mirage and still managed to turn my life upside down.

During my first visit to the hospital, my mother initially refused to speak to me. She was agitated, psychotic, obviously in need of drugs. But after a few days, we were finally able to see each other. It was hard and painful, for me and for her. I remember that when I pushed open the door, I had a backward movement.

Rebecca Prescott lying on her hospital bed, thin, IVs in her arms, her skin almost gray, wrinkles and white hair obscuring her once-perfect face. She's barely 40-years-old but life had aged her much past that. I approach slowly, wary. I felt like I was in *The Exorcist*. I don't know which version of her I will have today: the one who screams and refuses to see me or the one who is calm. Judging by the bright smile on her face, I get the calm version.

"Rocky, you're looking more and more like your father," she says, as if that's the most important piece of information to share right now.

The fact that she's been gone for months, that she comes back from nowhere to take Max away from me, then OD on the creepy tiled floor of a motel bathroom, leaving her son in a panic, doesn't seem to be the topic she wants to talk about. As always with her. The house burns down, but we talk about the color of the curtains. That's her specialty. But I'm sick of this bullshit. Sick of not facing things. I slam a legal document on her bed before her dumbfounded eyes. She frowns.

"What is that?"

"An official document that states that you give up your parental rights and that you give up custody of Max to me."

This document is far from official. It was written for me by Alyson. She used her father's office letterhead, but that's a detail my mom doesn't need to know. My strategy is to get her scared enough to agree to go to rehab. Isabella told me about a clinic in California that works miracles. Apparently, her actress aunt went there to fight her drug addiction. She made a generous donation to them afterwards, and they agreed to take my mother for a reduced price because of it. Otherwise, it would be impossible for me to pay the fees for this kind of institution. But the hardest part is to get Rebecca to admit that she has a problem and agree to go there.

"What? There's no way I'm signing this! I have no intention of giving up on Max. He's my son, and I love him."

I let out a bitter laugh.

"You have a funny way of showing it to him."

"So easy for you to judge me, you were never a mother."

"Mom, even a common alley cat has more maternal instinct than you. So, stop playing the loving parent and sign this paper. You'll officially be rid of all responsibility. Isn't that a dream?"

My tone is dry and cold, but Rebecca Prescott has, more than anyone else, the ability to make me angry, to turn me into a monster. She crosses her arms and shakes her head. I must admit that I am impressed, I thought she would jump at the chance.

"In that case, I hope you have a good lawyer, because it's going to be hard to justify the last six months," I say, heading for the door.

"Wait, Rocky! Stay..."

Her voice is almost inaudible and makes me hesitate. With my hand on the handle, I take one last look at my mother, who looks desperate. I sigh, then return to the chair next to her and try to calm my racing heart. I'm so mad at her that it's hard to look her in the eye without wanting to vomit. There is a lifetime of unsaid words and bitter resentment between us. I'm not sure I'll ever be able to forgive her. After an awkward silence, she starts, but as always, prefers to do small talk.

"How are your studies going?"

I roll my eyes and breathe out all my frustration.

"Where have you been all these months, Mom? Do you have any idea of the harm you've done to Max? Have you even once thought about him? To call him? To give him any news? While you were out on a date with who knows who and where?"

"I'm not asking you to understand me, Rocky! I know I haven't done the right thing as a mother."

"That's an understatement," I quip.

"But you don't know the pain I went through. Sam was my whole life. His death made me lose my footing. I couldn't stand being in that house constantly reminded of his death."

"In that case, move out, paint the walls, do yoga, but don't abandon your kids!"

My voice cracks, and I hate myself for showing her an ounce of emotion. She doesn't deserve it. She deserves only my cold and hard heart, forever closed to her.

"I'm sorry, sweetheart. I'll change."

This sentence exasperates me, and I feel the rage rising in me, again.

"Do you know how many times I've heard you repeat that same fucking speech? My whole life, Mom! MY WHOLE LIFE!" I yell, almost hysterically.

My voice must have attracted attention, because a young nurse opens the door and sticks her head in the doorway.

"Is everything all right, Mrs. Prescott?"

"Yes," my mother quickly replies, a little confused.

Her gaze shifts from my mother to me.

"Miss, could I talk to you for a second?"

I hesitate, but agree nonetheless. Spending a few minutes away from Rebecca will allow me to come to my senses and calm my urges to kill.

"Are you Rebecca's daughter?"

"Yes."

"May I talk to you about her health?"

For a moment, my heart stops beating, and I imagine that she's going to tell me the worst, like, I don't know, cancer.

"The doctor and I have been watching her reactions over the past few days, and we suspect she has a psychological problem."

"Yes, she's completely crazy. That's obvious!"

"No, I mean she has a real pathology. We think she suffers from Bipolar disorder."

"Bipolar? Do you think she's bipolar?"

"Yes. Does she tend to go from one mood to another? Sometimes does she think she's the queen of the world, and sometimes she has suicidal thoughts or an inability to get out of bed?"

"Yes… She used to do that when I was younger. Then she started drinking, and her moods became chaotic almost all the time.

"It's typical, many patients try to control their unhappiness with substances. Unfortunately, this only makes their illness worse. Your mother, however, doesn't seem to suffer from the most severe form, which makes the diagnosis even more difficult to make. To be sure, we need to test her."

"Why has nobody ever told us about this? I mean, it's not something she developed overnight."

"Many people don't know that they have a psychological pathology."

"Bipolar…"

I repeat that word to get used to it.

"Are you sure about this? My mother has always been an eccentric, irresponsible person, but before this major crisis, before my stepfather died, she had managed to calm down for years."

"Maybe your stepdad was just good at hiding or managing her crisis. But if our suspicions are confirmed, it's an incurable condition, so she has always suffered from it."

Now that I think about it, it's true that Mom could spend days locked in her room and Sam would tell us that she was just very tired.

"But nothing is sure. We would need to do some extensive testing first. And for that, I need your consent."

I nod, trying to take in this new information. How could his disorder have gone unnoticed all these years? My mom hates doctors and has no insurance, so if she had any illness, she clearly wasn't aware of it. This could explain a lot of things. All this time, I thought she was selfish, irresponsible. The eternal crazy lover. Could it be because she was sick?

"What about her addictions?"

"I think she needs to go to rehab, but if we don't treat the Bipolar disorder, she might relapse sooner or later. Now, you have to realize that this is an incurable condition, but the effects can really be lessened with daily medication and therapy. I invite you to come into my office and I will explain more.

***

When I go back to Mom's room with this new piece of information in mind, I'm more open to discussion. I'm not saying that I forgive her for her behavior, but let's say that I see things from another perspective. Besides, if I want my little brother to ever have the chance to have the mother I never had, I have to put my anger aside and try to understand her. However, my patience quickly disappears when my mother is unable to tell me what she has been up to for the past six months. She says she can't remember anything, that her memory is failing her, her age, blah blah blah. What I understand is that she spent her time high and, one day, she woke up and remembered that she had a son.

"How is my little boy?" she asks suddenly.

"Good, he's fine. He's a little shaken by what he's seen, but he's strong and he'll get over it."

Well, I hope so.

"I would love to see him. Do you think he can visit me before I get out?"

"I don't think that's a good idea. I don't want him to see you, get attached again, make a thousand promises, then disappear and break his heart."

"I won't do that! I told you I'm sorry and that I'm going to change."

"How can I believe you?"

"I promise you, Rocky."

"Promises won't cut it! Not this time, not when it comes to my little brother's mental health."

She sighs. "What do you want me to do to prove to you that I've changed, Rocky? That coming close to death made me realize things I didn't realize before? You have to believe me. Everyone deserves a second chance."

With tears in her eyes, she holds out her hand for me to take. I bite my lip to keep from yelling at her that in her case it's a dozen chances, but I swallow my bitterness for my brother's sake.

"I agree to believe you, to let you back into your son's life, but on one condition."

"Which is?"

"That you agree to go to rehab."

"These places are overpriced, Rocky. You know that as well as I do."

"Don't worry about it, I've already worked it out. There's a clinic in California that'll take you for less."

"In California?"

I confirm with a nod.

"How long?"

"Two months. After those two months, if you've followed the protocol and you're sober, you'll be welcome to see Max."

She thinks for a moment and adds, "And to you?"

She holds out her hand with a pleading look. It takes all the courage in the world to agree to touch her. I end up doing it. She smiles at me, "In that case, I accept."

40

Rocky

The days that followed go by so quickly. And it's in situations like this that I wish I had the gift of slowing down time. My mother flew to California thanks to the support of Isabella. Alyson told her father about my situation, and he pushed hard for me to get custody of Max while Rebecca was away. She will have to have her situation reviewed by psychologists and the courts if she wants her son back. I'm not doing this to punish her, but I have to protect my little brother. I cried when I received the official paper. No one can take him away from me anymore, and it's all thanks to my girlfriends. I thought they would be mad at me for lying to them for months, but no. They didn't blame me, just offered their help and compassion. I love them with all my heart. Our friendship is for life. Unfortunately, my happiness is marred by Jude's upcoming departure.

Objectively, I could visit him regularly, Chicago is a few hours away by plane. Except that his coach doesn't allow visits during the intensive training camp. The training camp is a preparation for playing in the NFL, and it requires intense concentration. I find that absurd, but it's their policy.

I can't afford to fly anyway, and bringing Max along seems like a really bad idea too. After what he's been through, he needs stability, not to wake up in an anonymous hotel.

So, I have accepted to watch the man of my life leave, the one who makes my heartbeat and gives flavor to my existence. Just thinking about it makes me want to curl up and cry. I will miss him so much! His smile, his laugh, his ability to be resourceful, his presence that brightens my day, his ability to take things calmly and solve all problems without ever flinching. It was nice to be able to count on someone for once, to be able to let my guard down. But it's almost over, and my heart is not prepared for it. There is no one to blame but me because I knew it was going to end sooner or later.

Six months is what it will take for him to realize that I am ordinary, not up to his standard. Last night I dreamed he was dating one of the many Kardashians and their pictures were all over Instagram. I woke up sweating and feeling like I couldn't breathe. I stayed awake and watched him sleep through the night to imprint his handsome face on my brain before he's just a distant memory.

I didn't want to fall in love with him, it happened in spite of me, and now I have to let him go, and that hurts me way more than I thought possible. However, seen from the outside, it won't be obvious. I continue to interact with the world as if nothing had happened.

Obviously, it's possible, the human beings have a great capacity for adaptation. Tear our heart out, and we'll keep smiling and baking cookies. Resilience. A concept I know well. So, since Jude broke the news to me, I've been on autopilot mode. I breathe, I smile, I go to class, I take care of my little brother. We have sex, we laugh, we spend time with our group of friends. No one would suspect that I'm devastated inside, that I'm about to lose the only person I've ever loved. How could it be otherwise? How many girls have watched their athlete boyfriend turn pro, rise to the top, and land in a world full of parties and Victoria's Secret models? And no matter how much he tells me otherwise, I'm not stupid enough to believe that I will escape natural selection.

Jude is gorgeous, adorable, and talented, soon to be famous, and I'm just... me. We are not part of the same world. We have never really been part of the same world. So, these last few days are like an extended goodbye to me. I'm enjoying my last moments with him because that's all I can do. I try not to show my sadness, nor spoil his moment of glory and joy.

When the petit fours are finished, I take out the hot dish under Mrs. Hartnett's watchful eye. She still doesn't trust me. It doesn't matter! After today, she will probably never see me again. We are in Warwick to celebrate Jude's official selection which will be announced on TV. That huge! For the occasion, the local press has come, and all those close to Jude too. Mrs. Johnson and Mrs. Hartnett act as conductors in the kitchen, while Isabella, Alyson, and I serve as performers, along with Clara and Evelyn, Jude's cousins.

"We could have hired a caterer," Isabella complains, wiping her brow dramatically after emptying the dishwasher.

Isabella is a Beverly Hills princess who has lived with maids and is not at all used to housework. But she couldn't say no to Mrs. Hartnett and her glaring eyes.

"Did you notice that there are only women in this kitchen?" Alyson grumbles. "Why don't the guys come and give us a hand?"

"Because they don't belong in a kitchen," Mrs. Hartnett replies casually, placing one of the many dishes she's made for the occasion in her hands. "Could you take this to the living room, please?"

Then she turns around without waiting for the latter to answer her. Alyson looks at her, outraged, and I see the hint of a smile on Mrs. Hartnett's lips.

My gaze meets Alyson's who is about to scream, but she doesn't. Like all of us, she gently obeys Mrs. Hartnett, who seems to love to rule her little world with a masterful hand.

Once the food is ready, we all gather in the living room, which looks tiny now that all the guests have arrived. Jude's friends are there, and most are gigantic football players like him, so space is quickly running out.

"Is it possible to have so many hot guys together in so few square feet?" Isabella asks with delight. "I'm glad I came!"

She licks her lips before going to speak to a very attractive and very tattooed blond man. I think his name is Raphael, if I remember correctly when we talked on Thanksgiving Day, and he played football with Jude in high school. Alec, who is standing on the other side of the room, glances furtively at Isabella, before redirecting his attention to Jude's two cousins who have been buttonholing him for a while. He doesn't seem more interested than that in the two brunettes with their piquant personalities. But that's just Alec. He's never interested in any girl. Yet, he is often their center of attention.

I scan the room. Everyone played the game and respected the dress code: a Bears T-shirt. A sea of blue and orange. Jude, for his part, also wears the cap. He looks so happy, surrounded by his family. As a result, I feel guilty for having dark and selfish thoughts.

My eyes meet his, and he winks at me, to which I answer with a big, bright smile. His eyebrows furrow slightly, and a flicker of doubt crosses his irises. Obviously, my smile wasn't that bright.

Pull yourself together, Rocky!

"The appetizers are ready, come and help yourself!" announces Mrs. Hartnett.

Everyone grabs a plate and lines up. Yes, this woman has the authority of a colonel, and I think she's caught the eye of Coach Callahan who spends his time admiring and complimenting her.

"This buffet is delicious, Elena! You've outdone yourself."

"And us poor slaves don't get any compliments," grumbles Alyson.

"You're the prettiest and the most talented," Scott says, hugging her from behind.

She puts a delicate hand on his cheek and looks at him tenderly.

"Thank you, my love. But don't overdo it either."

Things have progressed nicely between Scott and Aly, and they are more in love than ever, even if they continue to argue all the time. I find myself looking at them with envy. This summer, they are going to the Bahamas together. This summer, I'm going to find myself a little job and watch Jude have fun on a yacht with Kendall Jenner. My nightmare resurfaces, and I shake my head to clear the horrible images from my brain. A ball of energy crashes against my legs. I am happy to welcome this sweet distraction.

"How are you, sweetie? You're having a blast, aren't you?"

"Yes!" Max smiles. "Connor and Fred are super cool."

Jude's two little cousins stand right behind him. They're a little older than Max, but they seem to get along well. I'm glad to see he's having so much fun. After what he has just been through, it is a miracle that he's still able to laugh. He just started therapy a week ago, but I'm hopeful that it will work, especially at the price it costs me. *"Soon money won't be a problem anymore,"* Jude likes to repeat, and given the contract he signed, I don't doubt him. But it's his money, not mine, and I don't want him spending it on me or Max.

"Can I go play football outside, Rocky?"

"Erm… you should eat first."

"OK!

"And you too, boys," I say.

The three of them follow me to the buffet, I prepare them each a plate of different dishes. They sit down at one of the folding tables placed there for the occasion. The space is tiny, but Mrs. Hartnett has the talent of an Ikea engineer and has shown genius in making the most of every square foot.

Max smiles and devours his meal, as usual. A real glutton!

"Everything fine?" Jude asks, towering over me.

I look up at him, his caramel-green eyes looking into mine and asking me a thousand silent questions. Unfortunately, I can't answer any of them.

"Yes! Why wouldn't it?"

"I don't know, you're particularly quiet and distant, it's not like you."

"I'm letting you spend time with your loved ones and enjoy this wonderful moment."

He says nothing more, not the least bit convinced. So, I try a touch of humor to lighten the atmosphere and his doubts.

"Do you want me to climb on you in front of your mother? I don't have any problem with that, but I'm not sure she'll like it. She hates me enough already."

"She doesn't hate you."

He wraps his arms around my waist.

"And I need my dose of Rocky," he says, staring at my lips.

I stand on my tiptoes and give a chaste kiss. He arches an eyebrow as if to say, "Is that all?"

"Later."

He accepts and lays his forehead against mine.

"Later, I'll devour you."

"I can't wait."

I kiss him again, but my heart sinks when I realize that tonight we'll be spending our last night together. Is there any worse torture than the condemned man enjoying his last meal before going to the scaffold? I sigh despite myself.

"Are you sure you're okay?"

"Yes! Don't worry about me. Everything is fine, I promise."

I give him my best smile and hope it's reassuring this time. Thankfully, we're interrupted by Coach Callahan who offers to toast Jude. Everyone raises their glass. Beer and champagne clash, then Jude wraps his arm around me and kisses the top of my head.

"Are you hungry?"

"I'm starving."

After dinner, it's time to settle into the heart of the living room and wait for the Draft broadcast to begin. The conversations are flowing, and many are wondering who the other new NFL recruits will be. I'm perched on Jude's lap, listening with a distracted ear, because I don't know anything about it.

The famous credits of the show sound, and everyone immediately stops. It's a solemn, almost surreal moment. The moment when Jude goes from one reality to another. His dream will finally come true. I watch him enjoy it and I'm so proud of him. I'm not alone in this state, his mother is on cloud nine. Eyes riveted to the screen, everyone listens to the host listing the names of the selected. When Jude's turn arrives, the atmosphere is so electric you could cut it with a knife.

"And the sixteenth selected is Jude Hartnett, currently a student at Brown University, he will play wide receiver for the Chicago Bears."

Shouts, tears, applause ring out. Jude stands up, taking me with him. I let out a cry of surprise and joy and reflexively wrap my legs around him. He presses his lips against mine. Our noses crash into each other as our mouths merge. It's a messy, wild, and totally inappropriate kiss in front of this assembly, which earns us hisses. But neither he nor I care. We are way too happy!

"I'm proud of you, my love! You deserve it so much."

"Thanks, babe."

A flash brings us out of our mutual contemplation. It was the local journalist who took a picture of us.

He then drops me off and turns to his mother who is in tears. She immediately takes him in her arms and hugs him tight. Since she is very small, Jude carries her easily. She puts her hand on his cheek and whispers how proud she is of him.

"I couldn't have done it without you," Jude replies, just as moved.

It's moving to see them both like this.

"Now it's time to celebrate with your friends."

Jude nods, turns around and raises both fists in the air, while all his friends from past and present rush on him. He is carried away by this wave of cheerful people, and I stay behind to let him enjoy this surreal moment, trying somehow to ignore the ball of sadness that threatens to strangle me. I hate myself for feeling an abyssal void deep inside me.

The evening continues at The Logan until late. We end up at the hotel for our last night together.

41

Jude

I walk down the hallway of the luxury hotel where I've booked a room for the occasion. Rocky is in my arms, her legs around my waist, her slightly tipsy smile, and her pussy exerting delicious pressure on my aching cock as I squeeze her butt until it leaves marks. I make her move on me as I move forward, to relieve my urgency to take her here and now.

I don't know how I manage to contain myself until I get to the bedroom. I want her so bad. She's gorgeous in her Bears T-shirt and my cap, which she's wearing backwards. My biggest supporter.

To tell the truth, I didn't really contain myself, since I just threw myself on her in the elevator, pinning her against the wall and devouring her, like the sick person I am. I've been wanting it all day. I was this close to fucking her in The Logan's bathroom, after she danced lasciviously against me. However, I gave up. There were way too many people, and I didn't want to expose Rocky like that. Although she didn't seem against the idea. On the contrary, my little Balboa doesn't shy away from anything sexually, and I love her boldness. But in the confines of the elevator, all thoughts of preserving her virtue left my body and were replaced by pure desire. Desire to possess her, to make her mine, to fuck her till death.

Surprised at first, she quickly caught on and returned my kiss with the same fervor. As I was already tugging at her T-shirt, we were interrupted by the beep from the door. An elderly couple walked in, pretending not to see what we were doing. Of course, I immediately let go of her. I have plenty of vices, but exhibitionism is not one of them.

Then it was hard to contain our laughter, leaning against the wall facing each other, like two horny teenagers caught in the act. My hot gaze undressed Rocky, and from where I was, I could see her nipple poking out, her swollen lips, her hair disheveled by our short caresses, her breasts rising and falling to the rhythm of her frantic breathing, and her eyes filled with of desire. Pure torture! As for me, I must have looked arousal too. The sexual tension was razor sharp, and we were happy to get out of that fucking elevator. As soon as I crossed the threshold, I quickly slapped Rocky's ass, which earned me a yelp from her and an outraged cry from the old lady.

"Baby, I'm going to get so deep into this pussy that you won't be able to walk straight tomorrow morning."

She stifles a laugh, and her deep black eyes sparkle.

I have a tendency to speak raw usually, especially during sex, but when I'm drunk, I no longer have any filters.

"Is it a promise?"

I confirm with a nod. Her eyes are burning with desire. She bites her lips and brings them to my ear, I feel her sweet, slightly alcoholic breath,

"I want you to take me… from behind, this time."

"What?"

I literally choke on my saliva, as my cock jerks, especially loving the idea. I stop walking and grab her face with one of my hands. She tightens her legs around my waist so as not to collapse.

"Do you mean doggy style?"

I understood what she just said, but I want to be sure. No room for misunderstandings in this kind of situation. I've wanted to fuck her little ass since day one, so if she's ready, it's going to be fireworks. She nods and blushes. And that's all it takes for me to sprint to the bedroom. Rocky screams and bursts out laughing at my eagerness.

"Keep quiet! You're going to get us kicked out of this hotel!"

I pull the key card out of my back pocket in record time, while holding a laughing Rocky against me. My cock is aching, and if I don't release it right away, it's going to blow my fly off. We hear the magic click. Liberating. I grab my Balboa's face to devour her mouth. I advance in a chaotic way, hitting all the furniture as I go. Fucking modern and sharp decoration! I devour Rocky's neck, feel her butt, imagining the moment when I will spread it and insert myself…

Oh fuck! I have to calm down my excitement if I want to last.

We collapse on the bed, me on top of her. I get rid of her T-shirt in a second. She giggles, as her head gets stuck. I tug on it violently and throw it away.

"This T-shirt did not do anything wrong to you!" she laughs.

"It did, it prevents me from seeing that."

Her pretty tanned skin appears, she is not wearing a bra. That's my Rocky! I take her beautiful breasts before licking them eagerly.

"God, I missed you so much!"

Rocky giggles and props himself up on her elbows.

"Are you talking to my breasts?"

I give her a fake annoyed look. "Excuse me! Can I have a second of intimacy with my girls?"

My little Balboa shakes her head, amused, and lies down.

My mouth rushes to one of her nipples, which I circle with my tongue and suck while watching her react. Her skin is covered with goosebumps, and her soft, delicate body jerks with desire. I groan and move on to the next. My fingers unbutton her jeans at the same time. I get up on my knees, pull my T-shirt over my shoulders. She looks at me with admiration and wriggles in all directions, anticipating what's next.

I literally rip off her jeans, her thong, and her Vans with a quick gesture. She helps me by lifting her legs and laughs when I throw her shoes across the room like they were on fire. They crash with a deafening noise against the wall, almost exploding one of these state-of-the-art geometric lamps. To say I'm aroused would be an understatement.

"Take it easy, wide receiver!" mocks Rocky, hiding her pretty face with her forearm. "You're not on a field there."

"'Easy' is not part of my vocabulary, woman! Come here."

I grab her feet and pull her to the edge of the bed. She screams and laughs harder, but her laughter turns to gasps when I kiss her hot, pink, juicy pussy. It's delicious, and I can't help but pull out my cock and stroke myself while I taste her. I spread her lips and run my tongue over them. Heaven! I take my time, exploring every inch of her while my thumb caresses her clitoris. Rocky moans louder and squeezes her thighs around my head, tugging at my hair. She jumps when I literally fuck her with my tongue. I look up at her, she has this pleading, lost look, where she no longer knows where she lives, and I love making her lose her mind.

"Oh, Jude! Stop... Please... Ah..."

She tries to slip away, I stop her by squeezing and spreading her thighs, turning her on more.

"Oh, I'm going to cum!"

I replace my tongue with my fingers and penetrate her quickly, not wanting to miss a drop of the highlight of the show. She throws her head back, freezes, then hits the mattress several times with her fist. Gorgeous, she's gorgeous when she cums, when she lets go. I keep fingering her until she puts her hands on mine.

I step back, a triumphant smile on my lips.

"First orgasm, Balboa. The scoreboard is open."

Still on her little cloud, she doesn't answer me, but gives me a satisfied smile. I flip her over, she screams in surprise, then I place her as I wish. Her ass in the air is a vision that forces me to increase the pressure on my cock. I bend down and nibble her ass as I jerk off. Her ass is the most beautiful thing in the world. She has a tiny waist and a nice arch, but what I love is the beauty mark on her right buttock, as well as the dimples in the small of her back. I run my hand over her back, smacking her ass once. She gasps and turns her face to me. My hand caresses her slightly reddened satin skin. She is sweet, delicate. She looks over her shoulder, a little worried.

"Don't worry, babe. I'm not going inside like this without warning. No, you'll have to prepare."

I'm about to lick her from this angle, but she surprises me by getting out of bed. I follow her with a puzzled look, a little annoyed that she is going away, even temporarily. She searches through her bag before timidly returning with a tiny bottle in her hands. I raise an eyebrow, and she blushes even more.

"Lube? You walk around with lube in your bag."

"Yes..."

"Swiss army knife, lube, what else is in your bag, MacGyver? A crowbar, geisha balls?"

She smiles, and her cheeks flush more.

"Don't be silly! I don't walk around with lube every day. I

just thought tonight we'd… mark the occasion and do something special, before you… me…" she says, hesitating to finish her sentence. "I mean, before you leave."

I walk over to her, frowning, and take the bottle from her hands and place it on the bedside table. I then sit on the bed and invite her to sit on me. My jeans are open, and my cock is wedged between her belly and mine. I brush her hair and kiss her on the nose.

"Rocky, how about you tell me the real reason why you want me to take you this way?"

My hands can't help but touch her ass.

"What do you mean? You don't want to?"

"I'm dying for it, of course. My cock is so hard it might wreak havoc just thinking about it. But I have the strange feeling that you're offering it to me for the wrong reasons. Because you think that after tonight it will be over between us."

She says nothing but avoids my gaze. Sorry for my cock, but I just got the answer I was looking for.

"So, I'd rather wait until you're ready. Really ready. There's no rush. We'll do it later, when I get back, or after. We'll have a million nights together. Our relationship doesn't have an expiration date, Rocky."

She stays a little too quiet for my taste and swallows. She still doesn't believe me. So, I take her hand and put it on my racing heart.

"Can you feel that?"

I'm whispering and looking for her gaze. Her eyelids flutter and her black doe eyes stare into mine. I can read vulnerability in them. Rocky makes the whole world believe that she is a warrior and that nothing can touch her. But I know that's not true. She is sweet, sensitive, and needs to be taken care of, to be shown that she matters. Like everyone else. She just learned to hide it better than anyone, out of survival instinct.

"Can you feel my heart beating fast?"

She nods.

"How hard it beats for you?"

She takes a deep breath.

"Rocky, I love you. You're the best thing that has ever happened to me and I have no intention of losing you. I'm crazy about you, and nothing can stop me from coming back. Never. I don't know how we're going to manage with the distance, the six months of absence, but what I do know is that I want to do everything in my power to keep you."

Her eyes fill with tears, and I kiss her eyelids while I stroke her hair.

"How can you be so sure, Jude?" she whispers, as our foreheads touch. "We've known each other for a short time, a few months at most, so how do you know that you won't want something else? Like Kendall Jenner, for example?"

"Kendall, who?"

I shake my head.

"Listen to me, babe. You're talking to a guy who knows what he wants and has always known it. I have wanted to be a professional football player since I was old enough to walk. And I've done whatever it takes to make it happen. However, nothing was won in advance. The statistics were not on my side. Only one percent of players succeed. But never mind the stats, I was determined. And you know what else I want?"

She shakes her head no.

"You! I want you to be mine."

She sniffles in the most adorable way and wipes away her tears.

"Since the first day. Since the day I laid eyes on you. The first day you gave me a pool class, told me about *The Good, the Bad and the Ugly* and we made love against the greenhouse."

I don't add that I also want to marry her and drown her in babies, because she might think I'm crazy and run away. You have to take one thing at a time with her, I learned that the hard way.

"Do you believe me? Do you believe in us enough to trust me?"

She wet her lips, her gaze still a little uncertain.

"Tell me you believe me."

She ends up nodding. A relief invades all my body, and without thinking, I lift her up by the hips and sink into her. A moan escapes both of us. I swallow hers, kissing her passionately. The tight, humid heat sends an electric shock through my spine. It's way too good, and there's no way I'm stopping. I slowly move her up and down on me. She moans as I watch her being consumed, her face back and her throat rosy.

"Jude, the condom?" she says between two gasps after an eternity.

I keep moving inside her. My hips no longer obey me. I'm way too aroused.

"I'm clean. I always do tests for football. You?"

"Clean too!"

I smile like a cat that's just swallowed a canary, because she's just given me implicit permission to continue.

"At worst, you'll get pregnant with our first child, and we can start this large family a little early," I half-joke, because the idea doesn't seem completely crazy to me.

And then, at least, like that, she will finally understand that I am serious about us. But my remark quickly made her open her eyes.

"What?! What's wrong with you?"

She taps my shoulder while I laugh.

"I'm joking. Or not!"

"I'm warning you, don't end up inside me, Hartnett!"

"Yes, woman!"

She rolls her eyes.

"Now fuck me, Balboa!"

And that's what she does. She pushes on my shoulders, I lie on my back, and let her work on me. Take control, taking everything she wants. Her hands are on my pecs, and she moves her hips at a furious pace. Fuck! I grit my teeth and groan as she slides down my cock again, and again, and again. Her breasts move inches from my face. I can't take it anymore! I grab them and suck them, lick them. She moans. I grab her face and then pull her to me to kiss her with everything I have. My mouth says, "I love you!" my thrust tells her "You're mine!" and her moans tell me she's close to orgasm.

"Oh, Jude, I'm close!" she cries.

No sooner does she finish her sentence than she begins to tremble against me, eyes closed, mouth parted. Her chest turns pink, then she collapses. I continue to penetrate her through her orgasm. I'm far from done with her. Our first plan fell through, but that doesn't mean we can't have fun.

I turn her around, get on my knees, and thrust into her while activating her clitoris. I can hear how wet she is, and it's driving me crazy. Fucking her, in general, is a drug, but without a condom, it's ecstasy. I don't think I can ever leave this pussy again. I clench my jaw as Rocky is in a trance under me. She tries to escape, to impale herself, her gestures are messy, disordered. She puts her hands in her hair to tug on it, her eyes meet mine, I know she's going to cum again.

Her pussy contracts around my cock several times, squeezing me like a fist, and Rocky arches her back and screams in pleasure. I can't contain myself anymore. I thrust into her with all my might, trying to last as long as possible, pulling out just in time to empty myself onto her belly, her chest, her neck. Her tanned skin covered with my cum fills me with Neanderthal pride. After coming to my senses and calming my frantic breathing, I grab my T-shirt and clean her carefully.

Her hair is now soaked with sweat and so is her body. She looks, shiny, beautiful. I lay down next to her, exhausted, then wrap her in my arms.

"I love you, Jude," she breathes against my mouth, as I brush her hair away from that face I love above all else.

"I love you, Rocky."

My tongue is caressing her lower lip when I hear her say, "Forever?"

Our eyes meet, hers hopeful and mine determined.

"Forever."

Rocky

The next day, I drop Jude off at the airport. With a heavy heart, I watch him check in his suitcase, he will soon go through security. He will soon disappear. And don't we say, "out of sight, out of mind?"

"Did you take everything?"

"Yes…"

We look at each other for a long time. I sniffle, he pulls me into his arms and hold me tight.

Okay, don't cry, Rocky! Don't cry!

I swallow the knot in my throat as he strokes my hair. I end up straightening my face to look at his.

"Babe, don't worry. Six months will pass in the blink of an eye."

He strokes my cheeks with his thumbs while I try not to cry. But I fail miserably. He kisses my eyelids. I laugh and cry at the same time, feeling vulnerable and, at the same time, happy for him.

"We'll call each other every day."

I nod, sniffling. He kisses me. His tongue invades my mouth and intertwines with mine in a sensual dance that I love way too much.

I sigh in despair at the thought of never feeling like this again. He nibbles on my bottom lip, and when our mouths disconnect to catch our breath, our foreheads refuse to part. He puts his hands behind my neck and whispers, "I love you."

"I love you too."

"Goodbye, my love…"

He lets go of me, grabs his backpack, and walks hesitantly to security. I stand there, watching him go. My heart beats in my throat. I want to scream, want to collapse in grief, but I stay the course until he disappears from my sight and whispers, soul in pain, "Good-bye, my Love."

Back home, the reality of the situation grabs me by the throat. As long as I was moving, everything seemed unreal to me, as if it was happening to someone else, but now, but now I am overwhelmed. The house is so empty, so silent. The white walls send my loneliness back to my face.

"Sometimes, only one person is missing, and the whole world seems depopulated."

I had never understood the meaning of this quote until today, and Max is not even there to cheer me up. He's spending the day with Isabella and Alyson. They kindly offered to watch him, just to give us a few more hours of privacy.

I text them to let them know I'm home. They answer me with a selfie where the three enjoy an ice cream. It pulls a tiny smile out of me, as I curl up on the couch, trying to repeat all of Jude's encouraging speeches to myself.

"I love you and no one will stop me from coming back to you! Six months is nothing! I promise, you won't see the time pass."

"Kendall Jenner, who? She's no match for Rocky Prescott."

He is convinced that this long-distance relationship will work. Me, I'm afraid of losing him, afraid of being eaten up by my jealousy, but I'm ready to take the risk. I love him too much. Am I wrong? Am I right? The future will tell.

Bursts of laughter echo behind the door and bring me out of my torpor. I wipe away my tears and comb my hair. I must look like a wet rag. I don't want Max to see me like this.

My little brother rushes towards me, followed by my two best friends.

"Rocky! We had so much fun, it was great. The girls took me to the park and the Children's Museum of Providence. I built the biggest of all dinosaurs and... it was just... Are you okay? You're sad?"

He questions me with his big hazel eyes. Alyson and Isabella stare at me with the same concern.

"No, sweetie, it's just allergies," I say, rubbing my face, before asking him to tell me more about his day.

He gives it his all, repairing my heavy and bruised heart with his little voice and his funny anecdotes. I hug him tight. My little angel, he has the incredible ability to make the unbearable bearable, to turn storms into rainbows.

As I listen to her laughter and enthusiasm, I tell myself that I'll be okay, that I'll be strong, that I have a billion things to do while I wait for Jude to come home. For starters making sure my mother receives the treatment she needs, do my best to brighten up my little brother's day and validate my year. Yes, I can do it. I can survive his absence.

Max decides to stop the submachine gun that serves as his mouth and go play in his room. I have a hard time taking him out of my arms, because right now, he serves me as a human bandage.

I am often congratulated for taking good care of my little brother, but the truth is that he takes care of me as much as I take care of him. He is my fuel, my reason to move forward. For him, I can't let the pain drown me. For him, I have to be strong!

As soon as he turned on his heels than my girlfriends take over the tenderness. One on each side, they wrap me in their affection. And in front of them, I can no longer hold back my tears.

"How did it go?" Alyson asks, stroking my back.

"Well, he's gone… I didn't think it would hurt this much to see him walk away. I know I'm being ridiculous. He's only leaving for six months, but I don't know, I'm afraid of losing him."

"You won't lose him! He's crazy about you."

"Is he?"

"I have no doubt. You're a wonderful girl, Rocky, and Jude is smart enough to have figured that out. He'll come back."

Failing to be convinced, I'll take my girlfriend's certainty and Jude's as a guarantee of truth.

"Thank you, girls, you are the best. I love you guys."

"We love you too. And while we wait for him to come back, we're not going to let it get us down. And it starts with a tacos and tequila night!"

Alyson waves the grocery bags she has placed on the table.

"Yes!" says Isabella with enthusiasm.

We spend the rest of the evening bullshitting and eating. Girlfriends, good food and giggles, the universal remedy for all sorrows. Nothing is settled, but thanks to all this love, I feel like I can move on.

Epilogue

Rocky

Six months later

"Are you coming tonight, Rocky, to the prom?" asks Maria, one of my cafeteria co-workers, as she opens her locker.

It's our last shift today, so we're hanging out in the locker room, just to chat a little.

"No, that's not my thing. I'm going to spend the evening watching a good old movie instead."

The truth is, I don't feel like going without a date when everyone else is going to be with them and talking about their vacation plans. No, very little for me. A movie, popcorn, that's how I plan to celebrate the last day and my exam success.

"Damn, I envy you… It's not really my thing either, but my boyfriend really wants to go, so like the good girlfriend that I am, I sacrifice myself," she says, rolling her eyes.

"I'm sure it will be fun! We've been hearing about it for weeks, and besides me, everyone else is going."

I put my uniform away. This is the last time I wear it, at least until school starts in the fall. I throw the hairnet and the gloves in the trash. My colleague does the same, and we leave the cafeteria together before going our separate ways.

Brown's campus is abuzz. Summer is special in that it puts everyone in a good mood. The bodies are stripped bare, and the smiles are more frank, more massive. All classes are over, but the students don't want to leave. Groups have formed all over the lawn:

there are improvised football or volleyball games, ukulele players humming the famous "Somewhere Over the Rainbow," and picnics with chips and rosé. You know it's summer when the students swap vodka or beer for rosé. Some chicks are even doing yoga.

Everyone enjoys the sun and this unique atmosphere that Brown offers, between architectural jewels, festivities, and intellect. I take a deep breath before leaving. I love my university. it has been the witness to so many things, and the ground of all opportunities for me.

I see myself at the start of the school year: terrified at the idea of screwing up my school year, my shoulders weighed down by all the responsibilities that fell on me after my mother left. If I had known that this year, I was so dreading would also be the one where my life would take a completely different turn…

These last six months have been difficult, and that is an understatement.

Our separation was a great ordeal, especially for me, but Jude was able to reassure me. During his entire absence, he managed the feat of managing my moods and my family problems from a distance.

When my mother came home from rehab and I didn't know if she was going to relapse, he was there to reassure me. When my insecurities got the better of my will to make our relationship work, he was patient, gradually rebuilding the trust I never had in myself or in humanity.

After six months, I can finally say it: he was right. It can work, even from a distance. And in a few days, he will finally be back.

I reread the text he wrote to me this morning, and my heart skips a beat.

**D-7, baby! I hope you're ready
to not leave the room for weeks.**

Oh yes! I am ready!
I'm even more than ready. And the avalanche of steamy text messages that I send him is there to attest to it.

After a last visit to the library, I take the way back.

"I'm home," I shout, with the delicacy that characterizes me.

I put my keys on the kitchen table.

Nobody answers me, and for good reason, they are all in the yard. Max, his friends, Mrs. Johnson and my mother.

My little brother is playing football, while Mom and Carol are crouching in the dirt and planting flowers or vegetables, according to Rebecca Prescott's latest whim. Who could believe that a few months ago, she was high? Now she swears by organic food and meditation.

Since coming home from rehab where she learned to deal with her bipolarity other than by abusing substances, my mother is unrecognizable.

She found a job selling flowers, volunteered in the hospital that treated her, and even decided to get her GED. A true resurrection that we owe to the wonderful doctors who were able to diagnose and treat her mental illness.

The three of us live together and slowly rebuilding our relationship. Sometimes it's hard for me to think of her as the responsible adult in charge of the household. I'm still very possessive when it comes to Max, but little by little I'm making room for her, and so far, she gave me no reason to doubt her. The important thing is that Max is happy, and he is. He even stopped his therapy, the psychologist believing that it was no longer necessary.

My Max, he is growing so fast! This summer, he is going to a summer camp in Colorado for three weeks. Thanks to my mom's job and mine, we can finally offer him what other kids his age get to do.

This is the first time he's left me for so long, and I'm both excited for him and sad for myself, because I'm going to miss him so much. But Dinosaur Trail Camp is going to be a blast. He can't stop talking about it.

I approach him and his friends and give him a long kiss on the head. He gives me a hug before slipping out of my grip to grab the ball.

"Look! I'm a wide receiver!"

"Congratulations, big guy!"

I can't help but smile when I see how much he loves football now. He owes this newfound passion to Jude. The two of them have been talking and FaceTimeing each other for the past six long months.

Jude was not only supportive of me, but he was also there for my little brother, with little attentions, discussions around boyish topics that I, was not supposed to understand.

Max told him about his adventures at school, and Jude introduced him to the great players he had the chance to train with. Max even got a video of the entire Chicago Bears team for his birthday. Video became viral on social media and was the talk of every mom in school for weeks.

"What are you planting?" I ask as I walk into the garden.

"Ah, Rocky, you're home!" Rebecca exclaims, wiping her brow. "So, how was the last day?"

"Nothing to report. I passed all my exams and I'm free to do nothing for the whole summer."

"Oh, honey, I'm so proud of you! You're the first Prescott to go to college. If I didn't have my hands full of dirt, I'd give you a huge kiss," says my mother, exposing said hands in front of me.

"I have the impression that, apart from you and me, there are no other Prescotts, and calm your enthusiasm. You know I don't really like being touched."

I mean, I don't like HER touching me, but I don't want to tell her that, because she makes an effort, I have to let her have it.

But I'm not used to new Rebecca yet, and I don't know if I'll ever get used to it. This sweetened version of my mother who cooks and likes to garden always seems unreal to me. I am wary, watching for the slightest crisis, the slightest relapse. Years of neglect don't just go away.

On the other hand, my brother is very happy with this new maternal version. He immediately accepted her back into our daily lives, not blaming her at all for her absence. My brother has a huge heart, and that delights me as much as it despairs me.

"Well, I'm going to change, and then I'll give you a hand."

"No, you can't!" yells my mother, as if I'm giving her the worst news.

"Why can't I?"

"Because you can't. That's the way it is."

"That's not a solid argument!" I quip.

I cross my arms over my chest waiting for her to explain the reasons for her rejection.

Mrs. Johnson makes big eyes at Rebecca. The latter turns red as a peony and starts to ramble incoherently.

"You have better things to do, Rocky! You're not going to bother with gardening. It's for eldery people."

"Yes, Rocky, you should take a shower instead," adds Mrs. Johnson.

"A shower? But it's barely six o'clock… and I…"

"Yes, but you stink!" says Rebecca.

"I stink?"

"Yes, you smell bad, Rocky. You stink. There, I said it!"

Am I dreaming or Mrs. Johnson just insulted me?

I lift my arms and sniffle under my armpits, suddenly feeling dirty. The two gardeners continue to exchange bizarre glances. I end up retreating. Maybe they just want to be quiet. It must be said that, against all odds, Mrs. Johnson and my mother get along wonderfully and spend a lot of time together. Sometimes I even feel like I'm bothering them. Yet another miraculous thing.

"Well, if everyone insists, I'll relieve you of my presence and go wash up."

"Yes, and don't forget to straighten your hair too," suggests my neighbor.

"Very good idea!" my mother adds. "And wax," she says confidently, looking at my crotch.

Have they gone crazy or what?

"Straighten my hair? I never straighten my hair, let alone for a quiet evening at home."

"Well, maybe you should! Your sloppy look is driving me nuts," says my mom.

"Okay! I'm glad to be back home," I say, running a hand through my brown hair, suddenly feeling like Mowgli.

They both look at me, an enigmatic smile screwed to the corner of their lips.

"Are you hiding something from me?"

My mother flushes. She is unable to hide her emotions. She wouldn't last two seconds in front of a lie detector. On the other hand, Mrs. Johnson, she could play poker without problem.

"We're not hiding anything from you, Rocky, you're completely paranoid. Now, get in the shower, girl!"

My neighbor punctuates her words with an authoritative gesture for me to comply.

Just as I'm about to take them at their word, I hear the bell ring.

"It must be Tyler and William's mothers picking them up."

"Yes, that's probably it," mum says, clapping her hands. "Can you get the door?"

I don't understand her sudden excitement. But I don't usually understand this woman's reactions.

"Uh… yeah, but I'm afraid to gas them with my radioactive armpits," I joke.

"Hold on."

She tucks my hair behind my ears, pinches my cheeks to make them blush and tugs at my cleavage.

"What the hell are you doing?"

I gently swat her hands to get her to let go.

"There, you're ready to open the door. I love you, honey."

I squint, wondering if my mom is having a bipolar relapse. Maybe I should check the medication dosage, you never know. I meet Mrs. Johnson's eyes, who is just as moved.

"Are you sure it's not hallucinogenic mushrooms you're planting?"

They don't have time to answer me that the doorbell rings again.

I decide to go open. And damn, if I expected this!

"Jude!"

The cry that escapes me must set off the whole neighborhood, but I don't care. I jump on him and wrap my legs around his waist. He catches me like a champion and spins us around.

"Babe, I missed you so much!"

"Oh my God! Jude, you're here!"

I kiss him full on the lips, and he kisses me back with the same fervor. I cry, I laugh, I eat him with my eyes, then squeeze him closer, before bombarding him again with kisses on his face, on his neck. He laughs.

"Looks like you're happy to see me."

"It's the least we can say."

Jude, my Jude!

I take a deep breath. His amber scent invades all my senses and instantly soothes me.

I pull my head away from his neck, he grabs my chin and looks up into mine with his caramel-green eyes.

"It's so good to see you again, Balboa!"

He kisses me again before dropping me to the ground. My wobbly legs barely support me.

After the surprise effect, my brain goes on alert. He was supposed to be back in a week, not now, for a moment, I imagine the worst. Besides, why is he wearing a suit?

"What are you doing here? You're hurt? You weren't fired, were you?"

"No, not at all, the training camp ended a week early. Obviously, we have worked well, we are ready! So, the coach did us a favor. I took the first plane this morning, I couldn't wait another minute to see you."

I smile and wipe away my tears.

"Come here!"

He pulls me to him and kisses me again, hugging my waist. I had missed his caresses, his presence, his smell, everything.

His firm body, which seems even more muscular to me, seems to want to integrate with mine. He showers me with kisses, I moan into his mouth. If he continues to melt me with his tongue, I no longer answer for anything. Neighbors or not, I risk climbing on him and making love to him, here and now.

I hear hissing behind him and recognize Alyson's voice. I open my eyes and see a limo. My two crazy girlfriend's wave to me from the window, they are accompanied by Scott and Alec.

"But what…"

"Do you remember that I promised to take you to a ball one day? With suit and limo? Well, that day has arrived."

He gives me his big, charming smile that dazzles me and scrambles my brain.

"What? Are you talking about Brown's prom?"

"That's right!"

"But Jude… do you really want to go? Don't you want to make up for lost time in the bedroom?"

"One thing at a time, princess. First the ball, then the sex. I made you a promise and always keep my promises. Come on, baby, I know this isn't exactly what you expected from our first day back together, but you've never had the opportunity to go to a ball before, and I really want to share this new experience with you."

He kisses my neck and whispers, "I want to share all your first times."

He runs a hand over my ass, and I understand what he's referring to. I've made a thousand sexual promises to him over FaceTime. He's demanding his due, now that he's back, he's not going to be disappointed with the trip.

"Okay! But I have nothing to wear."

"I had a dress delivered yesterday to Mrs. Johnson's when I knew I was coming home. She should be waiting for you in your room."

"What? Mrs. Johnson was in on it?!"

"Yes! I asked her not to tell you. I wanted it to be a surprise."

"I can see what she was doing with Rebecca earlier."

"Speaking of which, I would love to meet your mom in the flesh. So glad she's feeling better! And my little man, how is he?"

"Fine, everyone is fine. Come in, they're all in the yard."

I gather my wits and calm my heart, which is pounding with happiness. I motion for my friends to come in as well, but they refuse.

"We'll stay here waiting for you! We have champagne," Isabella replies, showing me her glass.

I nod and close the door. I'm completely shaken. I need someone to pinch me to make sure I'm not dreaming and that he's really there.

"Jude," Max yells, rushing towards him.

My boyfriend kneels down and hugs him tightly before ruffling his hair. I will never tire of seeing them together.

They exchange a few tender words, while his two friends, William and Tyler, ask for an autograph.

Mrs. Johnson greets him warmly in turn, while Jude thanks her for keeping the secret of his return.

I can't believe she didn't tell me anything!

I then introduce him to my mother who doesn't hide her admiration.

"Jude, the famous Jude. I have heard a lot about you. Please to meet you, I'm Rebecca, Rocky, and Max's mom, but you already know. I know, no need to tell me, she laughs and combs her blond hair, I look younger than my age. Besides, everyone thinks that Rocky and I are sisters."

That's news to me! I bite my lip to keep from contradicting her. The Rebecca *Seduction Show* has started.

She holds out her hand to him, he takes it enthusiastically.

"The pleasure is all mine."

Jude smiled, she blushed. Yes, he has this effect on all women, and my mother is not immune.

I clear my throat. "I'll let you two get to know each other better and go change."

When I come back down thirty minutes later, Jude gets up from the sofa where he had settled down to wait for me. I hold on tightly to the railing. When he looks at me like that, I don't trust my ability to put one foot in front of the other.

I'm wearing a black and silver sequin dress that comes to my knees. I straightened my hair and applied more makeup than usual. Even though I don't like makeup on a daily basis, I must admit that, tonight, it's had its little effect. Heart pounding, I walk over to my boyfriend.

"Wow! You're beautiful, babe."

He looks me up and down, his feline eyes caressing every inch of my skin. His gaze is so intense it gives me goosebumps. I cleared my throat.

"Really? You don't find me too… too much!"

He shakes his head no.

I take this opportunity to watch him. He's wearing a classic Gucci suit that fits him like a glove, showing off every one of his powerful muscles. He's styled his hair back for elegance, which intensifies the perfect angle of his jawline even more. He's breathtakingly beautiful. Will I ever stop falling in love with him? The depth of my feelings seems endless, and I'd be lying if I said it doesn't scare me at all anymore, but I'm treating myself.

The ball lives up to all the clichés that I had for this kind of event, but I must admit that I had a great time. Between frenzied choreography and strong cocktails, this party is just like the craziest parties organized by Kappa Omega. The only thing that differs is that everyone is dressed up, no one does an improvised striptease or pukes their guts out. But you never know, the night is still young.

I'm completely exhausted, after having sweated on the dancefloor to latest hits of the moment, we return to our table.

"So, are you having fun?" Jude asks, stroking the inside of my wrist.

"Yes, it's great! A lot less boring than I thought it would be in high school."

"When you had blue hair?"

"Ha! Ha! You remember that!"

"I remember everything, babe, even…"

He approaches and whispers in my ear the most unmentionable fantasies that I shared with him during our torrid night discussions.

I blush.

"I think I got a little carried away. You know me, I was alone and very, very turned on by all your Instagram photos."

And for good reason, on the Bears' official team website, I've lost count of the number of photos of Jude working out, his perfect chest glistening with sweat.

Unfortunately, I'm not the only one who enjoyed these pictures, and his account grew to one million followers, including many celebrities, just days after he arrived at training camp. This obviously fueled my jealousy and my desire to run away from him, but once again Jude was able to calm my anxieties.

"A promise is a promise, and I believe in always honoring your promises," he whispers before nipping my neck.

His hand slides under my dress, lighting the fire on my skin.

"Yo, Hartnett! I think it's time you got a room!" scoffs Scott. "Otherwise, you'll be climbing all over yourself in front of the whole campus."

"Wouldn't be the first time," Alyson chuckles.

"Leave them alone, they haven't seen each other for months," Isabella adds.

But they're right, we need to calm down before I rip his clothes off.

Conversations turn to vacation plans. Alyson and Scott are excited to go to the Bahamas together. Isabella plans to do a cinema internship in Hollywood. Only Alec remains unclear about his plans. He has been contacted by a few teams to play in reserve, but for the moment, nothing concrete, and I think it depresses him a little.

A few guitar notes that we know only too well resonate from the speakers and make us smile silly.

"*Tell me something, girl, are you happy in this modern world?*"

"We need to dance on this song, Balboa!"

Jude holds out his hand to me, and we head back to the floor. He wraps his arms around my waist as I place mine around his neck. And eye to eye, we let ourselves be carried away by the melody of "Shallow" by Lady Gaga.

I rest my head on his chest, listen to his heartbeat as it makes my world spin more than ever, and I am suddenly overwhelmed with emotion.

Fuck, the shame if people see me crying. They won't understand.

We keep dancing slowly until Jude taps under my chin. His brow furrows when he notices my confusion.

"Babe, why are you crying? Is there something wrong?"

I shake my head, wipe away my tears.

"No, for once, everything is fine! These are tears of happiness. I love you so much, Jude, and I can't believe you're here. That we're both here with our friends and… I was afraid that you'd never come back… So used to things going wrong. I was prepared for the worst, but not for the best. When everything is going well, I don't know how to handle it."

He cups my face, tenderly caresses my cheeks with his thumbs. "Oh babe, I love you with all my heart too. I promise you everything will be fine from now on, and I have something to tell you, but I think you've had enough emotions for one day."

He spins me around before pulling me back into his arms. "Unless you really want to know?"

He has his playful smile and a challenging glint in his eye. He knows how much I hate it when he holds me in suspense, and he loves torturing me.

"Oh no, Jude, you can't just make me wait."

"Are you sure? It can wait until tomorrow…"

"Yes, I'm sure! Spit it out."

I get slightly annoyed, he laughs, proud of his little effect.

"OK, well… You told me that Max was going to camp for three weeks."

"Yes…"

I squint because I don't really see what he was getting at.

"Well, we could use this time to go on vacation together. I know that your biggest dream is to go to Europe, to visit all those architectural buildings and thousand-year-old cities that you have so often studied."

I swallow because, yes, he's right, I have always dreamed of it.

"So, I think we should go to Europe for three weeks."

"That's a great idea, Jude, but I can't afford it. I'm doing better financially since my mom came back, but not to the point where I can afford this kind of trip."

"You don't have to worry about it. It's a gift."

"You're crazy! I can't accept. It's too much.

"I knew you would say that. Stubborn that you are! But know that all reservations are already made. Either we go or it will be a big waste, the choice is yours."

I bite my lip and smile at his legendary determination. That determination that conquered all my fears and made me fall in love with him.

"You never take 'no' for an answer!"

"You don't say no, you hide behind rules that are supposed to protect you. Am I wrong?"

I smile at the remark that I made to him in the cafeteria, when he shamefully flirted with me.

"I accept!" I finally give in. "But I'll pay you back every penny and I—"

He growls, puts his mouth on mine. His warm tongue forces its way through my lips and silences me in no time.

More catchy music follows, but we both remain entwined in the middle of the dance floor devouring each other.

When he lets go of me, I'm just a fragile little thing. My brain has forgotten why I was arguing five minutes ago.

"We're going to Europe," he whispers in my ear, and I feel his erection rub against my belly.

"Is this the Eiffel tower I'm feeling?" I scoff, raising an eyebrow.

"Yes! Rocky, you're driving me crazy. I thought I could hold myself, but you look so gorgeous in that dress that I just want to rip it off. I've been holding myself back for hours."

His eyes land on my cleavage, then he closes them brutally as if he was in pain. He rests his forehead against mine and breathes to calm his ardor. But I don't want him to calm down, that's why I hear myself say to him, "So, let's go?"

"Where?"

"To the greenhouse! Where it all began."

Acknowledgments

I would like to thank Julie, Caroline and Lætitia. Three great girls, three outstanding beta readers who were able to guide me, give me confidence, and make me believe in my story.

I would like to thank the Addictives team, but especially Émilie, my editor, for her enthusiasm, her professionalism, and her advice. Working with you is a real pleasure.

And finally, I would like to thank the talented Camilla Simon for her sincerity, her relevancy and, above all, her boundless generosity.

Thank You for Reading!

We sincerely hope you enjoyed reading this book as much as we enjoyed publishing it. If you did, we would appreciate a short review on Amazon or your favorite book website. Reviews are crucial for any authors, and even just a line or two can make a huge difference.

Other novels from
WARM PUBLISHING

Scan to easily acess all of Warm Publishing books:

Join also our Facebook Group, Book Warmers, to get the lastedt updates and talk about books and more!

Myrina Holmes Demons and Wonders
by *Anna Triss*

I'm Myrina Holmes, the top Tracker of Infernum, tasked with neutralizing supernatural creatures who disobey our laws.

In my world, demons have legions. Fourteen to be precise: seven dedicated to the cardinal virtues and seven ruled by the deadly sins.

As a marginal hybrid, I belong to neither camp, which suits me just fine. I love my job and my life on Earth when I'm not on a mission. Except, of course, when mysterious corpses literally fall from the sky to torture my brain and when my succubus half-sister starts hanging out with the most detestable Hybresang there is, Kelen Wills.

A supremely powerful sinner, commander-in-chief of an elite army, he doesn't embody one deadly sin. No, he possesses all seven-with a penchant for lust, anger, pride, and gluttony. But keep that detail to yourself...

Anyway, this guy has made it his mission to seduce me, probably because I'm the only woman who can resist his dubious charms.

This Hybresang can go to hell, because I have other midnight demons to deal with.

Kalliopee: A Princess's Sacrifice
by *Koko Nhan*

After years of violent battles, Kalliopee agrees to sacrifice her freedom by marrying the prince of the enemy kingdom in order to bring peace.

In a world where women are treated as slaves rather than wives, she is still delighted to be reunited with her first love, Karel.

However, life is unpredictable, and the horrors of war have transformed Karel into a tough and ruthless heir to the throne, who despises the Viridians more than anything. While he has no qualms about mistreating Kalliopee, his determination wavers when confronted with her striking eyes. In the midst of desire and animosity, schemes and plots, dreams and disillusionment, will the princess's heart endure the price of her liberty?

The Cocky Heir
by *Ana K. Anderson*

She is about to get married. But not to him.

Quinn MacFayden, an accomplished expat businessman in New York, is set to return to Scotland in extremis to protect the precious family legacy. His 91-year-old grandfather is about to marry a perfect stranger sixty-six years his junior... And that is out of the question! Quinn swears it. Over his dead body will Dawn Fleming ever be part of the family!

But Dawn is not a future bride like the others. She is nowhere near the gold digger he imagined and, above all, she knows just how to stand up to him. And so a game of cat and mouse begins between them. A war with no holds barred and where surrender has never been so tempting...

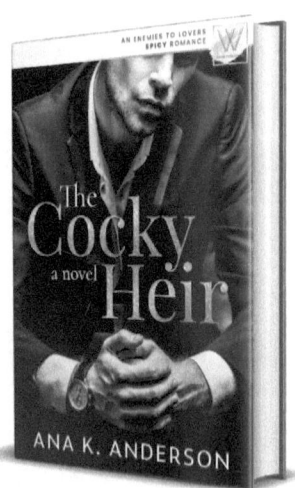

My Stepbrother: A Sexual Revelation
by *Sophie S. Pierucci*

Cassie is a highly intelligent young woman... Too much so for her own good!

And she is as daunting as she is intriguing. Carl, the son of his father's second wife, would hardly say otherwise!

Carl is the exact opposite of his steady father. He is a player and a slayer. Afraid of nothing and no one. Except for Cassie when she asks him to introduce her to the pleasures of the flesh.

And when the situation gets out of control, it is too late to turn back, and the two lovers find themselves ensnared in forbidden passion. Forbidden by everyone: society, their parents, their friends.

But how to resist the desire that consumes them?

Roommate with my Boss
by *Erin Graham*

Boss, roommate, fake fiancé... real lover?

Étienne is cold, charismatic, and he never shies away from a challenge.

He masters everything down to the smallest detail... until a little accountant with an unlikely look and flowers in her hair inserts herself into his daily life.

She is whimsical, full of life, laughs at the rules and gets around them, talks all the time except about her past... and she drives him crazy. Yet, it's impossible to fire her.

She needs a job and a roof over her head; he needs a fake fiancée...

Is it a deal?

Your Power Over me
by *Missy Heart*

A family home heavy with secrets, a dangerously charismatic owner.

Will her arrival at Iron House be the end of her?

Ever since she was a teenager, Lovisa has known it: at Iron House, anything can happen, especially the worst.

However, when she is forced to return to the family home for her stepfather's funeral, her heart races: she is going to see him again, this "brother" who she never wanted and who yet turned her whole world upside down.

Now at the head of a drug cartel, authoritarian and brutal, Niklas is nothing like the teenager she knew nine years ago. At his side, Lovisa finds herself immersed in a harsh, ruthless—but fascinating—world.

Irremediably attracted to this man who wants her as much harm as good, will Lovisa manage to fight her unmentionable desires? Or will she give in to Niklas' magnetic darkness?

Damn Roommate
by *Lou Garance*

Falling for your brother's best friend? Not a good idea!
Moving in with him? Even worse!

When she moves in with her brother's roommate and his group of friends, Scarlett feels like she's really in for it.

She couldn't get Nolan Jones out of her head while living

thousands of miles away from him, so how could she possibly forget him now that she's back in Boston? Especially now that she occupies the room right next to his?

Yet her lifelong crush gives her no reason to hope. Nolan teases her like she's his little sister! Scarlett knows she has to accept that he will never see her otherwise.

But between the evenings spent challenging each other, the unsettling closeness on the couch and the new spark she sees in Nolan's eyes, never might be coming sooner rather than later.

My Hipster Next Door
by *Mag Maury*

In Liverpool, the barbershop Hipster Maniac is an institution. Run by three bearded, tattooed friends, it is the place to listen to great rock, get a trim, and have a drink.

But for Line, it also spelled trouble. For starters, when she first got to the neighborhood, she rear-ended Jordan's car, who turned out to be one of the three barbers. Then she discovered that they were neighbors in business and residence! So no way can she escape this muscle-flaunting, smoldering man who is covered in tattoos and... completely insufferable!

He draws her near only to push her away. He toys with her shamelessly. But worst of all he hates Christmas whereas that is Line's very favorite time of year!

Beneath a backdrop of festive fairy lights, intoxicatingly passionate kisses, and blistering banter... It's on!

The Private Garden
by *Oly TL*

The most disturbing and transgressive of contracts...

Tiger Sexton seems to have it all. Charisma. Respect. Relentless business acumen. More fortune than he could spend in a life and a sublime wife, Sophia.

When Oceane is invited by Mrs. Sexton for a job interview in one of the restaurants that her husband gave her, the young French tourist knows nothing about this couple. Their name means

nothing to her, people are not her thing. She just wants a job, a place to live and to move on with her life... Sophia's proposal comes at the right time: the Sextons are looking for an *au pair*.

But by opening their doors to her, many other locks are likely to open. Is Oceane ready for this? And what about Sophia, and especially the Tiger lurking in this Secret Garden?

Keep in touch with Sonia Birdy

Instagram:
https://www.instagram.com/soniabirdy/

SONIA BIRDY
AUTEURE DE ROMANCE

About the Author

Sonia Birdy is an author of warm and emotional romances. Discovered on Wattpad France, she quickly made a name for herself thanks to her dynamic and addictive pen.

She loves chocolate, her loved ones, and travel but not necessarily in that order. Originally from the east of France where she works as a teacher, Sonia loves to spend her free time reading and watching people on the terraces of cafés, with a strong espresso, if possible. These slices of life from which she draws inspiration to write her novels. Her heroes, she likes them complex and endearing, her stories, torrid and impossible. So, are you ready to discover the world of Sonia Birdy?

www.ingramcontent.com/pod-product-compliance
Lightning Source LLC
Chambersburg PA
CBHW021237190726
48289CB00005B/1363